PRAISE FOR THE MAGICAL ROMANCES OF BARBARA DAWSON SMITH:

FIRE AT MIDNIGHT

"An unsurpassed historical romance that will keep you riveted with its intense suspense and intrigue. Her characterizations are unexcelled; her dialogue is sharp and witty. I couldn't put it down!"

—*Affaire de Coeur* (five stars, highest rating)

"With twists and turns galore, Barbara Dawson Smith has penned another wondrous, highly suspenseful and unique historical romance."

—*Romantic Times* (four plus, highest rating)

FIRE ON THE WIND

"Again and again, Barbara Dawson Smith stretches the boundaries of the genre . . . FIRE ON THE WIND is her most powerful romance yet."

—*Romantic Times* (four plus, highest rating)

"Superlative . . . definitely a fabulous treasure."

—*Rendezvous*

"Another five stars for Ms. Smith."

—*Affaire de Coeur*

DREAMSPINNER

"A page-turner filled with love and intrigue . . . make room on your bookshelf!"

—*Romantic Times* (four plus, highest rating)

"Barbara Dawson Smith is wonderful!"

—*Affaire de Coeur*

Barbara Dawson Smith

St. Martin's Paperbacks

A Glimpse of Heaven is fondly dedicated to all my dear friends who have been supportive and encouraging beyond the call of duty: Kathe, Jodi, Dora, Karen, Tory, Suzannah, Debby, Tanya, Penny, Pat, Carla, Marilyn, Heather, Bonnie, Anne, Anna, Jolie, Sharon, Elaine, Susan, Joyce, Betty, Janece, Christina, Mary Ellen, Alex, Thelma, Laurel, Marie, Jane, Debbi, Alaina, MJ, Hollis, Jan, Marian, Vicki, Vicki, Rita, Rita, Paris, Adrienne, Coral, Pat, Gail, Ginny, Cheryl, Betty, Harriet, Debbi, and Jen.

A GLIMPSE OF HEAVEN

ISBN: 0-312-95714-9

Printed in the United States of America

St. Martin's Paperbacks edition/December 1995

10 9 8 7 6 5 4 3 2 1

ACKNOWLEDGMENTS

For their unending support and valuable insights during the writing of this book, I am indebted to my critique group: Joyce Bell, Betty Traylor Gyenes, and Susan Wiggs.

A very special thanks goes to my editor, Jennifer Enderlin, whose guidance and support has been much appreciated.

Prologue

Waterloo, 18 June 1815

True to form, Burke Grisham, the earl of Thornwald, stood surrounded by beautiful women. But for once, he ignored them.

The brass ring of the spyglass pressed to his eye, he intently watched the battle that raged in the undulating landscape to the southeast. From a distance, the vast armies of England and France appeared as tin soldiers in mock combat. But with a horror that gripped his gut, Burke knew they were not toys.

They were men.

Men with wives and children and mothers and fathers. Men with flesh now torn by bullets and sabers. Men whose warm blood soaked the muddy earth.

Sunlight leaked through the clouds onto a scene of awesome carnage. Wave after wave of cavalry swept across the fields amid a thunder of hooves and the glitter of swords. Tiny stick-men lay crumpled in the dirt. Here and there, black smoke belched from the cannon and obscured the action. The rumble of the artillery mingled with the tattoo of rifle-fire, the faint roll of drums, the far-off screams of horses and men.

With the slowness of one submerged in a nightmare, Burke became aware of someone plucking at his sleeve.

Someone speaking words whose meaning failed to penetrate his stupefied mind.

He tore his attention from the battlefield and frowned at the woman beside him. A parasol shaded her dainty straw bonnet with the pink ribbons dancing in the breeze. Her limpid blue eyes blinked in a face of girlish purity.

But Lady Pamela Seymour was far from pure. Her morals were as low as his. No one knew that better than Burke.

"Well, answer me," she said. "Have we routed old Boney?"

We. He hid his shame behind a tight smile. "Not yet."

He raised the spyglass again, but she caught his wrist. Her lips formed a Cupid's bow pout. "Selfish man. Do allow me a peek. After all, my husband is fighting down there."

Handing her parasol to Burke, she took the telescope and surveyed the conflict. In a pale gauze gown that hugged her breasts, she might have been watching a stage play.

Burke clenched the parasol handle until his knuckles turned white. Never in his misbegotten life had he felt more worthless. He tarried here in supreme arrogance, clad in white cravat and spotless morning suit, his black Hessians polished to a high sheen.

While Englishmen lay dying down there.

How bold he had felt just hours ago as he and a few friends had set out in their carriages to view the warfare. Brussels had been in a state of frenzy with civilians fleeing to Antwerp for fear of a French invasion. But Burke had not crossed the Channel to run at the first cannon shot; he craved the chance to flirt with danger.

His own naïveté mortified him now. Only a braggart would call himself brave to watch from the safety of this ridge behind the British lines. Oblivious to such moral dilemmas, his companions chattered and gossiped. Now and then the shrill laugh of a lady punctuated the distant gunfire.

He forced his gaze to the battlefield. No, those below were not tin soldiers, but men of honor. Men whose belief in liberty and justice gave them the courage to die in defense of England.

Stinking coward. His father's voice rang from the cold vault of memory. Aware of a familiar pressure on his temples, Burke descended into the darkness of his own private hell. The broken weeping of his mother. The brutal reproach of his father. The body of his elder brother sprawled by the roadside in a great red pool of blood. As Burke ran away and hid in terror.

There was no escaping the awful truth. Colin's death was his fault. His shame. His alone.

Ever since, Burke had striven to prove his derring-do. He had raced the fastest horses. He had out-drunk and out-gambled his cronies. He had seduced more wives than he could count, even wounding the husband of one in a duel. He had earned his reputation as the most daring rake in London.

But in the end his father was right.

Burke Grisham, second son and—by default—heir to the marquis of Westhaven, was a stinking coward.

Pamela stamped her little foot. "Oh, bother. We're too far away to tell one regiment from the next."

Beside her, a lady flaunting an indecent bodice pressed a handkerchief to her rouged cheek. "Pray don't suggest we move closer."

Pamela shuddered. "Heavens, no. I wouldn't fancy seeing all those wounded men."

Burke heard their exchange as if through a fog. A fever spread through his cold limbs and upward, pounding in his skull. Sweat broke out on his brow, his chest, his back.

Men lying helpless. Crying out in agony. Bleeding to death.

As his brother had bled and bled and bled.

"How glad I am that you were not foolish enough to enlist, my lord." Pamela was leaning against Burke, her breasts pillowing against his arm as she whispered, "Just think, my stallion, after today your mare may be free at last."

Her pretty features suddenly looked hard and garish. He might have been gazing at a painted mask. Yet the loathing he felt was for himself.

Stinking coward.

The fever raged out of control. He knew only one way to silence that taunting voice, to entomb it in the black reaches of forgetfulness.

Blindly he turned, but Pamela clung to him, uncertainty on her face. "Darling, you look so fierce. I did not mean to speak out so plainly. Do forgive me."

"Go to hell." He jerked his arm free and plunged through the throng of ladies..

They stepped back, twittering like magpies. Some put their heads together, no doubt savoring the delicious drama of watching a notorious lord spurn his married lover.

Stinking coward.

He fled toward the cluster of carriages, shouldered aside the lolling coachman, and leaped atop the driver's seat. Seizing reins and whip, he urged the matched team of blacks down the rutted road. Vaguely he grew aware of someone shouting his name.

The carriage rocked. From the corner of his eye, he saw the door swing open. A man clung there a moment, then clambered up alongside Burke.

Alfred Snow plunked himself down, panting, his breath exuding brandy fumes. "Christ, Thornwald, I might've known it was you. Where th' devil are you going so all-fired fast?"

"Down there." Slowing the carriage, Burke nodded toward the battlefield. "I forgot you were inside."

"What do you mean to do?"

"I'm joining our illustrious fighting men. Now get off with you."

Alfred raked his hand through his fair hair, his blue eyes bleary and his cravat askew. He took another long swallow from his silver flask. "I'm going with you."

"No!" Burke spoke through gritted teeth; he couldn't stomach the guilt of embroiling a friend in his own penance. "You're drunk. Besides, you've a wife waiting for you at home."

Alfred sat silent a moment. "Perhaps Catherine is better off without me," he said, his voice bitter as he twisted the gold ring on his finger.

Not for the first time, Burke blamed the mysterious Catherine Snow for the bouts of angry melancholy in Alfred that turned him to drink so often of late. Burke had never had met the woman who caused his friend to brood so. She chose to stay at the Snow estate in Yorkshire rather than join her husband on his frequent sojourns to London.

"No woman is worth dying for," Burke said.

Alfred sent him a keen look. "On the contrary, I pray you'll someday know such love yourself."

A vast emptiness opened in Burke; then the rumble of artillery fire distracted him. "Let's not argue the merits of romance again. Get on with you now."

Alfred squared his shoulders. "No. Call it belated patriotic fever, but I want to fight, too."

"Suit yourself, then," Burke said with a shrug.

His own fever had little to do with patriotism and everything to do with subduing—at least for the moment—the demons inside him.

Stinking coward.

The frenzy in him resurfaced, compelling him onward. He snapped the reins and the carriage rolled at a fast clip down the rutted track. Almost immediately, they passed a straggly line of wounded soldiers trudging toward Brussels. Smoke from gunfire formed a pall over the scarred landscape, the farmland of trampled wheat and rye. Somewhere ahead, buglers sounded a rally in a series of staccato blasts. A dense column of red-coated infantrymen charged toward an unseen enemy over the next ridge. The bray of bagpipes from a Scottish regiment joined the cacophony of gunfire and shouting.

Bodies littered the field as far as the eye could see. Burke stopped the carriage and leaped down, snatching up a sword that lay on the ground. The blood beat hotly in his veins. He could not think beyond striking out against the enemy in the desperate hope of slaying the foe inside himself.

" 'Elp me, guvnor," croaked a boyish voice.

Burke looked down to see an English recruit, his face chalk-white, his leg cocked at an unnatural angle. The youth reached up his bloodied hand in supplication.

Burke hesitated, drawn by the lure of danger a few hundred yards ahead—the lure of morbid salvation. The boy's grotesque injury sickened him and made his own legs feel weak.

Then pity overtook his bloodlust and he threw down the sword. With Alfred's aid, he lifted the boy into the carriage. Other disabled soldiers cried out for mercy. The orderlies who carted off the wounded were woefully inadequate in number, and from that moment Burke found himself caught up in evacuating the injured to an open-air field hospital, where surgeons labored to save the overwhelming rows of wounded.

On through the afternoon, he loaded soldiers into the carriage. It was grim, filthy, wearisome work. Mud mired the wheels, forcing him or Alfred to clamber down and push. The air felt like a furnace, tainted by the stench of blood and smoke. From time to time, the ground trembled from the thunder of cavalry charges. Too often, a soldier expired of his injuries on the way to the hospital.

The voice inside Burke jeered his efforts. It whispered that cowardice, not compassion, kept him behind the lines. He continued doggedly, seeking the numbness of exhaustion. In London he would have gone to the pugilists' ring and fought until physical pain deadened his mind. But that, like this, was only a temporary respite. He knew he would never find peace.

As the fingers of sunset touched an earth consecrated by death, still the battle raged. Cannonballs whistled in the darkening sky as the English gained ground in a furious advance that left many more dead and wounded.

Returning from yet another trip to the hospital, Burke slumped wearily on the driver's seat. Patchy fog rolled in with the dusk, and the fire of musketry sounded hollow and distant.

As the carriage rattled up a rise, Alfred tilted his head back and drained his silver flask. He grinned suddenly, his teeth a smear of white in his begrimed face. "Christ, man, if the ladies could see you now, they'd call you a frigging hero."

Burke grimaced at his bloodied clothing, his boots caked with mud. His cravat had vanished, along with the coat he had used to staunch an infantryman's abdominal wound. "More likely they'd run screaming in the opposite direction."

"Bugger it. There's nothing a woman loves more than—"

A fusillade of pops drowned his words. As the vehicle crested the hill, grapeshot and shells rained like hail. A row of French artillery stood not ten yards away, firing at a British regiment of foot soldiers that surged out of the mist.

Cursing his misjudgment, Burke struggled to turn the horses. "Get down," he shouted to Alfred.

"Hell, no!" Alfred stood up, swaying as the carriage bumped along. "Let's grab some guns and charge th' devils. Tallyho!"

His body jerked suddenly. With nightmarish abruptness, he fell backward, clutching at his chest as he toppled from the carriage.

A shell whined past Burke's ear. He vaulted to the ground, landing ankle-deep in muck. The jolt half-dazed him.

He scrambled toward Alfred. In the twilight, a deadly patch of blood blossomed on his shirt. Horror pounded louder in Burke than the roar of the guns. "A doctor," he muttered. "You need a doctor."

Alfred didn't seem to have heard. He fumbled in his pocket, then pressed an object into Burke's hand. It was a cameo locket of a white-garbed angel reaching both hands toward a diamond star. Opening it, Burke stared at the miniature of a smiling woman with dark hair framing exquisite features, her eyes sparkling in a face so lovely it might have belonged to a goddess.

"Catherine." The din of battle almost drowned Alfred's agonized whisper. "You must take care of her . . . promise me."

Burke stuffed the locket back into his friend's pocket. "You'll care for her yourself, you fool."

Alfred clung to Burke's wrist as if summoning every fiber of his strength. "Watch over her. Swear it to me. You must."

His fingers were cold. Burke would do anything, say anything to ease his friend's pain. "All right, for God's sake. I promise. You aren't going to die, though. Damn it, I won't let you."

But Alfred's grip loosened and he slumped into a stupor. Burke scooped him up, staggering under the weight as he hastened toward the carriage, the mud sucking at his boots. Urgency throbbed with every beat of his heart. He couldn't fail again. Not as he had failed his brother.

Then Alfred shuddered once. The shallow rise and fall of his chest ceased.

Burke gripped him in a hard embrace. *"No!"*

In that instant something struck his upper body with violent force. White agony exploded outward, numbing his arms. He wheeled backward and fell into suffocating darkness.

Panic clawed at his throat. He couldn't breathe. An iron clamp squeezed his chest. Through it all, he felt an odd sense of surprise. He couldn't die yet. He was doomed to suffer on earth.

The battle sounds faded into blessed silence. Miraculously the pain slipped away like shed skin. He had a peculiar impression of detachment, of weightlessness, as if he floated high above the world. With startling clarity, he saw men fighting on the dusky field below. Beside the carriage, his still form lay near Alfred's.

The dream-like darkness became a river that carried him ever upward. As he strained to see into the pitch-black void, a bright star appeared on the horizon. The light streaked toward him and formed a shimmering tunnel.

Warmth washed him in glorious wonder. Unable to resist, he moved toward the light, drawn by its irresistible aura of . . . what?

Love, he realized in faint astonishment. *So this is love.*

Peace flooded him. Boundless and brilliant. The sensation was so extraordinary, he felt the urge to weep. All those years he had struggled, never dreaming such splendor existed, never guessing the magnitude of what was missing from his life.

The light flared brighter, dazzling him with the awareness of another presence. Alfred?

Even as Burke hesitated, a woman's voice called to him, not by name . . . and yet he knew her somehow. Her sweet entreaty rose from the shadows below and made him ache with yearning.

Don't leave me. Please don't leave me.

No woman had ever loved him. Not like that.

The voice lured him from the light, sucked him down, down, down. With jarring abruptness, the voice vanished into chaos. Pain burst inside him, as shocking as a plunge into icy water.

The radiance receded like the tide. Desperate, he strained to swim up toward it.

But the weight of his body doomed him to darkness.

Chapter 1

Yorkshire, August 1816

Catherine Snow clung to the ladder and contemplated murder.

A bitter breeze yanked at the black merino shawl knotted around her shoulders and threatened to dislodge the white-ruffled mobcap that protected her hair. Shivering, she gripped the top rung with one hand and carefully leaned over to wash the arched window of the drawing room.

It was the chilliest summer in her memory, and Catherine had lived her entire twenty-three years here on the moors of Yorkshire. A week of unrelenting rain left mud puddles everywhere. Today, the sun peeked from behind the leaden clouds like a coy debutante peering past her fan.

The day had gone from bad to worse when Martha, the downstairs maid, had succumbed to a bout of the ague. Never industrious under the best of circumstances, Martha had neglected to beat the rugs in the library. As punishment, Lorena had ordered the servant to wash all the outside windows. Every diamond-shaped pane was to sparkle by the time Lorena and her twin daughters returned from their afternoon round of calls.

The minute the family carriage had vanished down the drive, Catherine sent a feverish, sniffling Martha up to bed with a pot of honeyed tea. Then Catherine herself had mounted the wooden ladder. Two hours later, her arms ached and her fingers smarted. The stench of vinegar water from the pail stung her nose. Worst of all, looking down made her wretchedly dizzy.

Yes, murder might be in order, Catherine thought darkly. She inched downward, the heavy bucket bumping her black skirt. Perhaps a dose of rat poison slipped into her mother-in-law's tea. Or a timely tumble down the grand staircase.

Even as her own feet touched solid earth, Catherine battled her spitefulness. When she and Alfred had returned from Gretna Green four years ago, Lorena had raged about her son's impetuous marriage. But then, ever mindful of what polite society would say, she had taken Catherine in hand and molded her into a lady. Lorena had opened her home—if not her heart—at a time when Catherine despaired of having a family of her own.

Sadness unrolled inside her like an endless tunnel. Setting down the pail, she slumped against the damp, ivy-covered wall and inhaled the scent of crushed leaves. It was so easy to blame her mother-in-law. But Lorena was not responsible for Alfred's death at Waterloo the previous year. Nor was it her fault that Catherine had failed to conceive again after a hideous miscarriage early in her marriage.

The loss of her unborn child was Catherine's own cross to bear, the result of her impetuous behavior.

She swallowed the lump in her throat. The truth ached like a never-healed wound. By her rash conduct, she had driven Alfred to drink. By her unruly tongue, she had marked herself as common. When Alfred told her to act like a lady, she'd thrown an inkpot at him, barely missing his head. And proving his point.

Over the three years of their marriage, he'd changed from a flirtatious charmer into a morose stranger. Because of her aversion to faro and piquet, he sought amusement in the gaming dens of London. Because of her inability to give him a son, he had fallen in deeper with ne'er-do-wells like Burke Grisham, the infamous earl of Thornwald.

Resentment oozed over the wounds of the past. How dearly she'd love to give that scoundrel lord a dressing down, and the devil take any ladylike restraint. But she would never have the pleasure.

Catherine plucked an ivy leaf and twirled the stem between her fingertips. Life was no storybook where good always triumphed over bad, where tragedy drew husband and wife closer together. Now she was older and wiser than the dreamy country girl who had been swept off her feet by a dashing gentleman. Now she had a plan for her future, though it might take her another ten years to scrape together the funds—

A twig snapped in the underbrush. Straightening, she peered toward the woodland of oaks and wych elms that bordered the green lawn. Deep in the gloom, the pale oval of a face appeared past the trunk of a sycamore, then vanished again.

Someone was watching her. And she had a suspicion who.

Catherine marched onto the soggy grass. "Come out," she called.

Nothing moved. A pipit trilled its song into the silence. Sunlight flirted with the shadows in the forest, then ducked behind another cloud.

"Please show yourself," she cajoled. "I want to talk to you."

Someone stepped out from behind the thick trunk. A man.

"It's all right," Catherine said, hiding her irritation while motioning him closer. "Do come here."

With a hesitant, shuffling gait, he walked toward her, a small golden-haired dog trotting at his heels. He was a rather large man with sloping shoulders, dressed in country tweeds and muddy jackboots. A cravat wrapped his throat like an ill-tied bandage. Limp blond hair framed a face with a crooked nose and cheeks tinted pink with embarrassment. In one arm he cradled a long rifle; a red-stained sack dangled from his other hand.

Catherine curtsied with aplomb, as if Alfred's cousin hadn't been lurking in the woods and spying on her from afar. "Good afternoon, Mr. Snow. How pleasant to see you today."

Fabian Snow's blush deepened. "H-hullo, M-Mrs. Snow."

"Thank goodness the rain has stopped at last. I see you've been taking advantage of the fair weather."

His pale blue eyes blinked guiltily, as if he were a poacher rather than master of the estate. He opened his mouth, then closed it. Abruptly he thrust the sack at her. "F-for you."

"Thank you, but you shouldn't have." Hiding a grimace, she took the bloody bag and held it at arm's length. "If I may ask, what is it?"

"R-rabbits. For d-dinner."

He looked so painfully proud of himself, squaring his shoulders for once, that she lacked the heart to refuse his gift. For all his dearth of social skills, Fabian Snow was a crack shot and an avid huntsman. It was the third time this fortnight that he had brought her wild game for the table, once a brace of pheasants, then a pair of mallard ducks. His gifts disconcerted her not because she was squeamish but because he acted as eager for praise as a dog laying its kill before an adored owner.

Catherine didn't know how to discourage Fabian's bashful admiration without hurting him. "This is very helpful of you," she said. "Perhaps Cook can make a pie and you can join us for dinner. I'll take this 'round to the kitchen straightaway."

"M-Mrs. Snow?"

His squeaky voice stopped her. "Yes?"

"Y-you shouldn't be c-climbing that ladder. Or washing windows l-like a servant."

"It's only for today. And I'm nearly finished."

"But Aunt L-Lorena w-will be angry." He cocked his head, his lank hair blowing in the cold breeze. "Is that her c-carriage now?"

Distant hoofbeats drummed on the drive. But the long row of oaks shielded the bend in the road.

"I don't hear carriage wheels," Catherine said. "But thank you for expressing concern. You're most thoughtful."

His cheeks flushed crimson. He slowly backed away, bobbing his head and clutching the gun, the barrel pointed at her. "Er . . . goodbye then."

A horseman rode into view. He shaded his eyes and peered toward them. Abruptly the canter of hoofbeats accelerated into a gallop. At breakneck speed, man and horse came thundering down the drive.

Catherine clutched the sack to her drab mourning gown. Mane and tail flying, the black horse plunged across the lawn, clods of earth spraying. The rider bent low as if he were on a racetrack.

He meant to run them down!

Gasping, she jumped backward. Fabian Snow swung around and uttered a squawk of fright. The horse rushed into the gap separating him and Catherine.

The rider leaped from the saddle and down onto Fabian, knocking the rifle out of his hand. Both men went tumbling over and over on the lawn. The riderless horse ran to the edge of the trees and then slowed, prancing in a circle. Fabian's dog, Lady, barked furiously at the newcomer.

The sack of rabbits dropped from Catherine's nerveless fingers. Paralyzed by disbelief, she watched the stranger shove Fabian face down on the muddy lawn, then yank his arm behind his back. Who was this madman?

She certainly intended to find out.

She darted forward and snatched up the rifle. Clutching the gun and willing her hands not to shake, she advanced on the two men. Fabian moaned pitifully.

"Move away," she ordered.

Without turning his dark head, the stranger crouched beside Fabian and held him in an armlock. "Not until I subdue this bastard."

"I-I . . . *owww!*" Fabian sputtered.

The plaintive cry roused Catherine to fury. Though she had never held a gun before, she sighted down the barrel and caressed the trigger. "Release him this instant or I'll shoot."

The man lifted his head. He took a long hard look at her, and she stared in return, unwilling to let him see the shock of recognition that reverberated inside her.

His black hair in rakish disarray, his bone structure boldly masculine, he had a face of startling distinction. His fierce glower changed to an expression of surprise. His eyes widened, their color the gray of ashes after a fire has gone out. Yet there was nothing lifeless about him. Ablaze with intensity, his gaze burned into her.

Despite the brisk air, her skin felt overly warm. Her legs threatened to melt like tapers of hot wax. It couldn't be him. But that satanically handsome face was branded into her memory. For as long as she lived, she would never forget him—or the tragic chain of events set into motion by his act of depravity.

Burke Grisham. The earl of Thornwald.

"It's you," he said in an odd, guttural tone. "God help me, it's you."

"Pardon?"

The earl continued to stare at her, his tanned face gone pale. His expression softened and his lips parted slightly. His eyes drank her in as if she were a person who mattered to him.

Catherine shook off the fancy. They had never met. On the one occasion she had seen Lord Thornwald from a distance, he had been too caught up in his own debauchery to notice her.

Why had he come here?

A muffled groan wafted from Fabian Snow, who lay sprawled in the wet grass.

"Move!" she told the earl again, gesturing with the rifle.

He blinked. The keen absorption on his face turned to stony blankness. After a moment's hesitation, he released Fabian, who sat up, gingerly rubbing his arm.

Mud coated the front of Fabian's clothing. His hair stood out in wild blond spikes. Quickly he scooted back from his attacker. "W-why'd you h-hit me?"

Burke Grisham rose to his considerable height. His plum-hued riding coat and fawn breeches were immaculate, with only a few clods of dirt marring his shiny black top boots. As he straightened his cravat, he epitomized the wicked elegance of a London rake. "I should think that's obvious," he said. "You were threatening her with your gun."

"He most certainly was not!" Catherine objected, lowering the rifle. "Where did you get such a lack-witted notion?"

"I saw him point the weapon at you."

She subdued a fleeting thrill that the earl would ride to her rescue like a knight in shining armor. "From all the way down the drive, you drew this conclusion? Then without stopping to ascertain the truth, you attacked an innocent man?"

"I believed you to be in mortal danger—"

"You might have asked questions first."

"And see you killed?"

"The situation was entirely innocent. I wasn't in need of a savior. This is hardly a battleground, sir."

A dull red flush crept from beneath his starched collar. He rubbed his cheek and a crooked grin lent him a certain charm. "So it seems. Apparently I made a foolish blunder. Please accept my sincerest apologies."

She took pleasure in seeing him brought low. He deserved far worse for bullying Fabian. And for what he had done to Alfred. "Kindly direct your regrets to Mr. Snow. He owns this normally peaceful estate."

Lord Thornwald turned to Fabian and bowed. "Do forgive me."

Fabian scrambled to his feet. He brushed at the mud and only succeeded in smearing the mess over his baggy tweed suit. "Y-yes, of course."

"You'll want to clean up," Catherine said quietly, stepping to Fabian's side. "I shall deal with our visitor."

Hands grimy, he took the gun from her. "Are you q-quite certain?"

She nodded. "Yes. Go on home now."

He hunched his shoulders and trotted off with the dog at his heels, crossing the lawn and disappearing into the woods.

"I thought you said he owned this place."

Catherine turned to find the earl devouring her with alert, hungry eyes. A fluttery warmth took wing inside her, a sensation that appalled her. Curtly she replied, "He does."

"Then where is he going?"

"He lives in the dower house." Upon Alfred's death last year, his cousin had inherited the entailed estate. Fabian had voluntarily given up residence in the manor house rather than evict Lorena, her daughters, and Catherine. But she didn't owe this man any explanations. "Now that we've settled that, you can be on your way."

"But I came to see you, Catherine Snow."

He spoke her name with such confident familiarity that she wondered if he *had* noticed her peering at him all those years ago. The memory brought a sickening roll of nausea to her stomach.

She groped beneath her shawl and touched the delicate oval at her throat, warm from her skin. The locket. Of course, that explained why he'd recognized her. Alfred must have showed the earl her miniature.

"You claim to know me," she said coldly, "yet we have never met."

"Quite regrettably true." All of a sudden, the earl stepped closer and yanked the servant's cap from her head. Her hair came half undone with several tortoiseshell pins popping loose and tendrils spilling around her shoulders. He fingered one glossy brownish-black curl.

His unorthodox action stunned her momentarily. Did he treat all women with such callous familiarity? Yes, she had seen as much for herself.

She snatched back the cap. "You're a rude, arrogant, and insufferable man. I must ask you to leave."

"I shan't leave. Not until I find out *why* . . ." His voice deepened, enriched by mystery.

"Upon my word. State your business and be gone."

"First," he said, "allow me to introduce myself."

The sullen clouds parted. A sunbeam streaked down from the heavens to bathe him in golden light. All of a sudden his dark, wind-blown hair shimmered with life. Tiny green sparks glowed in his gray eyes. The forceful angles of his face took on a striking male beauty, the luster of a bronzed hero.

"The name is Grisham," he said. "Burke Grisham."

Any feeble hope that she might have been mistaken died a quick death. "The notorious earl of Thornwald."

"At your service, ma'am."

He reached into his breast pocket and handed her his visiting card from a slim gold case. Anger and aversion swelling inside her, she stared down at his engraved name.

Dear God. She had imagined this moment a hundred times while lying alone in her bed and watching the play of shadows on the ceiling. She had savored the idea of heaping contempt on this scoundrel, then consigning him to the sewer where he belonged.

But now her mouth went dry. The oft-rehearsed lines fled her mind. She could only manage to say, "You were at Waterloo. When my husband died."

The ray of sunlight vanished, robbing Burke Grisham of that superhuman brilliance. He lowered his eyes, as if peering at painfully private memories. "Yes."

Wrath formed a great clot in her throat. She threw his card down into the mud and ground her heel into it. Then she snatched up the sack of dead rabbits and stalked toward the house.

Footsteps scraped on the pebbled path. The earl caught her arm, his grip gentle yet masterful. "Catherine, wait. I've come halfway across England to speak to you. At least hear me out—"

With all her might she swung the sack and smacked his midsection, leaving bloody dots on his plum-colored coat. "I am Mrs. Snow to you."

He cautiously held up his hands, palms out. "As you wish, Mrs. Snow. I came to offer my condolences—"

"You're rather tardy, then. All my husband's other *friends* managed to do so last year."

"I was . . . otherwise occupied. But I hope you'll invite me inside. Your mother-in-law would want you to do so."

He confused her with the gleam of a smile, the sincerity in his eyes. No wonder the ladies of London found him so charming. In spite of her fury, she heeded his words. Lorena would be furious if Catherine dismissed the scion of one of England's first families.

Even if his lordship was the blackguard who had corrupted Alfred. And then lured him to his death.

"What a rare honor, my lord! To think you've journeyed all the way from Cornwall for a visit. I daresay you're every bit as dashing as dear Freddie said, God rest his precious soul. Did he mention his two sisters? They'll be the toast of London when they're launched into Society next spring. They should be back downstairs at any moment now. . . ."

While Mrs. Lorena Snow rattled on, Burke resisted the urge to fidget on the velvet chair. The blaze in the hearth cast waves of suffocating heat into the stately drawing room. He had met women like Lorena Snow before, ambitious and formidable, gushing praise to their social superiors and extolling their own virtues to anyone polite enough to listen.

Like a broody hen, she roosted on the settee across from him. She wore a gown of lavender silk and over it a gold shawl bristling with embroidery. Her sultry blue eyes and unblemished skin hinted that she had been a beauty at one time. But now her flesh had gone soft and an indefinable coarseness repelled him. Perhaps it was the vulgarity of too many diamonds glinting at her ears and throat, or the coquettish way she leaned forward, making cannonballs of her breasts. How incongruous that this self-absorbed snob had produced a son as amiable as Alfred.

At the thought of his friend, bitter loss flooded Burke. He cursed the futile sentiment. For the past year he had flayed himself with the scourge of regret, and to no avail.

With all his heart, he wanted to snatch back that fatal moment on the battlefield. But he couldn't change the past. He could only hope to atone for his mistakes.

That was why he had come here. He had intended to make a brief sympathy call, to purge himself of his strange obsession for the lovely widow Snow and assure himself of her comfort, then ride away a free man.

Instead, he had made a bloody ass of himself.

The flickering fire shimmered out of focus. In his mind he gazed across the lawn and saw the barrel of the rifle pointed at Catherine Snow. He felt anew the surge of unthinking horror, the paralyzing fear that he was too late.

Too late again.

Panic stung him. He relived the bone-jarring gallop. The jolt as he leaped onto her attacker. The moment of utter shock when she spoke from behind him.

He had heard that very voice calling to him after he'd been shot at Waterloo. Calling him back to earth, luring him away from the radiant light.

Don't leave me. Please don't leave me.

And then, crouched on the muddy lawn, he had reeled from the force of another shock. He had looked up into the face that had haunted his waking dreams for the past year—

". . . what do you think, my lord?"

He blinked. Her hands folded in her lap, Lorena Snow was gazing expectantly at him. He had no earthly idea what she had asked him. But he flashed her his warmest smile. "I'm sorry. You caught me woolgathering."

"La, it's my fault for boring you with my prattle when you must be weary from your journey. I only wondered how long you planned to stay on in Yorkshire."

One look at Catherine Snow had turned his intentions topsy-turvy. "A week at least," he said, making an instant revision in his plans. "Perhaps longer."

"How marvelous. Please allow me to extend an invitation to stay here with us."

"That's very kind of you. But I wouldn't wish to impose."

"Nonsense. It's no trouble, no trouble at all. My darling Freddie would have wanted you here. He was such a dear boy, so generous with his friends and family." She dabbed at her eyes with a black-edged handkerchief. "Look at me now. This talk of my son has turned me into a watering pot. Do forgive me."

Her sorrow sliced into Burke. "There's nothing to forgive," he said with the gruffness of true feeling. "Alfred was a fine man and a hero at Waterloo. I'd give my own life to have him back."

"You must humor a mother and allow me time to reminisce with you," she said, sniffling. "Do say you'll accept my invitation."

Stay under the same roof as Catherine? "With pleasure."

A beatific smile creased her face. Peering toward the door, she squirmed off the settee and onto her feet. "There they are at last! My two precious daughters."

Burke stood up as three women glided into the doorway. In the background, near the carved oak doors that opened to the foyer, hovered Catherine Snow, a dark and slender nightingale behind the colorful plumage of her twin sisters-in-law.

His heart jerked into an erratic drumbeat. The devil take his misgivings. He had been right to come here.

Unlike her companions, she hadn't changed gowns. The black bombazine dulled her complexion, and the ruffled cap hid the richness of her hair. But her beauty put the other ladies to shame. She had the qualities of an angel, from the sweet curve of her lower lip to the delicacy of her profile. The oversized shawl could not disguise the delectable shape of her breasts or the womanly indentation of her waist. Burke reminded himself that he was here to fulfill his vow, nothing more. But his body spoke a different language; it urged him to ravish her.

No wonder Alfred had never brought her to London.

Married or not, she would have caused a riot among the gentlemen eager to win her favor.

When she glanced his way, he was struck by the lack of a sparkle in those amber eyes. Gone was the spirited woman who had threatened to shoot him. Now she lowered her gaze to the Persian carpet.

Lorena Snow drew her daughters toward Burke. "My lord, this is Miss Priscilla Snow and Miss Prudence."

"Good afternoon, m'lord," they chirped.

Lorena made a surreptitious motion of her hand, and the two girls dipped a curtsy. Though not great beauties, they were presentable. At Almack's, they might even be all the rage due to their identical, fresh-faced innocence. Bobbing up again, they looked like a pair of sleek pheasants, Prudence in rusty orange and Priscilla in greenish gold. Or was it the other way around?

Burke didn't much care. His attention kept straying to Catherine, who remained in the doorway as he dutifully kissed the milk-white hand of each twin. "How rare to encounter such grace and elegance even once," he said by rote. "Twice is astounding."

They glanced at each other and giggled, yellow curls bobbing against flawless skin.

"Shall I fetch your tea now, ma'am?" Catherine asked.

Lorena inclined her head. "Thank you. That will be all."

Burke had been anticipating the chance to speak to Catherine, and now he watched in disbelief as she turned to go. She had been sent off like a parlormaid. That dismissal, added to her unattractive garb, summed up a grim situation. Lorena and her daughters regarded Catherine as their servant.

"Excuse me a moment, madam," he said with a terse bow to his hostess.

"But my lord—"

"Wait here."

He hastened through the doorway and caught Catherine in the outer passageway. Despite the daintiness of her stature, her upper arm felt firm and well-muscled. For the first time he noticed her chapped and reddened hands.

Unbidden, a surge of protectiveness coursed through him. "I shan't allow you to be treated this way," he said in a harsh undertone.

Her eyes shone a startled, luminous gold. "What way?"

"Like a slave, curse it." On a whim, he seized her hand and kissed the roughened back. A spark of connection seemed to leap between them and into his chest. "You should be wearing silks and painting watercolors."

She snatched back her hand and rubbed the place his lips had touched. "With all due respect, my lord, my artistic talents run to arranging hair and creating desserts. Besides, my life is no concern of yours."

If only she knew. He took a deep, calming breath. "I'd like you to join us for tea."

"I'm sorry, but there are household duties that require my attention—"

"*I* require your attention."

"Oh, do you now?" The luster of life shone in her eyes again, radiating a luminous beauty. "Surely three admiring ladies are enough to amuse even a skirt-chaser like you."

"You know nothing of my tastes in women, then."

"I know enough to decline any association with *you.*"

Glowering at him, she clutched something half hidden by her shawl, something suspended from a thin gold chain around her neck. The locket.

With a jolt of recognition, he spied the white sculpted shell against a coral background, the cameo of an angel reaching toward a diamond star. It was the locket Alfred had shown Burke on the battlefield.

An unnerving sense of familiarity struck him. He had seen that locket somewhere else, too.

An eerie tingling raced over his skin. The walls seemed to shrink, crowding in on him, pressing on his temples. With the inevitability of a tide, the image swept over him.

Catherine sat in the wing chair in the library, her head bowed, exposing the dainty mole on the nape of her neck. An indefinable sadness in her solemn eyes, she regarded the jewel case in her lap and touched her fingertip to the gold lettering stamped into the leather.

"Thee needn't have brought me a present from London," she chided, even as she opened the lid.

With a gasp of awe, she drew forth a pair of cameo lockets from their nest of white velvet. She undid the tiny clasp on each and examined the miniatures within.

A tender smile lit her face with radiance. "How perfect. One painting of me for thee, and one of thee for me." She held the locket containing his likeness to her muslin gown. Eyes misty, she vowed, "I'll keep mine close to my heart forever."

The image faded away. Burke found himself standing in the passageway again, the woodwork biting into his back and sweat chilling his forehead.

It had happened again. A scene had unfolded in his mind like a play. No, not a play. A real event. As if he truly *had* given her a jewel case containing identical lockets.

Impossible.

Over the past year, similar fantasies had plagued him without mercy. Obsessed him until he felt as if he were going mad. He had felt compelled to come here in the desperate hope of exorcising the demons that controlled his mind.

Instead, this vision had been the most vivid one yet. Before today, he had glimpsed her likeness only once, in the locket belonging to her dying husband. Yet Catherine looked and acted in real life exactly as Burke had seen her in his mind.

He groped for a logical explanation. No matching locket existed. Alfred's personal effects had been sent back to his widow. Naturally she wore his locket for its sentimental value.

The pronounced Yorkshire accent proved the scene was mere illusion. Because she spoke in the cultured tone of the upper class.

"My lord? You're pale of a sudden. Are you all right?"

Catherine's face swam into focus. One of her dark eyebrows winged upward in a quizzical look that he knew somehow. *Knew.*

Ask her, a voice whispered inside him. *Ask her if there are two matching lockets.* But his mouth felt drier than a wad of wool.

She looked achingly familiar, from the rich brown hair peeping out of her ruffled cap to the amber eyes so wide and mysterious, hinting at a sensuality that had tormented his dreams. He burned to press her against the wall and kiss her, taste her, touch her, to measure fact against fantasy.

Christ, he *was* going mad.

With effort, he fabricated a smile. "Never mind the tea," he said. "It's time you and I had our private talk. Why don't you show me to my room?"

Her eyebrow arched even higher. "You aren't staying here."

"Ah, but I am. Your mother-in-law invited me."

An attractive flush tinged her cheekbones. Her breasts lifted beneath the black shawl as she took in a breath.

Even as she parted her lips to speak, an angry rustling of petticoats came from the drawing room. Lorena appeared in the doorway. "What is all the whispering out here? Catherine, you mustn't pester Lord Thornwald. Go on back to the kitchen."

"I asked the lady to escort me to my chamber," Burke interjected. "I confess to a sudden weariness from my journey."

"Oh, but Priscilla or Prudence would be more than happy to accompany you—"

"Your daughters and I will have ample time to get acquainted over dinner."

Lorena compressed her lips, shot a suspicious scowl at Catherine, then composed herself with a pleasant smile aimed at Burke. "Whatever pleases you, my lord. Catherine, take his lordship to the Blue Velvet Room."

Catherine lowered her eyes. "Yes, ma'am."

Her sudden meekness exasperated him. It was as if in the presence of her mother-in-law, Catherine locked away all verve and vitality and became a shadow figure.

He offered Catherine his arm, but she swept ahead of him and headed for the grand staircase, her heels clicking on the marble floor. A strange sensation rushed over him. He had been here before. He knew these surroundings, the gilded balustrade, the three-tiered chandelier, the gold-striped wallpaper.

As quickly as the fancy had arisen, he scorned it. This dwelling was decorated with a marked similarity to the Regent's ornate style at Carlton House. That was all.

His hallucinations about Catherine were just as absurd. There must be a logical explanation for his seeming knowledge of her. He would stay here until he solved the mystery.

As he followed Catherine up the steps, the shawl slipped from her shoulders. She had a beautiful back, slender at the waist like an hourglass, curving upward to feminine shoulders and a graceful neck. In a flash he recalled the illusion of watching her open the jewel case containing the lockets.

And seeing the tiny mole on her nape.

Looking at her now, he felt the prickling of a ghostly chill. There, on the back of her neck, precisely where he had imagined it, was a tiny beauty mark.

Chapter 2

His stare unnerved Catherine.

Her fingers taut around the doorhandle, she glanced at Burke Grisham for the first time since leading the way along the twists and turns of corridors. She had walked purposefully fast. She had a few things to say to this man. His presence as an honored guest galled her.

Standing outside the bedchamber, she found herself distracted by his scrutiny. In dark splendor he towered over her, his broad-shouldered form lit from behind by the flickering candles in the wall sconces. His subtle scent of horses and leather made him more manly, and somehow more threatening. Cast in half-shadow, his eyes were hard as granite and a sulky tension firmed his mouth. As if *he* were angry with *her*.

Audacious scoundrel. Just wait until she gave him an earful.

She pushed open the door. "Your room, m'lord."

The earl waved her inside. "Ladies first."

She didn't feel like a lady, yet that was the second time today he had referred to her as such. Prodded by an ingrained courtesy, she walked into the room and heard the door close after him. When she turned, his lordship loomed mere inches away, still watching her. His attention never strayed to the large chamber with its expensive furnishings and dark-blue draperies. His brow was furrowed as if he were working through a puzzle.

Catherine cast about for the right words. But there was no manner book that stated how to address the man who had robbed one of the chance to have a family. There was no protocol for how to speak to the person who had caused one's husband to die. "My lord, it's best that I get straight to the point. There are certain things I have to say to you—"

"Were you wearing that shawl outside?"

His abrupt question took her aback. "This?" She plucked at the merino wool. "Yes, I suppose I was. But—"

"Was it higher?"

"Beg pardon?"

"You know what I mean. Up more." He made an elevating gesture at the black shawl, the ends of which were knotted at her bosom. "Perhaps high enough to conceal your neck?"

Was the man mad? "Upon my word, I don't know," she said, exasperated. "However, now that we have a moment of privacy, I trust we can speak frankly to one another."

"Whatever you like."

"It isn't a matter of *like.* It's a matter of saying what must be said, however unpleasant." Lorena would have an apoplectic fit when she found out her daughter-in-law had driven away their aristocratic guest. But Catherine would find a way to placate her later. "Firstly, I was surprised that you would dare pay us a social call considering your role in the death of my husband."

She paused. Lord Thornwald didn't appear to be listening. He circled her, the click of his bootheels sharp on the floorboards, rattling her confidence. Directly behind her, he lifted the shawl higher on her shoulders.

The brush of his fingers on the nape of her neck sent a flurry of shivers over her skin.

Catherine took an undignified leap sideways. Her hip struck a gilt writing desk and set a tray of quills to rattling. "What do you think you're doing?"

"I merely wanted to see if your mole is still visible when your shawl is raised." A peculiar satisfaction deepened his voice. "And it is, by God."

He *was* a madman. First he had attacked poor Fabian. Then, outside the drawing room, his eyes had glazed over as if he had fallen into a trance. Now, of all things, he was obsessed with her shawl.

Surreptitiously she rubbed her sore hip through the folds of her skirt. Even so far north, people gossiped about his notoriety as a gambler, a rake, a daredevil. And certainly she had witnessed with her own eyes the depths of his depravity. But what else did she really know of him?

Perhaps the battle of Waterloo had unhinged the earl's mind.

Too late, Catherine saw the folly in closeting herself alone with him. Who could guess what he might do next? With those large hands, he could overpower her easily. The thought took the edge off her anger and roused a sense of alarm.

She inched toward the door. "Here I am chattering when you must be weary. If you'll excuse me, I'll send the footman to make up the fire. Dinner is served at eight o'clock. If you require anything else, the bell rope is by the hearth."

He prowled after her. "Don't run off, Mrs. Snow. We haven't had our talk yet."

"I've reconsidered," she said, her voice catching. "It's ill-mannered of me to disturb you any longer."

She reached for the door handle; he flattened his palm against the oak panel and held it shut. "On the contrary," he said in a suddenly silky tone, "you have my permission to disturb me for as long as you like."

His smile took her breath away. It transformed his face into that of a charming rogue. She felt helpless to move, like a rabbit pinned by a predator. Though he didn't touch her, his arms and chest formed an impregnable prison. There was no space to retreat; the door handle poked into the back of her waist and the door felt hard against her spine. She was well and truly trapped. Yet a glow of warmth started low in her belly and somehow she lost the urge to flee.

"You know," he mused, "underneath that black shawl, you're a very pretty woman."

Deep in his gray eyes lurked a seductive darkness that called to her. Digging her fingers into her palms, she resisted the urge to touch the shadow of stubble on his cheeks, to invite the pressure of his lips on hers, to draw his weight down to cover her. She wanted more than anything to ease the ache of loneliness that she had lived with for too long.

Lord Thornwald's gaze strayed to her bosom. Without warning, he slid his fingers beneath her locket. "This is a charming piece. Is it one of a kind?"

The heat of his hand penetrated her bodice, and the warmth inside her became a river of bittersweet desire. Shameful desire for the worthless rake who had corrupted her husband and made her a widow.

Her body's betrayal was more than Catherine could bear. With a vicious swipe, she struck his arm away. "Stop touching me. Now get away. Go on!"

He stepped back, his palms raised as if *she* were the lunatic. "Catherine, forgive me. I never meant to cause offense. Yet there are things I must find out. Things I need to know—"

"Then know this," she broke in, fighting tears. "You're a contemptible scoundrel. You aren't welcome in this house. You should never have come here at all."

Fumbling with the handle, she wrenched open the door and fled.

A glass of brandy at his side, Burke lounged in a copper tub, the hard rim supporting the nape of his neck. From the cheroot in his mouth, a curl of blue-gray smoke wafted toward the ceiling of the opulent dressing room. The heat of the steaming water soothed the dull ache in his upper chest where more than a year ago a musket ball had ripped through flesh and muscle and changed his life forever.

The episode haunted him. As if it had happened yesterday, he was floating above his own body. He saw the white light shining through the black void, streaking toward him, enveloping him in an aura of perfect peace and wondrous love.

He grimaced in automatic denial. A dream, he told himself for the umpteenth time. A pain-induced delirium. Love like that didn't exist. It belonged to the make-believe realm of fairies and angels. Yet ever since, he had guarded the memory, never revealing it to anyone. Its luster would be tarnished if he reduced it to a war story to be laughed over by his friends.

He ran his tongue over the end of the cheroot and tasted the tang of tobacco. Not that his friends had cared enough to ask after him. None of them had visited during the long weeks he had lain in an overcrowded Brussels hospital. Until one afternoon, exhausted from his daily walk, he collapsed on his pallet and saw a woman in a clinging gauze gown approach his bedside.

He'd struggled to pluck her name from the parade of beauties in his past. Lady Pamela Seymour. A handkerchief held to her nose, Lady Pamela had cooed and fussed over him before admitting that her husband had also survived the battle. Stroking Burke's hand, she offered to resume her position as his mistress.

He had gazed at her painted features and seen her for

what she was: a tawdry tart, less a lady than an East End whore. When he bluntly told her so, she slapped his face and flounced out in a huff. At that very moment, with his ears still ringing, he had been afflicted for the first time by the astonishing vision of another woman. A woman with dark hair and amber eyes. A woman of quiet grace and rustic charm.

Catherine Snow.

Then as now, longing poured through his body. Burke clenched the sides of the bathtub and mastered his unruly emotions. Curse it. Never before in his life had he dreamt of a woman. He must be teetering on the brink of insanity to lust after the shrew who had caused Alfred such unhappiness. Besides, Burke could never betray the trust of the man who had been like a brother to him. He would fulfill his promise to Alfred by making sure Catherine received fair treatment from her in-laws. Beyond that, she meant nothing to him.

Nothing at all.

At least now he had an explanation for his knowledge of the mole on her neck: he could have noticed it while following her into the house. But were there two matching lockets? He had bungled his chance to charm the answer out of Catherine.

You're a contemptible scoundrel. You aren't welcome here. You should never have come here at all.

Her hostility was a sour tonic to his sick obsession for her. Granted, she had the body of a goddess, and like any red-blooded man he had burned to kiss her deeply, to carry her to the bed and make love to her long into the night. Would she be hot or cold? The latter, no doubt. If she had displayed her touch-me-not antagonism toward Alfred, it would explain why the poor wretch had been driven to drink the final year of his life.

Burke scowled at the candle, its flame shimmering over the mahogany clothespress. To hell with sharp-tongued women. They brought a man nothing but trouble. Give him a soft, scented lightskirt who knew how to use her mouth for more than talking. A woman who knew how to please a man in bed.

A queer jolt scurried over his skin. His temples began to throb. What the devil . . . ?

He drew deeply on the cheroot in an attempt to avert the vision. But the hot relentless tide washed away his willpower.

In the yellow halo cast by a candle, Catherine sat reading in the gilt poster bed with its hangings of green velvet. A pair of silver-rimmed spectacles was perched on her nose and a haphazard collection of books were scattered on the coverlet. The candle glow illuminated the glorious spill of dark hair on the mound of white pillows. Beneath the modest nightrail that reached to her throat, she would taste as delectable as the finest brandy.

She looked up. Eyes widening, she removed her spectacles and lay down her book—

A soft rapping noise yanked him back to reality. Sweating and disoriented, he crouched in the tub and struggled to regain control of his mind. Knocking. He had heard knocking.

The sound had come from the half-opened door that led to his bedroom. *Trotter,* he thought. Yes, the valet must have brought his trunk from the posting inn.

Steeling the shameful trembling of his hand, Burke removed the cheroot long enough to grunt, "Come in."

The hinges creaked. An unmanly rustling accompanied the dainty scuffing of footsteps. Into the dressing room walked a fair-haired girl dressed in tangerine silk.

Burke sat up straight in the tub, thought better of it, and slouched beneath the meager concealment of soap-scummed water. "What the devil—"

Prudence—or was it Priscilla?—stood with her gaze demurely downcast. "Mummy asked me to escort your lordship down to dinner. But I must be early. Oh, dear me."

With her hands clasped prayerfully at her waist, she might have been an angel. But there was nothing pure in the way she peeked at him from beneath the veil of her lashes. There was nothing virtuous in the come-hither smile that perked her lips.

He stubbed out the cheroot in the soap dish. "I was just getting out," he said. "If you care to avoid further embarrassment, I would suggest you leave now."

He planted his hands on the scrolled rim of the tub and slowly pushed himself upward. The invigorating air cooled his skin. Droplets of water sluiced through the mat of hair on his chest and the mottled scar tissue there.

The girl's eyes rounded. Pink tinged her cheeks as her sham sophistication altered to maidenly alarm. She fled like a startled kitten out the door.

He chuckled, not from mirth but from the grim specter of trouble. In the future, he'd have to keep an eye on those twins. The last thing he needed to complicate his plans was an outraged mother hen threatening a scandal if he refused to marry one of her precious chicks.

Burke stepped out of the tub and dried himself with a towel. He was here for one purpose and one purpose alone. To find logic in the madness, to end the obsession that ruled his mind.

This latest dream only strengthened his resolve. At least now he had a few more things to check. Did Catherine wear spectacles? Did she have a habit of lying abed with a stack of books?

He knew just the way to coax some answers out of her. He would do so tonight.

And God help him if his fantasies proved to be true.

"Dinner is served," Humphrey intoned from the doorway.

Catherine slipped past the cadaverous butler and into the drawing room. Coming from the kitchen where she had been overseeing the food preparation, she had timed her entrance to avoid having to chat with their guest. He made her distinctly uneasy and undeniably angry. She had spent the past two hours fuming over his outrageous presence.

Touching her locket for courage, she waited unobtrusively near the gilt-edged mirror. Her gaze was drawn to the circle of people who rose from their chairs at the summons: Lorena, the twins, Fabian Snow . . . and Burke Grisham.

She had meant to ignore him, but his magnetic, mist-gray eyes commanded her attention. Once she looked at him, she couldn't tear her gaze away. He was the paragon of masculinity in a cutaway navy coat over buckskin breeches, the white cravat setting off his swarthy complexion. The feelings she had denied inundated her again—the melting warmth in her belly, the tightening of her breasts, the vulnerable yearning to be held close and kissed. How mortifying that her body responded to him of all men.

He started toward her. She hadn't considered that he might lead her into dinner. Taking a step backward, she clamped her fingers into fists. She could not bear the thought of touching him. She could not. Yet the surging of her heartbeat declared otherwise.

Then Lorena stepped into his path and slid her arm through his. "My lord, it seems we ladies have a shortage of escorts this evening. How kind of you to squire me and my eldest daughter. Priscilla!"

Preening, the blonde girl glided forward, a vision in emerald silk as she took her place at his other side. Pouting, her sister Prudence flounced toward Fabian Snow, her tangerine gown rustling. Fabian cast an appealing look at Catherine, but knowing she was expected to take up the rear, she gave a little shake of her head.

As Burke walked past, flanked by Lorena and Priscilla, he flashed Catherine a woeful grin. The expression made him look surprisingly boyish and astonishingly handsome. And not at all like a man unhinged in his mind. An unexpected bubble of warmth rose within her. She had to bite the inside of her cheek to keep from smiling back.

She trailed the small party through the entrance hall and down the passage to the dining parlor. There she bumped into Fabian, who halted abruptly in the doorway.

"Oh, this will not do," Lorena wailed. "It will not do at all. Catherine? Kindly come here, child."

Catherine wondered what she had done wrong this time. She walked to her mother-in-law, who surveyed the sparkling china on the linen-draped table, the gold epergne dripping with fragrant roses, the liveried footmen standing ready to serve. Even the white-painted woodwork gleamed against the ocher walls.

"The candelabra on the sideboard isn't lit," Lorena complained. "Nor is the one by the chimneypiece. What is the meaning of this?"

"You've told me never to waste candles—"

"Never mind, never mind," she said, shaking her plump, diamond ringed fingers. "We have been favored by an important guest. He deserves only the best."

The scolding made Catherine defiant, ready to snap another retort. Out of long habit, she controlled the impulse. "Yes, ma'am."

As she started to turn away, Burke touched the back of her waist in a staying gesture. The contact sizzled like the heated metal of a pan. But he was gazing at Lorena. "Surely you have servants to attend to such tasks."

A placating smile creased her face. "Oh, la, m'lord, Catherine doesn't mind. She has a knack for household matters, though she does require a firm guiding hand."

"Sh-she's an angel," Fabian blurted. He aimed an adoring look at Catherine.

"I hardly think it necessary to speak in sacrilegious terms," Lorena said.

Prudence and Priscilla giggled behind their fans. Fabian blushed crimson, and Catherine could have slapped all three women for embarrassing him.

Taking the earl's arm, Lorena guided him to the table. "Come, m'lord, take the place where my dear Freddie used to sit. As I was saying, Catherine has been well trained in menial duties like all the common girls hereabouts. Why, I myself can scarcely tell the difference between wax and tallow candles . . . ."

As her mother-in-law droned on, Catherine took a lighted candle and moved about the room, touching the tiny flame to the wicks of the unlit tapers. She felt a queer twist of pleasure that Burke had troubled himself to champion her. Of course, that was his way, to charm every woman who crossed his path. And to bed as many of them as he could.

By the time she slipped into her seat at Lorena's left and opposite Fabian, she had regained an emotional distance. The talk turned to gossip. The twins monopolized Burke, who sat between them at the head of the table.

"What did you think of Princess Charlotte's wedding this past May?" Priscilla asked.

"Was Prince Leopold as dashing as they say?" Prudence added.

"Tell us about her gown," Priscilla intruded. "I hear she wore silver with garlands of diamonds."

"Is it true the prince has kept her ever since on a honeymoon at their house in Surrey?" Prudence said.

The earl gave them a bland smile. "To my regret, I must confess to ignorance in matters involving our future queen. I've spent the past year in Cornwall overseeing my flock of sheep. In truth, I thought I might purchase a few purebred rams during my stay in Yorkshire."

"You? A shepherd?" Catherine blurted in astonishment. "I should think you'd be more at home in a gaming hall."

"Catherine!" Lorena said. "Apologize to his lordship at once."

"No apology necessary," he said with a wave of his hand. "Sheep hold a curious appeal to us jaded sorts. They're docile creatures who never talk back. They're content to eat grass and yield a pretty profit. Besides, how else am I to get money to squander?"

His eyes twinkled at Catherine. She was tempted to scoff at such mummery. What a bald-faced liar he was, to pretend an interest in sheep. She forced her attention to the watercress soup ladled out by a footman. Likely, the earl had been forced to retreat to his estate in order to escape his London creditors.

"If business delays you, m'lord," Lorena said, "you will be staying for some time yet."

"It would seem so."

"Then you must allow me to arrange a gathering on Wednesday next. A few of our dearest friends in the neighborhood." The chair creaked as she shifted enthusiastically. "Not that we could ever hope to match the parties given by your London friends. La, you'll think us hopelessly countrified, but we would adore having a man of your stature in our humble midst."

"The honor is mine," Lord Thornwald said.

To Catherine, the flavorful soup tasted like laundry soap. He meant to tarry here for another week and a half? The prospect formed a tight coil of tension inside her.

The twins excitedly discussed the party. "We cannot forget to invite Lieutenant Galbraith," Prudence said, artfully placing her hand on her bosom. "He looks ever so dashing in his uniform."

Priscilla batted her blonde lashes at Burke. "Did you

meet Lieutenant Roger Galbraith at Waterloo?" she asked. "He served in the 16th Light Dragoons."

The earl set down his spoon. "No, I was never a member of our illustrious army."

"But weren't you and Alfred in the very thick of battle?" Prudence asked, her blue eyes wide. "Why, we received a letter of commendation signed by Wellington himself. You're both heroes."

"Not I." His voice deepened to a growl. "Alfred alone is. He was courageous beyond compare. He should be sitting here with you today, not me. It's my fault that he died."

Silence crawled over the dinner table. Lorena paused in the act of wiping her mouth with her napkin. Fabian Snow held his soup spoon frozen in midair. The twins stared, goggle-eyed, at their guest. Lord Thornwald's face might have been carved from granite. Beyond his immaculately starched cuffs, his strong fingers pressed into the white tablecloth, and Catherine fancied he kept dark secrets tightly harnessed behind the facade of a gentleman.

So, her anger at him was justified. Yet she felt deflated somehow, cheated of the satisfaction of shaming a confession out of him.

Lorena lifted the napkin to dab at her eyes. "What happened was a tragedy of war, my lord. You are not to blame."

The coil of emotion inside Catherine tightened. She couldn't stop herself from speaking out. "On the contrary. Let us hear his lordship's story and judge his actions for ourselves."

"I shouldn't have spoken now," he said, looking at her. "Such a grievous tale is hardly a topic for dinner conversation."

"Yet I would know from an eyewitness the circumstances of my husband's death."

"This is outrageous," Lorena protested. "Catherine,

what has gotten into you tonight? You must stop badgering our guest."

For once, she ignored her mother-in-law. Catherine felt locked in combat with the earl as she stared at him down the length of the dinner table. He made a formidable opponent, his jaw set and his mouth tight. The only sound was the clink of china as the footman cleared the soup bowls and served the fish course. She was determined not to give in, no matter what retribution Lorena visited upon her later.

He studied her face a moment longer before his gaze dropped to her bosom, where she clutched her locket.

"As you wish, then," he said. "But I'd like to begin by telling you everything I know of Alfred, from start to finish."

From his cynical smile, she had the oddest feeling he had planned all along for her to pressure him into talking about Alfred. She didn't understand why. What game of cat and mouse was he playing with her?

He sipped his wine. "When I met Alfred, it was late one night at Boodle's. He was trying to persuade a doddering old gent deep in his cups to go on home. You see, the two of them had been playing ecarte all evening, and the poor fellow had lost a bundle. Alfred cancelled his debt and arranged a ride home for him. That was the sort of magnanimous man he was."

"My darling son." Lorena sniffled, her eyes watery. "He was always so thoughtful of others, so ready to help."

Catherine sat rigid, her thoughts anguished. Yes, she had loved the man he described. Alfred had been generous when the mood suited him. But soon after their marriage she had discovered he was as likely to gamble away the revenues from the estate. How she had despised his addiction to the gaming tables. A disease fed by the company of dissolute men like the earl of Thornwald.

All during the rabbit pie and the sausages, the braised onions and parsnips, the gooseberry fool and the cotherstone cheese, Burke spoke eloquently of Alfred—his kindness, his compassion, his sense of humor, his love of adventure. Until at last Burke broached the topic of Waterloo.

"As we all know," he said, looking solemnly around the table, "when Napoleon escaped from Elba Island and marched across France, London was abuzz with rumors about the impending battle. Some even placed bets in clubs like White's and Brooks's as to when the attack would occur. But the real excitement lay across the Channel in Belgium. I arranged for a group of friends to go there, to witness the action."

"To frolic while courageous men died," Catherine couldn't resist commenting.

He stabbed a lone gooseberry, then set down his fork. "That's a blunt way of looking at it, yes. The British held parties to pass the long days of waiting. In fact, on the eve of battle, the duchess of Richmond gave a ball and Wellington himself attended. Surely you wouldn't question *his* judgment."

Why was she feeling so quarrelsome? Catherine wondered. He accepted the blame for Alfred's death. He didn't make excuses for his own culpability. And he painted Alfred in a favorable pose. She should be grateful, yet resentment churned inside her. "Tell us about the battle."

"As soon as word came that Napoleon was marching on the city, most of the British civilians fled to Antwerp. I was determined to stay. I persuaded Alfred and some other friends to accompany me to a bluff where we could observe the fighting from a safe vantage point."

"How frightening," Priscilla exclaimed.

"How brave of you," Prudence gushed.

"Brave? Hardly." Burke shook his head, scowling at his wine glass as if its ruby depths held dark scenes from his past. "I wanted to vicariously experience the danger and excitement. But watching the battle through a spyglass didn't satisfy my taste for adventure. After a time, I left my friends and drove off. Alfred came along, too. When we reached the battleground . . ." He paused. "I don't think you want to hear the rest."

"Yes, we do," Catherine insisted. "Tell us everything."

He shrugged. "The ground was littered with dead and dying soldiers. Men with their limbs shattered. Men with bloodied wounds in their chests or heads. Men crying out for help."

The twins gasped. Lorena moaned. Fabian gulped. Catherine bit her lip so hard she tasted blood.

In an anguished whisper, she said, "Alfred was no soldier. He didn't belong on a field of battle."

"I know. I came to my senses then and would have turned back, but Alfred insisted upon aiding our fallen soldiers. Under his direction we loaded the injured into the carriage and transported as many as we could to a field hospital. Alfred labored tirelessly until nightfall. He risked his life time and again to daringly rescue the wounded from enemy gunfire."

Burke paused, his mouth twisted into a moody grimace, his gaze shadowed and downcast. He gripped the stem of the wine glass, his knuckles white. Against her will, Catherine felt an outpouring of sympathy for him, that he had lived through such a nightmare.

While Alfred had died.

"So what happened?" she whispered. "I should like to hear the rest of it."

He slowly lifted his gaze to her. Catherine stared at him, shocked by the pain there, the self-loathing. She hardly knew what to think. Did he downplay his own role in saving lives? Was he hero or villain? She sat on the edge of her seat, waiting impatiently for the end of his narrative.

"Madam?" Holding a silver salver in his white-gloved

hands, the butler appeared in the doorway. "I have a message from Lady Beaufort."

Her eyes reddened, Lorena waved him away with her napkin. "Not now, Humphrey."

"Her footman said it is most urgent."

"Oh, all right." Lorena plucked the missive from the tray. "Do pardon me, m'lord. Her ladyship is a dear friend."

Lorena broke the sealing wax and unfolded the note. Her eyes widened. Her face paled to a pasty white hue. The paper trembled like a leaf, then slipped from her fingers and fluttered into her empty dessert bowl.

Catherine frowned. "Is something amiss? You look ill."

"What does her ladyship say?" Priscilla asked. "I do hope she isn't inviting us to another of her tedious theatricals."

Lorena looked as if she had seen a ghost. She pushed to her feet, took a few wobbling steps, then crumpled to the floor in a dead faint.

Chapter 3

His stricken hostess weighed more than he expected.

Gritting his teeth, Burke lifted Lorena into his arms. He might as well be hefting a dead ewe. The old wound in his chest throbbed from the strain. At least her steady breathing assured him she had merely swooned.

"Mummy," Priscilla said, recoiling in dismay. "Oh, Mummy, have you died?"

" 'Tis a fit of the vapors," Prudence said with great interest. "I've never seen her so overwrought."

Ignoring them, Burke turned to Catherine, who stood nearby, her amber eyes so full of tender anxiety that he found himself wishing he, too, could manage a swoon. "Where shall I take her?" he asked.

"Follow me." Wheeling around, she hastened out the door, with the twins and Fabian bringing up the rear.

Lorena's dumpling form bobbled against Burke. She lay with her mouth agape and her eyes closed. Her huge bosom was squashed against the front of his shirt. A blend of cloying perfume and body odor assailed him.

Catherine ushered him into a morning room decorated in gold and red. Taking care, he lowered his burden to a crimson velvet sofa. Catherine tucked a needlework pillow beneath her mother-in-law's head.

"Fetch the hartshorn from Mrs. Earnshaw in the kitchen," she told Fabian.

"Y-yes." The young man rushed off.

"Oh, this is terrible," Priscilla said, wringing her hands. "I don't know what to do."

Prudence pressed her hand to her brow. "M'lord, I feel rather dizzy myself. Do catch me if I fall."

Burke reached for a Chippendale chair and nudged it against the back of her knees. "Then perhaps you'd best sit."

Uttering a squeak of surprise, she plopped down hard on the seat. She glanced up at him, her mouth set in a sulky pout.

Catherine reached behind Lorena and unhooked the neckline of her gown to loosen the stiff lace. Then she picked up a doily and fanned her mother-in-law's pallid features. "There now," she murmured. "I'll take care of you."

The gentleness of her voice brought forth a memory in Burke, a hazy picture of his mother tending to him as a little boy when he was fretful and ill with a fever. He could feel her hand, cool against his brow and hear her voice, crooning a lullaby. . . .

His chest tightened with the vestiges of pain. That childhood event had occurred before Colin's violent death. Before Burke had destroyed his mother's love. Before he had lost his father's esteem forever.

Stinking coward.

His hands felt cold and clammy. Pressure throbbed against his temples. Mastering himself, he propped his elbow on the mantelpiece and assumed a pose of idle indifference. The devil take love. It was a worthless emotion that caused only misery. Look at Catherine Snow. She was a fool for catering to her mother-in-law. The old bitch would only continue to misuse her.

Fabian loped back into the room, his fair hair flying. Taking the small vial he thrust at her, Catherine removed the cork and waved the bottle beneath Lorena's nose.

The woman snorted and coughed. She turned her head from side to side in an effort to evade the ammonia scent. With a shuddering gasp, she opened her eyes and shoved Catherine away.

"What are you doing? Trying to poison me?"

"No, ma'am. Now lie still. You've had a shock."

Catherine's quiet tone seemed to soothe Lorena. She lay back, her eyes half closed, her breasts rising and falling like a pair of plum puddings. "A shock," she muttered. "Yes . . . a shock."

Now that she was conscious, her daughters crowded in closer.

"Mummy, whatever did Lady Beaufort say?" Priscilla asked.

"Yes, do tell," Prudence added, half dancing with excitement. "It must have been something perfectly dreadful."

Lorena weakly nodded, her double chin jiggling. "It was the theft of her jewelry. A robber broke into her home."

"She owned but a few trifling pieces," Priscilla said with a sniff. "I don't see why such news would make you swoon."

"It wasn't that. The talk of dear Freddie upset me. Yes, I was overcome by grief over my darling boy." Lorena wept noisily into her handkerchief.

Burke clenched his hands. He shouldn't have spoken at length about Waterloo, not even to portray Alfred as a hero. Not even to satsify his own zeal to find a rational explanation for his visions.

"You should rest upstairs," Catherine told Lorena. "Lord Thornwald, may I ask your assistance again?"

Burke shunned the appeal in her eyes and motioned

to Fabian. "No doubt a relation would be more welcome in the lady's bedchamber."

"M-m-me?"

"You're a strong fellow. Let her lean on you."

Fabian straightened his sloping shoulders and awkwardly slid his arm around Lorena. Her mouth pursed, she appeared old and shaken as he helped her out of the room, Catherine and Priscilla close behind them.

Prudence lingered, a slight curve to her ripe young lips. "Now that we have a moment alone, m'lord, I must apologize for walking in on you before dinner. It was a deplorable accident. Pray, don't think ill of me."

"How could I ever think ill of someone so enterprising?" he said with great irony.

"Enterprising . . . ?" She frowned uncomprehendingly.

Then Priscilla reappeared in the doorway and yanked on her sister's arm. "Come along. Mummy is asking for you." She fluttered her blonde lashes at Burke. "Unless, m'lord, you would care for us to keep you company."

"Your thoughtfulness is amazing. However, be assured I can entertain myself."

As they left, Burke felt the oppressive weight of frustration. The women he didn't want were falling all over him. The one woman he *did* want . . .

No, he wanted only information from Catherine, to determine if a matching locket existed. He had been leading up to that question when the butler had appeared with the note. Burke had to prove his dreams of Catherine were pure delusion, perhaps a form of self-flagellation for causing Alfred's death.

The maddening flights of fancy had begun the very moment when Burke himself had nearly died. He could have sworn he heard a woman's voice calling him back from the light. A voice as gentle and melodious as Catherine's. *Don't leave me. Please don't leave me.*

A wave of desperate need inundated him, weakening his legs. The need for love.

Curse it. What he really needed was a drink.

He stalked to the dining room to fetch his glass and a decanter of wine. On Lorena's dish lay the crumpled note, stained by green gooseberry sauce. No decent man read another person's private correspondence.

What the hell. He picked up the sticky paper between his forefinger and thumb and scanned the page.

My Dear Lorena,

Do forgive my wobbly penmanship, but my hands are shaking with fright. I beg to warn you that a thief is loose in our neighborhood! Upon returning from my afternoon calls, I discovered the strongbox in my bedchamber standing open and my jewels missing. Yes, even the pearls I wore on my wedding day! The ruffian had the effrontery to leave a single copper farthing inside the strongbox. As if that would pay for the loss of my treasures! Do take care and lock your doors and windows.

Your Devoted Friend,
Mary, Lady Beaufort

Burke frowned. Lorena struck him as too strong a woman to faint from reading a report about a burglary. Guilt stabbed him, sharp and deep. It *was* the dinner-table conversation, then. The deliberate revelations he had made were meant to coax information from Catherine about her locket.

He ought to leave here. But he couldn't, else he would be plagued forever by images of Catherine Snow. In the future, he'd simply refrain from mentioning Alfred to Lorena.

Burke dropped the note back onto the table. Petty thievery was none of his affair. All that mattered to him was exorcising himself of those strange visions. Visions of Catherine with her maddening beauty. Catherine with her prickly resentment. Catherine with her tender touch.

Catherine.

Children swarmed through the tiny vicarage, chasing each other in a circle from the dining room to the parlor and then back to the library. Their happy shrieks floated through the air, and Catherine found herself smiling wistfully. The sound of children playing, the musty scent of well-thumbed books, filled her with nostalgia.

As usual, the library was in comfortable disarray. Someone had left a buttered bread crust on a lower shelf. A skipping rope dangled from the back of a wooden chair. On the desk lay a quill pen, the tip weeping black ink onto the blotter.

How different from the formal library at Snow Manor. Though hundreds of books lined those pristine shelves, Catherine could not read a single one. Lorena cared only to create the illusion of aristocratic snobbery. She had bought the volumes at a bargain price from the estate sale of a scholar of Greek and Latin. Unfortunately none of the books were written in plain English.

A middle-aged woman emerged from the kitchen, wiping her chapped hands on her apron. Worry lines scored her broad face, and she sagged from face to shoulders to breasts. "Thomas! Sally! Peter! Alice! Jemima! Stop this racket at once."

The children dashed past her, laughing and shouting in blissful disobedience.

Mrs. Harriet Guppy snatched up a ruler and whacked it across the palm of her hand. "Stop, I say, ere I take a switch to thy bottoms!"

The boys and girls skidded to a halt by the mullioned bay window. The elder tow-haired lad bumped Catherine's pile of books. With a thump, the heavy tomes landed on the floor.

"Peter Allen Guppy!" his mother exclaimed. "Pick those up, then come straight here."

"Sorry, Mum." He hastily heaped the books on the writing desk, aided by his brother and sisters, who cast wary glances at the stick wielded by their mother.

"Thee needn't fear," Catherine said, lapsing into the Yorkshire speech pattern of her own youth. She ruffled the boy's hair. " 'Twas an accident, I'm sure. Mrs. Guppy, might I read them a story?"

"Aye! Aye!" the children burst out as one. "Mum, please!"

Their mother lowered the switch and sighed. "Will thee have time from thy duties at the manor?"

Catherine hoped Lorena was still napping. "Aye, for a short tale—"

"Gulliver's Travels," Peter put in, his face shining.

"That's far too long. Perhaps a fable from Aesop."

She plucked a book from one of the shelves and sat down on a stool by the hearth. Peter and Thomas jostled for position at her feet. Alice and Sally sat on the sofa and primly arranged their skirts as if they hadn't just been running like hoydens. The youngest, five-year-old Jemima, climbed onto Catherine's lap and poked a thumb into her little mouth.

Catherine's throat prickled with unshed tears. Eighteen years ago, when she was no older than Jemima, Catherine had come here to live as the ward of Reverend George Guppy after her mother and father died of a fever. She had been Catherine Yardley then, an orphan whose situation had been halfway between servant and family member. Growing up in the vicarage, a child herself, she had earned her keep by taking care of each Guppy sibling from infancy, in addition to the cleaning and washing and cooking. Jemima had just learned to walk when Catherine had married and moved away from the vicarage.

How naïve her dreams had been back then. As much

as she loved her charges, she longed for a devoted husband and a family of her own. A child with adorable eyes and wispy brown hair. A girl or boy who would snuggle to her breast in perfect trust. A little one who would need her guidance and love.

But fate had snatched the fulfillment of motherhood from her. The flaw was her own, a result of her rash behavior. And Lord Thornwald's vile act. . . .

The memory pressed at her. She resisted the pain of it, for the children sat looking at her expectantly. With a sigh, she drew out her spectacles from a hidden pocket in her skirt and put them on, opened the book, and read the familiar fable.

At the end, Jemima pulled out her thumb and asked, "What doth it mean, Mith Cathy?"

"It means thee must be a good person and not a braggart. Thee mustn't run wild like the hare, but work slow and steady like the tortoise."

"I'll wager his lordship runs fast," Peter said.

Jolted by surprise, Catherine frowned at the boy perched at her feet. "The earl of Thornwald? Have thee met him?"

"Nay," Peter said, crestfallen. "But I saw him riding a fine black horse on the moor. I'm going to grow up to be just like him."

"I should hope not." Catherine brushed dirt off the boy's cheek. "He's the biggest gambler in all London."

"And the handsomest," fifteen-year-old Sally said with a sigh.

"He's handsome, but outward appearances are sometimes no reflection of what's inside a person." Catherine removed her spectacles and tucked them away again. "Storytime is over. Alice and Sally, go help thy mother in the kitchen. Peter and Thomas, sit down and finish thy Scripture readings."

"What shall *I* do?" Jemima asked.

Catherine kissed her sweet brow. "Tell thy mother I'm leaving now."

The children groaned and protested. Jemima slid off Catherine's lap and scampered after the older girls. With much dragging of feet and grumbling, the boys settled at the desk and Peter took the first turn at reading the Bible aloud.

When Catherine had gathered up her armload of books, Mrs. Guppy followed her out of the gabled house and onto the stoop. She shook her head in bafflement. "Thee always did have such a way with 'em," she said on a weary sigh. "Ah, but the room in the garret would seem poor now to a fancy lady such as thee."

Strangely, Catherine did think fondly of the cramped attic room that she had shared with each Guppy baby in succession. It wasn't elegant things she craved, but a future of her own choosing. "I do miss this family," she admitted. "I'll always visit as often as I can."

Mrs. Guppy nodded in resignation. "Go straightaway to the manor house, then. Yesterday, Mr. Guppy said Lady Beaufort's jewels got stolen. The thief could be lurking about still."

Gooseflesh crept over Catherine. "I'll keep an eye out."

She set off down the road that led out of the hamlet of Warrenby and over a humped bridge, where a brook trickled musically over rocks. Her route hugged the perimeter of the moor that stretched for miles in rolling majesty. Dark clouds lurked on the western horizon, but overhead the sky was so blue it hurt her eyes.

Fear of robbers had no place on such a heavenly day, she reflected. The sweetness of warm grass hung heavy in the air along with the scent of heather. The blooms spread across the moor like an endless, pinkish purple sea.

Tugged by irresistible whim, she walked over the springy turf and clambered onto a dry stone wall. Setting down the books, she lifted her face to the radiance of the sun. She needed to get back to the manor house. Her housekeeping duties marched like tin soldiers through her mind. Jelly-making . . . laundry . . . dinner . . . Lorena . . . the twins.

Yet the rare moment of freedom called to her heart. Today her mother-in-law had spent the morning in bed, complaining of an indisposition. She had fallen asleep after lunch, and Catherine had made her escape. When Lorena awakened, let her silver-tongued devil of a guest entertain her. She and Burke Grisham deserved one another.

No. That wasn't fair to her mother-in-law, who was guilty of nothing worse than an overbearing manner. Even she could never descend to his depths of depravity.

Without warning, the memories Catherine had held at bay came rushing over her. In her mind she returned to that idyllic time after her whirlwind marriage to Alfred at Gretna Green, when they had spent four romantic weeks traveling through Scotland and northern England. Alfred had been a charming companion by day and a passionate lover by night. How strange and thrilling it had been to dine at small inns on food she did not have to cook, to sleep on linens she did not have to tidy, to see places she had only read about in books. And to revel in the attention of a handsome gentleman who was head over heels in love with her.

Then one morning she had awakened to an empty bed, and when she went down to breakfast in the dining parlor, she came upon Alfred deep in conversation with a serving maid. He bent his head to murmur in her ear, and the girl blushed prettily.

Catherine felt a shock at their air of intimacy. Was he flirting with the girl? The question burned stronger when he turned and his gaze widened guiltily on her. Smiling, he came forward to greet her, and she couldn't help making a sharp query about his chat with the maid. Alfred laughed and teased her about being jealous. With a kiss and a glowing compliment, he soon reassured Catherine that she was the only woman in the world for him.

Yet, that very day, the autumn weather changed to a blustery chill, and with it went Alfred's buoyant mood. Seeming restless and distracted, he ended the honeymoon trip and conveyed his new wife to Snow Manor. His mother's reception was icier than winter on the moor. Alfred and Lorena disappeared into her boudoir, and for a time Catherine heard their raised voices, then the sound of a door slamming. Her husband returned, grim-faced, to announce his imminent departure for London.

"Forgive me, love. I've business in the city. Dreadfully dull stuff."

Catherine threw her arms around him. "Take me with thee."

"Ladies never cling," he chided, disentangling himself. "In my absence, Mother will teach you how to dress and act. If you progress well, you can come with me to London next spring."

Catherine's continued pleas only seemed to annoy him, and when the time came to depart, he entered his carriage with an eager step. She worried that her husband had grown weary of her already. He had married her on a whim which he now regretted. He wished to hide his country mouse in the wilds of Yorkshire.

He was ashamed of her.

The thought was galling, and out of the depths of her despair she made a silent vow. She would transform herself into the type of woman he admired. She would become a lady of fashion.

Over the next fortnight Catherine gave herself up to Lorena's stern tutelage. She learned to walk straight and haughty with the aid of a backboard strapped to her spine. She memorized the intricate dance steps of the quadrille and the reel. She took lessons in elocution so that someday she could speak with the clipped syllables of an aristocrat.

She worked until a deep lethargy crept up on her, and she found it difficult to rise from bed in the morning. Gradually the truth dawned in Catherine. She was pregnant.

Joy bubbled inside her like the fine champagne she and Alfred had drunk to celebrate their nuptials. She couldn't wait to tell him. Now he wouldn't think his impulsive marriage was a mistake. All men wanted a son to carry on the family name. How delighted and proud he would be!

But her husband wouldn't be returning to Yorkshire until Christmas—nearly a month away. And a letter was too impersonal for such momentous news.

Disobeying Lorena, Catherine set out for London on the public coach. She carried a small valise and the pin money Alfred had left her. She would surprise him with the announcement that she would soon bear his child. They would be a family. In less than eight months, she would have a baby to hold and hug, a wondrous creation of their love.

The journey took three and a half days, and the coach left her at a depot near Covent Garden. She asked directions of a street seller and then made her way through the crowded, bewildering city, resisting the urge to gawk at the strangeness of it all. There would be time later to see the sights, safe in Alfred's company.

By the time she found the street, the evening was growing late, and a cold wind blew across the darkened square and tugged at her skirts. A passing carriage splashed her shoes with icy water from a puddle. Trudging beside the kerbstone, she felt a return of misgivings. What if Alfred weren't home? What if he were out to dinner or at a party?

The four-story town house was small but elegant, sandwiched in a row of terraced dwellings, with a stately pediment crowning the doorway. The golden candlelight that spilled from the upper windows cheered her.

But no one answered her knock. How odd that no footman was stationed nearby. After a moment's hesitation, she turned the polished brass handle and stepped into the warmth of the house. Setting down her valise, she studied the pretty foyer with its crystal chandelier ablaze with candles. To the left lay a dining parlor, the table set with gleaming china as if in preparation for a dinner party. There was no one about. She felt like an interloper, a servant who ought to have used the tradesmen's entrance in the rear.

But this was her home now, too, she reminded herself. She was mistress here. The notion seemed a strange and fantastical dream.

The muffled sound of male voices came from upstairs. She mounted the marble steps and at the first floor landing, she came to a set of closed doors. The voices and laughter rang louder here. Alfred must be entertaining visitors.

Catherine smoothed her travel-stained garb. She knew so little of polite behavior. Would it be considered rude of her to inform him of her arrival?

Then she spread her palms over her midsection and felt a warm surge of elation. How could she possibly contain her news one more moment?

She tugged at one of the great oak doors, opening it a crack and peering into a luxurious reception room decorated in blue and gold. The chamber was filled with fashionably dressed gentlemen. And ladies in gowns so revealing that Catherine gaped in startlement. One woman draped herself across a man's lap and pressed her painted mouth to his. Another giggled when her partner plunged his fingers inside her bodice. The smells of spirits and tobacco smoke set Catherine's stomach to roiling.

She squeezed her eyes shut a moment. She must have entered the wrong house. She must have.

When she opened her eyes, she spied Alfred.

He stood at the far end of the room, deep in conversation with another gentleman. Catherine blinked at her husband's appearance. He was red-cheeked with drink, his fair hair disheveled and his cravat hanging askew. He laughed uproariously in response to something said by the other man.

By contrast, his companion looked immaculate in a black frock coat and snowy cravat. He was tall and dark with boldly chiseled features and an imposing presence.

Then Alfred swung rather unsteadily toward his guests. "Quiet down, m'friends, and heed th' earl o' Thornwald." As all eyes turned toward them, Alfred clapped the earl on the back. "You organized this little gatherin', Burke, old chap. Let's hear what you've planned for the rest o' th' night's entertainment."

Burke Grisham, the earl of Thornwald. Alfred had described his rakish friend in glowing terms, but now Catherine took an instant dislike to the earl. This party was his doing?

"You cheated us out of celebrating your final days of bachelorhood," his lordship said, with a few convivial assents from the crowd. "Worse, you've kept your little jewel of a wife hidden away for your private amusement. Nevertheless, I've a wedding gift for you."

He walked out of Catherine's narrow line of vision. A moment later, he returned with a blonde woman who wore a crimson gown that clung to her voluptuous curves. He said, "May I present Miss Stella Sexton."

As Catherine watched in disbelieving horror, Miss Stella Sexton engaged in a provocative dance in front of Alfred. To the accompaniment of cheers and catcalls from the male audience, she peeled off her long red gloves. She slipped out of one sleeve and then the other, so that her ruby beaded gown hung suspended from her milk white bosom. Finally, ever so slowly, she lowered the bodice and unveiled enormous, rouge-tipped breasts.

"No more cold autumn nights." The earl aimed a lazy smile at Alfred. "She'll keep you warm until you feel obliged to return to Yorkshire."

Stella took a hand from each man and placed it on her breasts. "Why not share me?"

The earl cocked an eyebrow at Alfred. Alfred grinned and said something that Catherine couldn't hear over the obscene shouts from the guests. Then the earl very deliberately cupped one of Stella's breasts, bent down, and suckled her. Swaying drunkenly, Alfred followed suit.

Catherine backed away from the door. Nausea clenched her belly and she pressed trembling hands to her womb. The breath stabbed her chest; she felt as if she were suffocating. This was Alfred's business in London? This disgusting frolic with a whore? And these vile people were his friends?

In the midst of her bewilderment, she saw the facts clearly. The earl of Thornwald had reduced the intimate act of love to a sordid spectacle. And Alfred . . . !

Her husband had encouraged the sport.

Somehow, with no memory of descending the stairs or opening the front door, she found herself standing outside. A drizzling rain fell in icy drops that pricked her skin. Bile burned in her throat. She stumbled down the walkway.

Moisture blurred her vision. She couldn't face Alfred. She wanted only to flee, to escape back to the country. To stop herself from remembering.

It was no use. The scene played over and over in her mind. With a shuddering sob, Catherine ran blindly into the street.

The carriage hurtled out of the night. She heard the jingle of harness. The rattle of wheels. The shout of the coachman.

She surged backward and nearly slipped on the wet pavement. A hoof slashed into her belly. The sharpness of pain emptied the breath from her. She bent double, hugging herself as she slid to the cobblestones, too late to protect the unborn life inside her. . . .

Catherine blinked and found herself sitting on the stone wall in Yorkshire again. A brisk wind blew over the moor. Though the sun was shining, she shivered from the memory of that long-ago night. She would never forget the shock of waking up in a crowded hospital ward and hearing the news from a busy doctor that she had lost her baby.

Alfred had found her there. The morning after his party, he had discovered her valise in the foyer, learned of the accident out on the street, and traced her to the hospital. To his credit, he had expressed his horror, made abject apologies, and grieved with her.

He had taken her to a specialist, too. There, the calamitous verdict had been delivered: she had been injured in such a way that she would never again conceive. The half-moon scar left by the horse's hoof was a constant reminder of her loss. Even so, Catherine had clung to the frail hope that if only she and Alfred tried, a miracle might happen. But the next three years had proven the diagnosis. She was barren.

It was a tragedy, an accident. She knew that in her head, though it didn't prevent her from feeling as if a vital part of her womanhood had been stolen. Eventually she forgave Alfred for his indiscretions, and she made him promise that he would never tell anyone of her private sorrow.

But she had never absolved Burke Grisham of guilt. She despised him now as much as she had back then.

And she scorned the society that required rigid standards of behavior in public, yet allowed gentlemen their secret vices. She had refused to visit London ever again, and Alfred prudently never invited his cronies to Yorkshire.

Catherine gazed out over the moor, its wild beauty a healing balm to her soul. Here, she had sought sanctuary many times in the past four years. And here, she had come to the realization that she would never marry again. Having a husband wasn't worth the pain of shattered illusions, the distress of constant strife, the quarreling over mismatched dreams.

What decent man would wed her, anyway? She could not bear his children.

Yet at times she felt an errant yearning rise like a flame from the ashes of her heart. The yearning for a man to hold her, to cherish her. Sternly, she reminded herself that now she had a different dream. A future that would be useful and rewarding.

The breeze blew away her dark emotions, and she indulged the urge to dream her secret dream. As soon as Prudence and Priscilla married and no longer needed her, as soon as she had enough money saved, Catherine intended to leave Snow Manor. She would purchase a house of her own and open a school, where she would teach reading, geography, and arithmetic. No child in the district should be cheated of schooling as she herself had been.

She donned her spectacles and picked up a history text, determined to study the Plantagenet and Tudor monarchs since she didn't know one Henry from the next. There were appalling gaps in her education; it was self-taught and sporadic, squeezed in whenever she'd finished her chores. She had to hide her books and study late at night, for Lorena frowned on reading.

Reluctant to spoil the lovely afternoon by pondering past unhappiness, Catherine soon lost herself in reading about royal pageantry and knights riding destriers to save ladies fair. Some time later, the tickle of a damp breeze on her neck drew her back to reality. Raising her head, she removed her spectacles and blinked up at the leaden clouds that boiled across the sky.

"Upon my word!" she breathed.

She hopped off the fence, scooped up her pile of books, and struck out across the moor. The shortcut would save her nearly half an hour. She knew every stone and cranny along the way, from the peat bogs to the scree-strewn track, barely visible in the thickness of heather. If the storm broke, there was an abandoned shepherd's hut where she could take refuge.

The stark landscape unrolled before her—no farmhouses, no barns, no sign of man or beast. A cold wind whipped up, pushing her along like a monstrous hand with fingers that plucked at her hair. She had only herself to blame. She knew how swiftly storms could blow in, even during the summer. But this morning she had left her kerseymere pelisse behind because she had been overly eager to slip out of the house.

Before she encountered the earl of Thornwald again.

If he stayed another fortnight, then so be it. She planned to go about her duties and stay out of his way. Let him flirt with Prudence and Priscilla, perhaps even court one of them. Let him use his charm, his false flattery, his oh-so-handsome smile. None of it would work on *her*.

Catherine hastened along the stony path. Black clouds hung low as the belly of a pregnant ewe. A chilly dampness crept into her bones, and she prayed her borrowed books wouldn't get drenched. How horrid if Reverend Guppy forbade her the use of his library!

Thankfully she saw the halfway point ahead. It was Resurrection Rock, named for its uncanny resemblance to a crouched giant lifting his hands to the heavens.

Perched on top of a steep rise, the boulder was massive enough to hide a man.

A robber.

Mrs. Guppy's warning rang in Catherine's mind. For the first time, she pictured the thief furtively opening a window from the outside and creeping through the house. Dressed in a black hat and coat, he would jimmy the lock to the strongbox. Then he would stuff his sack with jewels and sling it over his shoulder, escaping undetected.

He could be hiding anywhere now. Even lurking in the shelter of Resurrection Rock. Waiting to rob an unsuspecting passerby.

Catherine tightened her hold on her precious burden. She fancied she heard the thudding of hoofbeats over the whoosh of the wind. But nothing human moved in the desolate emptiness that stretched for miles around. Even the sparrows and peewits had taken cover. A few cold raindrops splashed her face. Shivering, she wrapped the books in her apron and forged up the hill toward the boulder that loomed at the top of the path.

Common sense overrode her uneasiness. Better she should fret about the impending storm than fear a thief who likely had fled far from the scene of his crime. No fool would wait for travelers along this lonely expanse of moor.

Then she heard the hoofbeats again. Louder. Coming fast over the crest of the hill.

A jagged bolt of lightning split the dark sky. Amid the crashing of thunder, the horseman appeared beside the mammoth rock. It was no knight in shining armor come to save her, but a stranger clad in black from hat to cloak to boots.

The robber.

She panicked and ran. Ran on a swerving path up the slope, heading around the opposite side of the boulder.

She ran until her breath stabbed like sharp daggers into her ribcage.

The man shouted, but the wind whipped away his words. Horse and rider chased after her. Holding her books in one arm and her skirts with the other hand, she stumbled past clumps of heather, heedless of the stones that cut into the soles of her shoes.

Cresting the hill, she spied the hut. It was barely visible against the brooding moorland, a distant shape that offered scant protection.

From behind her came the jingle of harness, the snort of the horse. Alarm sent her rushing onward, bolting headlong down the slope. Abruptly her toe caught in the burrow of a small animal. The books spilled as she wheeled for balance. Her bottom struck the ground. Pain zig-zagged up her spine. Stars spun in crazy cartwheels across her vision.

The black horse circled in front of her. Through her dizziness, she heard the thump of feet as the rider leaped from the saddle. "Catherine! For the love of Christ . . ."

Blinking, she struggled to focus. Before her swam a man in a black hat with a low curled brim. She saw clean-shaven features. Raincloud eyes. Proud cheekbones. A mouth thinned by concern.

" 'Tis thee." Half sobbing in relief, she clutched at the folds of his ebony cloak. Never had she been gladder to see anyone. "Oh, Burke, 'tis thee."

"Of course it's me." As if she were made of precious porcelain, he lightly ran his hands down her arms, then over her ankles and calves. "Are you hurting anywhere? If you've broken a bone—"

"Nay. I'm shaken, that's all." Her skin tingling from his touch, she skidded backward on her bruised bottom. A thought distracted her. "Merciful heavens, my books!" Ignoring the weakness in her limbs, she crawled on her knees, searching the low bushes and retrieving two leather-bound volumes.

He found the other three, but ignored her outstretched hand. "Why the devil did you run like that?" he asked. "Do you despise me so much?"

His accusing tone snapped Catherine to her senses. She felt too foolish to admit the truth, that she had mistaken him for a brigand. "Think what you will. It matters not to me."

"Lorena sent me out here to look for you. She thought you might be too stubborn to come in out of the rain."

"Lorena?" Catherine said with a stab of guilt. "She must want me for something. I must get back—"

"All right, then. It wasn't her. What if I said *I* was worried about you?"

His crooked smile set her heart to pounding again, this time a slow rhythm deep inside her. Dismayed, she shot to her feet, and her head reeled again. "I don't need your help, thank you. Kindly give me the rest of my books."

In that instant, the heavens opened. The rain pattered over her hair, her gown, her skin. Thunder rolled and crashed. Burke sprang up and led his horse over to her.

Water dripped from his hat and onto his cloak. He looked infuriatingly dry beneath. With a sardonic grin, he held out his hand. "So, Catherine. Will you be proud and wet, or practical and dry?"

The rain fell faster and faster. She had but one choice.

Reluctantly accepting his aid, she let him boost her up into the saddle, his hands warm and firm at her waist. He mounted behind her and arranged his cloak to cover the both of them. She was determined to sit rigidly upright, to minimize contact with his body.

But the rain came in sheets now. Its wet, icy fingers slipped down her neck and leaked onto her books.

She glanced up at Burke. He frowned straight ahead, seemingly intent on guiding the horse along the treacherous rocky track. He didn't appear aware of her at all. Perhaps he had held so many women in his life, he was indifferent to one more. Ever so slowly she nestled herself against him.

His body exuded warmth like a fireplace. The heat soothed her aching muscles and chased away the chill. She grew aware of the rise and fall of his breathing, the beating of his heart, the solid muscles of his chest. His male scent wrapped around her like a loving embrace. Each rocking step of the horse rubbed her bottom against the portion of his anatomy that was made to join man to woman.

She ought to be mortified. She ought to blush. But she was no maiden, and though her mind fought against it, her body remembered too well the joys of intimacy.

In a rush she knew the poignant longing to have a man hold her again. She wanted to feel his mouth kissing her breasts and his fingers stroking her lower, carrying her to that glorious peak where she could forget strife and unhappiness. She craved it with a bittersweet yearning that veered close to pain.

The horse came to a halt. Catherine lifted her head and peered through the driving rain. Instead of the manor house, she saw the thatched roof of the shepherd's hut. Instead of her gentle lover, she looked up at the face of the man she despised. The man who would give a whore as a gift to his newly married friend. The man who, by his own admission, had led her husband to his death.

"Why are we stopping?" she demanded.

"Lightning," Burke said succinctly.

"I want to go home."

Rain misted his skin and somehow enhanced his masculine allure. Beneath the brim of his hat, his eyes narrowed with uncompromising purpose. "Not yet," he said. "First, there's the matter of finishing our private talk."

Chapter 4

The door of the cottage creaked open as Burke gave it a push. He ducked to avoid the low lintel. The single room was cold and dank with the musty odor of neglect. Despite the dense shadows he could see a stool by the hearth. Against the stone wall, a mat lay bleeding its mossy stuffing.

Catherine loitered in the doorway. The flash and glow of the storm silhouetted her womanly form. The damp bodice embraced her bosom, and from it cascaded the clinging folds of her black skirt. Even wet and bedraggled, dressed as drab as a governess, she had an uncommon, waiflike beauty that seized his jaded heart.

Desire lingered like a stubborn ache in his groin. He could still feel the imprint of her lush body cuddled like a kitten's against his. He could still smell her pure feminine essence. He could still recall his compulsion to shelter her from harm's way.

But Catherine Snow meant nothing special to him. He would have had the same reaction to sharing a saddle with any shapely woman. He had to believe that or he'd soon be breaking his vow to protect her.

She cradled her books in one arm and shivered. Muttering an oath, Burke strode forward, yanking off his cloak and draping it around her dainty shoulders. Despite the overhang of the roof, chilly rain spattered his face.

"Come inside," he said.

She leaned back against the doorframe. A bolt of lightning lit her wary expression. "It's dark in there."

"Afraid?"

"No. But it's hard to see. I prefer to wait out the storm right here."

Her lack of trust irritated him. He derided himself both for showing her courtesy and for being cut by her suspicion of him. "You're quite the tempting piece, Mrs. Snow," he said, scanning her from head to toe with rakish deliberation. "However, I promise not to bite."

She gave him a withering look. "How decent of you. One might mistake you for a gentleman."

"But you never will, thank God. You'll always know me for the blackguard that I am."

Turning on his bootheel, he walked away. Let her get wet. All that mattered to him was achieving his purpose.

He snatched off his hat and hung it on a peg by the door. This time he would keep her to himself, away from distractions, until she answered every bloody last one of his questions. And while she did, he wanted to study the nuances of her expression. To make certain he got the entire truth.

Groping along the stone mantelpiece, Burke found a tinderbox. He shook off a sticky cobweb; then he squatted on the earthen floor before the hearth. He had never in the thirty-one years of his life had to lay a fire. Yet he had observed servants at the task; it couldn't be too difficult.

Opening the small tinderbox, he took up the steel and the chunk of flint. He hit several glancing blows, throwing sparks downward onto the shreds of linen inside the box. He worked doggedly with the flint. At last the rags gave off a faint glow. Then he blew in gentle puffs until a tiny blaze danced up.

Just as he reached for the stub of a candle, a gust of wind whooshed in from outside and doused the flame.

Swearing under his breath, Burke repeated the tedious process, this time shielding the tinder with his body. In grim triumph he lit the candle. Within moments, he would be interrogating Catherine.

Taking kindling from a nearby basket, he threw a handful on the grate. Then he stuck the candle flame to the pile. The wood merely smoldered. He gritted his teeth, crawled closer to the ash-strewn hearth, and tried another corner of the pyre. He succeeded only in dirtying his coat sleeves and cuffs.

"Curse it," he muttered. "Bloody stinking green wood."

"Don't blame the kindling." Catherine sank to her knees beside him. "It takes skill to light a fire."

A trace of humor enriched her voice. Bristling, he peered through the shadows at her unsmiling face. "Skill?" he said in a scoffing tone.

"The kindling is set too close together. You can't get a proper draught of air that way."

She rearranged the branches on the grate, stacking them in neat crossbars. After rummaging in the bottom of the basket, she produced a few dark lumps of peat and placed them atop the kindling. Then she held the flame of the candle to the lot and waited.

He crouched on one knee and propped his elbow on the other. "See?" he said. "It won't light for you, either."

"Patience, m'lord. Nothing worthwhile comes quickly. Some things require a slow and steady hand."

His mind instantly put a sexual slant on her comment. His body reacted with swift, searing vigor. He peered sharply at her, but she was gazing at the fireplace, intent on her task. The glow of the candle gilded her fine-boned profile and the rich damp mass of her hair. Despite his enveloping cloak, her tight nipples were outlined against the rain-wet gown.

Dark and undeniable, desire sank its velvet talons into him again. He burned for her so hotly his muscles trembled. He wanted to make love to her, to rouse her with slow and steady patience. He wanted to hear her sigh in ecstasy beneath him.

The trouble was, Catherine despised him.

"You're glowering." She stood up, dusting the soot off her hands. "Is the fire not to your liking?"

Burke realized that a blaze crackled cheerily on the grate. And that caution had returned to her eyes.

"The fire," he said with bitter irony, "heats things quite beyond my expectations. Fancy, all it took was a woman's touch."

"A practiced touch," she said without reference to his innuendo. "Any manservant could have done as well."

A lady of the *ton* would have flirted in response, fluttering her lashes, touching him, encouraging his attention. It was perfectly acceptable for a widow to lie with any man of her choice, so long as she conducted her affairs discreetly.

But Catherine watched him as if he were a wolf intent on devouring her. Flicking dubious glances at him, she dragged the stool close to the opened door, sat down with her books, and began to lovingly dry the leather binding of one with the corner of her apron. As she did so, she leaned forward slightly, snapping his attention to the locket that dangled at her throat.

In his baffling fantasy, he had seen that cameo: the white shell angel stretching her hands toward a diamond star.

How much of his hunger for Catherine sprang from those obsessive illusions? And how much from the real, flesh-and-blood woman sitting before him?

He meant to find out.

"The thunder is abating," she said, her beautiful lips thinning into a polite smile. "We should be able to leave soon."

He didn't smile back. "On the contrary, I have a feeling the storm is only just beginning."

Catherine's pulse surged as he stalked past her and shut the door, blocking out the damp chill and giving her the uneasy sense of being trapped. The wind rushed and whistled around the eaves. The steady drumming of rain on the roof, the crackling of the fire, lent the cottage a cozy aura of privacy. Yet tension vibrated in the air.

Lord Thornwald seemed like a coil wound too tightly. He paced back and forth, hands on his hips, his tall shadow wavering on the stone wall. She thought about how oddly he had behaved on the day of his arrival, and how she had feared he might be a madman.

The possibility was even more unsettling now.

To give her hands something to do, she blotted raindrops from the spine of another book. A jittery warmth lurked low in her belly, and to her chagrin, the feeling was half alarm, half desire. In defiance of common sense, she felt drawn to him, and wondered bitterly at her weakness for scoundrels.

He stopped before her. "Where did you get all those books?"

Catherine had to bend back her head to view his saturnine features. "From the vicarage in Warrenby."

"Do you read a lot?"

"Whenever I can. Have you an objection?"

"I simply hadn't thought of you as a bluestocking." He plucked a book from her pile and riffled the pages. "Hume's *History of England.* Rather a weighty topic."

"Perhaps for you, m'lord." It wasn't like her to be so openly contrary, but he set her teeth on edge.

"You may be right." Handing the book back, he cocked his head. That peculiar intensity smoldered in his eyes. "Tell me, Catherine, do you wear spectacles when you read?"

His question took her aback. It was her one vanity, to hide the fact of her poor vision. "Why do you wish to know?"

"We may be hours here. I am merely striving to pass the time. So, answer my question."

She hesitated. "Yes. Yes, I do."

He seemed less than pleased by her answer. Glowering, he snatched up a few chunks of peat and flung them, one by one, onto the fire. The flames spat and hissed. She felt an unexpected jab of disappointment. Like Alfred, the earl must find spectacles unbecoming on a woman.

Over his shoulder, he said, "When I met you on the moor, you spoke with a thick Yorkshire accent. Why?"

"I grew up a country girl." Anxious to point out the differences between them, she added, "Ever since I was orphaned at five years old, I worked as a servant at the vicarage. 'Tis where I learned to lay a fire. Sometimes I fall back into my old habits of speech."

"Who taught you to speak like a lady?"

"Lorena did." The memories swirled like brown autumn leaves across Catherine's soul. Memories of being left to Lorena's training while Alfred vanished to London for weeks on end. Until one day she realized her efforts were in vain. Proper manners could not keep her husband from the gaming tables. Perfect deportment could not stop him from drinking to excess.

He had needed the stabilizing influence of the family she could not give him.

Burke Grisham prowled into a corner, leaned his shoulder against the wall, and crossed his arms. The gloom there veiled his features so that she saw only the glitter of his silvery eyes. He asked, "Did Lorena favor your marriage?"

"No, but she couldn't change the fact of it. You see,

Alfred and I were married over the anvil at Gretna Green."

"Ah, I'd heard of your hasty elopement. Quite romantic. Yet you and he are from two different worlds. How did you meet?"

He sounded skeptical, as if she had deliberately set out to entrap Alfred. "You're saying gentlemen don't marry common girls like me. I'm only suited for an affair."

Like Miss Stella Sexton. Catherine stopped herself from adding the spiteful remark. Much as she wanted to lash out at him, she had no wish to describe the painful events that had ended in her miscarriage.

He didn't react to her sarcasm. "Just tell me."

The truth was, one Sunday, Alfred had made a rare appearance in church and cornered her in the vestry afterward. With honeyed phrases, he had praised her beauty and melted her maiden's heart. Catherine had resisted his efforts to seduce her. Until one night, reeking of brandy, he had come to their secret meeting place in the churchyard and talked her into the elopement. Ever since, she'd wondered if he'd only wanted what he couldn't have.

Catherine lowered her gaze to the fire. That naïve girl had lived a lifetime ago. She saw no reason to open her memories to the scorn of Lord Thornwald.

She looked up to see him standing silent as a predator in the shadows. "My life is my own," she said. "At any rate, you should know the story. You were Alfred's best friend."

"He was never one to gossip. Especially not about you." His voice lowered until she could scarcely hear it above the lashing of wind and rain. "Now I can see why he kept you hidden away here in Yorkshire. You, Catherine, are a jewel too lovely to share."

Her breath quickened as she strained to see him through the darkness. Despite the hard lesson she had learned about flattery, she felt her insides turn to warm butter.

Her hands made fists around the stack of books. "And you, sir, are an impertinent scoundrel. Your questions, your poking into my private life—"

"How else are we to get to know one another?"

"Upon my word," she snapped, beyond caring if she were rude. "I don't want to know you. I'm here only because of the storm."

"Ah, but *my* interest in *you* runs deeper."

The earl walked back into the firelight. Some secret meaning colored his words, something inscrutable, almost diabolical. She sat tense and silent, shaken by the implication of his words.

He wanted to have a sordid affair with her.

The knowledge pulsed in her blood. Unwillingly she recalled him kissing the whore's breast, and she felt a shameful tightening in her own bosom. Surely even he wouldn't be so brazen, to try to seduce his friend's widow. Surely he knew she would throw him out on his aristocratic ear.

Like a man of purpose, he came straight to her and crouched on one knee. His hair was in disarray, and she felt the errant urge to comb her fingers through the wet black strands. Breathlessly she waited for him to make his move. To lay his hand on her thigh. To touch her breast. To declare his lewd intentions.

She savored the prospect of revenge. Of condemning him to the gutter where he belonged. The anticipation was so strong, she had no room left for fear.

Quite unexpectedly, he tapped her locket with his forefinger. "I've seen this before. It belonged to your husband. There's a miniature painting of you inside."

She managed to shake her head. "No. No, this one is mine."

"This one?" He pounced on the statement. "What do

you mean, this one? There can't be more than one of a locket so unique."

"But there are." She didn't understand why his features looked taut with concentration. "There are two matching lockets. Alfred picked them out as . . . as our wedding gifts to each other. His had my picture, and mine his."

Of course, she didn't mention that hers was now empty; she still felt guilty about burning his likeness in a fit of anger after he had walked out on her that last time. Ever since, she wore the locket as a reminder to hold her temper.

"My God. Oh, my God."

Burke sat back on his heels. Squeezing his eyes shut, he plunged his fingers into his hair. He gritted his teeth and a muscle jumped in his jaw. His stark expression of torment both confused and alarmed Catherine. He looked like a madman.

Yet his pain reached out to her. Against her will, she felt a softening inside herself. She wanted to gather him to her breast and comfort him.

"What's wrong?" she whispered.

He opened his eyes. For an instant she glimpsed an unnamed vulnerability in him; then he mastered his emotions and his face went blank. "I . . . was thinking about the time I saw Alfred's locket. On the battlefield, after he'd been shot. He brought it out and showed me your picture."

A cold stream of regret ran through her. "He truly thought of me . . . in his last moments?"

"Yes." Burke took hold of her hand, his grip warm and strong. "There's something else I haven't had the chance to tell you. Your husband asked me to watch over you."

"You?" The softness in her withered away, and she gave a brusque laugh. "No man would entrust his wife to your care."

"It's the truth, Catherine. I wouldn't lie to you. Not about something so important."

Alfred had done that? He had given her into the keeping of a man he knew she despised? What could he have been thinking of?

The rain had slowed and thunder rumbled in the distance. Her awareness of the storm receded as she stared at Burke. His eyes were fathomless, compelling, magnetic. His hand weighed heavy as sin on hers. A deep heat stirred inside her. She wanted to taste his mouth. She wanted to feel his bare skin pressed to hers. God help her, she wanted to succumb to the urges within herself.

Shocked, she wrenched her hand free. The pile of books fell to the floor. She sprang to her feet and paced the length of the tiny cottage.

"Lay what little conscience you have to rest, m'lord. You've fulfilled your obligation by coming here. Go back to London. Go back to your women, your gambling, your drinking."

He stood up, too. "I haven't been to London in over a year."

She doubted that. "Then crawl back into whatever hole you came from. It matters not to me, so long as you leave here."

"I'm staying," he said flatly. "Make no mistake about that. If I thought you could understand why . . ."

That aura of tortured mystery surrounded him again. It tugged at her, threatened to draw forth her softness. She held her anger around her like the folds of his cloak. "I don't need any smooth excuses. Over the years I heard enough of them from my husband."

"Oh? And I believed you two had made a perfect love match."

His biting comment made her fury rise like the wild wind. "He was a devoted husband, except when you threw temptation in his path. Like Miss Stella Sexton."

Burke stood very still. "He told you about her?"

"Suffice to say that I knew you encouraged him to break his marriage vows. And then there is the matter of the gaming tables." She jabbed her finger at Burke. "He might have conquered his addiction if not for *your* wicked influence."

"You were his wife. You could have stopped him."

"I tried. But I could never hold him here."

Catherine had never voiced that failing to anyone before, and without warning the tension in her chest ascended to her throat. Her eyes burned and her nose prickled. Choking back a sob, she spun away before Burke could witness her humiliating tears.

She flung open the door and rushed outside into the drizzling rain, his cloak falling from her shoulders. The chilly air struck her hot cheeks. By the time she reached the black horse sheltered beneath the overhang of the cottage, the pressure inside her burst and she fell weeping against the saddle.

A man's grip came down on her shoulders, turning her toward him, pulling her to his chest. He muttered something that could have been a curse or an endearment, or perhaps both. Craving the closeness of human warmth, Catherine burrowed deeply into his embrace. She needed to draw on his strength; for too long she had held her emotions in check—the anger and the frustrations of her marriage, the pain of isolation, of living with people who did not understand her dreams.

She cried until her sobs slowed to jerky breaths and she grew aware of the man who comforted her. With lulling strokes, he rubbed the tense place in her upper back. Her head fit perfectly into the lee of his broad shoulder, and his shirt felt damp and smooth against her cheek. His male scent enticed her. The strong beating of his heart and the steady rise and fall of his chest made her conscious of his energy, his aliveness.

And the vitality of her own spirit.

His lips brushed her temple in a whispery soft caress. She felt as if she were awakening from a trance of misery and regrets. Into the darkness of her soul flowed a light, warm and clean and nurturing. Its glow spread throughout her body and fired the embers of yearning deep in her center, the yearning to experience life to the fullest.

Burke's hand cupped her cheek as if he truly cared for her. In her heart she knew the gesture was more consoling than erotic, yet she turned her head and kissed his palm.

"Catherine?"

Surprise vibrated in his voice, but she kept her eyes shut. She wanted only to feel, to grasp the shining light before it vanished. Lifting up on tiptoes, she reached for the wildness within herself.

A rough moan surged from his throat in the moment before his lips crushed down on hers. Instinctively she opened to him, inviting the mating of his tongue. He tasted of heat and mystery, the essence of desire. A primitive passion beat in her blood and drummed in her ears. It was like a hot river rushing through her veins, washing away her inhibitions, consuming her mind and heart.

The same stormy need radiated from him. She felt the unleashed energy in his hands, exploring her face and throat and breasts. She felt it in the harshness of his breathing, in the slanting fervor of his lips on hers. She felt it as their bodies pressed together, making her aware of his manhood, thick and hard, aroused for *her*. Mindlessly she reached down to caress him there.

He shuddered and groaned. Abruptly he broke the kiss and thrust her away, his hands gripping her shoulders. "Catherine," he muttered. "Catherine, don't."

She opened her eyes to the stark hunger on his face. "Don't?"

"Don't tease me," he said in a harsh voice. "Unless

you bloody well want me to carry you inside and make love to you."

Longing quivered through her as she looked up into Burke's uncompromising features, the dark eyebrows, the sensual lips, the aristocratic cheekbones. His hair was tousled and a midnight strand dropped over his forehead in boyish vulnerability. A part of her hungered for the bodily repletion he offered. But that would mean embracing the man who had led Alfred to his death. The man who had stolen her chance at happiness.

A flurry of cold raindrops struck her cheeks and restored her common sense. As the wildness receded to the secret depths inside herself, Catherine felt a flush of mortification. She had behaved with unladylike abandon, even touching him intimately. The heat of him still burned her fingertips. What must he think of her?

Even worse, what lunacy had seized hold of her?

Thoroughly confused and shaken, she lashed out at him. "Love? I very much doubt, m'lord, that *you* know the meaning of the word *love.*"

Slipping past him, she struck out over the open moor. The ground was soggy with puddles and the rain fell in a sporadic drizzle. The brooding gray sky reminded her of Burke's eyes. Despite her scathing denunciation of him, she felt saddened by the vague sense of having lost something precious.

Something she might never find again.

Chapter 5

"This simply cannot be." Lorena snapped the morocco-bound account book shut. "It is a mistake."

Fabian Snow shuffled his large feet on the carpet of the boudoir. Beside him, Lady wagged her golden tail. "But nearly t-t-two hundred guineas are missing. I-I thought you would wish to know straightaway."

Dressed in a high-waisted gown of imperial purple muslin, Lorena sat enthroned on a stool, a formidable figure in front of the satinwood dressing table with its delicate turned legs. "Thank you for informing me, nephew," she said dismissingly. "You have done your duty."

Standing to one side, Catherine heated the curling wand over the candle flame. Fabian's cheeks were pink with embarrassment, his shoulders hunched. "That *is* a rather large sum," she said in his support. "It should be accounted for."

He sent her a look of gratitude. "I-I thought so, too. D-d-don't forget Lady Beaufort. Her j-jewels were stolen and the robber is still loose."

Lorena drew a raspy breath. She leveled a glare first at Catherine, then at Fabian. "Are you suggesting that our steward is a thief? Mr. Rudd has sterling credentials. Why, Freddie himself hired the man. My son would never have engaged a criminal."

"I-I never meant t-to question his judgment. H-h-however, about the lost money—"

"La, you needn't bother yourself with the household accounts in the future. No doubt the discrepancy is an error of arithmetic. It is of no consequence."

"Perhaps if I had a look—" Catherine offered.

"No, no, no," Lorena said, making a downward slash with her beringed hand. "How many times must I tell you? Ladies do not tend to matters of finance." She thrust the ledger at Fabian. "As to you, kindly return this book to Mr. Rudd, where it belongs. I will confer with him on the issue later."

"Y-yes, Aunt Lorena." Hugging the account book to his cavernous chest, Fabian scurried out of the boudoir, the dog trotting at his heels.

Lorena pivoted on the stool, her derriere overhanging the seat with its flounces of rose-colored silk. After examining herself in the oval looking glass, she uncorked a crystal pot from the table and dabbed a small amount of rouge on her cheeks. "Such an odious creature, that Fabian, to interrupt me at my toilet. And over such a trifling matter."

"Two hundred guineas is hardly a trifling amount."

"La, the money went toward a good cause. My daughters and I needed a new wardrobe after coming out of mourning, that's all."

Catherine stood frozen as Lorena preened in the mirror. Her mother-in-law had taken the money? "That's stealing."

Lorena glared at Catherine's reflection. "How dare you make accusations? The household funds are under my jurisdiction, and I will use them as I see fit."

"But it's dishonest—"

"The matter is closed. Now kindly attend to your duties."

Catherine's jaw ached from gritting her teeth. She resumed curling Lorena's hair with the hot wand. "Fabian deserves to know the truth. He's head of the family now."

Lorena harumphed. "Fabian should never have inherited. This splendid home would belong to my grandchild if only *you* had done your duty and borne a son."

The reminder of her barrenness struck Catherine like a slap. She felt empty and aching, haunted by the secret sorrow that never went away. Yet she kept her face expressionless, for she was unwilling to let Lorena know how much her thoughtless remark hurt. "Thanks to Fabian's kindness, we haven't been driven out of Snow Manor. He deserves credit for allowing us to live here."

"He could put us out in a ditch any time he chooses." The older woman lifted her chin, the fleshy folds beneath like the dewlap of a cow. "Of course, you wouldn't understand. You are accustomed to laboring for a living, while I am of a more delicate constitution."

A rebellious anger surged past Catherine's self-control. "I can see that," she muttered under her breath.

"What did you say?" Lorena set down the pot of rouge with a click.

"Only that these curls enhance your delicacy. Don't you think so?"

As always, Lorena succumbed to the flattery and turned her head to and fro. Her faded blonde hair was arranged a la grecque, with curls falling loosely around the temples and the rest drawn up into a cluster of ringlets at the top of her head. Privately Catherine thought it a style more suited to a fresh-faced debutante in her first Season.

"Quite satisfactory," Lorena proclaimed. "You have a talent with the curling wand. My old abigail would scorch my hair most dreadfully."

Catherine felt the reckless urge to scorch Lorena's tongue. Shocked at herself, she set the implement in its wire stand. These bouts of temper had troubled her more than ever in the past few days—as if she were opening her eyes after a long sleep and becoming impatient with the restrictions of her life. The restless wind that blew through her soul had been stirred by the arrival of Burke Grisham.

Her cheeks warmed as she recalled their passionate kiss the previous day. Outside the cottage, in the midst of rain and thunder, she had clung to him like a lover. Worse, she had touched him . . . *there.* She had wanted him, all of him, with a desperation that shamed her.

He must think her as vulgar as Miss Stella Sexton.

Turning away from Lorena, Catherine straightened the jars of perfume and pots of cosmetics. She had been so flustered that she had forgotten the books she had borrowed from the vicarage. She had not had a free moment to slip away and fetch them.

The memory of her carnal passion still baffled her. From what hidden wellspring had that wildness arisen? That craving to draw his strength into herself? That hot hunger to mate with Burke Grisham, of all men?

More than the kiss, though, she kept remembering how good his embrace felt, and how she had wanted to stay there forever. So easily she could have let him sweep her up in his arms and carry her into the cottage. How tempting to bask in the worship of a man, to feel beautiful in his eyes, to feel worthy and well loved—if only for a few brief moments.

She stifled her untimely yearning. After the disappointments of her marriage, she knew better than to entangle herself with a wicked Corinthian who gave whores as gifts to married men. Even if she were willing to jeopardize her dream of opening a school, her last choice as a lover would be a nobleman who walked the path of self-destruction.

Lorena rapped her knuckles on the dressing table. "Catherine! Stop woolgathering and attend to my words. I do not care to feel as if I am addressing the wall."

Guilt enfolded her like a familiar cloak. "Yes, ma'am."

"I have decided on a plan to secure my rightful place in Snow Manor once and for all."

"Plan?"

"I see only one course to follow. Fabian must wed my dear Prudence."

Catherine drew a sharp breath. Pairing the painfully shy man with the seductive girl boded misery for both. "Prudence will object to the match. She has her heart set on a London Season next year."

"Oh, la. The girl can enjoy a long engagement, then."

"But what about Fabian? I've never noticed him paying particular attention to Prudence."

"I beg your pardon." Accusation pinched Lorena's expression. "In light of your objections, one might think you've set your own cap again for the owner of Snow Manor."

Stunned, Catherine protested, "Nothing could be further from the truth. I wish only to assure their happiness—"

"Then you will discourage his attention. *My* daughter shall become mistress of this manor. The announcement will be made on the night of our ball next Wednesday." Rising from the stool, Lorena smoothed her hands over the mountainous terrain of her tea gown. "Soon I will see both of my girls settled most admirably."

"Both? Do you have a suitor in mind for Priscilla, too?"

A shrewd gleam entered Lorena's eyes. "Can't you

guess? My elder daughter is destined to become the countess of Thornwald."

Like a mottled gray cloud hovering on the horizon, the pedigreed ram grazed the sedge grass atop the hill. It was a majestic specimen, big and strong-boned, with massive horns curling from a proud head. Its face bore the patches of black and white that typified the breed. Its broad shoulders and stocky legs displayed latent power, and the breeze stirred the tips of its thick fleece.

" 'Tis a bonny Haslingden," said Eli Tweedy, his gnarled fingers curled around his shepherd's crook. "Thee'll never see finer nowhere."

Burke grunted distractedly. Leaning on the stone wall, he rubbed a piece of clipped wool between his fingers. The strands felt springy and surprisingly oily. He had spent the better part of the day bartering for sheep in the bleak hills of Yorkshire. The task was, after all, his excuse for tarrying at Snow Manor.

His head throbbed from the effects of imbibing too much brandy the night before. So much for his attempt to obliterate yesterday from his mind.

Though an entire day had passed, the memory of Catherine lingered like the perfect fantasy. The softness of her in his arms. The ragged catch to her voice. The outpouring of tears. The surprising fervency of her kiss. And incredibly, her fingers skimming low . . . and lower . . .

He ached as he had ached all night. How wrong he had been to think her passionless, as cold as the Snow name. He cringed to know that she had been hurt by his thoughtless gift to her husband. Miss Stella Sexton—he had been too drunk to recall the whore's name. The incident had been one of countless acts of recklessness, part of the dark period in his life when he hadn't cared who he'd dragged down in the gutter with him.

The pulsebeat in his loins became a thrust of pain.

From the moment the kiss ended and Catherine looked at him in dawning horror, he had seen himself through her eyes. An unprincipled rogue. A man of dishonor. A stinking coward.

I very much doubt that you know the meaning of the word love.

She was right. Love held no appeal for him. It was a sham emotion, the delusion of women and poets.

And so what of his strange twilight dream on the battlefield, when the white fire of a musket ball had struck him? He had no answer. Yet how vivid was his memory of floating high above the earth, suspended in the shining light of eternal love.

Somehow he had felt that same elusive peace while holding Catherine. She fit his arms in some strangely familiar fashion. He wanted to explore all the mysterious facets of her. He wanted to make her smile, to embrace her again, this time with her eyes wide open. Accepting him.

Curse it. She had wept and he had offered her solace. A unique experience for him, but then, maybe he had missed a great opportunity all these years. Drive a woman to tears and she'd fall into his arms. A useful method he might try again sometime.

It was only a kiss. Better he should brood about a far more dangerous problem. The soundness of his mind.

His visions of Catherine were not fantasy, but *reality.*

The spectacles. The Yorkshire accent. The matching lockets. He had seen them in his head before she had confirmed the truth.

A cold sweat broke out on his brow. Darkness hovered at the edge of his consciousness, a darkness he held at bay only with strict control. Was he deranged? Had that French bullet forever altered his grip on reality?

He grew aware of someone clearing his throat. "The beastie's a right hardy one," Eli Tweedy said, nodding at the ram. "Get close to twenty pounds o' wool off him. Maybe more."

Sheepbell clanking, the ram walked downhill and stopped to forage on a clump of bilberry. Half of Burke's mind concentrated on the magnificence of the creature.

The other half of his mind remained preoccupied. From where had his foreknowledge of Catherine come? He had sat awake most of the night, slumped before the fire in a brandy-induced haze, his brain worrying the possibilities over and over.

Maybe he had glimpsed the spectacles in Catherine's apron pocket. Maybe he had guessed at her accent since she was country-born and -bred. Maybe Alfred had mentioned the twin lockets and Burke had forgotten.

Hell, he was grasping at straws. Before he had even met her, in the painful months of recovery after Waterloo, other visions of her had obsessed him. Catherine laughing in the garden, the sunlight gliding her hair. Catherine reading to a group of children, spectacles perched on her nose. Catherine walking toward him, her hands stretched in welcome.

Then yesterday, he had recognized the sweetness of her kiss. He had known the soft curves of her body, the fresh rain scent of her hair. He had known the husky sound of her voice, even the desperation of her tears.

The terrible question was, *how?*

" 'Tis a ram of rare value, m'lord." Eli Tweedy lifted his slouch hat and scratched his sparse hair. "Thee'll not find a better one to sire prize lambs."

Burke pressed the flat of his palms to the hard stone wall in an effort to erase the silky feel of Catherine's skin. The rough texture of the stone kept him anchored to reality. Yet his inexplicable knowledge of her drummed against his temples.

How . . . ?

She had settled into his thoughts like a lover who

shared the same memories. Ate at the same table. Sat before the same fire. Slept in the same bed.

The darkness crept closer. Christ. If he weren't careful, he would end up a drooling lunatic like the king, slumped in the corner of a locked room, a vacuous stare on his face.

He could hear the rasp of his own breathing, in and out, in and out. It seemed to be speaking to him. *Run. Run. Run far and fast and leave the torment behind.*

Even as his muscles tensed, he resisted the call of madness. He had run once before in his life. When his brother had been shot and killed.

Stinking coward.

With effort, he thrust the darkness back to the verge of his consciousness. God, how he craved peace. He had sought it in the solitude of his estate in Cornwall, on the windswept cliffs, the grassy downs, the land which had become his sanctuary this past year. Yet even there he had been plagued by visions of the ingenuous woman who now burned like a fire in his soul.

Perhaps there was no peace for him anywhere on earth.

Burke flung away the bit of wool, and a gust of wind sent it dancing on air. He pivoted toward the horse that cropped the damp grass by the road. "I have to go," he muttered.

"Buy now," Eli Tweedy wheedled, "and 'twill give thee time to mollycoddle the beast afore tupping time in November."

Burke had lost interest in the ram. He could think only of his aching need to see Catherine again. To make her desire him. To change her miserable opinion of him, however well-deserved it was. What a glutton for punishment he was.

Then he thought of a way to please her. Not with trinkets or perfume as he would give other ladies. No, he knew the one thing Catherine really wanted. Impatient to put his plan into action, he swung into the saddle.

Eli Tweedy planted himself in front of the horse. "I'll lower me price by ten shillings."

"No."

"Fifteen shillings."

"No."

"Twenty?"

"Oh, for Christ's sake." Digging into his coat pocket, Burke found a gold piece and tossed it to the farmer. "I'll send my man after the ram."

Tweedy clutched the coin and bobbed his head. "A right sharp gent thee are, m'lord . . ."

Without listening to the rest, Burke urged the horse onto the dirt track. The rolling green hills bordered the moor, a distant grassy sea that led back to Snow Manor. The northerly wind had a knife edge that cut to the core of him. Contrary to what Catherine thought, he hadn't yet fallen so low that he would violate the promise he had made to watch over her. He would look into her financial affairs and assure himself that she had sufficient funds. Enough to loose herself from Lorena's yoke and perhaps set up a house of her own.

And then he would leave for good.

A jangling noise interrupted the clattering of pots and the chatter of conversation in the kitchen.

Catherine paused in her task of rolling dough for mince pie, brushed the wisps of hair from her brow with a floury hand, and looked up at the row of bells beside the huge door. The hollow thudding of her heart filled her ears.

He was back.

Burke had gone riding for the entire day. And all day she had wondered about his destination. She couldn't believe a rustic jaunt through the countryside would content him. Had he joined a friend for a game of cards? Alfred had gambled away many an hour at the Fox and Hound.

Or had Burke gone to visit a lady? To spend hours making love, dipping his fingers into all her secret places. . . .

"I'll see to his lordship," said Martha. "He'll be wanting his wash water."

Leaving a mound of unpeeled potatoes, the maid tore off her stained apron and straightened the mobcap on her curly brown hair. Her pretty face glowed as she pinched more color into her cheeks. Then she hastened to the hearth and tipped hot water from the cauldron into a tall can.

Usually Martha required a reminder to tend to her duties. It wasn't that she was lazy, only young and dreamy, more inclined to flirt with the male servants than to work industriously.

A strange tightness squeezed Catherine's chest. "That container must be heavy, Martha. Let the footman carry it up."

"Walter is laying out the silver. And the missus sent Owen to deliver invitations to the ball."

"Well, then, don't linger. We've lots of work to do before dinner."

"Thee needn't fret. I can manage this—and his lordship." The skirt swishing around her shapely figure, Martha lugged the can out the door.

Catherine slung the dough into the pie tin. Fret, indeed. As if she were an old maiden aunt with prissy proprieties.

Fetching the mincemeat from the larder, she tried not to think about Martha swinging her hips as she walked into Burke's chamber. Or smiling the sensual smile that begged for a kiss. Or bestowing the wink that hinted of her willingness to obey his every command.

Unbidden images flashed in Catherine's mind. Burke stripping himself naked. Standing in blatant splendor with his strong body aroused. He would crook his finger and invite the giggling maid into his arms. . . .

Catherine realized that mincemeat overflowed the pie shell. An empty ache throbbed in her. Doggedly she resisted examining the feeling and concentrated instead on cleaning up her mess. Mrs. Earnshaw and her helpers labored across the room, chopping lamb and leeks for dinner. Usually Catherine felt most comfortable in the kitchen amid the rich scents of cooking and the bustling of servants. This place was more home to her than the sumptuous rooms above stairs. But today her sense of belonging had been marred by an edgy distraction.

It was that kiss.

The kiss had reminded her of the intimacy that was missing from her life. The closeness, however fleeting, shared by a man and a woman. But marriage had proven to her that once the romantic luster wore off, love brought more pain than happiness, more bickering than companionship.

For over a year she had buried herself in the smooth running of the household. She had put away the bitter disappointments of the past by focusing on the present —and by preparing herself to open a school someday. The secret plan had guided her like a beacon shining on the horizon. Yet today she had a strange lost feeling, as if a fog shrouded the distant light of her dreams.

She opened the oven built into the stone hearth and slid the pie inside. When she turned around, Martha sauntered back into the kitchen, the empty can bumping against her leg.

A guilty gladness leaped in Catherine. They couldn't have done it so quickly. Still, she frowned at the maid's starry-eyed look. "It's time you're back."

Martha sighed. "Ooh, he's a handsome gent. Thee are indeed the lucky one."

"Lucky?"

A speculative smile danced on Martha's lips. "His lordship, he asked me directions to thy room."

Catherine felt a tightening deep in her loins. To give her trembling hands something to do, she picked up a rag and swiped at the counter. "I don't see why he would need to know that. If he had a message for me, he could have given it to you."

"He asked me not to say." The maid glanced over her shoulder and confided in a rush, "But I'll tell anyhow. He said he has a special present for thee."

Questions flocked to Catherine's tongue, but she stifled them. "That's enough. Now kindly return to your chores."

The servant girl bobbed a curtsy. "Aye, mum."

Busying herself with another pie, Catherine wondered what Burke wanted to give her. Perfume? Flowers? Probably some expensive trinket that lacked any heartfelt meaning.

She pricked the bubble of breathless curiosity inside her. More important than the *what* was the *why.* Now that she had thrown herself at him like a desperate lightskirt, he must think he could buy her affections. The notion was mortifying.

Well, he would have his arrogant assumption shattered. She would return his offering unopened. She desired nothing from him.

Nothing at all.

"Give me that."

"I had it first."

"Mummy bought it for me."

"It's for both of us, you widgeon-head."

Summoned to the bedroom by the sound of quarrelling voices, Catherine clapped her hands. "Girls, please stop!"

Wearing identical disgruntled expressions, Prudence and Priscilla turned toward Catherine. They clutched a fashion book between them, each girl clinging stubbornly. For all their ladylike appearance in muslin gowns and upswept coiffures, they acted like a pair of spoiled children.

"Perhaps you could take turns with the book," Catherine suggested. "Or look at it together."

"I need *La Belle Assemblée* all to myself," Prudence said, tugging at the book. "When I make my appearance at Almack's, I intend to capture the eye of every eligible lord there."

"Ha." Her sister yanked back. "That won't capture you anything but a smirk."

"Certainly you can't think they'll be looking at *you.*"

"What I mean is, you'll already be affianced." Priscilla gave a sly grin. "T-t-to our d-d-dear Cousin Fabian."

Prudence's jaw dropped. She loosed her hold on the book so that her sister stumbled backward and bumped into the bedpost. "You're lying!"

"I'm not. I just came from Mummy's room. She told me all of her plans."

Tears swam in Prudence's baby blue eyes as she looked at Catherine. "Make her stop telling fibs. Please do."

Catherine hardly knew what to say. The twins had been only thirteen years old when she had come here as a bride four years ago, and she felt an exasperated affection for them that was both sisterly and maternal.

The poor girl. Marriage was difficult enough without going into it so ill-matched. Gently she said, "Your mother mentioned as much to me earlier. But she does love you, and she only wishes to see you happy—"

"Happy!" Prudence stamped her foot. "I won't be leg-shackled to that loathsome milksop. *I'm* going to wed Lord Thornwald."

"Oh, no, you aren't," Priscilla taunted. "Mummy says he's intended for me."

"You ninnyhammer! He's mine."
"No, mine, cabbage-head."
"I'll seduce him first."
"And I'll tell Mummy on you . . ."

An hour later, after mediating the squabble and calming the distraught Prudence, Catherine ran up the servant's stairs, the narrow wooden steps creaking beneath her feet. She had sent a note to her mother-in-law, pleading a headache and begging to be excused from dinner. Avoiding Burke was the coward's way out, she knew. But it was far less awkward than facing him with the memory of their kiss so fresh in her mind.

Besides, she burned to know if he truly had left her a gift. Even if she didn't open it, maybe she could guess the contents by the size of the box.

Catherine reached the second floor landing and slipped into the main passageway. The small door clicked shut, its frame almost indistinguishable in the wall paneling.

Click.

Echoing down the length of the corridor came the sound of another door closing—or opening.

Only Prudence, Priscilla, and Lorena shared this wing with Catherine. But it was too early for them to retire. Especially when they vied over entertaining their eligible guest.

Catherine walked cautiously down the dim-lit corridor. Her footsteps echoed as if down a long tunnel. The hairs on the back of her neck prickled. She had the uneasy sense that someone was watching her.

And not for the first time.

Thick shadows shrouded the passageway with its chairs and tables, the portraits on the walls. Had Fabian ventured up here? On a few occasions, she had discovered the timid man in hiding, watching her, apparently screwing up his courage to speak to her on some household matter.

"Mr. Snow?"

Silence.

Her heart hammered. She ought to have brought a candle. But her mind had been distracted by too many other thoughts.

Rounding the corner, Catherine reached her door, turned the knob, and went inside. The banked fire cast a frail glow into the darkness, and the wind wuthered a lonely lament around the eaves. Feeling her way through the gloom, she located a candle stub on her desk. She crouched before the grate and lit the wick from the red-orange coals.

The candle flame danced to life. She held the taper aloft and looked around. To her sharp disappointment, she saw no present decorated by pretty ribbons.

The pale light flickered over the modest room with its tester bed, the dressing table with the age-speckled mirror, the cozy wing chair that Lorena had consigned to the attic. Unadorned by gilt trimmings and green velvet, the chamber lacked the splendor of the master suite Catherine had once occupied. Yet it was more comfortable than a servant's garret and somehow symbolic of her place at the manor: in limbo, caught between two worlds.

Then she spied the unexpected.

With a cry of delight, she scurried to the bedside table and set down the candle. Hands shaking, she brushed her fingertips down the leather bindings. Her precious books!

They were the volumes she had borrowed from Reverend Guppy's library. Shaken by that tempestuous kiss, she had forgotten them at the cottage and had meant to go back.

A piece of paper stuck out of the topmost book. She drew out the note and unfolded it.

My dear Catherine,
For distressing you yesterday, I hope this will make amends. As to the rest, I make no apology. It was merely a kiss.

Scrawled in bold black ink across the bottom was the letter *B.*

She held the square of paper to her swiftly beating heart. Her feminine vanity experienced a surge of fierce pleasure. He had taken the trouble to fetch the books from the cottage and deliver them to her. She pictured him penning the note, sanding the ink, folding the paper with his proficient male hands.

Hands that had touched her with tenderness. Hands that had held her close and stroked her back. Hands that could comfort as well as arouse a shivery warmth over her skin.

Even now, she felt her body softening, suffusing with heat. With desire for the man who had destroyed her marriage.

Jolted to painful awareness, Catherine gazed down at the message. How could she be so witless? This was a ruse calculated to win her trust. She was nothing more than another would-be conquest to Burke, a challenge to the charmer.

Slowly she brought the paper to the flame of the candle. The edge began to burn. The fire licked across the inked phrases and reduced them to ash. But even as she dropped the pieces into the grate, his words were seared indelibly into her heart.

It was merely a kiss.

Chapter 6

The next day, Burke strode down the long corridor, his footfalls muffled on the carpet runner as he searched for Catherine. His head ached from eyestrain. After a night of broken sleep and strange dreams, he had spent hours checking tedious columns of figures in the steward's room. Two entries in the estate books had roused his suspicions. Mr. Rudd, who had been wringing his manicured hands all morning, claimed the accounts were accurate and disavowed any knowledge of wrongdoing.

Burke couldn't fault the finicky steward, at least not before ferreting out another key piece to this devilish puzzle. That was why he wanted to find Catherine. He didn't trust anyone else to give him an honest explanation.

There was a fair chance that she, too, might refuse to help him. Clearly she had been avoiding him, declining to join the family for dinner last night, not acknowledging the fact that he had returned her books.

No doubt she regretted their kiss. It had been a momentary aberration for her, and a transcendent experience for him. His attraction to her was as strong and persistent as his visions. She had become an addiction he couldn't resist.

Salvation lay in staying away from her.

Yet she alone might know the answers to his questions.

Catherine wasn't upstairs in any of the stately bedrooms, where he interrupted Lorena in the midst of berating a housemaid over a towel folded wrongly in the linen cupboard. Lorena promptly pasted on a smile and begged him to take dearest Priscilla for a walk in the garden. Burke escaped on a vague promise.

Catherine wasn't in the music room downstairs, where the off-key tinkling of the pianoforte ended abruptly when Prudence and Priscilla caught sight of him and leaped up together from the stool. With effort he managed to unstick himself from their clingy competition for his attention.

Catherine wasn't in any of the storerooms belowstairs, either, where behind a rack in the wine cellar, he startled a couple locked in a furtive embrace. The girl, who had her bodice lowered to her waist, was the giggly maidservant who brought his wash water. The man, who turned beet red and fumbled to cover her, was Fabian Snow.

Interesting, Burke thought as he beat a retreat. The master of Snow Manor was not so bashful after all.

At last, drawn by a commotion of voices, he found Catherine outside under the great oak tree that shaded the west wing. She stood surrounded by a cluster of servants—the stout Cook, several chattering young girls, and prissy Mr. Rudd, still twisting his hands. Humphrey, the butler, his gray hair combed carefully over his bald spot, mediated a quarrel between a short stable boy and a tall footman in a powdered periwig.

Everyone kept glancing up and pointing into the spreading branches of the tree. At the base of the oak,

Fabian's spaniel ran back and forth, barking, its golden ears flapping.

"Run and fetch a ladder," Catherine told the freckle-faced stable lad. To the footman, she added, "Owen, you help carry it."

"But such is not my job," Owen protested, his handsome nose stuck in the air. "*I* am a household servant."

One of her dark eyebrows shot upward. Though he towered over her, she gave him a glower that would have done a duchess proud. In a no-nonsense voice, she said, "Go."

"Yes, ma'am." He bowed, then rushed off to the stables.

Burke walked toward Catherine, and the servants gave way, opening a path for him. Shading her eyes with the flat of her hand, she peered up into the branches of the tree again. The sleeves of her high-waisted black gown were rolled to her elbows as if she had been interrupted at some domestic task. Wisps of hair clung to her swan-like neck. She looked so delectable that Burke promptly forgot his purpose in coming to find her.

The aroma of roses wafted from her. Odd that, for he didn't remember Catherine wearing scent. Not even in his visions.

He followed her gaze aloft. Into her ear, he whispered, "What's the crisis?"

Uttering a breathy gasp, she whirled to face him. "M'lord! I thought you'd gone out again today."

"Sorry to disappoint you. Now what are you looking at?"

"Lady chased one of the stable cats up the tree. There, on the topmost limb."

Now that she pointed it out, he could see a tiny lump of tortoiseshell fur huddled high in the thicket of leaves. A weak mewling drifted to him over the noise of Lady's barking. "It's a kitten?"

"Yes." Catherine glanced around. "You haven't seen Mr. Snow, have you?"

"Ah . . ." Burke settled for a half truth. "I believe he was going for a ride. On a mare."

Her eyes rounded in mild astonishment. "Upon my word. He never goes anywhere without locking Lady up first."

"This ride won't take him far afield."

She frowned upward distractedly. "Poor kitty. Lady is frightening her."

The look of loving concern on Catherine's face caused a peculiar tightness inside Burke's chest. He felt frustrated by her neglect of him. He wanted to seize the center of her attention. He wanted kiss her again. And more.

Curse it. He wanted to become *her* obsession.

He scooped up the yapping dog, strode through the swarm of servants, and deposited the wriggling animal in Mr. Rudd's arms. The steward yelped and jumped backward.

"Don't drop her," Burke ordered. "Take her inside."

"Yes, m'lord."

Satisfied to see the man scurry away, gingerly carrying the squirmy dog, Burke stripped off his coat and waistcoat and dropped them into the hands of a kitchen maid. Then he went to the tree and grasped a stout, low bough.

"What are you doing?" Catherine asked as he hoisted himself into the crook of two limbs.

"Rescuing your kitten. Isn't that what heroes do?"

"But Owen and Willie are coming with the ladder." She pointed to the stables. "See?"

"Devil take it. I grew up climbing trees."

He had been a barefoot lad back then, Burke thought too late, as the soles of his polished Hessians slipped on the bark. Grimly determined not to make a fool of himself, he made his way steadily upward, moving from limb to limb. The bower of green leaves whispered in the wind. In the distance, beyond the manicured lawn and the rose garden, rolled the endless stark expanse of the moor.

The higher he went, the thinner the branches grew. One creaked ominously beneath his weight. Abruptly it broke, dangling by a shred.

Just in time, he latched his arms around the trunk. The rough bark abraded his cheek. The tree swayed, his stomach along with it. The servant girls oohed and aahed.

Looking down, he caught a glimpse of Catherine with her head tilted back and her arms clenched to her breasts. As if she were truly concerned for his safety.

Filled with a renewed strength of purpose, he worked his foot onto another limb. His muscles strained as he carefully elevated himself. The scar on his upper chest began to throb. He could almost touch the kitten now.

Shinnying upward, he slowly reached out his hand and brushed downy fur. Tiny claws raked his skin.

"Dammit!" He shook his stinging fingers, bringing one to his mouth and sucking on it.

The creature backed farther out on the unsteady branch. A pair of green eyes peered sullenly at him.

Burke gritted his teeth to contain a string of oaths. Bloody females. This one needed to be coaxed.

"Here, kitty," he crooned. "Come here, love. I won't hurt you."

Still talking nonsense, he inched out on the branch. The kitten gave another plaintive mew.

In his most seductive voice, he murmured, "Darling, don't try to fool me with that sorrowful cry. You're a little tigress. But I'm ready for you this time."

Burke snaked out his hand and seized the kitten, dragging it against his chest. The feline hissed and spat. He sheltered it in the crook of his arm, heedless of the claws that pierced like pins through the fine linen of his shirt.

With a grim lack of grace, he managed to descend the tree, guiding himself with one arm. The kitten never gave up on its fierce attack. By the time Burke's feet hit the ground, his side felt shredded.

"Oh, my poor darling," Catherine said.

Burke tried not to swagger as he met her halfway. He fought to keep the pride of the conquering hero off his face.

But she didn't even look at him. She snatched up the kitten and cuddled it to her bosom. The creature had the audacity to settle down and purr.

Of course, Burke thought darkly, he'd do the same were he snuggled to those delicious breasts.

Curse it. Now he was envying a damned cat.

"Thee were like a pirate climbing the mainmast," said the stable lad, his brown eyes big with awe.

"Jolly fine show," added the footman who held the long ladder.

The other servants murmured their agreement. Burke scarcely noticed them crowding around. He wanted Catherine's admiration. But he might as well wish for sainthood in heaven.

She gave the kitten a fond pat and set it on the grass. The cat scampered to the kitchen garden, bounded onto the low stone wall, and began to daintily wash its orange-and-black fur.

"She clawed you," Catherine said, frowning at Burke.

A few specks of blood dotted the lower part of his shirt, and the white linen was snagged. Now that he finally had her attention, he felt like a schoolboy facing up to his governess. "I'll live."

"If you'll excuse me," she said, "I'll fetch some ointment and bring it to your room."

"Don't trouble yourself on my account. I'll come with you."

He retrieved his coat from the maid and strode after Catherine as she disappeared though a back door of the mansion. He found himself in a huge kitchen with copper pots hanging in rows and an enormously long table bisecting the room.

Catherine's heels clicked purposefully over the flagstone floor. Burke followed her through the scullery and ducked his head to enter the still-room, a tiny stone-walled chamber with a single window. A flowery scent permeated the warm air.

Catherine made an exclamation of dismay. "My rose water."

She darted to a diminutive hearth, where a spiral tube curled from a gourd-shaped vessel set on the hissing fire. Bending over to stir the pot, she looked like a beautiful sorceress brewing a love potion.

She reached into an earthen jar and ladled preserved rose petals into the gourd-like pot. Steam from the bubbling vessel dewed her cheeks and curled the tendrils of hair at her temples. The fire glow cast a golden sheen over her enchanting profile—the long eyelashes, the pert nose, the luminous skin.

"There," she said, putting down the spoon. "I was so intent on saving Tigress that I nearly ruined my distilling."

"The kitten is called Tigress?"

A smile gently bowed Catherine's lips. "She is now. You named her."

So she had overheard his seductive coaxing of the cat. Burke felt exposed somehow, for Catherine had observed his romantic soliloquy and found it amusing.

Amusing.

Stretching up to get a brown bottle off a shelf, she said over her shoulder, "I'm terribly sorry about your shirt. If you'll give it to me, perhaps I can mend it."

"Why, Mrs. Snow," he drawled, determined to irk

her. "Are you suggesting I disrobe right here? Oughtn't we at least retire to the bedroom first?"

A becoming pink tinted her cheeks. "I meant for you to send me your shirt after you change upstairs." She thrust out the bottle. "Clean those scratches with soap and water so they don't fester."

He ignored the ointment. "I'm terribly inept at caring for wounds. Why don't you do it for me?"

She pressed her pretty lips spinster-tight. "I'm sure you can muddle through on your own."

"Ah, don't be shy now. It's not as if you've never seen a man's chest before. But if it makes you feel better, I won't take my shirt off."

He tugged out his shirttails and made a show of undoing the buttons. She stood watching him, unmoving. Something sparked in the amber depths of her eyes. Desire? Shock? Disgust? Before he could know for sure, she swung away and fetched a pan of water and a folded cloth.

He sat down on a ladderback chair. Catherine hesitated, then came forward with a resolute spring to her steps. Sinking to her heels before his chair, she lay her supplies on the stone floor. She took hold of his shirt and drew it back slightly, just enough to expose the scratches that criss-crossed his lower right side.

She pressed a damp cloth to the lesions. The warmth stung and he sucked in a breath.

Wincing, too, she looked up. "Did I hurt you?"

"Only my manly pride."

She gave him a look guaranteed to wither a lesser man. "Your overweening conceit, you mean."

She was teasing him. The novel idea seduced him more than her exquisite face, more than her shapely figure. She had surprised him in many ways. He had traveled to Yorkshire prepared to dislike her, to disprove the appealing woman of his visions, to find a conniver who had married for money and position. But

Catherine Snow had a beauty of the spirit and a strength of character uncorrupted by the people who would suck her dry.

The thought was a disturbing reminder of the questions he had yet to ask her.

In a moment.

Right now, he wanted to savor the feel of her hands ministering to him. Her touch was delicate, nurturing, feminine. A frown of concentration furrowed her brow as she focused her attention on him. He could almost imagine she cared for him. That he was the most important man in the world to her. She aroused in him the desire to caress her, to make love to her.

But she tolerated him, nothing more. He would do well to remember that.

"Thank you for saving Tigress," she said.

"It was my pleasure."

She dabbed ointment onto the scratches. "I haven't expressed my appreciation for the books, either. They were a wonderful surprise. I hope you haven't thought me ungrateful."

"Never," he said, beguiled into a rare candor. "You're a refreshing change from the ladies of Society. You seem incapable of an unkind thought."

Her troubled eyes met his. She knelt before him in a pose of wifely intimacy: her arm rested on his thigh, her bosom touched his knee, her fingers lay warm inside his shirt. An earthquake of yearning shook him. He wanted to seize hold of her, to draw her into himself and guard her from harm.

"You needn't flatter me," she said. "I'm hardly a saint. . . ."

He heard no more, for the image of her earnest face shimmered like a mirage. His head pounded and his skin prickled. For the first time he welcomed the madness and leaned his head back. He hungered to know so much more about her.

Catherine marched toward the fireplace in the master bedroom. With a furious sweep of her arm, she flung something into the flames. Small oblong pictures scattered over the blazing logs. A few spun onto the marble hearth, and she bent to scoop them up.

Jack of hearts. Nine of spades. Ace of diamonds.

She hurled every last playing card into the fire. Then she wheeled around, her face tear-stained and accusing.

"This addiction to the gaming tables disgusts me. You squander your life, then try to get back into my good graces by flattering me . . ."

Catherine stared at Burke in disbelief. He had dozed off in his chair! Just a moment ago, she had been speaking to him, and in the midst of her words, a glazed look had stolen over his face. He had tipped his head back and shut his eyes.

How peculiar. How mortifying. Did he find her so tedious?

Yet he had scaled the oak tree to retrieve her kitten. In a secret part of her woman's heart, she had been thrilled to think he acted to impress her. Now she wondered if he was motivated solely by the desire to show off his derring-do before an audience of awe-struck servants. The strutting cock.

Her fingers still lay against his flat abdomen, where ointment smeared the thin red scratches. It had been so hard for her to focus on that one area, so hard to keep her touch impersonal when she ached to explore every part of him. Logic told her he was not the man for her.

But, oh, what a man he was.

Freed from his watchful eyes, Catherine shifted her gaze to the black arrow of hair that disappeared into the waistband of his breeches. Temptation proved impossible to resist. Ever so cautiously, she moved aside the edges of his shirt, exposing the breadth of his chest inch by inch. The power of his physique entranced her. His hard-honed muscles had a sleek symmetry that belied his self-indulgent style of life.

She acknowledged the disgraceful heat within herself, the melting desire to lie with him, to relearn the mysteries of lovemaking. She had felt such stirrings before and managed to scold her willful body into obedience. But this time, an unquenchable hope flared within the empty core of her.

It was foolish. It was imprudent. It was heart-threatening.

Of all men, this nobleman rake could never give her the emotional nourishment that her soul craved. She had already tried to love a Corinthian once. Burke Grisham was far worse. He had plumbed the foulest depths of wickedness.

Yet her gaze feasted on his chest, the dark mat of hair, the flat circles of his nipples. Emboldened, she opened his shirt wider. Abruptly she gasped. Across his upper left chest twisted a mass of scar tissue, white against his swarthy skin.

He had been shot. At the battle of Waterloo.

The sight stunned her even though she had known he'd been wounded. With Alfred's effects had come a letter from the British corporal who had found the two men lying near their carriage. In her anger and grief, she had hated Burke Grisham for surviving the ordeal. She had wished him dead in place of her husband.

Now she could think only of how Burke must have suffered. The pain. The agony. The long recovery. No wonder it had taken him a year to come and pay his respects to the family.

Her hand moved involuntarily toward the scar. He shifted position on the chair, and she looked up. His eyes were open now, observing her with a strange, assessing light.

The deep heat of embarrassment washed through

Catherine. He had caught her gawking like a shameless hussy.

Letting loose of his shirt, she scrambled for a plausible explanation. "I-I wondered if you had a scar."

His expression was impenetrable, fraught with secrets. "So now you know."

"Yes."

Quickly Catherine gathered the cloth and ointment and stood up. As she walked away, he caught hold of her wrist.

His hard grip imprisoned her. An intent perplexity scored his brow. She braced herself for a taunting comment about her unladylike behavior. Instead, he asked a most unexpected question.

"Did you and your husband quarrel over his gambling?"

A lingering chagrin made her defensive. "I can hardly see how that's any concern of yours."

"Just answer me."

"Fine," she snapped, pulling away and retreating behind the work table. "Of course we argued. Alfred would disappear to London for weeks at a time and then return home, expecting me to welcome him with open arms." She clamped her lips shut. Burke didn't need to hear how she had failed to be a good wife. How Alfred had loved the glitter of the city more than he had loved her.

Frowning, Burke sat with his elbows on his knees and his shirt gaping open. "I saw him occasionally toss the dice. He played cards, but no more than other gentlemen of the *ton.*"

"He lost large amounts of money. That's all I know."

But Catherine did know more. She remembered their tense encounter after she had found a dun notice in Alfred's pocket. She had been so angry that she had burned his deck of cards in the fireplace.

She would never tell Burke about that—or her inability to bear a child. The unhappy details of her marriage were too private to share.

"The estate appears to have recovered from whatever money he lost." Burke stood up and rebuttoned his shirt. "I spent the morning in the steward's room. I've been checking into your financial affairs."

Catherine bristled. "I never asked you to do that."

"But your husband did. I made a solemn pledge to him."

"Then I hereby release you from your vow. I can look after myself."

"Can you?" Burke walked forward and planted his palms on the table. His dark gray eyes were serious. "Catherine, you're a kind, hard-working woman. Forgive me if I wish to make certain that no one has taken advantage of your good nature."

Her heart fluttered. Disliking herself for being swayed by his praise of her, she snatched up the spoon and stirred the bubbling rosewater. "If you're criticizing my role in this house again, please be assured I am not being forced to work. I've chosen to keep busy at useful pursuits."

"My concern has to do with your inheritance," he said. "The account book lists two entries of dower payments from the estate this past year, totaling over four thousand pounds. The checques were made out to Lorena. Did you get your portion of the money?"

Catherine swung around to stare at him. "My portion? You're mistaken. I'm entitled to nothing from the revenues."

"On the contrary, as Alfred's widow, you are."

"But he left me only a small annuity in government funds. There was nothing in his will about additional payments from the estate."

"The law entitles you to the right of dower. That means that one-third of the income from the estate goes to the widow. Since both you and Lorena are widowed, the four thousand pounds should have been split between the two of you."

"Two thousand pounds for *me?*" Disbelieving, Catherine shook her head. "I can't imagine. That's a fortune. Well, perhaps not to you, but to me. I've only a fraction of that amount saved for . . ." She bit down on her lip. No one else knew of her dream to open a school.

"So your mother-in-law has been pocketing all the money herself," Burke said in a hard-edged tone. "I suspected as much."

A pained furrow formed on Catherine's brow. Lorena had already admitted to purloining money from the household account to pay for new gowns. Yet Catherine didn't want to think ill of the woman who had trained her to be a lady.

She walked to the tiny window that looked out on the gardens and the stable yard beyond. "Lorena hasn't a head for figures. She probably didn't realize she was expected to divide the payment. After all, she's accustomed to keeping that lump sum herself."

"Then I shall have to disabuse her of the notion. Though I have a feeling Lorena is cracking sharp on money matters." He paced to Catherine's side. "In the meantime, you have the resources to move away from here. To set up your own household."

Could he peer into her mind and see her plans? She felt invaded, wary. "I am perfectly content right here."

"Are you? You have no time to call your own. You spend hours helping with the meals like a servant. And too often, you don't even join the family to eat. I'd say you're at the mercy of Madame Napoleon and her twin lieutenants."

The irreverent description shocked a giggle out of Catherine. She tried to cover her humor with a sober look. "You should show a little respect for your hostess."

"I don't believe in doing as one *should.*" He propped

his shoulder against the wall and studied her, his head cocked to one side. "However, you should do that more often."

"Do what?"

"Smile." He took the spoon from her hand and linked his fingers with hers. "The afternoon is still young. Let me take you away from all this. We'll go for a drive."

She thought about sitting beside him in the phaeton, the wind blowing her hair, the sun warm on her skin. Reluctantly she said, "I have work to do."

"Don't be a spoilsport. Everything will be here when you return. Now come."

He drew her toward the door, and she found herself walking without having made any conscious decision to accompany him. Flecks of green sparked in his smoky eyes. The lock of black hair on his brow made him appear boyish. The charming crook of his lips beckoned her onward. She could see why women adored him.

Many women. Women far more worldly than she.

Catherine halted in the doorway. "No. I'm staying here. And that's final."

His appealing smile vanished. He cocked a dark eyebrow at her. "There's nothing I can say to convince you otherwise?"

"No."

"Ah, well. I don't suppose I can force you to enjoy life."

With a look of regret, he brushed his thumb over her mouth, turned away, and disappeared out the scullery door.

She stood in the steamy air of the still-room, the only sound the bubbling from the pot. The touch of his finger on her lips tingled like a ghostly kiss. Once before, she had made the mistake of believing in a rogue. She wouldn't do so again.

Nevertheless, Catherine found herself wishing she had gone with him.

* * *

Burke was drunk.

He took another swig from his glass and grimaced as the gin burned down his throat. It was cheap, nasty stuff. But this rural pub offered only two choices, and it took too much ale to intoxicate him.

He tipped his chair back against the wall and blearily surveyed the tiny taproom of the Fox and Hound. Pipe smoke hazed the air. The five tables were occupied by farmers and shepherds. They cast glances at him and murmured amongst themselves, no doubt wondering why his fine and fancy lordship deigned to enter their humble alehouse.

They'd never guess why.

He had needed to get away from Snow Manor. Away from the woman who haunted his mind. Away from his growing desire to possess the wife of his dead friend.

The one woman immune to his charm.

"G'day, sir. The other chairs are taken. Mind if I join you?"

A wiry stranger appeared beside the table. The blue of his eyes was startling against teak-brown features weathered with age. Clad in nankeen pantaloons and a dark coat, his cravat tied in an old-fashioned style, he looked to be a gentleman down on his luck.

Preferring anyone's company to his own, Burke waved his glass at the empty chair. "Help yourself."

"That's right kind of you, sir." The man sat down and propped his ivory cane against the table. He peered closely at Burke. "Or shall I say . . . 'm'lord'?"

"Thornwald will do."

He shook Burke's hand. "Hullo, Thornwald. The name's Ezekiel Newberry. I'm new to the district. A traveler seeing the sights. How about yourself?"

Burke wondered what insanity had induced him to invite this gregarious man to sit down. It must be the rotgut he was drinking. "I'm visiting a friend."

"That wouldn't be the Snows, now would it? It's rumored they're entertaining a noble visitor." Newberry gave an abashed laugh. "Not that I'm one to listen to gossip, you understand. I merely overheard the mates over there."

Ezekiel Newberry had an odd accent that Burke couldn't place. His gin-soaked brain worried the thought, then abandoned it. "I am indeed staying with the Snows."

"Well! You're quite the lucky fellow. To live in close proximity to such a handsome widow lady."

Catherine. Just the thought of her made his chest tighten. He couldn't stop himself from asking, "You know her? Where did you see her?"

"Why, in church last Sunday. And a more lovely angel a man could never hope to gaze upon. To set my lips against hers would be pure heaven."

The randy old bastard. Burke was seized by the urge to dive across the table and throttle Newberry. Curse it. Did every man in the district lust after Catherine?

Burke swigged the last of his liquor. She might fall in love with one. Marry him. Bear his children.

"Aye, she did find a place in my heart," Newberry sighed. "I understand she's having a party in a few days. 'Tis my fondest dream to attend, to dance just once with her. Of course a passing wayfarer like me could never hope for such an honor."

This oily stranger was fishing for an invitation. He was taking his infatuation with Catherine too bloody far. "No," Burke said coldly, "you couldn't."

" 'Tis a shame. But I suppose she'd be too busy to pay mind to an aging gent like myself, anyhow. I understand she plans to launch her daughters at the ball."

Befuddled, Burke stared. "Daughters?"

"Aye, twin ones she has. They're pretty enough, but not so seasoned as their dear mother."

"Lorena." He released his breath in a guffaw as the

truth penetrated his mind. "You've been talking about *Lorena.*"

"Aye. The widowed Mrs. Lorena Snow. Ah, what a woman. Some might think her a bit stout, but I like my pigeons plump."

"A man who knows his own taste." Feeling expansive, Burke slapped Newberry on the back. "My friend, consider yourself invited to the ball. By the express request of Lord Thornwald."

A one-sided smile creased Newberry's face, lending him an oddly sinister aspect. "Why, m'lord. You are too kind."

"Nonsense. I'll wager Lorena will be delighted to have a suitor."

"Speaking of wagers." Newberry reached into his coat pocket. "Perhaps you would care to join me in a game of ecarte. No one else in this backwater village knows how to play."

He drew forth a deck and began to shuffle the cards. Burke felt a familiar rising excitement. The money didn't matter, only the thrill of taking a risk, bluffing his opponent, winning.

He hadn't gambled in months. Not since . . .

The colored symbols flashed past. Jack of hearts. Nine of spades. Ace of diamonds.

His head swam. Not since Catherine had thrown his cards into the fireplace. He could see her standing there, her slender body limned by the flames. As she hurled accusations at him.

And wept.

He blinked, and the smoky taproom reappeared. Christ. That scene was only a made-up fantasy, a madman's nightmare. Yet for a moment a strange twilight had crept over him, and he had fancied the scene was his own memory. As if it had happened to *him.*

Newberry lay the deck on the scarred table. "Your cut, m'lord."

Burke felt the dark pull of the cards. Luring him toward the world that had been his home, his hell. Perhaps if he returned to his former life, he could escape the dreams that haunted him.

Dreams of Catherine.

Abruptly he shaped his fingers into a fist. "I'm sorry. I have to go."

Burke stood, the legs of his chair scraping the wood floor. He threw a gold coin onto the table. Staying upright by dint of willpower, he wove his way past the other tables.

Zeke Newberry watched him go out the door. Odd blokes, these aristocrats. Couldn't hold their liquor.

Ah, but a man might as well take advantage of opportunity. He could make use of the coin that glinted in the lamplight.

Zeke rapped his cane on the table and summoned the proprietor. "Gin, if you please."

When the drink came, he downed it quickly. He had acquired the habit from years of hard living in a place where a man had to quaff his grog fast or see it stolen.

Zeke mulled over his plan. Things were going better than expected. He could swagger through the front door of Snow Manor instead of stealing through the back like a thief in the night.

He smiled. Lorena would be so surprised to see him again.

Chapter 7

The tinkling notes of the pianoforte invaded the music room. Twin voices shrilled in a wobbly duet.

Priscilla missed a high note and Prudence snickered. Priscilla jabbed her sister in the ribs and Prudence gasped. Side by side on the piano bench they sat in muslin gowns, one of myrtle green and the other of canary yellow, while Lorena beamed with maternal pride.

When Prudence struck a flat in place of a sharp, Catherine winced. Their faulty rendition made it difficult to focus on the song instead of staring at Burke as he sat politely listening.

At least that was the excuse she gave herself.

Oh, sweet heavens. Why not indulge herself in the rare chance to gawk at him? This was her first sight of him since their encounter in the still-room yesterday. She knew by the servants' grapevine that he had come in late last night and spent the day out again, not returning until dinner.

She burned to know how he whiled away the hours. Or more precisely, with whom. A rogue always sought out cronies of his own ilk—or loose women of his own moral depravity.

Slightly in front of her, he sprawled in a chair beside Lorena. His inky hair brushed the back of his high collar. His buff coat was so superbly cut it might have been molded to his form. His long legs were stretched out, the polished black boots crossed at the ankles. She remembered too well his muscular chest and the twisted white scar that enhanced his daredevil aura. The scar was a reminder that he was human . . . and vulnerable.

A delicious languor stole through Catherine. The pleasurable sensation was reminiscent of how she had felt upon awakening in the dark these past few nights, fevered and restless, with a fleeting memory of having dreamt about a shadowy lover whose caresses carried her almost to the pinnacle yet left her aching and unfulfilled.

Gazing at Burke's distinctive profile, she let herself drift into a daydream where he took her into his arms and kissed her again. Only this time their kiss led to intimate touches and whispered words of yearning—

"Do you play, Mrs. Snow?" he asked.

The pianoforte music had ceased. Burke had turned in his chair and his gray eyes bored into her.

Catherine blushed as the heat from her loins surged to her cheeks. He couldn't possibly guess the shameless thoughts that had cast a spell upon her good judgment.

Or could he?

"No, I don't play. Do you?"

Before he could respond to her tart question, Lorena said, "Poor thing, she grew up without the advantages of my girls. Priscilla, in particular, is quite the accomplished young lady. She would be delighted to play a solo piece."

"Oh, Mummy." Sitting on the piano bench, Priscilla pouted charmingly. "Must I?"

"I could never ask a delicate girl to strain herself,"

Burke said. "She's already played so long and so beautifully."

"Pray, don't leave yet. Why, the evening is young." Lorena put out her diamond-ringed hand to stop him from rising. "Catherine, find your spectacles and entertain us with a pretty sonnet from Lord Byron."

"Read my favorite," Prudence said, patting her blonde curls. " 'She Walks In Beauty.' "

Catherine got to her feet. The thought flitted through her mind that Lorena wished to show Catherine in a less than favorable light by requiring her to wear the unbecoming eyeglasses. Then she scolded herself. Vanity lay at the heart of her reluctance. During their unfortunate interlude at the cottage, Burke had made plain his distaste of her poor vision.

She straightened her shoulders. He could take his shallow beliefs and go to the devil.

Defiantly she drew the silver-rimmed spectacles from the hidden pocket of her skirt and perched them on her nose. Then she sat down on a stool before the fire, opened the slender volume, and began to read aloud.

The lovely rhythm seduced her. By the time she reached the last melodious line, her rebellious mood had softened. " 'But tell of days in goodness spent,/A mind at peace with all below,/A heart whose love is innocent.' "

The verse died into the whispery hiss of the fire. She couldn't stop herself. She lifted her head and looked over the top of her spectacles at Burke.

Their eyes held. A silvery light shone in his, and the demon bright intensity seemed to peer straight into her soul. As if he could prey upon the thoughts and feelings that belonged to her alone. Catherine shifted on the stool and lowered her gaze. For the briefest of moments, she had felt exposed in all her dreams and longings. But her private life was something she would never again share. There was no sense in making herself vulnerable to a scoundrel whose only goal was to seek out his next amusement.

"Just three nights until our ball," Prudence said, shattering the spell. "Who knows, perhaps I shall meet a handsome blade who will compose an ode to *me.*"

"You must save your best dances for your cousin Fabian," Lorena chided.

Prudence scowled. "I will not. He's a silly clod-pate. Thank heavens he didn't dine with us again tonight."

"Bide your uncivil tongue. Be a good girl and I'll allow you to wear my diamond necklace at the ball."

Her sullenness vanishing, Prudence rushed to her mother's chair. "Oh, dear, sweet, kind Mummy. May I, truly?"

Priscilla leaped up from the piano bench. "That's not fair. What of me?"

"You may wear my pearls with the matching tiara. They show off your beauty to its greatest advantage." Lorena slid a glance at Burke. "Do you not find her lovely, m'lord?"

He continued to look at Catherine. "Mere gemstones could never match the sparkle in her eyes."

The reading glasses distorted his image into that of a dark stranger. His compliment sent a forbidden thrill through her. Telling herself that he was teasing, Catherine removed her spectacles and tucked them away.

Priscilla glided around the music room as if dancing with an invisible partner. "Oh, by the by, Catherine. As you're still in mourning, you may wear my black satin if you like. It's finer than anything in your wardrobe."

Catherine hugged the volume of poetry to her breast and felt a stab of hot denial. It was sensible to accept a castoff rather than squander her precious money on a new gown that she might never wear again. Yet she found herself saying, "Thank you, but I've decided to set aside mourning."

Lorena gasped. The girls stared. Burke raised one eyebrow.

Catherine had shocked even herself. She didn't know where the decision came from, but she was glad, fiercely glad, she had said it. The gloomy garb had weighted down her spirit for too long.

"A widow has an obligation to wear black for at least two years," Lorena said in a huff. "It is the convention."

"People may talk for a short while, but they will find a more interesting topic quickly enough."

"I forbid you to do this," Lorena snapped. "You will bring disgrace on this family. And on dear Freddie's memory."

Catherine swallowed past the tension in her throat. Quietly she said, "I'm sorry to displease you, but I have made up my mind."

"And Alfred would cheer your decision," Burke said.

"Alfred?" Lorena said, turning toward her guest. "M'lord, you surprise me. He would not want his widow to forget him."

"And she won't. Yet your son despised black on women—said it made them look like a flock of crows. He'd have told Catherine to wear bright gold and the devil take anyone rude enough to gossip. You wouldn't invite any small-minded people to your ball, anyway, would you?"

He deftly guided Lorena into a discussion of the guest list, and Catherine sat in stunned amazement that he would come to her defense. An image floated into her mind of herself garbed in a gold silk gown and whirling around the dance floor in the arms of a tall stranger.

A gown in which she could feel radiant. A gown in which she could become a girl again, starry-eyed and innocent. A gown that was not someone's made-over discard. There had been a time when she had dressed like a fairy princess in silks and lace, but her frivolous wardrobe had been packed away more than a year ago, and her hopes and dreams had been shelved long before that.

Temptation whispered that she could afford to dress in the latest fashion now. Caution argued that she had yet to receive the two thousand pounds from the estate.

That reminded her. Had Burke requested her share of the dower right from Lorena yet? No, her mother-in-law would have made some cutting remark.

Yesterday she had automatically accepted Burke's determination to handle the situation. But today, away from his distracting presence, she'd had time to think. And to realize that an independent woman faced up to her own obligations.

She rose from her stool and set down the book of poetry. "Your lordship, if I may speak with you a moment."

"My pleasure." Burke followed her to a private corner. With the white cravat and pale coat setting off his swarthy handsomeness, he made a magnificent picture. He leaned close and murmured, "Bravo. As lovely as you are in black, you could do without a somber air."

Catherine sternly disciplined a rise of pleasure. Conscious of her mother-in-law's watchful eyes, she whispered, "I only wanted to tell you that you needn't bother Lorena about my dower rights. I've decided to address her myself."

He frowned. "That's out of the question. She's more likely to listen to me."

"She'll listen to me, too," Catherine said with more conviction than she felt. "I depend on her sense of fair play."

"Fair play," he scoffed. "She'll play on your kind heart and keep your money on a pretext."

"I won't allow that to happen."

"And how will you stop her?"

Catherine blew out a breath. "This argument is illogical. The situation will never come to that."

"You're right. Because *I* shan't permit her to take advantage of you."

"Burke, it's my problem. Not yours."

His stern expression softened. A rakish smile lifted one corner of his mouth. "I'm glad you've decided to address me by my first name."

Catherine's heart skipped a beat. How did he always manage to unsettle her so? "About Lorena—"

"I'd rather talk about the ball," he broke in. "I trust you'll save every dance for me."

"Every one?" The preposterous remark teased a smile from her. "As a widow, I very much doubt I shall dance at all."

"What, you'll sit by the wall with the crones? I'll drag you out if need be."

"Then perhaps I shall settle the matter by remaining in my room."

"Do that, and I'll have my dance regardless." His voice lowered to a husky whisper. "The notion is rather appealing. The two of us. Alone. In your bedchamber."

He gazed blatantly at her mouth. Looking up at his stunning features, she shuddered from the rise of that unladylike wildness inside herself, the mad impulse to grant him free access to her most private places. To feel his mouth on her breast as he had done to that whore. . . .

"What is all this whispering about?" Lorena asked. Clad in a blue-and-white striped gown, she advanced on them like a female version of Bonaparte. "Catherine, you naughty creature. You mustn't steal his lordship away from the rest of us." Though her tone was light, a forbidding tightness pinched her mouth.

Catherine felt her vitality slipping away and struggled to hold onto her resolve. It was now or never. "I was inquiring if his lordship would please keep Prudence and Priscilla company. You see, I need to speak to you—"

"I would speak to you first, Mrs. Snow, on a matter of grave importance." Burke took hold of Lorena's arm. "If I may request the honor of your attention?"

Her expression melted into a simpering acquiescence. "Of course, m'lord. We can find privacy in the library."

Catherine clenched her fists in vexation. With arrogant disregard for her decision, he would talk to Lorena himself. Well, he would get an earful from *her* on the morrow!

The instant he escorted Lorena out the door, Priscilla clasped her hands to her heart and wilted dreamily into a chair. "Oh, is it not wonderful?"

"It is horrid," Prudence snapped. "His lordship is gone and *I* am left with you two for company."

Priscilla smirked. "You poor jealous thing."

"I have nothing to be jealous of, Mistress Muttonhead."

"Yes, you do, Countess Crack-Brain. Right now his lordship is sure to be asking Mummy for *my* hand in marriage!"

"I have a most serious question to ask you, Mrs. Snow."

"Pray, m'lord, do make yourself comfortable first." Lorena led the way to a matched pair of leather chairs by the fireplace.

As Burke followed, he noticed an odd fact. All the books on the shelves appeared to be written in Greek and Latin. Was that why Catherine had to borrow books from the vicarage?

"May I pour you a brandy?" his hostess asked.

The prospect of a drink lured him. Clasped in the dark embrace of alcohol, he could forget that the one woman he burned to possess didn't want him. He could remind himself that the widow of his best friend was the last woman on earth he should seduce.

Lorena waited expectantly. Despite her abundant proportions, she must have once been a handsome woman, judging by her sultry blue eyes, her smooth skin, her majestic carriage. A stranger might well admire her from afar.

Who was that fellow again? Newton? Newland?

No, Newberry. Ezekiel Newberry.

Burke knew he ought to tell Lorena about inviting the man to her party. But at the moment he wasn't feeling charitable.

He sat down, leaned his elbows on his knees, and clasped his hands. "I would rather get straight to the point."

Beaming, she settled her broad bottom on the chair opposite him. "It is my Priscilla, is it not? You'll think me impertinent, but she will make you a fine wife. So obedient, so accomplished, so dainty. And an heiress, too. Her paternal grandfather left her quite a valuable estate in Lancashire."

"I am not here to speak of Priscilla."

"It is Prudence, then?" Lorena's blue eyes rounded. "Oh, la, my lord, you are a sly one. I never guessed of your interest in her. I assumed you would prefer my elder daughter. But dear me, Prudence is promised to someone else. Though nothing has been settled yet. If you give me a few days, I can perhaps arrange matters to your liking—"

"I am not here to ask for Prudence's hand, either. It is Catherine who concerns me."

"Catherine?"

Burke relished the shock on Lorena's face. Let the woman believe that despite her matchmaking, he meant to tender a proposal for Catherine's hand. Let her think, if only for a moment, that he found Catherine a superior choice for a wife.

It was not far from the truth. Were he bent on matrimony, he would prefer an intelligent, mature woman. The realization startled him. He was accustomed to women who chattered about frivolous topics like fashion and gossip. Women who spent hours each day dressing and pampering themselves. Women he could charm with easy compliments and stolen kisses.

Not a stubborn bluestocking who wore spectacles and treasured books more than his companionship.

His affairs were legendary among the risqué members of the *ton.* His stable of *chéres amiès* had included married women and widows eager for a romp in his bed. Ambitious mamas overlooked his proclivities and sought his status and fortune. He had even sunk so low as to bed the mother instead of wooing the daughter.

But after nearly dying at Waterloo and then experiencing the mysterious visions of Catherine, he could see that his life had become a series of meaningless, self-indulgent episodes. He had comported himself like a spoiled juvenile, ever seeking the thrill of the next conquest. All in the vain hope of silencing the voice that tormented him.

Stinking coward.

It was true. He lacked honor. He had no moral backbone. Why did he think he could change?

"M'lord," Lorena said, her voice faint. "You surely cannot mean what I think."

Burke focused his eyes on her. "And what do you know of my thoughts?" he said coldly.

"You spoke of Catherine. And . . . marriage."

He shrugged. "And if I did?"

A wooden smile bared Lorena's teeth. "I'd advise you to reconsider. She's a common girl who worked as a servant at the vicarage. How she managed to bewitch my dear Freddie, I never understood."

"Then you'll be relieved to know my question concerns not marriage, but a financial matter."

Lorena's stiff posture relaxed, though wariness entered her expression. "Mr. Rudd mentioned that you had been examining the estate books. I cannot imagine why."

"Your son entrusted me to look after Catherine. In the moment before his death."

"My poor boy—lost to me forever." Lorena drew her lacy handkerchief from her sleeve and dabbed at her eyes. "I do miss him so. If only there were some way to bring him back."

Burke felt an uncomfortable twinge of compassion. There was yet another guilt to dwell forever in his black soul. With effort he forced himself to think of Catherine's welfare. "Please accept my sincerest regret for your loss. However, you must honor your son's wishes for his wife."

"I am doing the best that I can. And if I may point out, Catherine is a grown woman. She doesn't need a guardian."

"Then consider me her financial advisor. As such, I must ask when you intend to pay her portion of the dower right."

Lorena's cheeks went pale except for twin spots of rouge. "Her portion?"

"Yes. Half the revenues you received from the estate this past year. Two thousand and twelve pounds, to be precise."

Plucking at the folds of her gown, Lorena loosed a nervous laugh. "Oh, but the money has been applied to Catherine's share of the household upkeep. The expenses here are overwhelming—the salaries of the staff, repairing dry rot, repapering the ballroom. Surely you are familiar with the tremendous cost of maintaining a mansion such as this one."

"Fabian Snow is responsible for the household expenditures, whether he lives here or not. Besides, Catherine has more than paid her way in servitude."

"Has she been complaining to you? After we welcomed her into the bosom of our family and gave her so much?" Lorena fanned her face with a handkerchief. "Oh, the girl is so ungrateful. Considering the inferior circumstances of her birth, the honor of the Snow name is a gift she can never repay."

His temper snapped. "Catherine is too much the lady to complain. So I will act on her behalf. I must ask that you deposit the money in her bank account by tomorrow."

"Tomorrow? That's impossible. Where would I obtain so large an amount on such short notice? You must give me more time . . ."

All of a sudden, a familiar tingling swept over Burke's skin. His temples began to throb and darkness encroached on his mind.

A vision. Now?

Even as he gripped the arms of his chair and fought the madness, the library dissolved into another scene.

Lorena sat moaning on the bench in her boudoir. Her breasts heaved beneath the apricot gown. She twisted a handkerchief in her hands and the fine lace was shredded. Today, no smile lightened her face.

"This will destroy the family honor," she cried out. "We'll be ruined. All I have worked for, gone!" She looked up, her eyes stark with fear. "We must pay him off somehow. I can obtain the money if you give me more time . . ."

Someone was shaking Burke's shoulder. The motion made his war wound hurt like the very devil. He growled a protest and opened his eyes to find his mother hovering over him.

No, he thought on a wave of dizziness. Not *his* mother. Lorena.

She said, "You were staring so fiercely into the distance. I feared you had fallen into some kind of fit. Are you quite all right, m'lord?"

With effort, Burke controlled his shaking hands and waved her away. "It's nothing. A sudden headache."

"Then I will pour you that brandy. My son, God rest his soul, believed brandy to be a great restorative." She bustled toward the sideboard and reached for a decanter.

In truth, Burke craved a drink. Anything to help him forget the threatening darkness. His head felt thick, off-kilter. For the first time, someone other than Catherine had entered the dark realm of his dementia.

Who had Lorena felt obliged to pay off?

And to whom had she been speaking?

Alfred.

Icy fingers tiptoed down Burke's spine. That answer defied logic. It pointed toward a solution so unthinkable, he might as well dive into the bottomless black pit of insanity.

It meant he was privy to Alfred's private memories.

Chapter 8

A shriek pierced the party preparations in the kitchen.

Everyone stopped to stare: the maids peeling mounds of potatoes, Mrs. Earnshaw stirring the huge kettle of spiced punch on the range, the pantry boy staggering under a platter of plucked quail.

Catherine looked up from the pile of raspberries she was sorting, too late to avert disaster. Martha dropped her basket of onions and made a dive for the long table, where a half-grown kitten had its nose stuck in a pitcher of cream.

"Thievin' bugger! Get off!"

Tigress streaked along the table like a bolt of black and orange lightning. Cutlery and plates clattered. The egg bowl crashed to the floor, yellow slime oozing across the flagstones. The flour bin tipped over and a white cloud rose to the rafters. Several servants backed away, waving their hands and coughing.

The kitten jumped onto a tall cupboard and leaped upward from shelf to shelf. Atop the high vantage point, it settled down to clean its whiskers.

"Upon my *word.*" Pressing her hands to her cheeks, Catherine regarded the mess littering the floor.

Martha snatched up a broom and stalked toward the cat. "I'll get the little beast."

"Leave her be. I'll put her outside later," Catherine said. "In the meantime, go fetch more eggs and cream from the dairy. Timothy, put down that platter and get a mop and pail. The rest of you, return to your work or we'll never be ready in time."

With much murmuring, the servants did her bidding. Catherine turned back to the raspberries. The ball loomed a mere eight hours away, and the monumental task of preparing a banquet for nearly two hundred guests fell to her. She had already dealt with the butcher's boy who had forgotten to deliver the hams, a dairy maid who had trapped a mouse in the butter crock, and a tweeny who had been caught kissing a stable lad.

Just when Catherine thought matters could get no worse, the back door burst open and Alice Guppy rushed inside.

The nine-year-old ploughed through the field of servants and came straight to Catherine. She stopped, panting, her freckled cheeks rosy. "My brother's gone, Mrs. Cathy. Peter's run off."

"Are you quite sure, darling?" Catherine grasped the girl's bony shoulders and peered into her round blue eyes. She smelled of wind and sweetness, and Catherine felt that mysterious tug of longing for her own child, a longing that persisted despite her new plan for the future. "Perhaps your brother has gone fishing. Or he's out with a friend on the moor."

Alice gave a vigorous shake of her carroty braids. "He's gone for good. Papa caught Peter sneaking out of the Fox and Hound last evening. He'd wagered away the watch Grandpapa gave him for Christmas. Papa was so furious he thrashed Peter and banished him to his room. This morn he was gone, his bed not slept in."

"Perhaps he straightened the sheets before he went out to play."

Alice screwed up her nose. "Peter?"

"Aye," Catherine sighed. " 'Tis impossible to imagine. What have your parents done to find him?"

"Papa's out searching with the dogs. Mum's at home, weeping into her apron. Please, Mrs. Cathy. Thee must come."

"Beg pardon, ma'am." Owen strode up, his manly jaw braced atop a towering stack of china plates. "I brung these up from the storeroom. Shall I put 'em in the dining room?"

"The scullery," Catherine said. "They'll have to be rinsed before we set them out for the guests."

"Yes, ma'am." The footman shouldered a path through the busy kitchen.

Biting her lip, Catherine surveyed the army of servants, from the pantry boy cleaning the floor to the scullery maid tottering under an armload of dirty pots. Besides the refreshments, there were scores of tasks for Catherine to oversee: the airing of the guest chambers, the washing of hundreds of champagne glasses, the arranging of cut roses from the garden.

And if she left she might not get back in time to dance with Burke.

But in her mind she could picture a dejected Peter Guppy with his freckled face and the lick of tow hair that drooped perpetually onto his brow. He could be in trouble.

"Mrs. Cathy?" Alice said. "Please?"

"All right." Catherine untied her apron and snatched her pelisse from a hook near the door. Maybe she could return before Lorena discovered her absence. In any event, her mother-in-law's disapproval meant nothing beside the safety of a little boy.

Dear God. Where would Peter go?

* * *

Peter Allen Guppy trudged along the high road to London. His stomach rumbled. The bread and cheese he had snitched from his mother's kitchen was long gone, wolfed down at midnight while he hunched his back against a stone wall to block the cold wind off the moor.

His legs ached. Determined to put as much distance as possible between himself and home, Peter had walked much of the night. The darkness had been spooky with only a fingernail moon to light the road. When at last he came upon an inn, he sneaked into the stable and slept in a stall filled with smelly straw.

At dawn he had been rudely awakened by the stable master. The smack of a broom against Peter's already-sore backside had sent him scrambling out the door, abandoning the rucksack that held a change of clothes, his pocketknife, and the ten shillings he had hoarded since his tenth birthday back in February.

So much for daring adventure. In the past hour, only two carriages had gone by. The first, a post chaise, had nearly run him down. When Peter flagged down the second, the driver had flicked his whip at Peter's ear so that now it stung as badly as his rump.

He sighed. Right now, Mum would be frying rashers of bacon for breakfast. The family would be sitting down to eat scones dripping with butter and coddled eggs still steaming from the pan. Even the thought of porridge made his mouth water.

His Papa was an old porridge-head, Peter thought, brimming with defiance and crossness. So what if he had lost that frigging pocketwatch? It was his. He could do whatever he liked with it. Even wager it in a game of ecarte.

Anyhow, Mr. Newberry had played fair like the fine gentleman he was. He had been kind enough to teach Peter the rules of the game. Peter himself had dealt the losing cards.

He kicked a stone and sent it clattering down a slope.

All gentlemen gambled. Besides, he had to win enough to purchase a commission in the cavalry.

He lost himself in fantasy. Old Boney had escaped from the isle of St. Helena. The mad Frenchie could be stopped only by the bravery of Lieutenant Peter Allen Guppy. His saber flashing, he rode his warhorse into the thick of battle, killing Frenchmen right and left, dodging the bullets that whizzed past his ears. . . .

The clip-clopping of hooves broke his reverie. Coming at a spanking pace was the smartest vehicle Peter had ever beheld. It was a high-sprung curricle with yellow-painted wheels, drawn by a pair of bays and driven by a dashing blade with a lady at his side. A portmanteau was strapped in place behind the seat.

Feeling invincible from his imaginary fight, Peter stepped into the middle of the road and waved his arms. The carriage stopped so close he could feel the steamy breath of the horses.

The young gentleman stood up, scowling, the ribbons dangling from one gloved hand. "Ho there, brat. Move aside."

"Are thee going to London?" Peter asked.

"What devilish business is that of yours?" The stranger gestured with his whip. "Get off the road ere I run you down."

"I'd like a ride. Please."

"And why should I take you to London?"

"Because . . ." Peter improvised a lie. "Yesterday my parents went off to the city. I've a dozen brothers and sisters, and in all the confusion they left without me."

"Hobbledehoy, you're a runaway farmlad, more likely. Go on back to your pigs and sheep."

The blonde lady leaned forward so that her bosom looked like twin white udders. "Oh, come, Jervis," she said, "don't badger the little heeler. What's your name, boy?"

"Peter. Peter . . . uh, Wellington."

"Well, Peter Wellington, how old are you?"

He puffed out his chest and stretched himself taller. "Thirteen, m'lady. Old enough to be seeking my own fortune."

"Hmm." She gave her companion a long look. "He's a rather innocent-looking sort, is he not? Country-bred. Inexperienced."

"I'm no bumpkin!" Peter protested, planting his hands on his hips. "I know how to play ecarte."

She giggled. "Fancy, a junior Corinthian, no less. Jervis, just think. It might prove amusing to take him along with us."

Jervis glowered at her. He was a dandy of the first stare in his yellow waistcoat, pale-blue trousers, and black knee boots.

The corners of his mouth slowly tilted upward. "Stella, my puss, how your mind does work. I believe we must find a private place to stop after awhile. Hop aboard, lad."

His back to the sturdy trunk of a sycamore on the top of a hill, Burke lunched on a packet of cold chicken and a flask of brandy. A yellow butterfly flitted over the bushes of heather and furze. Down the slope grazed a flock of sheep, mirror images of the clouds that scattered the blue sky. The clank of bells mingled with an occasional bleat when a lamb got separated from its mother.

Burke took a swig of brandy, then drummed his fingers on the silver flask. Even in this bucolic setting, he felt no peace. Restlessness stirred within him like the everlasting wind that blew over the moor.

At one time he would have called it boredom and gone out to find a high-stakes dice game to amuse himself. But lately his discontent had a sharp edge. It was honed by his failure to break the bond of his obsession for Catherine Snow.

Lust he could understand. Deliberately he reduced her to a list of physical attributes. The waiflike face. The hourglass curves. The amber eyes that could tempt as well as taunt.

What he couldn't fathom were his eerie insights into her private past. A spasm of apprehension gripped him. Ever since his arrival at Snow Manor, his visions had become more vivid, more explicit, more maddeningly real.

There *was* one answer. One phenomenon too bizarre, too implausible for any rational man to accept. He might as well consign himself to a stark padded cell as believe *that.*

Refusing to consider it, he steered his thoughts back to Catherine. Madness or not, he craved her smile. He yearned for her respect. He ached to win her heart.

Curse it. He didn't need her. Coming to Yorkshire had been a mistake. As soon as he settled her finances and fulfilled his vow to Alfred, he would leave. For good. Forever.

Lorena had promised to have Catherine's money by Friday. In two more days, he would return to his estate in Cornwall. In solitude he could vanquish his bedeviling need for the widow of his dead friend.

In time the visions would fade. They must. He had to believe so or he was lost.

He took another numbing swallow of brandy, corked the flask, and tucked it inside his coat pocket. The chicken bones he scattered on the grass for the scavengers.

His horse grazed the hillside behind the sycamore. Mounting up, Burke gazed across the vast scrubby sea, looking for the cottage where he and Catherine had shared a stormy kiss. No wonder he couldn't forget her.

That single taste had whetted his appetite for the one woman who scorned him.

The one woman he must never, ever possess.

The cottage made a black speck against the lonely miles of moorland. Then he spied something moving nearby. Riding to the crest of the hill, he shaded his eyes with the flat of his hand.

Two females, one short and one tall, walked swiftly across the moor, heading away from Snow Manor and toward the village of Warrenby. The girl skipped ahead, pausing every now and then to pick up a stone or a flower.

His stomach tightened. He recognized the graceful stride of the woman. She drew him like a Corinthian is drawn to the dice table.

Responding to his command, the horse trotted down the hill, past the flock of bleating sheep. The day seemed suddenly brighter, redolent of warm earth and fresh air. Sunshine smiled on the rocky landscape covered by tufted grass. Puffy white clouds scudded across a sky that glowed a rare, deep sapphire.

Burke caught up to Catherine as she and her young companion neared the village. Clad in an old pelisse over a plain brown dress, with wisps of sable hair curling around cheeks flushed with health, Catherine had never looked more appealing.

He burned to kiss her.

Instead he asked, "Is something amiss? May I be of assistance?"

She glanced distractedly toward the village. "There's naught you can do."

Her furrowed brow belied her words. "Tell me," he insisted.

He could see the hesitation in her, the pursed lips, the judgment in her eyes as if she debated whether or not to entrust him with her secret thoughts. His good mood evaporated.

"My brother's run away from home," the girl piped up. "Mrs. Cathy's going to find him."

Only then did Burke take a closer look at the girl's freckled face. It couldn't be. Yet a cold spasm of unreality seized him. Darkness crawled from the brink of his consciousness.

He recognized the girl. He had seen her in a vision. She'd sat in a group of children who were listening to Catherine read.

Would this madness never stop?

"Alice, that's enough," Catherine said in a clipped voice. "Your mother's waiting for us at the vicarage. I'm sure his lordship has more important matters to attend to." Picking up her skirts, she hastened over the arched bridge.

Burke followed her. The horse's hooves clopped a hollow tune on the stone bridge that spanned the gurgling water. He rode down the dirt lane that meandered past thatched-roof cottages, a gabled inn, and the public house, where the painted sign of a hound chasing a fox creaked in the breeze.

At the other end of the village rose a stone church with an octagonal bell tower and a graveyard beautified by rhododendrons and a magnificent oak. Burke resisted the urge to take another drink from the flask in his pocket. Alfred should have been buried here, instead of lying in a common grave beneath a Belgian rye field.

Just beyond the church, Catherine disappeared into a dwelling with tall eaves and a brick chimney. The desire to unveil every facet of her life propelled Burke onward. He wanted to know why she would leave her duties at the manor house and rush after a runaway boy. He swung down, secured the reins to the filigreed iron fence, and knocked on the door.

Alice let him in. "Have thee come to help us, too?"

Something in her wide blue eyes caught at him. The pure trust of the innocent. "Yes."

A smile beamed across her freckled face. Surprisingly, she put her small hand into his and drew him into a cramped library.

Burke looked around with keen interest. Catherine had grown up at the vicarage.

A kite fashioned of newspaper dangled its rag-and-string tail from the top bookshelf. On the desk, a half-eaten piece of bread and jam sat beside a globe of the world, where someone had stuck a tiny Union Jack into France. A skipping rope snaked across the threadbare rug.

Catherine comforted a weeping woman on the sofa, her graying hair straggling to her shoulders. On Catherine's lap sat a tiny girl who hugged a rag doll and sucked her thumb.

At their obvious affection, Burke was aware of a hollowness inside himself. He felt like a penniless lad with his nose pressed to the window of a sweet shop. How extraordinary to meet people who could show tenderness and concern for one another.

Catherine frowned at him. "Why have you come here?"

"To find the missing boy, of course." Before she could argue, he crouched on his heels before the woman. "You must be the lady of the house. Can you tell me what's happened?"

"M'lord." She made a half-hearted attempt to tidy her hair. "I'm Mrs. Guppy, the vicar's wife. I'm fair ashamed to tell thee about our disgrace."

"Believe me, I'm well acquainted with disgrace."

She took a shuddering breath. "It all started when Mr. Guppy found Peter gaming last evening. Oh, what has my boy come to?"

"You've surely been to the Fox and Hound," Catherine said to Burke. "Have you ever seen a tow-haired boy there? Peter's ten years old."

Her accusatory tone lit the wick of his anger. "No," he said. "You force me to confess, I've been there but once."

She arched one eyebrow in disbelief.

Mrs. Guppy went on, "Mr. Guppy flogged the naughty lad and sent him to bed without his supper. 'Twas only what he deserved for his ungodly deed, wasn't it?"

"His rump did sting something dreadful," Alice said with unseemly relish as she hitched her bony elbows over the back of the sofa. "He could scarce sit down."

"When I went upstairs to rouse him for his chores this morning, he was gone. Gone! Where, oh, where is my dear little boy?" Mrs. Guppy fell to sobbing into her apron again.

The little girl whimpered, "Where'th Peter, Mith Cathy?"

Catherine snuggled her close. To Mrs. Guppy, she said, "Mr. Guppy will notify the magistrate. Peter'll be safe and sound back at home sooner than you think."

"The lad has ever been a trial," Mrs. Guppy said, sniffling, her broad face wet with tears. "Too adventuresome by far, always dreaming. And pestering his father and me about sending him to stay with his great-uncle in London. As if we could afford the coach trip with five young ones to feed."

"Let's make a list of all the places he might have gone," Catherine said. "I've a mind to try the fair at Middleton. He has a liking for the puppet show there."

"Or he could be hiding in the ruins of St. Mary's Abbey," Alice said, her eyes shining. " 'Tis haunted by spirits."

As the others speculated, Burke stood and paced the confines of the library. His gaze narrowed on a slingshot lying on the lowest shelf. There was something familiar about it.

The back of his neck prickled, the sensation extending up his scalp and down his spine. Pressure pulsed in his temples and darkness rushed out at him.

No, his mind screamed. *Not here.*

The dim library vanished under a wash of bright sunshine.

Peter Guppy sat on the stoop of the vicarage, took careful aim with his slingshot, and launched a stone. He watched as the missile hurtled over the wall and into the graveyard. Then the sound of hoofbeats must have caught his attention. Springing up, he dropped the slingshot and came running on bare feet.

He secured the reins to a post. "Morning, sir. Did thee just come from London? Mrs. Cathy said thee were away for a month in the city." He patted the horse's neck. "Someday I'm going to ride a handsome mount and live in London, too."

"How exciting. Now where is she?"

"Mrs. Cathy's helping Mum with the baking." The tow-headed boy heaved a sigh. "If I lived in London, I'd go off every day to see the sights. There's the torture room at the Tower and the changing of the guard at St. James Park . . ."

The scene wavered and faded. Burke stood blinking at the shelves in the vicarage library. The vision shook him to the core. He was sweating as if he'd run a long distance. Had he had truly seen Peter Guppy? He had no knowledge of the event, and yet the boy's freckled face was as clear as a memory.

He groped for a logical explanation. The lad did look rather like Colin.

Burke gritted his teeth against the rise of pain. His elder brother had died when he was just about Peter's age. They had had the same tawny blond hair, the same talkative manner, even the same love for slingshots and mischief.

So. Wishful thinking had conjured the vision. His mind was playing tricks on him.

A hand brushed his arm.

Burke felt his muscles jerk. Then he realized that Catherine hovered near him, a dark-haired nymph in the simple gown of a servant.

"You're scowling, my lord. If you've more important things to do than rescue a boy, pray don't let us keep you."

He relaxed himself. "I said I'd help you. And I will."

Her gaze traveled up and down his form as if doubting his worth. "Well, then. Since you've a horse, you can ride over to Swaledale and check the lead mines. Peter might have gone there to watch the men at work."

"No."

"No?"

Obeying his hunch was surely a sign of mental derangement. Yet Burke found himself saying, "I'll wager a hundred pounds our quarry has flown farther afield."

"How like you," she said scathingly, "to reduce a boy's safety to a wager."

Burke knew he deserved her censure. He could be proposing a wild-goose chase. But if he was right, maybe the chill of mistrust would melt from Catherine's eyes. Maybe for once she would look on him with warmth and respect.

"I believe," he said slowly, "that Peter's gone to London."

Catherine rode the dappled gray mare at a bone-jarring gait. The sunlit countryside might have been invisible, for she had to concentrate on keeping her seat. Determined to maintain pace with Burke, she gritted her teeth and gripped the leather ribbons like a novice.

Which indeed, she was.

Riding was a lady's pastime, and Catherine had taken lessons at Alfred's command. But she had never felt at ease perched high on the back of a monstrous beast. Only her concern for Peter could induce her to mount the borrowed animal.

At first she'd scoffed at Burke. Surely Peter wouldn't attempt so long a journey all by himself. But Burke's certainty about the workings of a boy's mind had swayed her, so she had insisted upon accompanying him.

At a posting inn along the great London road, they'd found a ray of hope. The stable master reported chasing away a boy fitting Peter's description that very morning. Catherine was almost certain the rucksack he'd left behind belonged to Peter.

Since then, they had stopped and inquired of every coach, every farmer's cart, every post chaise-and-four they passed. But Peter seemed to have vanished into the vast unknown.

Now, as the sun blazed past its zenith, they had only a few hours left to locate him. Heaven only knew what horror could befall a boy traveling alone after dark. Her stomach lurched at the possibilities.

To distract herself, she ventured a look ahead. Burke cut a dashing figure, sitting soldier-straight on the black gelding. His brown coat and buckskin breeches fit him to loving perfection. His coal-hued hair blowing in the breeze, he might have been out on a pleasure jaunt.

He rode with the effortless arrogance of an aristocrat. It was one more reason why he was the wrong man for her.

Yet always at the edge of her memory lingered the warmth of his embrace, the tenderness of his kiss. Catherine drew a shaky breath. She had to stop thinking about him that way. As if he could offer steadfast devotion and enduring love. Burke Grisham only cared where his next amusement lay.

Or did he?

Not for the first time, she wondered why he had elected to stay so long in Yorkshire. For more than a week he had been their guest, vanishing all day and only returning in time to dine with the family. He claimed not to frequent the Fox and Hound. But she couldn't believe he went out each day to see the sights like a tourist.

He must be visiting a woman.

Yet he showed no sign of sexual repletion. In fact, the opposite was true. More often than not, he seemed coiled as tightly as a spring. Could he have changed from the unprincipled rogue who had given a whore as a wedding gift?

I'll have my dance. The two of us. Alone. In your bedchamber.

He wanted to seduce her.

The knowledge curled warmly in her belly. Was that why he had offered to find Peter? To win her gratitude and thereby crumble the wall of her resistance?

If she wasn't careful, she would find herself in bed with him.

Clenching the reins tighter, she told herself that an affair between them could never be. She couldn't bare her body to him without also baring her soul. That was something she would never again give a man, the power to see into her private self.

The power to break her heart.

"We'll stop there."

She jumped at the growl of Burke's voice. He had drawn level with her and pointed at a posting inn that loomed ahead.

"Could Peter really have come this far?" she asked.

"If someone gave him a ride."

Alarmed, she urged her mount to a swift trot after Burke. All manner of folk traveled this great road, and she wasn't so gullible as to think every one of them were upstanding citizens.

Her apprehension grew when they reached the inn yard. The place was ill-kept, a crumbling stone structure with dirty windows and the heavy scent of manure emanating from the stables. There was a public house attached to the inn, and a burst of harsh male laughter rang from inside. A young groom ran forward to hold their horses.

"Well, I'll be," Burke muttered.

Catherine followed his gaze to the other side of the stables. She saw only a fancy phaeton with yellow wheels.

"What's wrong?" she asked.

"Wait here. I'll inquire within."

"No." With an utter lack of grace, she slid off the mare, half-stumbled, and caught herself. "I'm going with you."

He steadied her, his fingers firm and warm on her arm. "Catherine, be sensible. This is no place for a lady."

His protectiveness both pleased and irked her. "If Peter is here, I want to assure myself of his safety immediately. I insist upon it."

With a shrug, he let her go. "Suit yourself. But don't interfere."

Turning, he entered the inn and she trailed him inside. A musty odor combined with smoke assaulted her senses. Through a door off the anteroom, she could see into the public house, where men sat playing cards and drinking in a dim haze of tobacco smoke.

The lanky proprietor sprang up from where he had been slouching in a chair at the desk. He glanced over Burke's elegant garb and smiled, showing several blackened teeth. "Ah, yer grace. A room for you and yer fair lady?"

"No," Burke said. "We're looking for a boy about ten, fair of hair, who might have come here today. His name is Peter Guppy."

"Well. Kermit Wooster ain't one to be spying on customers."

Catherine had reached the end of her patience. She marched forward. "Upon my word," she snapped. "If you refuse to answer a simple question, we shall be forced to summon a magistrate—"

Burke clapped his hand over her mouth and yanked her against him. Over her head, he said, "Forgive my wife. She has an unfortunate habit of meddling in a man's business."

Catherine squirmed against his strong body, wanting to deny any relation to him although they had agreed to pose as a married couple to protect her reputation. She could taste the leather of his glove. No matter how she wriggled, he kept her locked in the vise of his arms.

Wooster looked on with approval. "Aye, a man couldn't run a fine establishment if he gossiped to every passerby."

"I admire your discretion. But perhaps you require a gesture of my sincerity." Burke drew forth a gold coin and tossed it onto the table.

Wooster's pale eyes bugged out. Snatching up the guinea, he took it to the window and examined it in the watery sunlight. "You've a generous heart, yer grace. Lemme think now. Short lad, you say? With freckles and tow hair?"

Catherine wrested her mouth free. "That's him. It's Peter. Is he here?"

Ignoring her, Wooster looked at Burke. "Might he've traveled with a young blade and his tart? A gent by the name of Jervis?"

"Quite possibly."

Wooster jerked his thumb toward the passageway behind him. "Second door on the right. Don't say as how you know."

"It'll be our little secret," Burke promised grimly.

He marched Catherine past the common room with

its boisterous gathering of men. The corridor was gloomy and narrow, the paint peeling from the woodwork. She wrenched herself away and rounded on him. "Don't you ever treat me so shabbily again."

"Let's skip the maidenly sensibilities," he said in a hushed voice. "I have to think of how to get Peter back."

"*You?* I cared for him since birth, I'll have you know. He's like my own child."

"Is that so?"

Burke's sharpened gaze made Catherine realize what she had revealed. She held her chin high. So what if he were repelled by her servant's background? His opinion didn't matter to her.

"You were right to think I recognized that phaeton outside," Burke said. "Peter's fallen into the hands of Sir Jervis Pendleton. He's a Corinthian of the worst ilk."

"Like yourself?"

He sent her a black look. "Exactly. I understand Pendleton's twisted mind. Now keep quiet and I'll tell you my plan."

Chapter 9

Peter sat opposite Stella at a small table in their lodging. He squirmed gleefully on his chair. For the past two hours, he had been winning. The pile of coins in front of him had grown into a mound.

Unlike the gaming dens of London, they didn't have a faro box, the little machine with a spring inside that pops up the next card. So Jervis was acting as the dealer, passing cards from the bottom of the deck. Stella and Peter would wager on the order in which certain cards appeared.

In between turns, Jervis idly polished his dueling pistol, using his handkerchief to shine the long barrel. Peter vowed to buy such a fine weapon when he set himself up as a gentleman.

If his papa didn't haul him back home first.

Home, where Mum would smooth back his hair and kiss him, home where he and his brothers would have sword battles with sticks, home where Mrs. Cathy would sometimes stop by and bring sweets.

Burying the wistful thoughts, he pushed a coin into the center of the scarred table. "I stake a guinea on spades."

"Greedy blade," Stella grumbled. "I'm down to my last few shillings. I'll gamble everything on hearts."

"Ready?" Jervis asked.

Stella lifted her hand in a languid wave. Peter leaned forward, propping his elbows on the table.

Jervis gave the pistol one last loving swipe with the cloth. With a flourish, he slapped down a card and lifted his hand.

The queen of spades.

Peter let out a whoop. He raked the coins onto his pile. His winnings more than made up for that silly timepiece he had lost yesterday. "I'm rich! I'm rich!"

"And I'm clean out of blunt." Stella bared her small white teeth in a smile. "At last it's time for our little nap, dear Peter. Remember?"

His happy mood vanished like a popped bubble. When they had arrived here, Stella had wanted the three of them to lie down together on the poster bed. They needed a rest, she said, from the tiresome carriage ride. Yawning broadly, Jervis agreed.

Peter protested that he hadn't taken a nap since he was a baby. Besides, he wanted to learn to play faro like all the dashing blades of London. She and Jervis could sleep, Peter said, while *he* went to the public room and found a partner.

Stella had looked exceedingly grumpy. She and Jervis went into the corner and had a whispered talk. When they returned, Stella was smiling again and Jervis suggested they play a few rounds on the condition that Peter promise to rest afterwards.

Now Peter regretted his bargain. Cramming coins into his trouser pockets, he muttered, "I'm not tired."

Stella placed her hand on his knee. "Darling, a gentleman never goes back on his word."

Several coins plinked back onto the table. He didn't like her touching him. It was different from when his mother or Mrs. Cathy gave him a hug. That only embarrassed him. *This* made him feel peculiar, all hot and dirty somehow.

He edged away and caught a rolling penny. "I'm hungry."

"Supper won't be served for another hour or two at least," Stella said, rising. "In the meantime—"

"I'm thirsty, too. I'm going to ask the innkeeper for another ginger beer." Peter started toward the door.

Stella moved swiftly to block him. Her blue eyes narrowed to slits. "Now see here, brat—"

"Sheathe your claws, puss," Jervis said. "The lad can have a sip or two of my ale. Might even mellow him a bit."

He and Stella shared a secretive look. Her mouth relaxed into a smile again as he filled a tankard from the tray on the bedside table. "Drink hearty," Jervis said.

Peter peered into the dark depths. The brew smelled like a wet sheep. "Papa will flog me again for drinking spirits."

"Papa shall never know," Jervis said, giving Peter a clap on the back. "If you mean to be a gentleman, you must learn to drink like a true Corinthian."

Gamely Peter uptilted the mug and took a swallow. Its bitter taste gagged him. By reflex, he spat out the liquid.

"Argghh!" Jervis scowled at the droplets staining his yellow waistcoat and blue pantaloons. "Frigging bastard! Look what you've done. My tailor charged me a pretty penny for this suit."

His anger alarmed Peter. Mum and Papa never called him bad names. "I-I'm sorry."

"Now, lambkin," Stella said, stroking Jervis's lapel. "Your clothes will dry. You were going to remove them anyway while we have our little nap, remember? Perhaps we should disrobe now."

"Ah, yes," Jervis said, his expression clearing. "Go on, boy. Off with the trousers."

Peter stood paralyzed. Undress? In front of Stella? How queer these Londoners were to sleep in the afternoon.

Then the truth slapped him. They were up to no good. Well, he was no bumpkin. He could guess exactly what they were after.

They must be planning to steal his winnings while he slept!

Jervis had stripped down to his drawers and shirt. Stella was pouring him another tankard of ale.

In a panic, Peter eyed the door. He could run faster than these city-folk.

But suppose they told the innkeeper he had stolen the money? He might get tossed into gaol forever. Sickness gripped his stomach. He wished he had never accepted a ride from strangers.

Then he squared his shoulders. Two thieves wouldn't get the best of Lieutenant Peter Allen Guppy. He had a plan of his own.

"*That's* your brilliant plan?" Catherine whispered. "To knock on the door and pretend you're the landlord?"

She glowered at Burke, who glowered back. They stood face to face in the murky corridor of the inn. She drew in a breath, catching the stale odors of rubbish and ale.

And the irresistible essence of man. In spite of her anxiety, she felt warmth trickle into her belly. Though more than a week had passed since that tumultuous kiss at the cottage, the memory washed through her with astonishing clarity. She wanted to lift up on tiptoe and press the length of her body to his again. She wanted to immerse herself in the heady sensation of being needed by a man. She wanted—

Catherine halted her runaway thoughts. She wanted to get Peter home safely, that was all.

"Sometimes the simplest plans are the best ones,"

Burke said in a low voice. "Unless you can offer a better idea, we'll go with mine."

"We should call in the law. If Sir Jervis Pendleton is half the blackguard you say he is, then the situation should be handled by the proper authorities."

"Jervis always manages to slide out of the stickiest of predicaments." Burke's expression hardened. "Few people know he also leads a secret life—he has a taste for young boys."

Catherine stared at him. Then realization rolled through her on a wave of horror. "You can't mean . . . surely he wouldn't . . . not to *Peter.*"

"He won't, if I have any say in the matter." Burke stroked her cheek in an unexpected caress. "Stay back now. Promise?"

Shaken, she could only nod.

He walked lightly down the passageway and listened at the door. Tall and athletically built, he looked ready for action in form-fitting buckskins and a superfine coat that stretched across his shoulders. A lock of hair dipped like a black crescent moon onto his brow, giving him the aspect of a pirate.

Catherine hastened to his side. "Do you hear Peter?" she whispered.

Putting his finger to his lips, Burke shook his head. The firmness of purpose glittered in his gaze. A sense of connection leaped between them, and the impression shook the core of her belief in their incompatibility. He could have squandered the day in his usual aimless fashion; instead he had volunteered to rescue a runaway boy. The knowledge glowed in her heart like the embers of a fire.

She squeezed in beside Burke and pressed her ear to the wooden panel. The muted rise and fall of voices reverberated from within. But the din from the tap room masked the words.

He rapped on the door. No one answered. A scrabbling noise drifted down the passageway, and Catherine shuddered as the small dark shape of a rat scuttled into a hole in the baseboard only a foot away.

Burke knocked again, harder. " 'Tis Wooster," he called out. "I've a parcel for you. Could be valuable. Open up."

Against the noise from the taproom, a muffled shot rang out. A female screech followed it.

"Dear God," Catherine breathed. "Peter!"

"Stay out here."

On that terse command, Burke thrust open the door and barged inside. Catherine hesitated only a moment; then anxiety for Peter overrode any concern for her own safety.

She entered a cramped room. In a fleeting glance, she saw a poster bed with faded crimson hangings. Clothing strewed the bed. Near the hearth, playing cards were scattered over a round table. An overturned tankard lay on the floor.

Then she saw Peter.

The smoking, long-barreled pistol shook in his hand. In front of him, a man wearing only knee-length underdrawers held a woman clad in her underclothes. A dark liquid soaked the front of her frilly shift and dripped onto the floor.

"Jesus God, he shot me!" she shrieked. "I'm dying."

The man pushed her away. "Damn it, you'll bleed on me."

Catherine stared. Her heart was thundering and the breath seared her lungs. She blinked to assure herself she wasn't imagining that woman.

It was Miss Stella Sexton. The whore Burke had given to Alfred.

"M'lord!" she wailed, staggering toward him with her arms outstretched. "You've come to rescue me."

Burke snatched a towel from the washstand and bent

to examine her shift more closely. "This isn't blood. It's ale. And a sour brew at that."

"Impossible." Her nostrils flared. "Well, perhaps I did drop my tankard. But it's all the fault of that pint-sized brute."

Peter crept forward, his eyes shiny with tears. "I didn't mean to shoot. Truly. I only wanted to scare thee—"

"Bedlamite!" Stella screeched. "Don't come near me, you horrid little beast! You'll shoot at me again!"

"For pity's sake, can't you see the child is terrified?" Burke gave her a shake. "And he can't fire again. The pistol only holds one shot."

Peter hunched his shoulders, his mouth quivering. Catherine slipped her arm around him. He turned his freckled face up to her. " 'Twas an accident, Mrs. Cathy. I'm most awful sorry."

"I know you are," she murmured. "Give me the gun."

Sniffling, he surrendered the weapon. The weight of it startled Catherine. She gingerly lowered the pistol to her side.

Stella put her hand to her brow. "Oh, I do believe I shall swoon."

"Then you'd best sit down," Burke said.

He guided her to the bed. There, she clutched at him and moaned artfully, her breasts like round melons half-spilling from the shift. A furious sickness roiled in Catherine's stomach. Was Burke remembering how he had kissed Stella in front of a crowd of cheering men?

"You're so heroic, m'lord," Stella said breathlessly. "What miracle of fate brought you back to me?"

"I came to find Peter," Burke said in a hard tone, "not you."

"That little wretch?" Her lower lip jutted in a pout. "To think of turning on me, after all I did for him."

"And what precisely *did* you do?"

"We gave the brat a ride, that's what. And I let him

win all my blunt. This is the thanks I get for my kindness."

"I see." Burke's keen gaze flicked to the bare-chested man. "And you, Jervis? You hardly looked dressed for doing good deeds."

Jervis reached for his shirt from the back of a chair. "I was merely changing my clothes. Not that it's any concern of yours."

"It concerns me when I find you sniffing after an innocent lad."

Jervis laughed. "Wanting him for yourself, eh, Thornwald? And all these years I thought you only went after the fancy pieces. Had I known of your other predilections, I could have procured any number of boys for you—"

Burke smashed his fist into Jervis's mouth. The blond man reeled backward and crashed into the chairs and table. With a thump, he landed in a heap on the floor amid a snowstorm of playing cards. Blood trickled from his lips.

Catherine blinked. It had happened so fast. A fierce satisfaction surged in her to see that foul-tongued beast laid low. Peter let out a hiss of awe.

Jervis sat up and moaned. Nursing his jaw, he spat out a small white object onto the floor. Then he stuck the tip of his tongue into the gap that his front tooth had lately occupied. "Damn you, Thornwald, you've thpoiled my mouth—"

"No, damn *you.*" Catherine advanced on Jervis. "You deserved that and more for your obscene insinuations."

"Who th' devil athked you—?"

"Certainly not the devil; you seem to be in league with him yourself." She handed the pistol to Burke, who watched her with one dark eyebrow cocked. "I'll see about summoning a magistrate. A charge of kidnapping is in order here."

Jervis got awkwardly to his feet, his shirttails flopping

around his drawers. "Go on, report uth. I'll be forthed to tell how the boy gulled uth out of our money, thtole my pithtol, and shot at a defenthleth lady."

"A gentleman wouldn't set himself up to be a laughingstock," Catherine retorted.

"Nevertheless, we shan't press charges," Burke said, tucking the pistol into his waistband. "We'll be on our way now."

"You'd let them go free?" She cast an incredulous stare at him. "What is this, honor among thieves?"

"Yes," he said, "we dissolutes stick together."

She knew she was being unfair to him, for the testimony of Sir Jervis would stand up in court over that of a common runaway. Yet she was too angry to retract her words.

Stella leaped up and rubbed herself against Burke. "Perhaps, m'lord, you'll allow me to repay you for your help."

A shuddering wave of fury broke in Catherine. She snatched a ha'penny from the floor and flung it at Stella. The woman uttered a squeal of surprise as the coin vanished into her shadowy cleavage.

"There," Catherine said, "that's all you're worth."

Burke took hold of her arm. His eyes gleamed though his mouth remained unsmiling. "I believe we've overstayed our welcome."

As they moved toward the door, Peter trotted along at their heels like a duck behind its mother.

"I thay!" Jervis called after them. "My dueling pithtol—"

"Will make a fine addition to my collection," Burke said. He shut the door, cutting off one last lisping curse from Jervis.

In the stableyard, Peter hung his head and scuffed the dirt with the toe of his boot. The late afternoon sunlight lit the vulnerable curve of his neck.

Catherine worried that something else had happened

inside the lodging, that Stella and Jervis *had* misused the boy and he was too ashamed to admit it. She hugged him tightly. "Are you quite certain you're all right? They didn't . . . press you to do anything you didn't want to do?"

Confusion clouded his blue eyes. "They wanted me to take a nap. But I never did."

Burke sank to his heels before the boy. "There are some adults who like to hurt children. Don't ever let anyone touch you in places where you don't want to be touched."

"Oh." Peter frowned as he digested the advice. "Mrs. Cathy?"

"Yes?"

"I daren't go home," he said, his shoulders drooping even lower. "Papa will lock me in my room for the rest of my life."

As Catherine breathed in his boyish scent, wistfulness swelled within her. Since she couldn't have children of her own, she looked forward to opening her school. "Thee mustn't worry, Peter," she said, reverting to the speech of her youth. "Thy parents love thee dearly. Remember the parable about the prodigal son? The father prepared a feast to welcome home his long lost son."

Peter's brow remained furrowed. "But I've been so wicked."

"A true gentleman faces up to his mistakes," Burke said, rising to his feet and clapping the boy on the back.

They shared a secret, man-to-man look. "All right," Peter said. "I'll go home."

As Burke helped Catherine mount her horse, she couldn't stop herself from murmuring, "How pleasant that you had the chance to renew your acquaintance with Miss Stella Sexton."

A faint ruddiness entered his cheeks. He cocked a wary glance up at her. "How did you know it was her?"

Catherine could have bitten her tongue. Too late, she

realized that Stella had never introduced herself. But perhaps it was time he knew at least part of the truth.

"I was there that night," Catherine said, bending down and whispering so that Peter couldn't overhear. "I came to London to tell Alfred . . . well, to pay my husband a surprise visit. But instead of finding him enjoying a quiet evening, I witnessed that sordid scene from the back of the room. Needless to say, I departed quickly."

A muscle worked in his jaw. "Alfred never told me."

"I asked him not to. It was hardly a situation in which any respectable lady would wish to be seen."

Burke placed his hand over hers on the reins. "I'm sorry, Catherine. It was a mistake. I never meant to hurt you."

A mistake. A tragedy that had left her barren. She could never reveal her secret sorrow to the likes of him.

Yet the gentle warmth of his touch swayed her. She struggled to retrieve her righteous rage. "Perhaps you'd care to go back inside now. Miss Sexton, you, and Sir Jervis could make a jolly threesome."

His mouth tightened. Then the familiar smoky glow smoldered in his eyes. "I've come to prefer twosomes. One on one."

Heat surged from deep inside her. She tugged the reins so tightly the horse danced sideways. "Oh, just take me home."

"As you wish." He strode away and gave Peter a hand up.

Catherine squinted at the lowering sun and forced her mind away from her infuriating attraction to him. The ball. She must remember her duties. The guests would begin to arrive at eight o'clock for the glittering event that would launch Prudence and Priscilla into local society. More importantly, it sounded the bugle-blast in their hunt for husbands. Lorena would never forgive her if Burke didn't lead Priscilla in the first dance.

Catherine set her chin. Let the woman scold. If it

hadn't been for Burke's quick thinking, they might not have found Peter in time. She shivered to imagine the lad stripped of his innocence in so foul a manner.

On the black gelding, Peter rode in front of Burke. The boy turned hero-worshipping eyes up at his rescuer. "I never met anybody what could knock another gent flat with one punch."

Burke laughed, flexing his gloved fingers around the reins. "I don't advise you to try it yourself. My hand hurts like the very devil."

"Could thee teach me to fight like that? Please?"

"It isn't something one learns overnight. I've practiced for many an hour in Gentleman Jackson's ring."

"Someday, I'm going to be a gentleman, too. I'm going to fight in duels. I'm going to win my fortune at the gaming tables—"

"Whoa, scamp. I've won from time to time, but I've also lost a bloody fortune. Gambling is like having a big bowl of sweets. If you eat too much, you'll end up with a stomachache." Burke winked at Catherine. "Besides, if you don't watch out, Mrs. Cathy will toss your deck of cards into the nearest fireplace."

Her fingers froze around the reins. She had done that once. When Alfred had gone deeply into debt from gambling, in a fit of fury she had burned his playing cards.

But how could Burke know that? Unless Alfred had told him.

She felt sick at the notion of their private quarrels laid bare to a man she hadn't even met at the time. No, it was more than that. She was hurt by the idea that Alfred might have confided his pain and frustration to a crony when he had refused to share his innermost thoughts with his wife.

Slowly she relaxed her grip. She might be overreacting to a chance remark. Not even to his mother had Alfred revealed every intimate detail of his married life.

Peter leaned trustingly against Burke and peppered him with questions about the *ton.* Catherine was struck by the way Burke pointed out the pitfalls in a life of dissolution. Odd, she had thought him a predator, intent only on satisfying his craving for amusement. Now she looked beneath the rakish facade and saw a man who showed kindness to an impressionable boy. Was he still the notorious nighthawk she had seen four years ago?

Or had he changed?

She suddenly realized how precious little she knew about Burke Grisham. He was heir to the marquis of Westhaven, and he owned an estate in Cornwall. But beyond the single glimpse she'd had of him in London, his life was a mystery to her.

As she watched him converse with Peter, she wondered if Burke wished for a son of his own. Of course he did, she reflected with bittersweet sadness. All men wanted an heir. And a fertile woman who could fulfill their fatherly ambitions.

The keen ache of loneliness assailed her. Yet as she gazed at Burke, something began to glow inside her, a warmth that slowly spread throughout her heart. It was surely just a grudging friendship, she told herself.

She was too sensible a woman to love a rogue.

Chapter 10

Where the devil was she?

Burke stood in an alcove and scanned the ballroom with its tall gilt columns, the high frescoed ceiling, the crystal chandeliers ablaze with tapers. By descending a little-used staircase in the west wing and entering through a back door near the orchestra, he had slipped unseen into the crowded chamber. The musicians were sawing away at a country tune, and Prudence and Priscilla were among the dancers, though Burke couldn't tell one giggling twin from the other.

Nor did he care to.

The air hung hot and stuffy from the press of people. Fêtes like this one had always bored him. He preferred to tempt his luck in gaming dens, to dine with cronies at his club, to amuse himself in the scented embrace of his latest *chére amiè.*

Or so he had done before a French bullet had shattered his life forever and thrust him into a tunnel of light so pure, so radiant with love that even now his throat tightened from the anguish of loss.

He locked the memory in the deepest corner of his mind. Tonight he wouldn't dwell upon that baffling delirium, the spark of his madness. All that mattered was his determination to find a certain woman.

Where the devil *was* Catherine?

The ballroom stretched out before him like a living tapestry, the ladies wearing gowns of rainbow hues, the men suited in formal black with white cravats. Seeking a better vantage point, Burke strolled along the perimeter of the room. He passed a group of women, who eyed him and murmured behind their fans. Several debutantes gawked in open admiration. Inured to gossip and speculation, he ignored them all.

Then one lady detached herself from the clique and slowly wound her way through the crush toward the main doorway, where Lorena stood welcoming the late guests.

The word would soon be out, he thought cynically. In a matter of moments, Madame Bonaparte would descend and take him prisoner. It was the price he had to pay to remain a guest in this house.

To stay close to Catherine Snow. To learn her secrets. To feed his obsession.

Where was she?

Pausing beside a curtained alcove, where a Grecian urn rested on a pedestal, he searched the assemblage again, but to no avail. When he had parted from her in the stables, after delivering Peter home safely, Burke had wrested another promise from her to dance with him. The beauty of her wary smile lingered in his memory.

She was softening toward him; he knew it.

He had dressed with undue haste, barking orders at Trotter and driving the poor valet to distraction over the tying of Burke's neckcloth. He felt as breathless and damp-palmed as a juvenile who agonized over an encounter with his first girl.

It was dishonorable to covet the widow of his best friend, the man whose death weighed heavily on Burke's conscience. Alfred had entrusted him to look after her. Not to break her heart.

By seeking Catherine out, he played a dangerous game. The stakes were too steep even for him, the risks were too great of causing her more pain. Nothing must ever come of his infatuation. Nothing.

Yet he couldn't resist prolonging the dalliance. Just for a little while longer. Just long enough to see if she truly cared for him. He'd sell his black soul for another of her smiles.

The curtain behind him moved slightly, and he turned. Through a gap in the crimson folds glinted one pale eye.

Startled, Burke drew back the drapery.

Alfred's cousin Fabian lurked in the narrow space. Uttering a squawk of dismay, he shrank deeper into the alcove. At his feet sat his dog, Lady, wagging her golden tail.

"Come out and join the party," Burke said.

Fabian shook his head, and his fair hair brushed the shoulders of his ill-fitting suit. "Can't," he whispered. "Aunt Lorena m-might see me."

"So you're avoiding her, too."

"She wants to announce my b-b-betrothal to M-Miss Prudence tonight. I d-don't want to marry her."

Burke felt a kinship with him. Both of them were targets for the arrows of Lorena's ambitions. Though master of the manor, Fabian Snow was reduced to skulking behind curtains.

On a hunch, Burke asked, "Have you another woman in mind for your wife?"

A flush reddened Fabian's cheeks; then he ducked his chin and nodded. "B-but she's too beautiful for me."

By God, he must be referring to the chit he had been kissing in the wine cellar. Burke had met the pretty servant once when she'd brought his wash-water; she seemed cheerful and sincere, though unduly flirtatious.

Still, with a bit of polish, she might be just the woman to draw Fabian out of his shell.

"Have you asked this girl to marry you?"

His expression hidden by a hank of untidy hair, Fabian bent to pet the spaniel. "I-I couldn't. I must win her heart first."

A queer longing gripped Burke's chest. How charmingly naïve to think a heart could be wooed and won, that love could bring peace instead of turmoil. "If you don't mind a bit of advice," he said, "I wouldn't wait too long. You might lose her to another suitor."

Fabian threw back his head and glared. Whiteness outlined his tensed mouth. Even as Burke wondered at the look, Fabian shifted his gaze to the ballroom. As abruptly as it had appeared, his glower vanished.

"Aunt Lorena!" He snatched the red curtain shut, setting the gold tassels to quaking.

Burke turned to greet his hostess who bore down on him like a general riding into battle. She wore a grape satin gown that hugged her great bosom and accented her broad shoulders. A cluster of purple feathers wagged in her coiffure. Behind her trotted a horse-faced woman with protruding teeth.

"My lord," Lorena said, extending her gloved hands. "Here you are at last. Did I see you speaking to someone a moment ago?" She frowned at the draperies behind the urn.

"Only to myself. You know what an eccentric I am." Taking her by the arm, he guided her a short distance from Fabian's hiding place.

She tapped his wrist with her folded fan and smiled. "Oh, la. You're a devil to tease me after vanishing all day. Catherine tells me she dragged you off on some cockle-brained chase."

Curse his stupidity. He should have realized that Lorena would take Catherine to task over her disappearance.

"Dragged is hardly the word," Burke said in her defense. "I offered Catherine my aid in finding a runaway boy. I felt sure that a woman as generous as yourself would encourage such an errand of mercy."

"Hmph. Well, I was forced to allow Lieutenant Galbraith the honor of opening the first set with my dear Priscilla. She was terribly disappointed to miss you."

"I shall endeavor to make it up to her," he said by rote.

"You and she will make a perfect match." On that bald statement, Lorena beckoned to the woman standing behind her. "Your lordship, may I introduce my dear neighbor, Lady Beaufort. My lady, our esteemed houseguest, Burke Grisham, the earl of Thornwald."

"Westhaven's heir." Her ladyship lifted her quizzing glass to look him up and down like a piece of horseflesh. "Why, you're the very image of Roderick Grisham. Handsome as sin, he was, and a hero in one of those tribal wars overseas. The ladies that Season were all agog over him." She sighed noisily. "Ah, can it have been thirty-five years ago already?"

Burke's lungs constricted. He held himself at rigid attention, every muscle under control. Politely he said, "I wouldn't know, my lady."

She loosed a neighing laugh. "Drat it, the young don't care to be bored with the reminiscing of an old moonling. The next time you see your father, lad, do give him my regards."

"As you wish." He hadn't seen the wretch in ten years, not since Burke had reached his majority and had come into an inheritance from his grandmother. To his father, Burke would never be more than a failure and a bitter disappointment, a stinking coward. It was galling how that memory still stung.

As Lady Beaufort chattered on, Burke's attention sharpened on the man strolling toward them. It was the chap he'd met at the Fox and Hound, and he was chatting up one of the twins. What was his name?

Newberry. Ezekiel Newberry. The man who professed to admire Lorena from afar.

Oddly, she stared glassy-eyed as if Newberry were a ghost. Her cheeks turned pasty white. Her generous bulk quivered like someone who had taken a chill. Her lips moved, but no words issued forth.

Burke frowned. Did Lorena know the man?

Fearing she might swoon, he poised himself close enough to catch her. "Are you quite all right, madam?"

She blinked unfocused eyes at him. Then she snapped open her fan and frantically waved it at her face. " 'Tis the heat," she said in a faint voice. "So many guests."

Lady Beaufort stepped to her side. "Perhaps we should remove to the refreshment room."

"I . . . yes . . . in a moment."

Lorena's gaze remained fixed on Newberry and her daughter. The elegant middle-aged gentleman wore a superbly-cut suit from one of London's best tailors. His ivory-topped cane was an affectation, for he walked as straight as any man. A charming smile showed a gleam of white teeth against the teak-dark tan of his face.

"Good evening, m'lord," Newberry said, nodding to Burke. "If I may intrude, I should like to pay my respects to the hostess. Ezekiel Newberry, at your service." Stepping forward, he placed a reverent kiss on her kid glove.

She snatched her hand back. "Have you an invitation, sir?"

Newberry's smile faded. "I never dreamt the presence of a lowly gentleman like myself would cause anyone distress. If I've inconvenienced you, I'll take my leave at once."

The twin set her crystal cup on a nearby table. "Oh, Mummy, don't send him away. Mr. Newberry was kind enough to fetch me a syllabub." She giggled. "I promised him a dance in return."

"My dear Prudence," Lorena said in a frigid tone, "you have not been properly introduced."

So that explained her peculiar reaction. She believed Newberry harbored romantic intentions toward her daughter.

Burke smiled to himself. Lorena would find out soon enough that Newberry's true interest lay with *her.* A lusty tumble might unpinch those lips and distract her from badgering Catherine.

"Forgive me," Burke said. "This situation is my doing. I forgot to mention that I'd invited Mr. Newberry. Allow me to present him."

After Burke made the introductions, Newberry bowed to Lady Beaufort. "My lady, I heard a tale hereabouts that you recently suffered an inconvenience."

"Inconvenience, bah," her ladyship said. "You needn't mince words—I was most foully robbed. The thief had the effrontery to leave a single copper farthing in my strongbox. As if he were playing a joke!"

Newberry tut-tutted. "Was the villain ever caught?"

"Never. The magistrate believes the scoundrel ran off to London to fence my jewels. Oh, to think of my mother's pearls in the filthy hands of some Whitechapel felon. It is too much to bear. Too much!"

As they discussed calling in the Bow Street Runners, Burke noticed the kitten slinking along the baseboard. Tigress jumped onto the table, stuck her nose inside Prudence's cup, and began to lap the remains of the creamy syllabub.

Good God. If Lorena saw the creature loose in the ballroom, Catherine would face more trouble.

He moved toward Tigress, but Prudence glided into his path. Flowery perfume wafted from her. A profusion of orange blossoms decorated her white gown, and a diamond necklace glinted at her throat. She looked rather like a fancy cake that would give a man indigestion.

"My dear Lord Thornwald," she said in her breathy little-girl voice. "I've been searching high and low for you."

"Then you've disappointed the other men present." He edged around her. "I'm sure they are all waiting to dance with the princess of the ball."

"They are naught but want-witted boys." She batted her golden lashes. "Now, you, on the other hand, know how to treat a lady—"

"Don't listen to her flummery." Priscilla swooped out of the crowd and took up a post beside Burke. She was an amazing copy of her sister except for the pearl necklace and tiara. "My lord, how wonderful that you are finally here. I was beginning to think you'd gotten lost down one of our many passageways."

"You're such a widgeon," Prudence said crossly. "I'm sure his lordship has an uncanny sense of direction."

"Yes, he's managed to avoid you all week." Priscilla wrinkled her nose at her sister, then aimed a brilliant smile at Burke. "Never mind Miss Cabbage-Head. Perhaps, m'lord, you might be so kind as to fetch a lemonade for me."

"My pleasure."

He seized the chance to walk away. Just as he surreptitiously reached down for the kitten, Prudence came up from behind and slid her arm through his. "I'll go with—"

A sudden furious barking drowned her out. The crimson draperies shuddered as a golden missile hurled forth. People fell back, out of the way of the projectile. Several women shrieked.

Lady bounded straight at the kitten. Tigress yowled and arched her back, her tail puffed. The table crashed to the floor as the cat took a flying leap and landed on the lacy sash of Prudence's gown.

"Eeek!" Using her fan, Prudence whacked the lump of tortoiseshell fur. The kitten slid downward, its claws raking trails in the white satin skirt.

Fabian loped out of the alcove and grabbed the dog. It squirmed and yipped in an effort to reach the cat.

Lorena stormed forward, Zeke Newberry at her elbow. "Ugh, a cat!" she said. "And who let that dreadful dog loose in here?"

His shoulders hunched, Fabian stuttered, "I-I'm sorry."

Tears blotched Prudence's cheeks. "Mummy, my dress! That horrid beast has ruined my dress!"

Lady Beaufort slipped her arm around Prudence. Priscilla gawked with her mouth open. The guests crowded closer, buzzing like excited bees.

In the confusion, Burke scooped up the spitting kitten and dropped it into his coat pocket, heedless of the stinging claws. Then, with a sense of deliverance, he strode out of the ballroom.

The tiny bundle squirmed madly. Frantic meows issued forth. Burke held his pocket shut. He remembered all too well the tree incident when the feline had shredded his side.

And Catherine had ministered so tenderly to him.

Where the devil was she?

He scanned the multitudes swarming the ground-floor chambers. Servants offered champagne to the guests in the drawing room. Card players thronged the tables set up in the library. The luscious aroma of roasted meats drifted from the dining parlor. Footmen scurried up and down the passageway, carrying trays of cakes and patés and cheeses.

Then suddenly Burke knew.

Pushing open the green baize door at the end of the corridor, he entered the kitchen. Steam rose from the stove where a portly cook stirred a bubbling pot and called orders over her shoulder. Maidservants rushed back and forth to do her bidding. By the massive fireplace, a boy turned the spit on which several hams sizzled and dripped.

And there, in the midst of the hubbub, in front of a long table littered with bowls and cutlery and food, stood Catherine.

She wore a white apron over a golden gown that shimmered in the lamplight. No jewelry spoiled the swan-like smoothness of her throat. Her upswept hair revealed dainty ears and the elegant curve of her neck. Clasping a wooden spoon in one hand, she squinted down at a book that lay open on the table. Absently, she pushed a wisp of curl off her cheek and left a smear of flour.

Burke scowled. He should have guessed earlier that she would be slaving here while her sisters-in-law frolicked.

A curious tenderness unrolled inside him, a depth of feeling that bore an aching sweetness. He wanted to whisper praise for her beauty and feel her melt in his arms. He wanted to carry her upstairs to his bed and bring pleasure into her dreary life.

But he had barred himself from seducing Catherine Snow. It was the only way he could prove to her—and to himself—that he had any honor left at all.

Needle-sharp teeth nipped his thumb. The kitten had poked its orange-and-black head out of his pocket.

Muttering an oath, Burke stuck the injured finger in his mouth. Catherine looked up and caught him sucking his thumb like an infant.

A smile bloomed on her face. He felt faintly foolish, yet his overriding sensation was one of warmth, the dangerous desire to bask in her good graces. He cringed to think that Catherine had seen him at his worst. Yet, miraculously, the events of the afternoon had eased the antagonism between them. He would rescue a hundred runaway boys if it would cause her to favor him.

As he approached, she smoothed the sides of her hair. Pink tinted her cheeks, and he couldn't tell if she was blushing or merely flushed from the heat of the kitchen. "You oughtn't have come back here," she said.

"Neither should you. We searched everywhere for you."

"We?"

The kitten chose that opportune moment to clamber from Burke's pocket and leap onto Catherine's book, where the animal settled down to wash its face indignantly.

"Tigress and I," he replied. "She's caused quite a ruckus, you should know. This fête will be talked about for years to come." Burke related the story of the upheaval in the ballroom.

An irreverent giggle escaped Catherine. "I was supposed to put her out. I completely forgot." Sobering, she stroked the kitten. "Poor Prudence and Priscilla. To have their first ball spoiled so."

"Better you should call it a miracle from heaven. Now Lorena won't dare announce the betrothal of Prudence and Fabian. She'll have to wait a few months, at least until the talk dies down."

"I hadn't thought of that." Catherine's face brightened. Then she ducked her chin and peered up at him with a charming shyness. "I'm making raspberry tarts. Would it be an imposition if I asked you to read the ingredients to me? I left my spectacles upstairs."

The light of trust shone in her amber eyes. He felt an exultation more uplifting than when Lady Luck smiled on him at the gaming table. Yet he had failed so many people in his life—his brother, his parents, Alfred. Burke hoped to God he wouldn't disappoint Catherine again, too.

"It *would* be an imposition," he said.

Her smile faltered, and she lowered her gaze. "Thank

you for rescuing Tigress, then. I'm sure you're anxious to return to the ball—"

"Bosh. I'm only anxious to claim that dance you promised me."

Her lips parted. Her wide eyes lifted to his again. "Oh. But I can't join the party. Lorena said—"

"The devil take that old biddy. This gathering doesn't need any more tarts than it has already."

He took the spoon from her and tossed it onto the table. Then he untied her white apron and flung it at a startled footman. Servants stared curiously as they bustled about their chores. Slipping his arm around Catherine's slender waist, Burke guided her toward the back door.

"This isn't the way to the ballroom," she said.

"I know."

A twinkle flashed into her eyes as if she had been infected by his recklessness. "So where are you taking me?"

Smiling, he bent to whisper in her ear, "To a place where we can be alone."

Chapter 11

They emerged into the starry night. Against the black velvet sky, a sliver of moon rose above the tangle of trees. Yellow candlelight spilled from the squares of windows and onto the shrubbery.

Burke was keenly aware of Catherine's fingers on his arm. Greedy with the desire to have her all to himself, he guided her away from the house and down a darkened path until they reached a small clearing at the edge of the formal gardens, where the scent of roses perfumed the evening air. The strains of a waltz floated like fairy music through an enchanted forest.

He sketched an elegant bow. "May I have this dance, my lady?"

"I haven't learned the steps to the waltz."

"You have only to follow my lead."

She curtsied. "Then I would be honored."

Catherine came into his arms with a willingness that made his chest clench. He nested her small hand in his and guided her other hand to his shoulder. The dance was daringly new and scandalously intimate, as near an embrace as a couple was allowed in public. He had no doubt Lorena had included it in the program because she'd meant for him to squire her daughter.

He smiled. Thank God he held Catherine instead.

As light and nimble as the breeze, her feet moved in rhythm with his. As dark and mysterious as the night, her scent wrapped around him. Though the evening veiled her face in shadow, the starlight touched her hair with gilt.

As they whirled across the grass, her body trembled . . . or perhaps he felt the quivering of his own muscles, the restraint that kept him from loosing the demon desires locked inside himself. She was not like his other women, free with their bodies, blatant with their lust. The last thing he should be doing was holding her in his arms.

And yet he remembered that kiss at the cottage, when he had glimpsed the passion in her, with the rain pouring down and her soft curves pressing against him, her mouth warm and wanton and welcoming.

A profound yearning coursed through him. If only he had met her at a different time, in a different place, under different circumstances. Before she had seen him at his worst. Before Alfred had stamped his claim on her heart.

Ashamed of himself, Burke shifted his gaze past her shoulder. An arbor of roses loomed in the darkness. The tall archway dripped white petals onto a stone bench.

His temples began to throb. He knew this spot. He had seen it before.

A familiar tingling swept over his skin. Curse it. Not now. Not here. Even as his fingers tensed on Catherine, the blackness of night gave way to the brilliance of sunshine . . .

Framed by an archway of fragrant white roses, Catherine sat slumped on the bench. Raising her head slowly, she crossed her arms over her bosom. Her face was ravaged by weeping. Tears matted her lashes and dampened her cheeks.

"I wasn't trying to hide from you," she said in a subdued tone. "I only wanted to be alone for awhile."

"I'm sorry she insulted you," he said. "I'll have a word with her."

Catherine quickly shook her head, and tendrils of hair brushed the milky skin of her face. "Please don't. I can't blame her for wanting grandchildren. She has every right to be disappointed in me. And so do you. . . ."

The light faded into a swirl of darkness. Disoriented, he blinked at the pale oval of Catherine's face through the gloom. They had stopped dancing. His mind registered that fact even as the tentacles of the vision slowly released their grip on him.

"You came here that day," he heard himself say hoarsely. "This is where you come when you've been hurt by someone."

"What day? How did you know I used to come here?"

Wariness edged her voice. She stepped back, out of his arms. He sensed a withdrawal in her, a resurgence of the wall between them. But he couldn't answer her. He had no logical explanation for his uncanny knowledge.

Her sorrow in his vision seemed as real as her presence now, a delicate shape in the evening shadows. She had been distressed over her failure to bear a child. He remembered suddenly that Alfred had mentioned her miscarrying a long time ago. Perhaps there had been other lost pregnancies—or a baby who had died in infancy. Could that explain Alfred's melancholy, his increased drinking during the final year of his life? Burke cursed himself for not knowing. He had been so caught up in subduing his own demons that he had paid little heed to the woes of his friend.

And who had been speaking to Catherine? Alfred himself?

A chill spread through Burke, numbing his hands and his head and his heart. Absurd. No, *madness.*

It was madness to think he could recall events that Alfred had experienced. Somehow, his guilt over Alfred's death had wrought these waking dreams. His mind had invented scenes with living, talking characters. The episodes had no basis in reality.

None. To believe otherwise, he would have to descend the dark shaft into insanity.

"Burke? Why are you staring at me so strangely? Perhaps you should sit down."

Her warm hand grasped his arm, tugging at him. He let himself be led to the bench and lowered to the hard stone seat.

Catherine hovered like an angelic apparition, her gown sparked by gold against the murky night. "Are you ill?" she asked. "Would you rather return to the house?"

By way of reply, he drew her down beside him, needing to absorb her warmth and life, her blessed sanity. He should ask her if she had ever become pregnant. He should find out if Lorena had badgered her about having children. Instead he imagined Catherine's belly beautifully swollen with his own baby.

He released a long breath. *That* was madness. Yet, unthinkingly, he lifted his hand to touch her cheek, following the velvety skin along her hairline and down to her dainty jaw and her soft, soft lips.

A shudder ran through her. "Burke?" Her voice emerged as a husky whisper. "What are you doing?"

"Making sure you're real." Unable to resist, he bent to her and brushed his lips over the whorl of her ear. She smelled fresh and floury, devoid of heavy perfumes. "I fancied for a moment you were an angel."

"An angel?"

For a brief moment, she leaned into him, and her sigh whisked against his cheek. His pulsebeat surged. She wasn't just any woman, but Catherine, who would abandon her duties to track down a runaway boy. Catherine, who could remain loyal to the family that treated her like an unpaid servant. Catherine, who could read a love poem with the same passionate intensity as she could kiss a man in the rain.

She drew back and put her hand over his on the bench. "You're the angel. Thank you again for rescuing Peter. I would never have thought to look for him on the road to London."

Her touch was a friendly gesture, nothing more. He despised himself for feeling so disappointed. "It was a lucky guess."

"Whatever it was, you deserve all the credit," she said, removing her hand. "By the way, just before I left the vicarage, Peter told me you promised to send him to Eton."

"Nothing like school to keep the scamp off the streets and out of trouble."

"He isn't your responsibility, though." After a heartbeat, she added, "I discovered something today. That you do have some goodness beneath all your swagger."

He shifted on the bench as her scrutiny filled him with a strange sort of panic. This was what he wanted, to convince her of his worth. Yet he felt uneasy, undeserving of her praise. "Peter reminds me of my brother, that's all."

"Truly?" she said, her voice rising in delight. "You never let on that you have a brother. He must be younger, since you're the heir."

Christ. His throat closed at his own stupidity. He never spoke of Colin. Not to anyone.

"He was older than me. He died a long time ago."

From his terse tone, Catherine knew instantly that she had touched a very private pain. She wanted to call back her thoughtless comment. A large black shape on the bench, Burke peered into the night-shrouded garden as if communing with the shadows in his past.

"I'm sorry," she whispered.

"Don't be," he said curtly. "It wasn't your fault. It was mine."

"Yours? What do you mean?"

He sat silent, arousing her curiosity all the more with his uncommunicative manner. It shook her to think he had suffered grief and guilt like any other human being.

"Tell me about your brother." Loving the textured strength of his fingers, she couldn't stop herself from touching the back of his hand again. "Please."

He turned toward her, and she sensed more than saw his burning stare. The tune of a country dance lilted from the house, but to Catherine, the ball seemed worlds away from this pocket of intimacy in the night, enfolded by the fragrance of roses. She was only beginning to conceive the depths of emotion in the earl. Burke Grisham was more than a dastardly rogue. She wanted to peel away the layers of his cynicism, despite her fear that learning more about him would strengthen the bond between them.

She thought back to his odd comment about this arbor. How had he guessed that it had once been her private refuge? She hadn't come here since the day she had learned of her husband's death. Yet somehow Burke seemed to know things about her as if he could peer into her mind. The idea made her feel invaded, uneasy.

They were strangers linked only by the memory of Alfred, she reminded herself. She shouldn't expect Burke to confide his innermost thoughts while she guarded her own secrets.

"Never mind my questions," she said softly. "I shan't pry. I haven't the right—"

"Maybe you do." He sprang to his feet, his fists clenched. "So you want to know the story? All right, I'll tell you. Then you'll see that I'm not as good as you mistakenly think."

His abrupt anger mystified her. She couldn't help but wonder if his agitation arose from the turmoil of deeper emotions. Perhaps he needed to talk, to release the bottled-up pain.

"I'm listening," she murmured.

"Colin was four years older than me," Burke said. "He was eleven that last summer we spent at our home near Wimbledon. I was forever getting into scrapes, and Colin was forever standing up for me."

"What sort of scrapes?"

"Oh, letting a crate of chickens loose in church, hiding under the stairs and peeking up the skirts of the servant girls, that sort of thing. It doesn't matter now." He gave a strange, harsh chuckle. "Life was never boring with Colin. He always managed to dream up new diversions for us. Until the time when everything went wrong."

The cynical twist to his voice tugged at her heart. "What happened?"

He prowled back and forth in the moonlight. "One day after tea, Colin had the idea to play highwayman using real weapons from Father's gunroom. The guncases were locked, but I snitched the key while the keeper wasn't looking and took a pair of pistols. Then we hiked to the London road, found a secluded spot near a blackthorn hedge, and waited for the next coach."

He paused, and she strained to view his features through the gloom. From memory she recreated the elegance of his brow, the boldness of his eyes, the strength of his jaw, and then softened them to fit a boy of seven. "And . . . ?" she prompted.

"It was getting on toward evening when we heard the rattle of wheels, the jingle of harness. As the coach rolled into sight, Colin told me to get out there and stop it. But for once . . ." Burke rubbed the back of his neck as if it pained him. "For once I was too afraid."

"That's understandable. Did your brother try to force you?"

"No. He called me a baby and said he'd do the job himself. I can still see him striding into the roadway, waving his pistol and shouting, 'Stand and deliver.' And the driver sawing on the reins. The horses snorting. A woman inside screaming. Then the coachman aiming his own weapon."

Dread gripped Catherine. She thought of another carriage hurtling out of the night, the squealing of the horse and the slashing hooves. "Surely the man realized Colin was only a child."

"He was big for his age, as big as some fully grown men. He'd tied a kerchief over the lower part of his face. And he'd deepened his voice." Burke drew a breath as if he were girding himself. "The coachman panicked and fired. The bullet struck Colin in the chest. There was blood . . . so much blood."

Catherine winced, sensing the depths of Burke's torment. A cool breeze fanned her hot cheeks. The bushes rustled as if murmuring sympathy. All that came to her mind were platitudes inadequate to soothe the little boy whose horror lived on inside the grown man. "Oh, Burke. You must have been terrified."

He shrugged. "The damned irony of it was that our pistols weren't even loaded. We were only playacting. It wasn't meant to be real."

She rose and went to his side, touching the smoothness of his sleeve and wishing she could erase that awful memory. "Of course it wasn't. There was nothing you could have done."

"I could have stopped Colin," he said fiercely, taking a step backward. "I should never have stolen those guns. I should have had the courage to step into that roadway myself."

"To die in your brother's place?" Catherine said incredulously.

"Yes! He deserved to live. He was smarter, more heroic, a far better son than I."

She shook her head. "For pity's sake, you were only seven years old. Colin was the one who should have known better."

He swung away as if rejecting her reasoning. "You haven't heard the worst of it. I got up and ran. I ran back to the house and hid in the cellar. I was afraid I'd get thrashed."

"So you panicked. Any child would in the face of danger. The coachman could have shot you, too."

"You don't understand. I just wanted to avoid a whipping. While my brother lay in the dirt bleeding to death, I was crouched between the wine racks, quivering and crying." He gave a harsh laugh. "I acted like a stinking coward, just as my father said."

Catherine went cold with shock. "Your father called you that? He couldn't have meant it."

"Why not? It's the truth."

"Upon my word! How could he be so . . . so *cruel* when you were already hurting?"

Burke paced as if he didn't hear her. "The least I could have done was to fetch the doctor. Or to stay with Colin, to comfort him in his last moments."

His self-flagellation troubled Catherine. All her youth, she had envied people who were blessed with a real family. Now she could also see the agony of losing a beloved brother. And blaming oneself for the tragedy.

"Surely your father must have forgiven you eventually."

"How could he? I was a constant reminder of my brother's death. I was sent away to school and stayed there, even through the holidays."

"What about your mother? Didn't she intercede for you?"

"She took to her bed and never recovered from her grief. She died the following summer."

Though his words were stiff and emotionless, Catherine could imagine him as a banished young boy, unloved, his spirit crushed by guilt. Fury at his parents lashed her. They had been so selfishly wrapped in mourning the dead heir that they had failed to love the living son who needed them.

And Burke had never healed from that wound.

She caught his arm. He tried to yank away, but she held on tightly. "It was an accident. And you were only a child. What matters is that you're a brave man now."

He muttered a strangled curse. "For God's sake, don't try to placate me."

"I'm not. You *are* brave. On that first day you rode up to the manor, when you thought Fabian was about to shoot me, you knocked the gun out of his hand."

"Don't remind me of that stupid blunder."

"It was an act of courage. So was climbing the tree to rescue Tigress."

"Any boy over the age of five could have done as well."

"You saved Peter this afternoon, too."

"Only because I wanted to win your favor." Reaching out, Burke stroked his thumb over her lips. "Tell me, love, did my ploy succeed?"

Her legs threatened to fold. He was trying to distract her by playing the rogue. Then the truth struck her. He *wanted* her to believe the worst of him. Because he was as afraid to trust again as she was.

She took his hand in hers and gently kissed his fingers. "Yes, it succeeded. Because I saw the compassion you hide so well. The same compassion that made you go out onto the battlefield at Waterloo and risk your life to save our wounded soldiers. I cannot imagine any act more courageous than that."

"I was looking for a thrill, that's all."

"I don't believe you. But I do believe you've suffered enough for your sins."

The bushes rustled as if from the passage of a small night creature, a rabbit perhaps. Catherine kept her eyes trained on Burke's shadowy face. She heard the rasp of his breathing, felt his warm fingers on hers, inhaled his masculine scent.

"You can't think well of me," he said flatly. "I'm a contemptible scoundrel, remember?"

"I said that before I knew you. But now . . ." She paused, rearranging the pieces of his character, making a new picture of him that surprised her. "Now I think you're as lonely as I am."

Burke wanted to shake some sense into her. She couldn't seem to understand that he *deserved* to suffer for his wickedness. She was supposed to revile him, to see the darkness in him and remove her tempting self from his sight.

Instead, she moved even closer, enveloping him in her body heat. He kept his arms rigidly at his sides. He wished to God she'd step away before he did something rash and wonderful. Like make love to her.

"I wish I knew how to make you stop judging yourself so harshly," she said. "But I don't know quite what to say or do."

"If you have any sense at all, you'll run like hell."

Her laugh was sweeter than music. "It won't work."

"What?"

"Growling at me. I'm not afraid of you. See?"

She lifted her hand to his face. Her caress felt like the brush of a butterfly's wing, soft and velvety as it glided over his cheek, his jaw, his chin. Her touch set off a yearning inside him that burned brighter than any passion he had ever felt.

It must be the result of denying himself for the past year. Or perhaps exposing the dark secret that had burdened him since boyhood.

How baffling that she could accept him, black soul and all. His plan to repel her had failed. Yet he felt no regret. Not with Catherine so close, so willing, so tantalizing.

He had vowed not to seduce her. But one kiss couldn't hurt.

With a groan, he embraced her, shaping their bodies together. He was keenly aware of the yielding pressure of her breasts and hips. She whispered his name even as he lowered his mouth to hers. The kiss was long and deep and ripe with hope. She tasted even sweeter than his memory served. Her lips held for him both the joy of homecoming and the thrill of discovery.

He cradled the warm roundness of one breast, then moved his mouth to nuzzle the silken mound of her bodice, though frustrated by the cloth that deterred him. She sighed, her trembling hands gliding restlessly over his hair, his face. She wanted him, too. The surety of her response shuddered through him. She was all goodness and light, a beacon in the gloom of his own soul.

Driven by the urge to claim her, he guided her down to the grass beside the rose arbor. Tenderly he cupped her neck, rubbing his thumb over her cheek. The usual romantic phrases seemed inadequate to express his feelings.

"I need you," he muttered. "God forgive me, I need you."

Realization crept into him, filling him with exultation and alarm. He felt more than physical lust for the woman who gazed up at him with eyes that sparkled in the starlight. His feelings for Catherine Snow came dangerously close to love.

She slid her hands inside his coat and over his chest. "Please, Burke. Don't stop. Not now."

Her breathy words aroused him to a fever pitch. He shouldn't listen, even though his loins ached to join with her and his heart cried out for her affection. She was the one woman he could not—and should not—have.

But the pleasure of her closeness clouded his judgment. He breathed in the scent of her, feeling her lithe, welcoming body move beneath his. He wanted to give her the glory of sexual release. It was the only way he knew how to make Catherine love him.

Yet even as he bent to kiss her again, he heard a sound. A shuffling movement somewhere nearby.

His senses snapped to alertness. He lifted himself into a crouch, positioning his body between her and the noise as he scanned the shadowy garden.

Other guests from the party might have wandered out here. If Catherine were seen in a compromising position, she would suffer the lash of gossip and the loss of her reputation. He cursed himself for not thinking of that earlier.

"What is it?" she asked.

He held up his hand in a silencing gesture. Peering into the gloom beneath a sycamore tree, he spied a black shape. It looked suspiciously human.

Wrath rose sharp and hot in him.

Someone was spying on them.

Chapter 12

Catherine watched in dazed astonishment as Burke leaped to his feet. A moment ago, he had been about to kiss her again. A moment ago, she had been about to surrender to him. The heat of anticipation still flowed through her veins.

Now he streaked like a dark blur across the grass and plunged into the gloom beneath the sycamore.

A squawk of fright disturbed the night air. The noise of a brief scuffle carried to her ears. Then Burke emerged, dragging a hunched figure by the scruff of the neck.

"D-don't hurt me. P-please don't."

Shocked awareness cooled Catherine's blood and abruptly returned her to reality. She scrambled up, the folds of her petticoat tangling her legs. She strained to see the captive through the shadows. "Fabian? Is that you?"

He snuffled loudly in reply.

"Fabian," Burke said in a hard voice, "was watching us from the bushes. Like a bloody Peeping Tom."

"I wasn't hurting anyone. I-I only wanted to protect Mrs. Snow."

"By invading her privacy?" Burke gave him a rough shake. "I ought to throttle you."

Catherine hurried forward. "Release him at once."

"Only if he apologizes."

"I w-will. Gladly." The gangly blond man sank to his knees before Catherine and held up his clasped hands. "Forgive me. I d-didn't mean to bother you. I-I would never do you harm."

"I know you wouldn't," she said, embarrassed by his humble posturing. "Please, stand up."

As if he hadn't heard, Fabian rushed on, "B-but I c-can't let him disgrace you like this. He-he's leading you astray. He'll b-break your heart."

Fabian had witnessed their kiss. And more.

Her skin crawled. He had been lurking behind the tree and observing that intimate interlude on the grass. In another few minutes, she and Burke would have been coupling out in the open for all the world to see. The beautiful sensations he had wrought in her now seemed sordid, illicit. Was she so starved for love that she could forget all scruples?

Burke stood watching her, his shadowed features inscrutable in the faint moonlight. Even now her insides clenched with wanting him.

Was he leading her astray, using his erotic appeal to lure her from the path of independence? Was she just another conquest to him, a challenge, like winning a high wager?

She had to admit, though, she been an equal partner in the seduction. She had invited his kiss and much more.

Fabian closed his clammy palms around her hands. *"I* would never dishonor you, Mrs. Snow," he said earnestly. "I-I know this is hardly the t-time to say so, b-but I must c-c-confess. I-I want to marry you."

Burke bit out a startled oath. "Like *hell!* I'm not the only one leading a woman astray. . . ."

Catherine waved him to silence. She kept her eyes on Fabian, who knelt before her, his pale hair spilling untidily around his shoulders. His proposal jolted her, and she regretted the prospect of hurting him.

"You're a dear, kind man," she said. "If only I shared your feelings—"

"D-don't say no. Please. I-I-I love you."

Dear God. His voice wobbled as if he were on the brink of tears. Her heart went out to him.

"I'm flattered that you would honor me with such an offer," she said gently. "But I've no wish to remarry. Not ever again."

Burke drew in a breath as if he were about to speak. Ignoring him, she tried to pull her hands away from Fabian, but he clung tighter. "I can be patient. W-we can have a long engagement. As long as you like."

The awkward situation made her increasingly uneasy. "I'm afraid you ask the impossible."

"B-but at least give me time to w-win your heart—"

Burke clapped his hand onto Fabian's shoulder. "The lady said no."

Fabian scrambled to his feet. "Y-you cad. You only want her to use her. I w-will not allow you to treat her so shabbily." He puffed out his chest and shook his fist. "Ch-choose your second, my lord."

Catherine gasped. Before Burke could answer the challenge, she stepped between the two men. "You mustn't duel with him, Burke. He's a crack shot."

"So am I."

"But he could kill you."

Even through the darkness she could see the glow in his eyes. He caressed her lightly under the chin. "Would you mourn my passing?"

That one brief touch reawakened the agonizing yearning in her. She *would* mourn him. More than he could imagine. "I don't want to see any bloodshed," she countered. "You're both behaving like two dogs who want the same bone."

His smile gleamed. "You're an uncommonly pretty bone."

Denying herself the pleasure of his compliment, Catherine turned to Fabian. "I must ask you to withdraw your challenge. For my sake."

"B-but I can't let him make you his lightskirt."

"He won't, I promise you. I have more integrity than to let a man misuse me." It was true. Because if she had an affair with Burke, she would choose to do so of her own accord.

"And y-you really won't marry me?"

"I'm afraid not." Somehow she had to ease the sting of rejection, yet make him realize once and for all that she would never encourage his suit. Silently she begged Alfred's forgiveness and lied, "You see, my one true love is dead."

"As y-you wish, then. I won't d-duel with the knave."

Relieved beyond words, she touched his shoulders and kissed him on the cheek. His skin was fuzzy and childishly soft in contrast to his muscled body. He put his hand to the spot and stood as if transfixed. Then he scuttled away into the darkness.

"Very touching," Burke said from behind her. "A kiss is sure to convince him to give up on you."

She whirled to face him. He stood in a cocky pose, his hands on his hips. The sight of him made her weak with longing, yet she also felt a constraint, a confusion over the wisdom of her desire for him. Fabian was right about Burke—he wanted only a fleeting affair. She had no illusions about anything more. After a few nights of splendor, they would go their separate ways, and she would be left with fond memories and a lonely bed.

She took a step back from him. "Save your sarcasm. At least Fabian had the good sense to call off the duel."

Burke remained as still as one of the tall shadowed trees. "You're overlooking one relevant detail."

"What's that?"

"There wouldn't have been a duel. I never agreed to it in the first place."

"Yes, you did." Yet when she thought back, Catherine realized guiltily that he was right. She had judged him by his rakehell reputation and leaped to a conclusion.

He lifted his hand as if to touch her, then let it drop to his side. "I hadn't told anyone yet, but I'll be leaving here the day after tomorrow."

Leaving? A sickening lurch hit her stomach. She had known he'd come for only a visit, to pay his respects to Alfred's family. But in a secret part of her heart she had hoped he would stay indefinitely. She had hoped to experience the glory of making love with a man who cherished her.

What a dreamer she was. Still.

Burke cocked his head and added quietly, "I trust we'll have the chance to say good-bye." Even as she stood dumbfounded, he turned on his heel and strode off toward the manor.

She crossed her arms over her breasts. He walked away as if they had never shared an impassioned kiss. As if he hadn't trusted her enough to reveal the tragedy haunting his past. He must be disappointed by her lack of faith in him about the duel. He must have decided she wasn't worth his trouble. He could find a score of ladies at the ball who would be willing to spend the night satisfying him. The thought of him with another woman pained her more than she wanted to admit.

Catherine walked slowly, aimlessly through the darkened garden. Perhaps it was better this way. To make a clean break. To say farewell with her pride intact. To avoid the torment of loving a rogue again.

She stumbled on the path and caught herself. The ache in her breast told her the bittersweet truth. It was too late to escape being hurt. The earl of Thornwald had already seduced her heart.

She was seized by the powerful impulse to run after him and restore the magical trust between them. But dare she engage in a brief romantic interlude? In order to open her school, she must be regarded as a respectable person. Not a lightskirt whose lack of morals might taint young children.

Catherine reached the rear of the manor house and paused in the shadows beneath the great oak tree which Burke had climbed to rescue Tigress. He was nowhere in sight now; he must have rejoined the party. The sounds of conviviality swirled from the candlelit windows—the clink of glassware, the music and laughter, the rise and fall of conversation.

As much as she had looked forward to the ball, she couldn't face people right now. She craved the quiet of her own bedroom over drinking and dancing in the company of strangers. She needed time to think, to ponder the right course of action.

She made her way to a side door that opened into the portrait gallery in the east wing. The door clicked shut behind her, and her footsteps echoed in the vast, empty chamber. The darkened pictures of strangers stared down from the walls. Since the Snows lacked an illustrious lineage, her mother-in-law had purchased an assortment of paintings at estate sales. Alfred had drolly referred to them as his sham ancestors. Or at least he had until the last year of his life when he had lapsed into melancholy and nothing could make him smile.

Catherine felt a pang at the memory. She had tried so hard to cheer him with tales about the villagers and the latest antics of the Guppy children. But he'd refused to speak of what ailed him, and she had suffered the heavy burden of guilt. It was her own barrenness that had changed him from an exuberant flatterer into a bitter stranger who sought oblivion in a bottle.

In the passageway outside the gallery, a lamp flickered on a sidetable to light the way of any guest who strayed from the main rooms. As Catherine made her way to a back staircase, the hushed rise and fall of voices carried to her ears.

One male, one female. She had the odd impression they were quarreling.

Hoping to reach her room unnoticed, she started up the stairs. Then she spied two people standing in the shadows on the landing.

The man gripped the woman by her forearms as if to prevent her from fleeing. The couple fell silent at Catherine's approach.

Her stomach sank. The stout woman in the purple gown was Lorena.

Her mother-in-law let out a hiss of surprise or displeasure, or perhaps both. Her posture rigid, she stared with glittering eyes at Catherine.

Her companion was an attractive, middle-aged gentleman with graying hair and a trim form. A genial smile flashed in his weather-seamed face. The familiar way he held onto Lorena struck Catherine as peculiar.

"Good evening," she greeted them. "Is something amiss?"

"Of course not," Lorena snapped. "Run along with you now."

Catherine had braced herself for an order to return to the kitchen. But Lorena seemed more anxious that Catherine leave them alone. So be it, then. She moved thankfully toward the upper stairs.

"One moment." The man released Lorena and stepped in front of Catherine, blocking her path. "So you're the younger Mrs. Snow." He made a courtly bow. "Ezekiel Newberry, at your service."

She afforded him a polite nod. "I'm pleased to meet you."

Newberry's sharp eyes studied her. "You're a pretty

sight even with your hair atumble and grass stains on your skirt." He turned to Lorena. "What do you think? Doesn't she have the look of a well-kissed woman?"

Catherine drew a quick breath. Automatically she touched her coiffure and found several curls hanging loose. Green smears marred the spangled gold silk of her gown. Dear God, he was right.

Lorena stepped into the candlelight and scrutinized Catherine. "You designing hussy. You've been with his lordship, haven't you?"

"We only went for a walk—"

"How dare you practice your wiles on the man intended for your own sister-in-law. No doubt seduction is how you lured my darling Freddie into your trap, too."

"That isn't true—"

"Lord Thornwald is heir to the marquis of Westhaven. The marquis would be irate to learn of your scheming to win his son."

"I'm not scheming—"

"The earl requires a wife of impeccable character. Not a drab from the gutter. Henceforth, you are to stay away from him. Is that clear?"

Catherine stood frozen. Not since she and Alfred had announced their impetuous marriage had she seen Lorena in such a rage. That she could attack so viciously in front of a stranger mortified Catherine. She wanted to hide her face in shame, to slink away like a scolded child, to obey as she had always done.

Even as she lowered her head, pride nudged her chin back up. She was a grown woman, not a guttersnipe. She would bow to no one.

She squarely met Lorena's glare. "I will act as I wish."

"What? You would defy me in this?"

"If I so choose. I am a wealthy lady in my own right."

"Rich and pretty," Newberry mused. "A winning combination."

"Stay out of this." Lorena pinched her lips tight and

regarded Catherine. "As to you, miss, I won't tolerate a sordid liaison under my roof. Remember that."

"So long as you remember that whatever I do in my private life will be my choice. Not yours." It took all of Catherine's courage to keep her gaze steady. "Even in matters involving his lordship."

As Lorena sputtered a protest, Ezekiel Newberry took her arm. "Ah, leave the girl alone. Come along and we'll finish our little chat."

The ugly glower vanished from Lorena's face, and she cast a wary, sidelong glance at Newberry. "Yes, of course," she muttered. As docile as a lamb, she let him lead her down the stairs.

Catherine slowly mounted the steps to her bedroom. A sinister quality to the man nagged at her. She reflected on the way he had pointed out her dishabille, something no true gentleman would have done. And Lorena obeyed him as if he were her master.

That in itself was extraordinary, for she was a woman of strong opinions. Why did he exert such influence over her? If they were old acquaintances, it was odd that she had never mentioned him.

Pausing in the dim corridor outside her bedroom, Catherine took a shaky breath as another realization struck her. By openly admitting to her interest in Burke, she had declared war against Lorena. Though apparently her mother-in-law didn't know he intended to depart on Friday.

A keen ache assailed Catherine. She had so little time in which to make the choice between following her head or her heart.

By tomorrow she must decide whether or not to ask Burke to stay.

Smooth skin. Sweet as brandy. Intoxicating as champagne.

Her body was a fount of heat. A wellspring of the finest wine. Breasts and thighs and cunt formed a temple of car-

nal pleasure. He kissed a path downward to the curved scar on her belly. Then he moved lower and tongued her essence.

She moaned. Eyes shut, lips parted, head tipped back. Her face went in and out of focus. As always, Catherine held a part of herself inviolate. She clutched at the tangled sheets instead of him. As if isolated in her passion.

Because she sensed the truth. He was nothing but a fraud. Yet he must go on living a lie, else destroy his whole family.

Another, stronger craving swept over him. The thirst for a drink blotted out his need for her.

Push up. Stumble away. Find a bottle. . . .

Burke sat bolt upright in bed. His rasping breath disturbed the quiet darkness. Cold sweat bathed his body, and the blood pounded in his ears. It took a moment to orient himself to his shadowy surroundings.

He had been dreaming about Catherine. Dreaming about making love to her. The hard evidence of his fantasizing throbbed in his groin.

Bowing his head, he plunged his fingers through his hair. He fancied he could still taste her. He could smell the fragrance of her skin. He could see the small scar on her stomach, a thin half-moon against her white flesh.

Not a dream. A vision.

The thought jolted him to full awareness. He threw back the counterpane and rolled out of bed, the rug cool against his bare feet. Feeling his way through the gloom, he stubbed his toe on the chair that held his dressing gown. Pain speared up his leg.

He growled an oath and thrust his arms into the silk garment, yanking the sash into a knot at his waist.

His tongue felt parched. He needed a drink. A strong one.

Out in the passageway, a candle sputtered low in a sconce, casting shaky shadows over the walls. The ball had ended in the wee hours, and he had stumbled to bed stone drunk in his campaign to forget Catherine. Several hours must have passed. Now, cold clarity governed his mind.

My one true love is dead.

He braced a shoulder against the doorframe as Catherine's statement stabbed his chest anew, a ghost of the blow she had dealt him in the garden. She would never love again. He thanked God the night had hidden the anguish on his face. He had managed to finish their conversation and walk away without her realizing what a fool he had almost made of himself.

He was leaving on the morrow, once he determined that Lorena had handed over Catherine's share of the dower right. He would leave without achieving his purpose here: to discover the source of his visions. Because staying posed a greater threat to his sanity than suffering the occasional fantasy.

When he had announced his departure to Catherine, he had waited a moment, buoyed by the rise of hope that she would protest, give him a reason to change his plans and prolong his visit. She had merely stood there, gazing at him with her beautiful eyes.

I have more integrity than to let a man misuse me.

Did she regret encouraging his passion? Did she wish she hadn't lain in the grass with him? Despite all her sterling words about his bravery, did she still think him a worthless scoundrel?

Please, Burke. Don't stop. Not now.

Desire enfolded him like a thick fog. God save him, he wanted to make love to Catherine without the barriers of the past between them. He wanted to kiss every inch of her smooth skin, right down to the scar below her navel.

Just like in his vision.

His pulse quickened, this time from a chilling realization. If she did indeed bear such a scar, only one man would have known of it.

Alfred.

A dizzying resistance swept through Burke. He felt a powerful urge to run, to avoid facing the truth. Instead, he pressed his brow to the cool wall. Only a bedlamite would believe that another person's memories had invaded his own mind. Indeed, he had found logical explanations for his knowledge of her spectacles, her locket, her lilting Yorkshire speech.

Yet how could he know of such an intimate detail as a hidden scar?

Then he thought of the one way to find out the answer.

He walked down the dim passageway, his bare feet making no sound on the Persian runner. Unerringly, he found his way through the labyrinth of corridors and into the east wing of the house. The house was silent, the other guests fast asleep. Rounding a corner, he stopped before a nondescript door.

Catherine's bedroom. He had come here once before to deliver the books she had forgotten at the abandoned cottage on the day he had first kissed her. Back then, he had wanted to please her, to inveigle himself into her good graces.

I think you're as lonely as I am.

The faint ticking of a clock somewhere mingled with his own uneven breathing. In that, at least, she was right about him. Over the last year, solitude had become his boon companion. Until now.

Now at last he had the chance to get the irrefutable proof that had made him ride halfway across England to find the one woman who had every right to despise him. The one woman who obsessed his mind to the verge of dementia. The one woman who held his misbegotten heart in the palm of her hand.

He gripped the cold metal doorknob. The hellish

irony was, in order to find out the truth, he must do the one act guaranteed to confirm her belief about his wicked nature.

He must seduce her.

Chapter 13

Warmth. Pressure. Arousal.

A man's body cradled her from behind. His breath tickled her cheek. His fingers ascended a path up her arm, along the side of her neck, over the hollow of her throat. Like the brush of angel wings, his touch tingled across her skin. After a moment his heavenly hand descended to her breasts, glided over peaks and valley, and cupped her fullness as if it were a chalice of wine.

Catherine drifted in the misty limbo between dreaming and wakefulness. Her spirit rejoiced in hazy wonderment. He did still want her; he had come to her after all. His caresses held both the promise of paradise and the fulfillment of the flesh. A sweet, heavy yearning flowed deep in her belly.

Down, she thought languidly. *Lower.*

As if he could see inside her mind, he slid his palm slowly, slowly down the front of her nightdress. At her stomach he paused, and his fingertips danced a waltz over her midsection. The contact was inquisitive, oddly searching. Somehow she sensed he sought her most mysterious secret.

Lower, the voice inside her cried out again. *Lower.*

Breathless seconds passed, and then his trek continued its descent, coming to the place that ached for him. She moved restlessly when he touched her through the nightgown. He raised the hem and unerringly found her pearl. A blissful sigh eddied from her; she gave herself up to the tender stroking of his hand. His clever, blessed hand.

The divine sensations lifted her higher and higher, and she felt her essence expanding, swelling, reaching for release. At last the ripeness burst in a shower of glory, and she sobbed out her joy before sinking back into the soft folds of darkness.

Her awakening came in small degrees of awareness. His hand still covered her mound. The front of him was pressed against her spine and bottom. His chest rose and fell in heavy breaths. No dream had ever wrought such pleasure.

She opened her eyes to the velvety night. Burke lay behind her; she knew the scent of him, the skill of his touch. A fierce exultation coursed through her and left her trembling anew. Needing to assure herself that he was real, she caressed his arm, loving the raspy play of hair on sinewy muscles.

He nuzzled the back of her neck. His tongue delved into her ear. On a shuddering sigh, she tipped her head back to meet his lips in a fleeting kiss.

"Catherine," he whispered. "You do know it's me, don't you?"

The thread of vulnerability in his voice tugged at her. Surely Burke didn't think she would welcome any other man into her bed.

She turned onto her back, and the faint glow from the banked embers on the grate illuminated his dark silhouette. She traced his form with her fingertips. Strong jaw. Noble cheekbones. Hair a bit long on his neck. Broad shoulders tapering down to a muscled waist. And the turgid proof of his desire.

"Of course I know," she murmured. "Even asleep, I knew." Through the shadows, she found his shoulder and pressed a kiss to the smooth ridges of his scar. "Upon my word, you have a unique talent for waking a woman up."

His laugh stirred her hair. "I'm relieved you didn't scream to the high heavens. To be honest, I wasn't certain I'd be welcome."

There it was again, that hint of anxiety, so at odds with his devil-may-care image. Her heart beat faster. Perhaps his coming here meant he needed more than physical release. Perhaps, like herself, he craved closeness on a deeper level. After thinking long and hard last night, she had made a decision to seize whatever happiness he offered her. She need only take care to keep their affair a secret from the rest of the world.

She caressed his face, and the trace of unshaven whiskers abraded her skin. "I could simply say you're welcome in my bed," Catherine murmured. "But I'd far rather show you."

Burke watched in speechless astonishment as she sat up to work at the buttons on her bodice. He couldn't believe how easily she accepted his presence, how swiftly and passionately she had responded to him. Her ecstatic cries still echoed in his ears, heating him to a near-painful arousal.

I have more integrity than to let a man misuse me.

He had expected resistance. Considering her wretched opinion of him, he had anticipated having to coax her into removing her nightclothes. So that he could look for the curved mark and settle once and for all if he were madman or merely imaginative.

But now he forgot his purpose as she lifted her arms and drew off the gown over her head. Through the veil of shadow, he glimpsed her nakedness. Alabaster limbs. Rounded breasts. Slender waist. Womanly hips.

His. All his.

She knelt beside him on the bed, her knees touching his ribcage. Desire flooded him with the stormy urge to hold her close. He started to push up on his elbow, but she gently grasped his shoulders and pressed him back down.

Leaning over him, she whispered, "You gave me pleasure. Now let me do the same for you."

Intrigued beyond his wildest dreams, he lay still while she explored him with her mouth, stringing soft kisses over his shoulders, his throat, his face. The clean fragrance of her wafted over him. The ladies he knew demanded to be wooed, bestowing their favors in exchange for extravagant gifts and lavish compliments. That Catherine would give so freely to him made the experience incredibly erotic and deeply moving.

As she bent to feather her lips across his cheek, her braid trailed down her shoulder and brushed his chest, sending tingles across his skin. Her hair formed a dark halo around the creamy oval of her face. He fancied she was his own angel, descended to earth to minister to his needs.

More than anything, he wanted to believe she cared for him, that she could heal the self-loathing that corroded his soul. She personified what had been missing from his aimless life. For too long, he'd had intimacy without true closeness, friendships without trust, attachments without devotion.

My one true love is dead.

He held back the impossible declarations that crowded his tongue. Her heart belonged to a dead man. He would do well to remember that.

Her breasts jutted tantalizingly close. Then again, he reflected, a flesh-and-blood man had a distinct advantage over the spiritual. Tossing willpower to the wind, he cupped one breast in his palm and suckled her. She uttered an inarticulate sound of pleasure, and he felt a flare of male pride, the primal satisfaction of owning her ardor, if only for a short while.

One of her hands caressed his cheek. The other stole down, down over his chest and his abdomen until she reached the source of his heat. Her fingers tiptoed over him as if discovering a treasure, and the reverence in her touch brought a stinging thickness to his throat.

"To hell with restraint," he muttered.

He rolled Catherine onto her back, covered her with his body, and laid claim to her mouth with all the tender violence of love unleashed. She tasted intoxicating, as if he were drinking from a wellspring of the finest wine. The velvet stroking of her tongue drove him to the brink of madness. Without taking his mouth from hers, he reached down between them and found her hot and wet and ready.

She moaned his name and opened her legs in the sweetest of invitations. In one glorious slide, he entered her sanctuary and united their bodies. Seeing her lovely features in the faint fireglow, he had the sweet-sharp impression of coming home after a long absence. He trembled with the need to make sense out of the illogical.

He nestled his hands on either side of her neck. "I feel as if we've done this before . . . somewhere . . . sometime."

Her lashes fluttered open. Her lips curved in a dreamy smile. "Impossible," she whispered, turning her head to kiss his palm. "I could never have forgotten something so beautiful."

She moved her hips beneath him, and the fierce urges inside him blotted all else from his mind. He sank deeper into her, commencing the age-old rhythm that held a shiny newness for him this time. The long months of celibacy sharpened his desire to fever brightness. The intensity of his feelings for Catherine plunged him into a white-hot river, a rushing surge of turbulence that carried the both of them up and up and up toward a wondrous light. Its irresistible aura beckoned to him, and he held tightly to her, bearing her with him on the mystic journey.

Her cries of ecstasy bathed him in splendor, and a long shuddering spasm delivered him into the brilliance. The ripples of radiance died away gradually, leaving him adrift in the sweetest peace he had ever known. He lay atop Catherine, their bodies still joined, their breaths mingling, their skin cooling. How wrong Alfred had been—Catherine held nothing back.

But that knowledge came from a dream. Or was it reality?

"Burke," she murmured. "That was heaven."

"Yes." The awesome truth left him shaken, stripped of defenses. "A glimpse of heaven."

Still holding her, he rolled onto his back and shut his eyes, wanting to preserve the sensations. The transcendent experience reminded him of his dream after being shot. Against his closed lids he could see the tunnel of light; he could feel the flooding of love, the boundless serenity. *Had* it been a figment of his imagination? Or an actual event? Had his spirit somehow left his body for a few moments and soared toward heaven?

Absurd, the cynic in him scoffed. Paradise existed only in the minds of pious preachers and faithful churchgoers who were foolish enough to believe in miracles.

And, of course, in a woman's arms.

Yet the maddening questions spun around and around in his head. *Did* a person's soul separate from his body at death? If he had nearly died at the same moment as Alfred, it might explain the impossible—

"Burke? You mustn't fall asleep."

Opening his eyes, he turned to Catherine. It struck him that he could see her more clearly now, the creamy smoothness of her skin, the feminine curve of breasts and hips, the lush outline of lips well kissed.

Pushing himself up onto his elbow, he glanced out the window and spied a pinkish glow against the dark tangle of trees. The pale light glinted off the spectacles lying atop a pile of books on the bedside table.

"My God," he said in bemusement. "It's near dawn."

She drew the sheet up almost to her breasts and murmured, "That's what I mean. The servants will be about their duties soon. You need to go now."

Her dismissal hit him like a slap in the face. A few minutes ago, he had lost himself in the most earth-shattering lovemaking of his life, and now Catherine wanted him to walk away as if they had shared nothing more than animal mating.

My one true love is dead.

He should have known. Yet he felt used and betrayed somehow, and the irony of it mocked him. He had always been the one to walk away. Now, for the first time he ached to linger in a woman's arms, and he was being chased away like a stallion who had fulfilled his stud duty.

Not yet, Burke thought grimly. He wasn't going anywhere until he had achieved his purpose here. The purpose he had damned near forgotten in his eagerness to bed her.

Kneeling, he let his gaze travel over her naked breasts and lower, where the sheet hid her midsection. He reached for the covering and found himself caressing the curve of her hip instead. The sweet warmth of her flesh unleashed the wild fever of desire in him again.

A tremulous smile illuminated her face. She placed her small hand over his larger one. Softly she said, "Will you come back tonight?"

It was an invitation he could never refuse. "Yes."

As he started to remove his hand, she gripped harder to him. "Burke. May I . . . ask you something else?"

"Ask away."

She bit her lip. With a hint of charming shyness, her amber eyes met his. "Would you consider postponing your departure?"

A rush of hope inundated him. Denying his foolish yearnings, he said without inflection, "That depends on what inducement you're offering me."

She bowed her head and studied their joined hands as if the words were difficult to say. "Only myself. If you stay on, we can meet like this every night."

"How long will our little affair last?"

Her gaze lifted to his again. "I . . . I'm not sure. As long as these things go on. You know more about such matters than I."

He did, indeed. But experience hadn't prepared him for the woman who had woven a spell around his heart. The woman who could listen to his darkest secrets without recoiling. The woman who was so intrinsically a part of him that he saw visions of her even in his sleep.

She lay against the pillows, her hair atumble and the precious weight of her hand still resting on his. He wanted so badly to believe in the vulnerability he saw in her eyes.

Unable to resist, he leaned closer and brushed a kiss over her soft lips. "Let's take it one night at a time, then."

Before she could distract him again, he drew back the sheet. The dawn cast a pearly pink glow over her skin. She had a perfect body, luxurious breasts and a waist that indented like an hourglass to the flare of feminine hips.

Slowly, with a strange reluctance to replace fantasy with fact, Burke turned his gaze to the flatness of her stomach. Then he saw it. Above the dark-thatched crown of her womanhood, a thin half-moon scar adorned her white flesh.

A chill penetrated his bones. Unable to trust his sight,

he ran his fingertips over the mark. A tiny bump, almost indiscernible. No wonder he hadn't noticed it in the dark.

"How did you get this scar?" he asked hoarsely.

She slipped her hand over it in an odd gesture of self-protection. "I . . . it was nothing. It happened long ago."

The pounding in his skull distracted him. He had wanted to prove the scar a figment of his imagination.

But it was real. He had seen it as clear as a memory.

The darkness came rushing over him. He could no longer fight the descent into the black abyss. He felt himself falling, falling. Into a glimmer of light. A radiant tunnel where he could see with unclouded perception.

The scar was the key piece to the puzzle that had been tormenting him for the past year, ever since he had nearly died at Waterloo and had come home to fantasize about a woman he had never met. His scattered thoughts fit together in only one logical way. It was incredible. Inconceivable. Yet *true.*

He got up from the bed and paced naked around the small bedchamber. "The transfer of memories," he mused aloud. "That's how I saw all those things. It must have happened when Alfred died just moments before I was shot—"

"What are you talking about? What things? What happened?"

He spun around to see Catherine frowning at him. She was sitting now, her back against the headboard, her knees drawn up beneath the quilted coverlet. She still had her hands pressed to her middle, hiding the telltale scar.

All of his dread disappeared beneath a bubbling rather like excitement. With acceptance came a sense of lightness, a freedom from the burden of fear. He wasn't insane. Rather, he had been the recipient of an awesome gift. And he wanted to share his astounding discovery with the only woman who mattered to him.

He sat down on the edge of the mattress, the bedropes creaking beneath his weight. "Catherine, do you think a person's spirit leaves his body after death?"

She tilted her head to the side. "I suppose so. The church teaches that we all go up to heaven . . . or down to hell, depending on how we lived our life on earth."

"Yes. Now listen closely. What I'm going to say will sound impossible, but it's true, I swear it." Needing to touch her, to feel the reality of living warmth, Burke gathered her hands in his. "After Alfred was shot on the battlefield, I picked him up and tried to carry him to safety. He died in my arms."

Catherine's eyes went misty. "I didn't know that part."

Burke felt a weakening in his chest, but he steeled himself against it. "He expired only an instant before I was shot myself. When the bullet struck, I felt an explosion of white-hot pain throughout my body."

She hissed out a sigh, and her gaze dipped to his chest before returning to his face. "No one should have to suffer so. But what has all this to do with spirits?"

"I'm getting to that. What happened next is something I couldn't accept as real until now. The pain slid away, completely vanished. I felt myself rising until I could look down and see my body lying on the muddy earth, beside the carriage we'd been using to transport the wounded."

Catherine arched one eyebrow, but said nothing.

He searched for the right words to express his mystical experience. "There was darkness all around me, dense yet soft. I saw a star shining in the distance, and without making a conscious decision, I felt myself flowing toward it. As I got nearer, it became a tunnel of brilliant light that stretched out and enveloped me. I felt . . ." His voice sounded rusty to his own ears; he forced himself to go on. "I felt a sense of utter love and peace. I know that sounds silly, and yet it was real."

"You must have been dreaming."

"That's what I told myself, too. But something else very peculiar happened. I sensed a presence there in the light with me." He paused, assessing her frowning features. "I believe now that it was the spirit of your husband."

"You're trying to tell me your soul left your body and went to heaven? And you *remember* it?" Catherine shook her head. "You must have been delirious, that's all."

"I didn't want to believe it, either. But ever since, I've had visions that I couldn't explain. Visions of you, Catherine."

"Of *me?*"

He nodded. This was the part that awed him, the part he feared she would reject outright. "I've finally come to the conclusion that my spirit crossed somehow with Alfred's in that tunnel of light. In the process, I absorbed his memories of you. At least some of them."

Catherine leaned back, stunned by his incredible announcement. Her mind branded the tale implausible, even insane. Burke sat in naked splendor, his demon-bright eyes glowing in a face so impossibly handsome that despite her wariness, she felt a melting surge of desire. Their joined hands still rested on her knees. Black hairs peppered the skin along his arm and over his chest, except for the white scar that twisted across his upper left chest. She wondered again if the horrors of war had unhinged his mind. A chill coursed through her, and she felt their astonishing closeness slipping away.

"Why would you invent such a tale?" she whispered.

His fingers tensed on hers. "It's no invention. Listen to this. Do you remember when we were caught in the rainstorm at the shepherd's cottage, and I asked you some questions about yourself?"

Catherine nodded. That episode remained luminous in her mind, for ever since, in the dark of night, she hugged her pillow and relived the excitement of their first kiss.

"I asked you about the locket you often wear," Burke said. "The one with the angel reaching for a diamond star."

She drew her hands free and pressed them to her bare throat. The locket lay in her drawer now; she hadn't wanted to wear it since discovering her attraction to Burke. "I remember."

He regarded her steadily. "Even though I pretended to be surprised, I knew there were two matching lockets. Because I saw you open the jewel case that Alfred gave you as a present."

Shock stung her. "What do you mean, you *saw* me?"

"The visions—no, the memories—unfold in my mind as if I were watching a play. In this instance, you were sitting in a wing chair in the library. I remember you holding the locket to your breast and saying, 'I'll wear mine close to my heart forever.' "

Her flesh crawled as if touched by ghostly fingers. Yet her mind scrambled to find a logical explanation. "Alfred could have told you that. Though why he would have, I can't imagine."

With a shrug, Burke reached to the bedside table and picked up her spectacles. He leaned close to her, and with a tenderness that made her chest ache, he perched the eyeglasses on her nose and tucked the earpieces behind the curve of her ears. "At the cottage, I also asked if you wear spectacles when you read."

She felt a pang, remembering that like her husband, Burke found eyeglasses unbecoming on a woman. "You made a lucky guess."

"No. I knew because once, I had a memory of seeing

you sitting in bed, reading." He glanced around. "Though it wasn't this bed. The hangings were of green velvet and the wood was gilt painted."

Her mouth dry, she whispered, "My room in the master suite. Lorena had it closed up after Alfred died."

"So I was right."

He stared at her with a strange intensity. She told herself it only was the reading glasses that made his image blurry. With trembling fingers, she removed the spectacles.

"I've seen lots of other things, too," Burke said. "That's why I came to Snow Manor in the first place, because I thought I was going mad. I kept seeing flashes of you, sitting beneath the rose arbor or reading to the Guppy children or speaking in that delightful Yorkshire accent. Once, you were walking in the portrait gallery, remarking on the fact that none of the paintings were of Snow ancestors."

Catherine shrank back against the pillows. Her mind clamored with all the odd little comments he had made to her, hinting at things he couldn't possibly have known, like the time she'd burned Alfred's cards in the fireplace. Yet skepticism warred with the persuasive proof Burke offered. "You've named things you could have learned since you came here. Though why you'd trick me like this, I don't understand."

"It does sound inconceivable," he said, sliding closer to her on the bed. "I've wrestled with the same doubts myself. But here's something I couldn't explain away. Last night, before I came to your bed, I dreamt I was making love to you. That's when I first saw the scar on your stomach. Seeing it a few moments ago only confirmed the truth, that some of Alfred's memories are locked inside my head."

Burke's expression *had* been strange as he'd touched her belly. At the time, her own mind had been gripped by the terrible memory of a horse's hoof striking her, the pain of waking up to learn she had lost her precious baby. And then she had been shaken by the impossible yearning to bear Burke's child. She had feared he might be thinking the same thing, that he would question her and learn of her flaw—that she was not a whole woman.

Shame swamped her. Unless he already knew. Perhaps he even preferred her to be infertile.

I feel as if we've done this before . . . somewhere . . . sometime.

Her blood ran icy cold. His tale had to be a disgusting hoax, a cruel prank . . . or the raving of a madman. To accept that he could peer into her most intimate memories was too shocking to bear.

Clasping her trembling hands over her breasts, she lashed out at him. "So you admit the true reason you came to my bed. To verify your own crazed imaginings."

"Believe me, Catherine, I had no other choice. One can hardly go up to a lady and ask, 'Perchance have you a scar on your stomach?' You'd have slapped my face."

She leaped out of the side of the bed farthest from him and yanked on her old gray dressing gown. Even its soft familiar folds could not soothe the agony gnawing at her. "I should slap you now for seducing me under false pretenses."

"For God's sake, it wasn't pretense. I certainly didn't have to pretend that I wanted you." His voice rang with a zeal she could no longer trust. He circled the bed and stopped before her. "Or that I want you still."

Her traitorous body ached for his touch. She couldn't believe him; she mustn't believe him. "You only wanted to use me. I should have guessed that from the start." Wildly she groped for a reason. "You're trying to prey on a grieving widow by convincing me that my husband's spirit lives on in you. Only a scoundrel could be so vile."

He stood still, his magnificent form sculpted by the clear light of dawn. "If you need more proof, I'll tell you something else I saw in my dream last night. In the midst of making love to you, Alfred got up out of bed and walked away." Burke took a step closer. "Did that ever happen, Catherine? Did your husband ever need a drink more than he needed his own wife?"

Yes, her heart cried out. *Over and over that last year.*

Turning sharply before Burke could see her tears, she stumbled to the window and gripped the sill. "He must have told you," she whispered. "He must have described our private life to you in great detail. Dear God. How could he?"

The tread of footsteps came from behind. Burke caught her shoulders and turned her to face him. "He didn't. Catherine, I swear it. Men don't speak of their failings in bed."

Fired by a sudden fury, she thrust against his bare shoulders. Caught off-guard, he staggered backward. "But they do boast of their successes," she snapped. "Is that what *you* intend to do?"

He flinched as if she'd slapped him. "I shan't honor such a question with an answer. We were speaking of Alfred's memories."

"Ah, yes. Your soul left your body and flew up to heaven, pausing on the way to learn a few choice secrets. Quite the plausible tale."

His mouth twisted in humorless irony. "I see. You think me so evil a man I'd have been singed by the fires of hell instead."

She didn't know what to think anymore. "You *are* a devil. Go. Get out of here. Stay away from me."

He bowed. "As my lady wishes. God forbid anyone should awaken early and see a seducer stealing out of your bedchamber."

Walking away, Burke picked up his dressing gown and slipped it on with studied casualness. Then without a backward glance he sauntered out the door.

She heard the click of the latch; then silence settled over the room. A gust of wind rattled the window panes.

Warmth seeped down her cold cheeks and wetness splashed onto her hands. Catherine blindly groped in her drawer for a handkerchief. She found one and pressed the crisp linen to her tears, wishing she could as easily wipe away the sickness in her soul.

Oh, Burke, that was heaven.

She had been played for a fool. Her very privacy had been invaded. All the time he had been caressing her, he must have been searching for the scar that he had seen in his dream. . . .

No. Not a dream or a memory. Alfred must have gotten drunk and confided the sordid details of their marriage bed. He must have described her body right down to the mark on her skin. She couldn't believe her husband had fallen so low. Yet he must have. *He must have.*

Because even more unthinkable was Burke's claim to spiritual intervention.

Washed by a wave of pain and frustration, Catherine flew to the bed and pounded her fists on the tangled sheets, where the scent of him still clung, still aroused her. "Vicious rascal. Trickster. Villain. I'll cheer your descent into hell."

Chapter 14

She needed desperately to be alone.

Catherine struck out over the open moor, following a rough path through an endless, pinkish-purple carpet of heather. After a brilliant dawn, the morning had turned cool and blustery. The north wind tugged at her kerseymere pelisse, and the overcast sky reflected her troubled mood. Though hours had passed, she still wavered between incredulity and trust, between anger and acceptance.

For awhile, cleanup chores had distracted her. She had directed an army of servants who even now washed hundreds of champagne glasses and china plates, swept up debris, and moved furniture back into place. The overnight guests had drifted down a few at a time to partake of a buffet breakfast in the dining parlor. Lorena and the twins had held court all morning, saying farewell to those departing. In all the confusion, Catherine had slipped out for a breath of fresh air.

She hadn't seen Burke since he had left her bedroom at dawn. According to a groom, his lordship had ridden away early on another of his mysterious expeditions.

Now, as her demi-boots kicked up pebbles on the

path, Catherine reluctantly considered their estrangement from his perspective. *If* he were telling the truth, he must be terribly wounded by her lack of confidence in him. She had rejected every word he'd said. On top of it all, she had denounced him as a devil and ordered him to stay away from her.

Yet how else could she have reacted? Did he expect her to take his amazing revelation purely on faith?

Last night, before I came to your bed, I dreamt I was making love to you.

Her cheeks burned. His voice had rung with the torment of a man who had forced himself to accept the impossible. No matter how she might scoff or accuse him of hoaxing her, Burke believed he possessed another man's memories. Memories that he had gained in an extraordinary spiritual exchange.

The firmness of his conviction rocked the foundation of her own skepticism. No longer was she so certain he was demented or determined to trick her for some nefarious purpose. If he'd wanted to delude her into thinking that her late husband's spirit lived on in him, Burke would have done so *before* they'd made love. Not after.

That left only one answer. He spoke the truth.

The moor undulated before her, wild and windswept, starkly beautiful. Here and there, a bog pool glinted like a dark mirror against the treeless landscape. The air was sweet with the scents of grass and heather and cool dampness. A kestrel glided with brown wings spread against the brooding clouds. If nature was a miracle of creation, then was it so impossible that miracles could occur in the souls of people, too?

Even as certainty soared within her own soul, Catherine cringed to think that Burke could invade her past at any time without her knowledge. To imagine him witnessing the quarrels, the gradual disintegration of her marriage, mortified her. What if he had seen that final, humiliating encounter? She swallowed the sudden sickness in her throat. The sense of violation she felt was far worse than her reaction to Fabian spying on her.

She knew why. Fabian was shy and harmless, a man to pity. Burke, on the other hand, was aggressive and fascinating, a man to admire. A man to thrill a woman's heart. A man to coax her body to flowering.

Her lack of restraint during their lovemaking still stunned Catherine. Though she had often enjoyed marital relations, nothing in her experience had prepared her for the intensity of feelings Burke had aroused in her.

Yet he had also betrayed her trust.

Troubled, she quickened her steps over the moor. He had come to her bed, driven by his hidden purpose, knowing he was looking for proof even as they had shared the exquisite closeness of intimacy, even as she had worked up her courage and asked him to have an affair. His deceit throbbed inside her like an embedded thorn.

As she crested a hill, the great weathered monolith of Resurrection Rock loomed ahead, its curious shape resembling a giant with two hands lifted to the heavens. Against her will, a soft mist of memories enfolded her. Here she had mistaken Burke for a robber and run from him. Here he had hauled her up on his horse and carried her off to the cottage in the distance. She had let down her defenses and kissed him with all the wild yearning inside herself.

That kiss had been a mere prelude to the magnificence of their lovemaking. The warmth and tenderness of his touch lingered within her as if their joining somehow had altered her forever. He had made her feel precious, cherished with the completeness of his body and soul. Even now, in defiance of all her doubts, the need for him rose from the lonely place in her heart.

"Well, well. If it isn't the younger Mrs. Snow."

The oily smooth voice with the trace of an odd accent

startled Catherine. A man stepped out from behind the huge boulder. He wore a brown coat unbuttoned over a checkered suit, and his curly-brimmed beaver hat added a dashing flare to his middle-aged attractiveness. His leathery skin told of a life spent out in the sun.

"Mr. Newberry! Where did you come from?"

"The village, of course." He cocked a leg in an old-fashioned bow. "Alas, I wasn't one of the lucky ones invited to spend the night at Snow Manor."

"I'm sure with the noise of the party, you rested more comfortably elsewhere."

"That's kind of you to say so." His voice dropped a notch. "And Lorena? How does my dear lady fare today?"

Catherine wondered at the familiarity of his address. "My mother-in-law is busy tending to the needs of her guests."

He took a step closer, leaning on his ivory cane. "And whose needs have you been tending to, m'dear?"

His blatant meaning shocked Catherine. Last night he had heard Lorena accuse her of leading Burke astray. Now, Newberry acted as if Catherine were fair game for his crude insinuations. Was this a taste of how men would treat her if the world learned of her affair with a notorious nobleman?

"I've been helping my mother-in-law, of course." Catherine cast around for an excuse to escape him. "She sent me on an errand to the village. I really must hurry along."

"One moment." Newberry caught her neatly by the arm. His fingers gripped with a wiry strength through the layers of her pelisse and sleeve. "Don't run off so quickly. I thought we might take the chance to chat a bit."

Catherine's heart tripped. To the north and east, the moor stretched out in rolling miles of desolation.

Should he try to press himself on her, the wuthering of the wind would mask her screams.

This time, she could not depend on Burke to ride to her rescue. She had only her own wits to rely upon.

Far to the west, at the edge of the moor, the village squatted like a broody hen. The needle-thin bell tower of the church pierced the gray sky, and a flash of silver marked the serpentine course of the beck. She had come out here to be alone, but suddenly the company of people appealed to her.

"Sir," she said, deftly withdrawing from Newberry's hold, "I never meant to offend you. Indeed, if you'd care to escort me to the village, we can talk on the way. Unless of course you had other plans."

"None that can't be changed. I only came up here to have a look at the famous landmark rock. I'm a traveler, visiting the sights hereabouts."

Why did she imagine deeper shades of meaning to his words? As they started along the scree-strewn trail, curiosity outweighed her scruples. "How do you know my mother-in-law?"

"Me and Lorena go back a long way. She was a fine-looking female in her time. We were quite close once, if you catch my meaning."

His vulgarity made Catherine all the warier. Was he bragging? Or had Lorena truly engaged in an affair with this stranger who dressed like a gentleman, yet betrayed a lack of refinement in his speech? "I'm afraid she's never mentioned you."

" 'Twas a tragic event that tore us apart. But I did love her. I was ready to devote my life to her."

"Truly?" Catherine said in surprise.

"Aye." For a moment his eyes softened, and he stared at the horizon as if lost in memories too painful to share. Then he clapped his hand over his breast and grinned. "I've never forgotten my precious jewel. She's kept my heart imprisoned all these long years."

Quite possibly he was a footman or valet who had dallied with the young lady of the house, and then had been sent packing. Catherine knew little about Lorena's upbringing, beyond that her parents had owned a modest estate in Norfolk. Upon their death, she had sold the property, married Alfred's father, and borne him three children.

No wonder she had acted nervous last night, so obedient when Newberry commanded her. She would hardly wish to make known the reappearance of a past indiscretion.

"Pardon my bluntness," Catherine said, "but Lorena has been widowed for many years. She's shown no interest in romantic attachments."

"Ah, there's the rub of it. Somehow I've got to get back into her good graces." Ezekiel Newberry cast a sly, sidelong glance at her. "I've a notion you could help me."

Uneasy with the turn of conversation, Catherine walked faster across the moor. "I hardly think my speaking to her would accomplish anything."

"Talking ain't what I had in mind. My plan was to stir up her jealousy."

"Her jealousy?"

Another grin flashed across his face, crinkling the skin at the corners of his blue eyes. "Aye. She'd be quick to notice if she thought you and me were carrying on together."

Revulsion crept through Catherine. Thank heavens they neared the dry stone wall that marked the beginning of pastureland and civilization. "That's out of the question."

"Come now, where's the spirit of generosity in you? The ruse won't take much effort. We'd just have to pretend a bit, let her catch us kissing, maybe touching each other. Like so."

With the swiftness of a fox, he lunged, his hands delving inside her pelisse and roughly fondling her breasts.

Catherine screamed. Thrusting him away, she flung herself backward and heard the tortured ripping of fabric. Her bodice gaped open, exposing part of her muslin chemise.

Newberry curled his lips in feral amusement. "There now. That should get a reaction out of the bitch."

Driven by fear and loathing, Catherine ran. A gust of wind hurled the scornful salute of his laughter in her wake. Then she could hear only the rushing of air against her ears, the thudding of her feet, the hiss of her breathing. She could feel only the imprint of his hands besmirching her, making a mockery of the caresses that had felt so beautiful with Burke.

She ran until her chest hurt, on across the humped bridge and down the high street of the village. The Guppy house. She would find safety there.

She dodged a horse-drawn cart, then a clutch of housewives gossiping in front of the gabled inn. A barking dog loped along beside her until the scent of the butcher's shop lured him away.

Catherine dashed past the graveyard, then the stone church. Beyond loomed her haven, the three-story vicarage with smoke drifting from the stone chimney. A black horse was tethered to the iron fence.

Burke was *here?*

Even as she flew up the front steps, the door opened and he walked out, donning his riding gloves. At his heels tagged Peter Guppy.

Uttering a cry of relief, Catherine cast herself at Burke. His arms enclosed her in the sweetest of embraces. His warmth chased away the coldness inside her and made her feel clean again. The steady beating of his heart thrummed against her ear.

He caught her face in his gloved hands and tenderly

tilted it up toward him. His black brows were cocked in startlement. "Catherine, darling. What's wrong?"

Her mind was so awhirl that she barely heeded his endearment. "He's out there," she babbled. "On the moor."

His expression darkened. "Who is? Who put you in such a state?"

"It must be Sir Jervis Pendleton! Don't worry, Mrs. Cathy, I'll defend thee." Peter Guppy punched the air, first with his right fist, then his left. "His lordship's been teaching me the finer points of pugilism."

"He has?" Pulled from the numb state of fright, she blinked at Burke. "I thought we agreed he's too young to be fighting."

"Every lad needs to know how to defend himself. Run along now, Peter. I want to speak to Mrs. Cathy alone."

Peter argued, "But I can help—"

"Go."

He hung his tow-haired head. "Aye, m'lord."

When the door closed behind the boy, Burke held her at arm's length. "Your bodice is torn," he said in a strange, hard voice. "Who did this to you?"

"A man named Ezekiel Newberry. He's an acquaintance of Lorena's." The horror of the incident washed over Catherine again, weakening her knees, making her glad for Burke's support.

"Tell me what happened."

"I met him while I was walking on the moor. He wanted to talk, and I saw no harm in that. Then . . ." She hesitated, seeing no purpose in revealing Lorena's checkered past.

"Then what?"

"Newberry professed to having a regard for Lorena. He wanted to make her jealous. By using me. He grabbed me, but I ran."

She shuddered anew, and Burke held her tightly against him, his fingers massaging away the knots of tension in her back. Strange, how she could feel so protected in the arms of the man who had come to her bed to pursue his secret goal of proving his memories. The man who could peer into the private agonies and ecstasies of her marriage.

After a moment, he drew the pelisse together to conceal her damaged gown. His arm around her shoulders, he guided her to the Guppy's door. "Wait for me inside."

"Where are you going?"

"To have a word with Newberry."

A devil darkness burned in his eyes. His tight expression of fury alarmed her. "Let him be, Burke. I won't let him bother me anymore."

"What do you take me for? A coward who can't defend you?"

"Of course not. But—"

"Just stay here. I'll settle the matter once and for all."

He opened the door and gave her a little push inside. The latch clicked shut. She found herself standing in the tiny, dim foyer of the Guppy household. From the library came the high-spirited noise of children chattering, punctuated by shrieks of laughter. From the kitchen drifted the yeasty aroma of baking bread and the heavier scent of sizzling sausages.

Leaning against the tall casement clock, she took several deep, steadying breaths. The familiar sounds and smells soothed her raw nerves, and the quaking inside her gradually subsided. Burke would handle Newberry; she needn't think about that horrid man anymore.

The realization slowly dawned on her. She planned to move out and live as an independent woman. But as always she was letting someone else fight her battles. She was bowing to Burke's authority.

Never again.

She opened the door and marched outside. Clouds hung low over the cozy village with its single dirt street lined by shops and thatched-roof cottages. Burke was nowhere in sight.

Buttoning her pelisse securely, Catherine walked briskly along the road, peering ahead for a tall man on a black horse. Several people hailed her. No doubt they were curious about her earlier headlong dash through the village. She spoke only a quick greeting in her haste to intervene before Burke engaged Newberry in a senseless bout of fisticuffs.

The more she thought about the reality of bloodshed, the faster Catherine walked. She must make Burke see that this was her conflict, and she would resolve the matter peaceably.

Emerging from the village, she saw his horse grazing the grasses alongside the stream. In the middle of the arched bridge, the two men stood face to face, Burke towering over the smaller man.

As she hurried closer, Newberry bared his teeth in a smile. "M'lord, I told you what happened, that the chit provoked me."

Burke seized the man by his starched neckcloth. His hat and cane tumbled to the ground. "Liar," he said, his voice steely soft. "You'll die for touching the lady."

"Let me go," Newberry choked out.

"Only when I'm through with you."

There was no mistaking the dangerous resolve on Burke's face. His defense of her honor caused an unbidden thrill to trickle through Catherine. Yet she seized hold of his arm. "You'll kill no one on my behalf."

His sharp glance sliced into her. "Would you let the villain go free to bully you again? What if he assaults someone from the village? One of the Guppy children, perchance?"

The question gave her pause. She tried to keep her voice calm. "You're leaping to conclusions. Besides, violence never solved anything."

"Listen to the lady, m'lord. You're making too much of a fuss over a misunderstanding."

Burke yanked Newberry up so that his shoes dangled a few inches above the bridge. "Misunderstanding, you say? I'd call it a fatal error."

A strangled squeak issued from Newberry's mouth. The dark tan of his face took on a purplish cast. His hands clawed at Burke's but to no avail.

Catherine launched herself at Burke. "Stop it! I said, I don't need you to fight for me."

He flashed a furious look at her that she countered with a glare of her own. The corded muscles in his neck revealed the strain he exerted to hold Newberry. "Let me be the judge of that," Burke said through gritted teeth. "The insult to you shan't go unavenged."

"I'll handle the matter in my own way. And *I* will settle for an apology. So let him down. Now."

Newberry's pitiful gurgles filled the silence. Then Burke said, "Very well."

In one mighty heave, he tossed Newberry over the bridge and into the beck. A loud splash sounded, followed by a startled yelp.

Gasping, Catherine ran to the side and peered over the low stone wall. Newberry sat waist-deep in water, his arms and legs sprawled out, his eyes rounded in an almost comical expression of surprise.

Burke dusted off his hands. "Well, aren't you proud of me? I managed to restrain myself. He's still alive."

For once, Catherine was speechless. She was too busy swallowing the laughter that bubbled up inside her. Even the stream seemed to chuckle as it flowed over the rocks.

Like a drowned rat, Newberry scuttled up the embankment, his ruined suit dripping. He shook his fist at Burke, who stood on the bridge. "Bastard," he croaked.

"You aren't the first to wish me so," Burke said. "But

save your insults. The lady would like to hear her apology now."

Newberry slogged over the paving stones of the bridge, snatched up his beaver hat, and jammed it on his head. His voice still rusty, he said, "I most humbly beg your forgiveness, Mrs. Snow."

"The affair is closed, then," Catherine said. "I trust we can all behave in a civil manner from now on."

"Mr. Newberry will do better than behave," Burke said. "He's going to collect his belongings and leave Yorkshire altogether."

The two men glowered at each other for a tense moment.

Then Newberry shrugged and picked up his cane. "I'm practical enough to admit I took a bite out of the wrong biscuit. G'day, Mrs. Snow." Leaving a trail of wet drops, he set off into the village, his water-logged shoes squeaking.

"Let's hope it's not a mistake to let him go," Burke said.

Catherine turned to him, her skirt swishing around her ankles. "How dare you speak of mistakes. You could have broken his neck, pitching him in that shallow water. Murder is a sin."

"I saw you almost smile."

She planted her hands on her hips. "I'm far from smiling. You cannot correct one wrong by committing another."

"But I *can* force the bully to think twice before he accosts you again."

Burke's protectiveness warmed her inside and out. She released an exasperated breath. "Oh, why are we quarreling? What matters is that you were solving my problems without my permission."

"Newberry is more than a mere problem." Burke stopped pacing, his eyebrows lowered as if he were mulling over a mystery. A faraway look in his eyes, he stood very still for a long moment. Then he blinked and focused on her again. "He knew Alfred."

At first she didn't follow Burke's line of reasoning. Then her stomach tensed. "Do you mean you *saw* Newberry? In one of your visions?"

"Only a glimpse." The distracted look on Burke's face sharpened into a keen scrutiny of her. In a lowered voice, he asked, "Does this mean you believe me now?"

A curlew trilled a song from the reeds on the embankment. Catherine's heart skipped a beat as she struggled for an answer.

"I believe you've seen things that defy another explanation." She swallowed uneasily. "Strange as your version of the truth may be, it's less disgusting than to think that Alfred gossiped about me."

"He never spoke ill of you," Burke said tonelessly. "I know that he cherished you."

His expression might have been sculpted of stone. Her throat closed on a rush of frustration. *And what of you?* she wanted to ask. *Do you cherish me? Could you, if I gave you the chance?*

"Alfred would not have wanted you to peer into our private times together," she said. "I must ask that you stop doing so."

"I can't control what I see, Catherine."

"You'll have to try. I won't have you scrutinizing my past."

He shook his head impatiently. "Be they curse or blessing, the memories surface without any prompting from me. This isn't some cheap carnival trick that I can manipulate at will." Then the tightness of anger slipped from his face. Burke sank onto the low wall of the bridge and stretched out his booted legs. "However . . ."

"However?"

"I was just thinking," he said slowly, "that certain objects *have* triggered a memory. Such as the first time I saw you wearing your locket."

Her blood ran cold. What would he see next? Would he notice the phaeton in the stables and recall that impetuous trip to Gretna Green, when she had been the starry-eyed innocent? Would he spy a silver inkpot and remember the time she had hurled it at Alfred, barely missing his head? Would he see the doctor pronounce her incapable of bearing a child? Worst of all, would Burke see her so desperate for a family that she had groveled at Alfred's feet?

The very thought threw her into a panic. The closer she let Burke get to her, the greater the risk of sparking a memory of her most private moments. She must end their association right here and now.

Yet in spite of her resolution, she wanted to kiss him, to postpone her own dreams and revel in bodily joy with him, however fleeting it might be.

Desire and revulsion and uncertainty wrenched at her. She forced herself to say, "I want you to leave tomorrow, as you'd originally planned."

Something flashed in his eyes. Surprise? Anger? Before she could read the emotion, the shuttered look came over his face again, and Burke rose to his feet. "And if I refuse?"

"I can't force you to go. But know that I *have* changed my mind about us. Certainly you can see why an affair is impossible now."

"No, I can't." His gaze wandered to her breasts and then lower, as if he were remembering all the places he had kissed her. "Last night, we found heaven together. You felt it, too."

She wove her fingers together to hide their trembling. "That was before I knew the real reason you came to my bed. You were searching for a telltale scar."

"Don't delude yourself. It was true at first, yes, but there's no denying the bond between us."

"You feel lust," she insisted. "So go back to London and find yourself a more willing woman. Perhaps Stella Sexton is now available."

She heard the cruel lash of her words, yet if she called them back, she might betray the depths of her own longing.

He stood silent a moment, slapping his riding gloves against the palm of his hand. His eyes were the color of rainclouds, she noted irrelevantly, a soft and moody gray. Eyes that could arouse her with just one look.

"There's something I haven't told you about my experience when I nearly died." He stepped closer to her, so close that she fancied she could smell the musky scent of his skin. "While my spirit was in that tunnel of light, I heard a woman's voice calling to me, drawing me away from the brilliance and back to earth."

"What is that supposed to mean?"

"It was *your* voice, Catherine."

"I called you down from heaven?" She tensed, staring at him. "That's the height of absurdity. We had never even met."

"I admit, you didn't speak my name. But I distinctly remember you saying, 'Don't leave me. Please don't leave me.' "

With a piercing ache below her breastbone, she recalled herself making that very entreaty to Alfred the last time she had seen him. She had gone into his bedchamber, clad in her sheerest nightgown, only to find her husband packing his valise.

No! Burke mustn't remember that humbling experience. "You suffered a delusion," she asserted. "There can be no other explanation."

"I know what I heard." Reaching out, he tenderly cupped her cheek in his warm palm. His eyes glowed with the intensity of conviction. "Deny it all you like, Catherine, but it's you who kept me from dying. It's you who brought me back to life. And I won't walk away from you now."

Chapter 15

Burke cast a glance over his shoulder. Chairs and statuary and urns stood sentinel against the paneled walls of the passageway. At this hour, Lorena and her giggly daughters should be dressing for dinner. And Catherine, too, he hoped.

From his pocket he produced an ornate iron key, filched from the spare ring kept in the steward's room. He fitted the key into the lock and the bolt clicked.

Picking up the lighted candle from a side table, he hesitated a moment. This was the one place at Snow Manor he had avoided since his arrival nearly a fortnight ago. But his latest memory called for decisive action.

Opening the door, he stepped into Alfred's bedchamber.

The air was musty and surprisingly chilly. Burke steeled himself for an overwhelming jolt of familiarity. Instead, he felt only a faint stirring inside himself, the eerie impression of memories hovering at the edge of his mind, eluding his grasp.

He closed the door and held the candle aloft. The circle of light wavered over a room of grand proportions. At the far end, ice-blue draperies hid a bank of windows. White covers shrouded chairs and ottomans. Painted Cupids and clouds cavorted across the shadowed ceiling. Dominating the room was a poster bed hung with blue-and-white striped silk.

He wondered if Alfred had ever made love to Catherine there. Or if he had always gone to her adjoining room to claim his marital due. Burke pictured her lying with her sable hair spread out on the pillows, her eyes glowing with passion and love, her arms lifted in wifely welcome.

Damning himself for feeling an ugly jab of jealousy, Burke decided it somehow was more painful to picture her fully clothed and chatting with her husband, sharing a companionable laugh or two, exchanging details of their lives with the comfortable intimacy of a married couple. Except that, strangely, he never saw them doing so in his visions. What had their marriage been like after he had thrown temptation at Alfred in the form of Stella Sexton?

Burke grimaced. How Catherine must have hated him. Even now, she withheld the fullness of her trust. He couldn't blame her. Coming so close to death had turned his life around—and yet he wondered if she was right to doubt him. Was the change in him lasting, or would he eventually slip back into his old ways?

Unable to answer the question, he walked about the room, touching a box of cigars, then a clock that had long stopped ticking. The mere act of accepting the memories didn't mean he would be inundated with them. He possessed no gypsy's crystal ball that would conjure up images at will.

Yet he had come here to Alfred's suite for that very purpose. He hoped to trigger a memory of Ezekiel Newberry.

Burke felt the rise of a murderous rage, a violence that simmered inside him, dark and hot and corrosive.

With effort, he restrained his emotions. He must think clearly.

When he'd caught up to Newberry after the attack on Catherine, the satisfied grin on the man's face had sparked the flash of a scene. Burke had recalled a time when those lips had been curled just so, speaking words that echoed from the dark reaches of the past: *Mind your promise, or all Society will learn the truth.*

That was it. A threat and nothing more. But the fleeting memory had revealed a troublesome fact.

Alfred had known Newberry.

Not only that, the man had possessed a hold over Alfred. What truth did Alfred want to hide? Something so damning it could have ruined him?

Burke walked slowly past the bed, attuning his senses to anything that might inspire a reaction. Unlike Catherine's bedroom, there wasn't a book in sight, not even in the mahogany secretaire. The glass doors revealed a row of crystal decanters that likely contained Alfred's favorite brandy. How different the husband and wife had been, Alfred with his craving for diversions and glittering nightlife, and Catherine who valued books more than new gowns and fancy parties.

Suppressing a hollow sense of loss, Burke examined the opened secretaire. On the blotter rested a tray of quill pens and a silverplate jack for melting sealing wax. Except for a fine layer of dust, the setting looked as if its owner had stepped away for a moment.

As if he were still present somewhere in the house.

A draught of cold air whispered across Burke's neck. The bedcurtains swayed slightly. As he started to turn back around, he spied the figure of a man standing in the shadows across the room.

On reflex, he spun toward the man. "Who . . . ?"

The question died on his tongue. He was gazing at his own dark reflection in an oval-framed pier glass.

Shaking his head, Burke set his candle on the desk.

He'd have to be mad to start imagining ghosts. Methodically he sorted through the papers stashed in the cubbyholes. A few duns. An invitation to a dance dated a fortnight before Alfred's death. An outdated list of horses for auction at Tattersall's.

And a torn-off corner of stationery with a scrawled message: *EN—Friday.*

EN. Ezekiel Newberry? Had Alfred set up a meeting time?

Burke rubbed the paper with his thumbs, closed his eyes, and focused his mind on the note. *Friday. EN. Friday.*

Nothing. No throbbing in his head. No involuntary tightening of his skin. No stirring of memory. Only the nagging impression that he knew something vital.

But what?

He tucked the scrap into his pocket. Perhaps Catherine could shed some light on the note. In the meantime, he concentrated on putting together the pieces of the puzzle.

We'll be ruined, Lorena had told her son in another memory. *We must pay him off somehow. . . .*

Newberry again, no doubt.

While going over the account books, Burke had noticed large sums from the estate revenues were missing during the final year of Alfred's life. Had he been settling a gaming debt owed to Newberry?

Alfred had kept to himself a great deal during the months before Waterloo. While others rolled the dice or dealt the cards, he sat in the background and drank with an air of quiet desperation, refusing to discuss what ailed him. No one in their circle of acquaintances had pressed him for a reason; every gentleman had an embarrassment of his own to hide—an undesirable relation, a pregnant mistress, a penchant for sodomy or other deviant practices. Burke had assumed Alfred was regretting his impetuous marriage to an unsuitable female, that his common wife had made his life a living hell.

If only Burke had known then what he knew now. Catherine was an angel. If she refused to come to London, it was only because during her one visit, she had witnessed the debauchery put on by Burke himself.

With effort he focused his mind on another of Alfred's memories. *He was nothing but a fraud. Yet he must go on living a lie, else destroy his family.*

Alfred had thought that about himself even while making love to Catherine. His despair had been so profound that he had abandoned his wife while he stumbled off in search of a drink.

But would a man who had lost money gambling think of himself as a *fraud?* A wastrel, perhaps. Or a fool. He hadn't bankrupted the estate, after all. The revenues were sufficient to keep his mother and his sisters in silks and lace.

Lost in thought, Burke wandered to the bedside table, where he uncorked a small jar and sniffed the pungent contents. Tincture of opium. Whatever the source of Alfred's melancholy, it had caused him to suffer from sleeplessness, too.

Burke set down the jar with an unsteady hand. Perhaps if he had not been so bent on fleeing his own demons, he might have pried the truth out of Alfred and helped him resolve his problem. His friend might have remained behind the battle lines, a drunken sot, but alive at least.

Catherine would still be a devoted wife. Not a grieving widow.

And Burke would never have made love to her.

In seducing Catherine, he had broken his vow to protect her, a vow made in blood to a dying man. For the rest of his life, he would live with that black mark of shame on his soul. Yet he wouldn't trade the memory of loving Catherine for an eternity in the tunnel of light.

Because it was *his* memory. Not one that came from the spirit world.

Something glinted in the gloom beneath the bed. Burke reached down into a nest of dustballs and plucked out a button. Larger than his thumbnail, the brass circle dangled several broken green threads. He knew this button.

A pounding started in his temples. His skin prickled and his muscles tensed. Yes! On a rush of elation, he opened his mind to the mystical memory.

In the doorway stood Catherine, clad in a thin nightdress that showed the shadows of her fine curves. He knew why she had come, and he felt the searing regret of having to disappoint her again.

Her eyes widened as she spied the opened valise on his bed, then the overcoat he wore. "You're returning to London tonight?"

He turned away, unable to bear the hurt on her face, and consumed by the greater pain inside himself. "Yes."

"But . . . why?"

He strode to the secretaire, seized the decanter, and splashed brandy into his glass. A long drink spread a false warmth through him. "I've an appointment on Friday."

Her footsteps padded toward him. She pressed herself to him, sliding her hands over his coat. "Take me with you. Please."

Her beauty stirred him. God forbid she should find out how easily he could ruin her, his mother, his sisters, himself. "No."

"Then at least come to bed." Her voice grew softer now. "You know how I want to have your baby. If only we try again . . ."

"No! It's useless. You know that as well as I."

He pushed her away, but with a sob she clung to his coat. A button went flying, striking the floor and rolling away.

She slid slowly to her knees and tilted her tear-wet face up to him. "Don't leave me. Please don't leave me."

The image wavered and vanished. Burke came back to an awareness of the musty bedroom and the metal button pressed into his palm. It wasn't the memory he had come here to find.

This one was more disturbing.

He had witnessed something extremely private, a scene Catherine would be appalled to reveal to anyone. She had had to beg her husband to make love to her, to give her a child. Even then Alfred had refused her, humiliating her in the process.

Damn him.

In a rush of fury, Burke hurled the button at the bed. The brass flashed in the feeble light of the candle, pinged against the headboard, and plopped onto the dusty pillow. But he couldn't hate his friend for long. Alfred had already paid for his sins.

No wonder Catherine's face had paled when Burke had spoken to her on the bridge. He'd told her that her voice had drawn him down from the light and back inside his body. *Don't leave me. Please don't leave me.*

She had known those words came from that wrenching memory. And she dreaded the moment when he would know, too. For that reason, he had no intention of ever revealing his knowledge.

But it made him all the more determined to woo her. He would win her heart. He would convince her to marry him. And then he would make damned sure he got her pregnant.

Catherine tapped the tines of her fork against her crystal water glass. Rising to her feet, she mastered the tension that tangled her insides. She had to speak now before the footmen returned to clear the dessert dishes.

"Excuse me, ladies and gentlemen. I have an announcement to make."

Everyone at the dining table turned to her. Fabian paused in the act of slipping a morsel to Lady, who hid beneath the table. Prudence and Priscilla stopped giggling and peered around the silver candelabra. At one end of the table Lorena glared with her mouth agape. And at the other end, Burke leaned back in his chair, his disturbing gaze focused on Catherine.

Even now, she felt a weakening surge of desire for him. His formal black coat and white cravat enhanced his devilish good looks. Throughout dinner, she had caught him studying her intently as if he were planning how to lure her into his bed, just as he'd promised to do.

But she had no time for the self-indulgence of an affair. In a moment, he'd realize why.

Lorena clinked her spoon into her scraped-clean pudding bowl. "What is the meaning of this? You interrupted my conversation with his lordship."

"Then I must ask that you finish your talk later." Over her mother-in-law's gasp, Catherine forged on: "While all of us are gathered here, I wanted to say that shortly I'll be leaving this household. Tomorrow I'll begin looking for a home of my own."

"A home of your—" Lorena's face turned pasty white as if the news alarmed her. Over the ticking of the mantel clock, her breathing sounded half-strangled. "That is outrageous. Unthinkable. You can't move out of this house."

"I don't wish to cause any ill feelings. Yet it's time for me to make my own life."

"You'll leave us in the lurch," Lorena accused. "Who will guide the servants at their tasks? Who will tend to the marketing and the mending?"

"Who will read to me at bedtime?" Priscilla demanded.

"Who will fix my hair?" Prudence wailed, patting her golden coiffure. "My maid always botches my curls."

Catherine's heart sank. It hurt to think they were

more concerned about losing her services than bidding farewell to a dear relative. "You can advertise for a French abigail. And a housekeeper as well."

"Balderdash." Lorena's nostrils flared. "I forbid you to go. You are putting us to needless expense, all because of a whim."

" 'Tis no whim. I've considered this move for a very long time." Catherine braced herself to reveal the dream that had sustained her hopes through the darkest hours. In a husky voice, she added, "In my new house, I plan to open a school. A free school so that every child in the county can learn to read and cipher."

She couldn't resist glancing at Burke. He sat watching her, his head cocked to the side, his chin propped in his hand. His bland expression gave away little of his reaction.

Did he see now? If he refused to leave Snow Manor, then *she* would go. It was just as well. She had been drifting along like a leaf tossed by the breeze. Burke had forced her to feel again, to *want.* And he had given her the means to attain her dreams.

"You, a teacher?" Priscilla said, her lip curled. "Why would anyone waste all day instructing little brats who are too stupid to learn anything?"

"Being a commoner does not make one a half-wit," Catherine retorted. "All children deserve the chance to learn and grow and broaden their minds."

"But how will you afford a house?" Prudence asked. "Mummy, she hasn't any money, has she?"

Lorena pinched her lips so that whiteness bracketed the corners. "We have a guest present. This is neither the time nor the place to discuss financial matters."

"Ah, but there's nothing like a vulgar discussion at the dinner table." Burke lifted his wine glass. "Go on, tell them. They're bound to find out sooner or later."

Lorena's pudgy hands pressed against the linen tablecloth, and the candlelight glinted off the diamond rings on her fingers. With a show of reluctance, she said, "Catherine has demanded a share of my dower right."

"But that's impossible!" Priscilla burst out. "She has no claim to our money."

"How will we buy gowns for our London Season?" Prudence cried. "I must have no less than thirty dresses in the latest fashion."

"Girls, girls! We will discuss our funds another time." As the twins settled into sullen silence, Lorena aimed a sour look at Catherine. "Do you see the turmoil caused by your selfish plans? You simply cannot go off and live unchaperoned."

"It is perfectly respectable for a widow to own a house."

"The neighbors will think ill of the arrangement. There will be talk all over Yorkshire and beyond."

"The gossip will die down soon enough. Especially when people see there is nothing the least bit improper about my living arrangements."

"I don't know what's come over you," Lorena fretted. "My darling Freddie would never have wished you to run off and leave us. How like you to disgrace his memory."

She lifted her napkin to dab at her eyes. With her mouth downturned, she looked so woebegone that Catherine felt a spurt of guilt. But she had known her mother-in-law long enough to recognize when tears were used as a ploy.

"Alfred is no longer my husband," Catherine said gently. "I make my own decisions now."

"Well!" Throwing down her napkin, Lorena glowered at Fabian. "What of you, Nephew? Don't sit there like a clod-pate. As head of this family, you must order her to stop this mad plan. Tell her that we cannot manage without her."

Fabian slouched in his chair and cast a heartfelt look

at Catherine. "I-I cannot like to see you go. Please, w-won't you stay?"

His sincere entreaty swayed her more than all of Lorena's arguments combined. Yet Catherine could not permit herself to turn back now.

"I'm sorry, but my mind is firm. There is nothing anyone can say to make me change my plans."

"Obstinate chit." Lorena pushed back her chair, and the legs scraped the carpet. "Such ingratitude. After all I've done for you. Raising you out of the gutter, turning you into a lady, enduring your country manners."

Catherine flinched as her last illusions of belonging to this family were shattered. Yet she held her chin high. "I always did my best to be a credit to Alfred."

"Then you've failed miserably. Perhaps it is a blessing that you never bore a child. Your common blood would have tainted the baby, too—"

"Enough." Burke rose from his chair, flattened his palms on the table, and glared down the length of white linen at Lorena. "I've endured your tirade out of respect for Catherine's desire to handle this matter herself. But if you say one more word against her, I shall stuff your napkin down your gullet."

"My dear lord!" Lorena gave a nervous laugh, and her hand fluttered to her mountainous bosom. "I never meant to offend you. It was imprudent of me to allow you to witness our sordid quarrels. But you've become so much a part of this family that I quite forgot your presence."

He regarded his hostess for a moment of grim silence. By degrees, a hard smile transformed his face into the heart-melting rake. "How gracious you are, Mrs. Snow. I have indeed felt welcome here. I trust you won't mind if I extend my visit for another week."

"Oh, that would be marvelous! Don't you think so, girls? His lordship shall remain our honored guest."

As he reduced her mother-in-law to babbling gratitude, Catherine wilted into her chair. The flood of pleasure she'd felt when Burke had leaped to her defense was dammed by the realization that he was staying, after all. Her announcement hadn't deterred him in the least.

Early the next morning, Catherine borrowed the pony cart and started her search for a suitable house. She had traveled no farther than the stone gatehouse when hoofbeats pounded the drive behind her.

Astride his black gelding, Burke drew up alongside her, and common sense told her to send him off with a tart dismissal. But he looked breathtakingly magnificent in buff riding breeches that outlined his muscular thighs, a military blue jacket that spanned his broad shoulders, and a snowy neckcloth that set off his bronzed skin. As usual he was hatless, and the breeze had already blown his hair into rakish disarray.

He leaned toward her, his hands loose around the reins. In the sunlight, his eyes twinkled silver with tiny sparks of green. "You left without me, Mrs. Snow. I confess, I'm wounded to the quick."

"Since you weren't invited," she retorted sweetly, "how could I have known to wait for you?"

"Nevertheless I'm here. And I'm all yours."

Her heart took a joyful leap, which she disciplined at once. "Certainly you have more fascinating things to do than to tramp through dusty houses all day."

"Name one thing more fascinating than you."

The lambent look on his face ignited a slow heat that spread through her midsection. "On behalf of your hostess, I can name two. Prudence and Priscilla."

He threw back his head and laughed. "So, you have a sense of humor today. That bodes well for our house-hunting."

He spoke as if they were husband and wife, seeking a quiet country home in which to settle down and raise a family. Irked by the appealing image, she snapped the reins and the pony started plodding down the dirt road.

It was hopeless to think Burke could be dissuaded. Sure enough, he rode alongside the cart. "Where will you start looking?" he asked.

"I'm driving to West Scrafton to meet with a house agent. He has a listing of the residences available in the area."

"Then you'll need me to examine the purchase agreement."

"I'm perfectly capable of handling the matter myself."

"Catherine, exactly how much experience have you had with legal contracts?"

She hesitated, then with a sigh, admitted, "None. But I can certainly read. No one's going to deceive me."

He raised his eyebrows. "I trust you brought your spectacles."

"Right here." She patted her reticule, then made a shooing gesture at him. "So you can ride away in good conscience. Go wherever it is you go all day."

His big mount easily kept pace with her pony. "Sheep," he said, over the clatter of the cart wheels.

"Pardon?"

She looked over at him, then wished she hadn't. Lord, he could make her heart tumble when he smiled. Today he seemed determined to charm her, and she was equally determined not to let him realize how well he succeeded.

"I've spent the past fortnight looking over rams in the interest of improving my flock," he said. "Particularly the Haslingden, one of the oldest breeds in these parts."

She glanced at him, curiosity rising in her. "You really do raise sheep?"

"Hard to believe, isn't it? Of late, I've become rather intrigued by the little beasts. Don't tell any of my London friends, though. This might just be a passing fancy."

"I won't." She spoke off-handedly so he wouldn't

guess at her amazement. Was he teasing her or not? "Have you always taken an interest in business matters?"

"Only this past year." Grinning, he waggled his eyebrows. "It keeps me out of trouble."

He went on to relate stories he'd heard about digging out sheep that had been buried in snow during a freak winter storm, about the ewe that had to be tricked into fostering an orphaned spring lamb, about the importance of mollycoddling the rams prior to tupping time. Catherine found herself totally absorbed by his animated facial expressions, by his eloquent descriptions. Here was yet another side to Burke Grisham, one that endeared him to her more than charming compliments and impassioned kisses.

But he himself admitted that his interest in sheep was only a whim. He would grow bored and return to his profligate life in London.

Even so, she couldn't stop glancing at him, marveling again at the splendor of his form. She had lain awake most of the night, half the time wishing he were there beside her, the other half combing her memory for all the intensely private moments of her marriage that he might invade without her permission.

But now, in the vivid light of day, her worries blew away on the breeze. The late August morning bloomed bright and balmy, the hedges and hills alive with birdsong and wildflowers. Green pastures formed a patchwork with fields shorn from haying. The sweet scent of grass and clean air refreshed her senses. As the cart jolted along, she tilted her head and let the sunshine warm the cold places inside her.

On such a beautiful morning it seemed silly to fret over possible embarrassments. Letting Burke accompany her today might be the wiser choice; being away from Snow Manor reduced the chances of triggering a significant memory in him. And the sooner she moved out, the sooner he would give up on her.

Catherine ignored her empty sense of regret. Even though she enjoyed being with him, the fanciful longings of a girl lay behind her. She was twenty-three, older and wiser now, and finally making her dream a reality. In a way, she owed a debt of gratitude to Burke. By prying into her personal affairs, he had prodded her awake from a long sleep. Thanks to him, she could buy a house, purchase supplies, and organize a school. If she made haste, she might even have everything ready by the time harvest was over and the farm children in the area would be free to attend classes.

A surprisingly companionable hour later, she and Burke reached West Scrafton, a quaint oasis of a village perched amid rocky crags and desolate moorland. Trees shaded a tiny green, and hollyhocks flourished in cottage gardens. Catherine guided the ponycart to a two-story house in the middle of town, where a small, gold-lettered sign beside the door proclaimed, SIMON L. HAREWOOD, ESQ., SOLICITOR/LAND AGENT.

At Burke's knock, Mr. Harewood opened the door himself. The agent was a fussy little man, as round as he was tall, and clad in a tweed overcoat and top hat. "May I be of assistance?"

Burke introduced them. "Mrs. Snow is looking for a house to purchase."

"Oh, bother. I'm due to advise Lady Sedgwick on a legal matter at eleven o'clock on the dot." Harewood snapped open his gold pocketwatch and peered importantly at it. "If you'd care to wait, my housekeeper will serve refreshments. I am sure to return by one sharp."

Disappointed, Catherine said, "Thank you, that would be most kind—"

"But we already have plans for luncheon," Burke smoothly cut in. "We'll meet you here afterwards."

He took her by the arm and escorted her outside. She

waited until the door closed before pinning him with a suspicious glare. "Plans, m'lord?"

He grinned. "Why confine ourselves to a gloomy house on such a glorious day?"

She could think of a dozen reasons why, first and foremost that she felt safer chaperoned by servants. Did he hope to set up a romantic encounter? Yet his good mood infected her with recklessness. "Why, indeed?" she murmured.

He left his horse tethered in the shade and joined her on the small seat of the pony cart, their thighs pressed close out of necessity. On their way out of the village, he ducked into a public house and emerged shortly with a farmer's basket, lashing it to the back. Then he guided the cart along a rutted road through the trees.

They spoke of inconsequential things—the scenery, the wildlife, the weather—yet to Catherine, each moment glistened. Every time he smiled, she remembered the flavor of his kisses; every time he moved his hands, she recalled the sensations they had wrought on her skin; every time he spoke, she thought of the sweet seductive praise he had whispered while making love to her.

She was secretly glad she had worn her prettiest gown today, a willow-green muslin trimmed with eggshell lace, and a matching bonnet. After wearing unrelieved black for more than a year, she loved the freedom in laying aside her mourning garb, for the time had come for her to live again.

They found the perfect picnic place in the dappled shade near a stream. Reeds grew along the stony bank, and a brilliant blue damsel-fly skimmed the surface of the water. A speckled trout leaped at the insect, forming a silver arc in the sunshine, then plopping into the beck.

Burke dropped the basket, stepped to the embankment, and studied the water. "Curse it. The perfect spot to ply a rod, and here I am without one."

"You're an angler?" she asked, still trying to reconcile the country gentleman with the London rake.

"Whenever I can spare a moment." He knelt beside her and took hold of her wrist, gently stroking her tender skin. "There are lots of things you don't know about me, Catherine. I suspect there's rather a lot about you I don't know, either."

At the warm pressure of his fingers, she nearly dropped the wedge of Wensleydale cheese back into the basket. The lazy cooing of a woodpigeon drifted from a chestnut tree. Of its own volition, her gaze flitted to Burke's mouth, and she felt the stirring of another hunger.

She forced a light laugh. "All you need to know is how surly I can get when someone prevents me from eating."

"Food is only an excuse for bringing you here." He released her and spread out a bleached linen cloth on the ground for their picnic. "I've a need to speak to you on a matter of importance."

Alarm jolted her. "You've remembered something else."

He peered into the basket and pulled out a bottle of wine, which he proceeded to uncork. "Not really."

" *'Not really'?* What does that mean?"

"It means nothing of consequence." He handed her a glass. "Let's drink a toast. To your successful hunt for a house."

He did know something. She could tell by the secretive way he studied her over the rim of his own glass.

But he refused to answer any more questions. They dined on roasted chicken and cheese and bread still warm from the oven. Upon finishing, Burke reclined on the grass, closed his eyes, and pillowed his head with his folded arms.

He looked so blasted content that Catherine wanted to lie down beside him. She wanted to brush back the lock of black hair that dipped onto his forehead. She wanted to kiss that sculpted mouth and feel his body respond to her touch.

The wine made her slightly dizzy. But that was only an excuse, she admitted. Her body longed for his loving, craved him with a woman's passion. Likewise, her mind craved to learn all the hidden facets to his character.

She placed her hands firmly in her lap. "Will you tell me now?"

Without opening his eyes, Burke reached into his coat pocket and drew forth a bit of paper, which he held out to her.

"What's this?" she asked even as she unfolded it.

"What I wanted to talk to you about."

The torn-off corner of cream-colored stationery held a cryptic message. " 'EN. Friday.' " Mystified, she frowned at Burke. " 'Tis Alfred's handwriting, I think. And the paper is his, too. Where did you find it?"

"In his secretaire."

The warmth flowed out of her, leaving her body frozen and her mind alert. "You've been snooping in my husband's bedroom?"

Burke regarded her through slitted eyes. "I was looking for clues—"

"There are only two keys to that room. Since you haven't got mine, you must have stolen the other from the steward."

"I borrowed it. But that isn't the point—"

"The point is that you were trying to call up more memories." The reminder that he could observe her past made Catherine feel raw and exposed. She hurled the scrap of paper at him. "You intruded upon my privacy when I expressly asked you not to."

He pushed up onto his elbow and snatched the note just as wind carried it aloft. "Stop interrupting me. I went into that bedroom because I want to protect you, not hurt you."

His irritation gave her pause. "I don't understand."

"Remember how I told you Alfred was acquainted with Ezekiel Newberry? I had a memory of Newberry saying, 'Mind your promise, or all Society will learn the truth.' " Burke plucked a blade of grass. "I believe Newberry had the means to ruin Alfred."

She clenched a fistful of green muslin skirt. "To *ruin* him?" she repeated, bewildered. "But how?"

"That's what I intend to find out. This note proves they had a meeting scheduled. Did Alfred ever mention such an engagement?"

She started to shake her head. Then she remembered that last painful encounter when she had implored him to give her a baby.

I have an appointment on Friday.

Burke lay sprawled on the grass, the breeze ruffling his hair, the note crumpled in his hand. His scrutiny of her raised an ugly suspicion in Catherine. Had he seen her on her knees, so desperate to bear a child that she would beg her husband to make love to her?

No. Surely Burke would say so if he had.

"I can't recall," she lied. "For all we know, *EN* could be someone else's initials. Or it could refer to a horse Alfred intended to bet on. Or a dozen other possibilities."

"Granted," Burke said, though one eyebrow remained in a quizzical arch. "Could he have owed Newberry a gambling debt?"

Alfred had always hidden the dun notices from her. Or at least he tried to. "He was a gentleman. And gentlemen don't speak to their wives of debts."

If Burke noticed her bitterness, he made no reference to it. "What did Lorena say when you told her about Newberry's attack?"

Catherine crumbled a bit of cheese onto the remains of their picnic. "I never told her."

A thrush twittered into the silence. "Never?" Burke sat up and gave her piercing stare. "Why the devil not?"

"Because he seemed to *want* me to tell her. I thought it best to stay out of their quarrel. To not let him use me as a pawn in whatever game he was playing."

Burke nodded. "Good thinking," he said approvingly. "The question remains, what game *is* he playing? Blackmail? Is there a family secret Newberry might have stumbled onto?"

"Not that I know of."

"Think, Catherine. It might involve Lorena. He seems to have taken an inordinate interest in her."

Catherine bit her lip. "There *is* something. When we spoke on the moor, Mr. Newberry claimed to have had a romantic affair with Lorena a long time ago. I gathered that it had ended abruptly."

Burke leaned forward. "Did he say exactly when?"

"No. I surmised he might have been a servant in her parents' household."

"But you don't know for sure."

"I only know that it makes sense. A young girl's head can be turned so easily by flattery."

"And what about a woman's head?"

One black eyebrow was still cocked at a pensive angle. She couldn't believe he would tease her during such a critical discussion. "Now is no time for your brand of flattery."

The ghost of a smile haunted his lips, then vanished. "You misunderstand me. What I meant was, what if Lorena had had an affair with Newberry not as a girl but as a woman. Not before she was married, but *after.*"

Catherine blinked. "I can't imagine that. She's so obsessed with what's proper. If she'd had an affair, I certainly never knew anything of it."

"You wouldn't have. I meant long before you joined the family." An arrested look came over his face; then his mouth worked into a grimace. As if he were pondering a repulsive secret. "Even before Alfred was born."

A discreet affair that had ended long ago was not so ruinous a scandal. Nor would it be sufficient to blackmail Lorena's son.

Her son.

"Upon my word." Struck by a horrid possibility, Catherine raised a hand to her mouth. But she couldn't stop the suspicion from spilling forth. "You think Newberry fathered Alfred."

Chapter 16

Two days later, Burke still didn't know the truth.

He and Catherine rode side by side in the phaeton. Ahead of them on the rural road, Simon Harewood bounced along on a sway-backed nag.

In the sunlight Catherine's eyes shone like amber, and the breeze tugged tendrils of sable hair from her plain straw bonnet. The high-waisted gown of primrose silk enhanced her glowing complexion. At one time he would have preferred a lady of the highest fashion and the lowest morals; now he felt hopelessly drawn to a woman of simple country charm.

Was he a fool to think he could win her heart? And why did it matter so much? Love couldn't last an eternity. Dependency bred pain; people only ended up hurting one another. He had learned that lesson at his father's knee.

He forced his mind back to the mystery surrounding Newberry. "So," he said to Catherine, "you spoke to Lorena and she refused to tell you anything."

"Twice already I've recited her exact words," Catherine said in exasperation. "She denied ever having an affair and denounced Newberry as a liar. Then she marched out of the room."

"Could you read anything from her expression?"

"She was furious, of course." Catherine's mouth formed a wry grimace. "She chastised me for making wild accusations."

"And the bitch insulted you as well, no doubt." Burke fixed his hand over hers in her lap. "If you'd allowed me, I would have spared you the pain of that confrontation."

She extricated her fingers from his. "Painful or not, it was my duty."

Duty. They had argued over that, but in the end, he had acceded to her wishes. She did not, after all, belong to him.

But she would. Little did she know, today he would launch the decisive battle in his campaign to win her affections.

The carriage rolled over a bump in the road, jostling them together. Seeking a handhold, she brushed his thigh, and that single innocent touch burned him with the fire of desire. From the way she snatched back her fingers, he could tell the flame had singed her, too.

Their lovemaking had awakened the slumbering passion in her, though she fought her feelings with admirable tenacity. He couldn't blame her. No decent woman would get involved with a man like him. Especially when that man could peer into her most intimate memories. He was a fool to dream of a lasting relationship with her. Catherine Snow could hurt him badly. Yet he felt a fierce possessiveness toward her that was startling in its newness. For the first time in his life he wanted a woman who could be a companion as well as a lover.

Hell, what was he worried about? She never had to know the depth of his need for her. He'd keep it light, carefree.

"At least we have an explanation for Alfred's melancholy," Burke said. "He was being blackmailed, quite possibly over his parentage. The scandal would have painted the family with the tar of disgrace."

Her haunted gaze lifted to Burke. "I should have been more understanding."

"But you didn't know."

"I tried to be a good wife. But I don't suppose I was suited for the role."

"Don't talk like that." He cradled her cheek in his palm. Because of his memories he could imagine the pain Catherine held inside herself. The caress started as a means to comfort her; then he couldn't resist feathering his thumb over her lips. Those soft, moist lips.

Ever so slowly he bent toward her, anticipating the rich sensual experience of her kiss. Her eyes grew dreamy, and the rise and fall of her breasts quickened.

Their mouths were nearly touching when, with a tiny shuddering gasp, she drew back. Her cheeks flushing pink, she pointed to the road ahead. "Look. Mr. Harewood is turning. This drive must lead to the house."

The land agent indeed motioned them to follow him onto a long, oak-lined avenue. *So much for romance,* Burke thought darkly.

Ah, well, it was only a delay. The reminder of his plan cheered him immensely.

"You're wise to leave Snow Manor," he said. "Lorena would smother the very life out of you."

Catherine sighed. "I only hope I'll like living on my own. Do you know, I went straight from the Guppys' house to the Snows? It seems odd to think of no one needing me."

"No one ordering you to fetch tea. No one berating you over an unswept floor or an unlit candelabra. No one reminding you that you've spoken out of turn." Burke gave her a pointed look. "I'd say you're well shut of them."

"Yet they're still my only family." Suddenly her eyes widened and she leaned forward on the leather seat. "Upon my word, look at that."

He followed her stare as the alley of ancient oaks gave way to a green lawn and a timbered, two-story house bristling with stone chimneys. A riot of pinks tumbled along the front and sides, creating the illusion of lavish ribbon wrapping a gift.

Catherine clasped his arm. "It's perfect, don't you think? Exactly the house I've been dreaming of."

He looked down into her radiant features and wished she would dream about *him.* With a violence that stunned him, he didn't want her to settle into a residence of her own. He wanted to kidnap her, then ride hell-bent for his estate in Cornwall, where he would keep her all to himself for the next fifty years.

But marriage was exactly what she was rebelling against. And the thought of a lifelong commitment made his own palms sweat.

Or was it worse to think of losing her?

"Let's hope this one doesn't have dry rot like the house we walked through yesterday," he said. "Or water damage like the one we saw this morning."

"Now, don't be a doomsayer." She withdrew her hand, and he missed its precious warmth. "Though I must thank you for pointing out those flaws. The repairs would have delayed the opening of my school. And the expense would have beggared me."

He didn't want her gratitude. He wanted her body, her heart, her soul. Yes, even her freedom.

Curse it. At this point, he'd settle for a kiss.

Burke guided the horse to a stop and set the carriage brake. He had to admit, the house had a quaint charm from the arched stone of the doorway to the tall mullioned windows. He could picture Catherine here, gathering bouquets of pink flowers or reading to a circle of children in the shade of an oak.

Mr. Simon Harewood slid off his horse with all the grace of a blob of melting butter. He drew out his pocketwatch and checked it as Burke gave Catherine a hand down.

"Welcome to Gilly Grange," Harewood said, beaming. "It's two-fifteen on the dot, just as I predicted."

"You're a model of efficiency." Burke took Catherine's arm. "Shall we?"

As they strolled toward the stone stoop, the heavenly fragrance of flowers drifted on the breeze. "It's a lovely house," she said with enthusiasm. "Is it Elizabethan?"

Harewood nodded. "Built solid in 1573 and renovated just last year. An elderly couple lived here most recently, a scholar and his invalid wife. They've moved to York to be closer to their grandchildren."

"A scholar?" Her face lit up. "Then there must be a library."

"A fine one, Mrs. Snow. Fine indeed." As they reached the front door, the rotund man fished in the pocket of his checkered suit. "I'll just open the door . . . oh, dear."

"Is something amiss?" Burke asked.

"The key." Astonishment creased the agent's moon face. "I could have sworn I brought it."

Burke tried the door latch. "Locked. What a pity. It looks as if you'll have to go back."

"Let's check the windows first," Catherine suggested. "You go this way and I'll go that."

Curse her. He couldn't let her ruin his perfect scheme. "You'll dirty your skirts in the flower beds. Allow me. It'll just take a moment."

He made a show of testing each window along the front, rattling the frames for good measure, then hastened along the side and back, and returned in short order. "Sorry, no luck. You'd best be on your way, Harewood."

The agent peered at his timepiece again. "The ride

takes precisely twenty-six minutes each way, so I should return within the hour. If you don't mind waiting, m'lord?"

"Of course not. Now run along. Time's a-wasting." Burke escorted the man to his sorry nag and gave him a leg up. "Don't forget to watch the road in case you dropped the key along the way."

"Oh, bother." Settling in the saddle, Harewood drew out his handkerchief, removed his brown hat, and mopped his bald pate. "Examining so much ground will add many minutes to my trip."

That was the idea. "Take your time. We can inspect the grounds at our leisure. And do keep a close eye peeled. We wouldn't want you to miss that key."

"Yes, m'lord." The man rode away, hanging over the side of the horse to stare at the road.

Burke restrained the urge to kick up his heels. He had an hour alone with Catherine. Much could happen in that time.

Whistling a tuneless ditty, he turned to see her at the corner of the house, standing on tiptoe in the pink-flocked shrubbery and peering into a window. Even as he walked toward her, she shook the latch in frustration and the window swung open on squeally hinges.

Surprise illuminated her face. "It's not locked, after all."

"Fancy that. I must not have tried it properly. All it took was a woman's touch."

Something in his tone made Catherine peer closely at him. A lack of surprise? A hint of laughter? Was he tricking her? Then he moved behind her and the chance to study his expression was gone.

"I'll lift you inside." His hands closed around her waist. "Are you ready for an adventure?"

His breath stirred the fine hairs at the back of her neck, and his question made her think of an activity that had nothing to do with examining a house. The sides of her bonnet hid the blush that warmed her cheeks, but the telltale pink traveled lower. It was her own fault for wearing a gown that showed too much bosom.

Willing her voice to steadiness, she said, "Go ahead."

Obligingly, he firmed his grip and lifted her. She hooked her elbows over the stone ledge, the toes of her demi-boots scrabbling for purchase on the outer wall. Burke shifted his hands to her bottom in what felt sinfully close to a caress. But before she could protest, he gave her another boost upward.

She half-tumbled into a dim, bare room with cabbage rose paper decorating the walls. She had only a moment to adjust her skirts. Then, with catlike grace, Burke hoisted himself onto the ledge and landed beside her.

"We're in," she said unnecessarily.

"We are at that." He whipped something pink from behind his back. "These are for you."

He held out a ragged bouquet, the blooms sticking out every which way. She felt a perilous thawing inside her breast and buried her nose in the pinks. It had been years since anyone had given her flowers. "They smell lovely. Thank you."

"Your pleasure is reward enough." The merest hint of green sparks gleamed in his silvery eyes. "Shall we go exploring?"

Again, he imbued the simple question with layers of meaning. She had the niggling sense that he was up to something. He crooked his elbow, and after a moment's hesitation, she slipped her gloved hand around his sleeve.

Immediately moving his arm flat against his side, he forced her to step closer so that her hand was trapped in a nest of his body heat. Then he took her on a stroll around the chamber.

"Morning room, I suppose." He craned his neck back. "The plaster appears cracked in a few spots."

With growing interest, Catherine examined the

cream-painted molding and the delicately carved fireplace. "Cracks can be patched. Everything else looks in perfect condition."

"Or so you hope. A house over four hundred years old is bound to have flaws."

"Less than three hundred years," she amended. "And don't forget, the place has been renovated."

"At least on the surface." He led her through the doorway. A musty aroma perfumed the air. Corridors led off in three directions. At the end of one dark passage, a narrow servant's staircase hugged a paneled wall. "A rather cheerless place," he remarked. "My home in Cornwall has much wider passages with windows at the ends to let in the light."

Catherine clutched the flowers and ordered herself to stop yearning for what could never be. "This will do me fine. Only picture this corridor with candles casting golden light on the wood." She smiled at the cozy image.

"You'd likely see wormholes in the paneling. Come upstairs."

She scurried to keep pace with his long strides. The wooden steps squeaked as he drew her to the upper story and along the corridor. He poked his head first into one bedroom, then another, and she caught only a glimpse of pastel walls and dormer windows.

"Stop," she protested. "I want to look more closely."

Burke seemed preoccupied as he glanced into a third empty bedchamber. "I could have sworn Harewood said this house was furnished."

"Did he? I don't think so."

Was that a curse Burke muttered under his breath? Through the dim passageway with its fine-striped wallpaper, their footsteps echoed, hers light, his heavy.

"Will you kindly slow down?" she said in exasperation. "We can tour the house at our leisure. Mr. Harewood won't be back for nearly an hour."

Burke halted so abruptly that she bumped into him. "You're right," he said. "We should take advantage of our time alone."

In a move as silky as his voice, he clasped her to his chest, his hands stroking down her back. Her breath caught at the suddenness of his seduction. The pink blooms in her hand stood in stark contrast to his dark coat. Her gaze lifted from his white cravat to his tempting lips to his smoldering eyes, and giddy longing washed over her senses. She knew exactly what he was thinking—exactly the thoughts that beguiled her own mind. He was remembering how perfectly their bodies had fitted together, how extraordinary the bond between them had been.

And still was.

He traced the contour of her face from her temples to her chin. "I've forced myself to be patient. These past few days, I've dreamt of you day and night."

He lowered his head toward hers until his lips were so close she felt the warm breeze of his breath. She ached to taste his kiss again, ached as she had in the carriage. But once his mouth touched hers, she would be lost.

Caging the wildness of her desire, she withdrew from his arms. "Were the dreams yours?" she had to ask. "Or Alfred's?"

"I'm hardly possessed by his spirit." Annoyance edged Burke's voice. "Other than an occasional vague flash of memory, my thoughts are entirely my own."

"So are mine. And I'd like to view the rest of the house."

She hastened down the corridor, her heels clicking on the floorboards. He called her name in a voice fraught with frustration, but she didn't stop.

A grand staircase loomed ahead. She flew down the oak risers, her hand grasping a smooth balustrade that turned at a landing and led into a charming vestibule. As she reached the bottom, the tranquil setting calmed the storm of her emotions. White woodwork accented the coral-painted walls and the parquet floor. To the left, a doorway opened into a snug drawing room. To the right lay the library.

She clasped the nosegay to her breast. This was what she wanted, this home where she could create a new life for herself in an atmosphere of quiet contentment. Here she could find lasting solitude away from the torments of love.

Burke came down the stairway, and in defiance of all logic, a pang of longing struck her heart anew. Would she never learn?

Resolutely, she turned her back on him and entered the library. Empty shelves stretched across three walls from floor to ceiling. A stone chimneypiece decorated the fourth wall, and she saw herself sitting there on a rainy day, curled up in a chair with a book. Alone.

But never lonely. She would spend her days in the company of children. Laughing, happy, wonderful children.

Other people's children.

Conquering the ache in her chest, she went to the window facing the rear of the house. "Here's a seat for Tigress to sun herself. And there's a terrace overlooking the garden." She absently rubbed her hand over a glass pane and her glove came up gray with dust. "Upon my word. I wonder why no one's bought such a lovely place."

"Ghosts," Burke suggested. He had one shoulder propped in a lazy pose against the doorframe. "Hauntings in the dead of night. Quite common in these old dwellings."

Gooseflesh tiptoed over her skin. "Don't be an addlepate." A half-formed thought took shape. "You're trying to discourage me from buying this house. Why?"

"Just playing the devil's advocate." A mischievous smile on his face, he pushed away from the door and swaggered toward her. "You've declared me a devil. I may as well live up—or perhaps down—to the image."

As he loomed closer, her heart danced against her ribcage. Instinctively she walked backwards. But there was no fleeing the urges inside her. "I won't be seduced, Burke. I thought I made that clear."

He stalked toward her. "Very well. Then you seduce *me.* You do want to."

A protest died in her throat; the blaze inside her bespoke the truth. Quiet freedom paled in comparison to tempestuous joy.

"I can't deny that," she said on a rush of sweet anguish. "But there are other considerations—"

Her back thumped into the wall. Her mind scattered as he braced his hands on the bookshelf above her. His broad chest and long legs hemmed her in, and even though she could have escaped to either side, she didn't. She stood transfixed by the desire to touch the shadow of stubble on his clean-shaven cheeks.

Bending nearer, he whispered in her ear, "You were saying?"

She gathered her thoughts. "Other considerations. My plan to open a school, for one. I have to be respectable. And I can't just forget those memories—"

"Curse the memories. Would you reject me if I had a limp? Or a patch over one eye?"

"Of course not," she said, momentarily taken by the fantasy of him as a pirate, and herself the captive he was about to ravish.

"Then don't hold me to blame for recollections I can't control." He untied the ribbons of her bonnet and tugged gently on them to tilt her face up to his. "The memories needn't be a barrier. Think of them as a means to bring us closer together." His lips brushed hers. "As close as a man and a woman can be."

With searing insight, Catherine knew she wanted him to remember making love to her himself, not as a second-hand experience from the spirit of another man. She longed to line a treasure chest with their own memories, bright and new and cherished ones, rather than the twisted remains of the past.

"Oh, Burke, yes." On a surge of liberation, she opened her trembling fingers and the pink blooms showered to the floor. Then she reached down to cup his hardness. "I want you. I do."

A primal growl vibrated in his throat, a sound of pure male need that fed the wildness spilling forth from deep within herself. Their mouths met in a deep, consuming kiss that set fire to her, body and soul. She couldn't wait; the frantic need for him overpowered her. "Now," she whimpered. "Please, *now.*"

She wrested free the buttons of his breeches even as he lifted her skirts and shucked her drawers. And then blessedly he was filling her, and she locked her legs around him, awash in the fierce sensual bliss of the mating that brought them both to a swift and shattering release.

The sounds of their pleasure died away into the silence of the library. Catherine opened her eyes to find herself supported between the shelves and Burke, his hands cupping her bottom.

He wore a smile of shameless satisfaction. "When you change your mind, you certainly do it with panache."

"I had an excellent teacher," she said, her voice unsteady.

"Partner," he corrected, and kissed her again.

His tongue tasted her, tested her, with slow relish this time. They were still joined, and she felt the magical feelings swell within her again, the irresistible need to touch heaven once more.

He nuzzled her ear and the bonnet tumbled to the floor. Next he peeled away her glove and kissed her delicate inner wrist, then her work-roughened palm, stroking the length of each finger. He afforded the same devotion to her other hand, unfurling a silken strand of sensation that streamed up her arm and knotted her chest.

Impatient, she moved her hips. "If only we had a bed."

He grinned wickedly. "Darling, there's always a way."

He shrugged out of his coat, and folded it to make a pillow on the floor. Then he tumbled her down on top of him. Lowering her bodice and chemise, he suckled her breasts until she moaned in delight.

Catherine had a sudden mental picture of how brazen she looked with her legs sprawled out and her skirt hiked to her waist, revealing the garters that held up her plain white stockings. Yet she felt curiously free and alive, joyous and rejuvenated, unfettered by duty or servitude. She need only please herself and Burke for this unbearably sweet stolen moment.

Her upper body flowed downward, breasts brushing his chest as she bent to kiss his face, the crooked grin she loved so well, the arrogant cheekbones and high brow that marked his noble lineage. He did indeed have a trace of stubble although he must have shaved that morning, and she loved the roughness of his skin against her tender lips.

While they kissed, he delved beneath her skirt again, seeking the bloom of her womanhood and unfolding the petals to the nectar within. He explored her as if she were his own precious discovery. And she was his, Catherine acknowledged. His alone. He was branded so deeply on her heart that the memory of their closeness would remain with her forever.

Wanting him to remember as well, she braced her hands on his shoulders and poised herself to welcome him. "Come home," she invited in a husky whisper. "Come into me, my lord."

The expression on his face was dark and smoldering,

yet with a quality akin to wistful yearning. "Only if you meet me halfway."

She did so with exultation, melting down to meet his upward thrust so they became two halves united into one glorious whole. Catherine closed her eyes to concentrate on the voluptuous sensations coursing through her, sensations that sharpened and quickened each time she moved.

He uttered an inarticulate growl and matched her rhythm in seductive strokes. Her breasts felt heavy, swollen, and she leaned closer so that he could drink of their sweetness, her head tipped back as she reveled in rising passion.

"Catherine," he whispered. "Love me."

Her breath caught at the vulnerability in his gaze, as if she were being granted a rare glimpse into the mysterious depths of his soul. Did he truly long for her love? Or was he only speaking in the physical sense?

She couldn't think; she could only feel. The intimacy of their bodies drew her deeper and deeper into the mindless realm of ecstasy, and this time their coupling held a mystical quality, a quiet madness. At last her body convulsed in endless rapturous spasms, and he too cried out the joy of his completion.

Bonelessly, she dissolved onto him, his shoulder hard against her cheek, his heart beating against her breasts. She marveled again at the utter contentment a thorough loving could bring, a contentment she had never felt until Burke had awakened her slumbering emotions. Whatever the future might hold, she would not regret this golden moment.

A bird trilled somewhere outside. She opened her eyes to see dust motes dancing in a ray of sunshine. Rows of empty shelves stretched to the ceiling, waiting for all the books she would buy. What a fine christening for her new library.

Awareness broke into her dreamy state. She sat up,

supporting herself on Burke's chest. "What time is it? Mr. Harewood could return at any moment."

"I shouldn't worry. He won't be back so soon."

His confident tone stirred suspicion in her. "Did you do something with the house key?"

"Who, me?" For a man who had just proven his unrivaled virility, he could look boyishly innocent.

"Yes, you." He still wore his waistcoat, and Catherine probed for an inner pocket. "So where have you hidden the key? If you had it on your person while you made me climb through that blasted window, you're in terrible trouble."

Chuckling, he stayed her wrist so that her palm lay flat against his warm chest. "I don't have it. I swear, I don't."

"Then where is it?" she said in her best schoolmarm voice.

He lowered his chin like a chastened pupil. "The key is lying in the bushes outside Harewood's house. I managed to sneak it out of his pocket as we were leaving."

She cherished the secret happiness that he would scheme to be with her. "Then you planned this seduction."

The laugh lines that crinkled the corners of his eyes suddenly vanished. He reached up and brushed back a stray curl from her forehead. "Do you mind?"

When he regarded her with such wary tenderness, she felt her heart take flight on wings of hope. "No," she said fiercely. "I'm glad. So very glad."

She leaned down to seal her avowal with a kiss, and his arms closed around her, his mouth slanting over hers with a fervor that reawakened the passion so recently sated. On a rush of poignant awareness, she knew she loved him. And would love him forever, even when he tired of her.

When at last she drew back, she was determined not to mar the moment with demands about the future.

"Now I see why you wanted the house to be furnished," she teased. "You must be sore from lying on the hard floor."

Unsmiling, he watched her, his half closed eyes hiding his thoughts. "You can kiss all my bruises later."

"Come to my room tonight, and I'll do so in a proper bed."

She ached to lie with him longer, but a lost key could be found. Sliding off, she knelt to adjust her chemise and bodice. The brush of fabric tingled through her, and she savored the sensitivity of her skin like a badge of honor. She had been afraid for too long—afraid of Burke's memories, afraid of ruining her reputation, afraid of opening herself to the pain of loving.

The time had come to embrace life to its fullest. She would have her love affair and damn the consequences.

Burke was standing now, tucking his shirt into his breeches. He helped her to her feet, then held tight to her hand. A muscle worked in his jaw. He looked almost nervous.

"Catherine, I've something to ask you . . . ah, *hell.*"

He bit off the oath and cocked his head to the side in a listening pose. Even as she wondered what he had meant to say, she heard the unmistakable clopping of hooves outside.

Catherine gasped. "Mr. Harewood!"

She flew across the library and snatched up her drawers, stepping into them and half-falling in her haste. Burke steadied her, then buttoned the back of her gown as she brushed ineffectively at the telltale wrinkles.

"Oh, my, he's going to know what we were doing," she said on a moan, snatching up her bonnet and jamming it onto her head.

"He'll only know you look as beautiful as ever." Burke picked up a pink bloom and tucked it into her bodice. "Radiant, in fact. Like a satisfied woman."

"That's reassuring."

Chuckling, he tied the ribbons beneath her chin. "Stop fretting and leave the explaining to me."

With the swaggering assurance of a seasoned rake, he led the way to the vestibule just as the key rattled in the lock and Mr. Harewood trotted inside.

To her relief, he didn't notice her surreptitiously tugging on her gloves; he was too busy checking his pocketwatch. "Only fourteen minutes past my estimation. I vow, I've never dropped my keys before."

"We all make mistakes." Burke put his arm around the shorter man and walked him outside, explaining how they had entered through a window and Mrs. Snow would give the agent her decision on the morrow.

Within moments, Catherine was seated beside Burke in the phaeton as they rode at a spanking pace down the oak-lined drive. She craned her head around for one last wistful look at the gabled house. Already it seemed like home, for it held the special memory of her interlude with Burke. "I should have told Mr. Harewood to prepare the sale papers. What if someone else buys it in the meantime?"

Burke placed his hand over hers on the leather seat. "In that unlikely event, I'd pay the other party to retract their offer."

The mellow warmth slid from Catherine. He made her feel like a kept woman. "The house is my responsibility. You're to put out no money on my behalf."

He regarded her with a moody gaze. Briefly he turned his attention to the trotting horses and the reins. "What if I said I wanted to take care of you? In every way?"

A cold flush swept over her. Feeling elated and insulted all at once, she pressed her fingers into the folds of her gown. She should have known that loving him would hurt. "I'd refuse you. While I'm happy to carry on a mutual arrangement, I'll not be your paid lightskirt."

"I'm not suggesting you be my mistress." His voice

was controlled, almost casual. "I'm asking you to be my wife."

Certain she had misheard him, certain the rattling of the carriage wheels had distorted his words, she studied his handsome profile. He couldn't have uttered such an offer.

Could he? Could Burke Grisham, renowned rake and confirmed bachelor, wish to marry *her?* When she searched his face for the answer, she saw only a bland smoothness as if his thoughts were closed to her.

Dear God. He wanted to be her husband. *Her husband.*

"Well?" he prompted. "If you're thinking I make a habit of asking women to marry me, you're wrong. This is the first time I've ever done so."

"I wasn't thinking that," she whispered. "I just don't know what to say."

He lifted her gloved hand and kissed the back. "It's quite simple. Repeat after me: 'Yes. Yes, m'lord, I'll marry you.' "

She swayed toward him, drawn by the dream of happiness, by the lure of impossible yearnings. The anguish of reality intruded. How could she be so foolish again?

She reluctantly withdrew her hand. "You must have had affairs with hundreds of women. Why would you offer for me?"

His gaze slid away as he looked back at the road. "I promised Alfred I'd take care of you. Marriage seems an ideal way to do so."

Her heart sank like a stone. She couldn't help asking, "And what about love?"

"Let's not get caught up in sentiment." He sent her a swift, shuttered glance. "We're both mature adults. We get along well, and that's a sound enough basis for marriage."

He made it sound so simple, so rational. Could she ever win his heart? Her own heart was beating with slow, painful strokes of hope. Never in her wildest fantasies had she allowed herself to imagine spending the rest of her life with Burke. "But I want to open a school."

"The children on my estate need an education. You could teach them." A half-smile warmed his face. "And my library is thrice as large as the one we just left. It's crammed to the ceiling with books—more books than you could read in a lifetime."

He knew how to tempt her. "You need a woman of your own class at your side. I can't be a countess. I don't know how."

"Catherine, you're more a lady than any other woman of the *ton.* You could give the aristocracy lessons in nobility." The firm, reassuring weight of his hand came down on hers. "Say yes. It's time I married and fathered an heir. Just think, I can give you a family of your very own."

Pain lanced her anew, and the brief moment of blissful hope bled into the darkness of her soul. Aware of a burning behind her eyes, Catherine turned away and blinked at the stands of oak and chestnut shading the country lane. Dear God. He didn't know. He hadn't remembered her quarrels with Alfred, or the terrible moment when the doctor had pronounced her infertile.

How appalled Burke would be. All men wanted an heir, proof of their potency, continuation of an old and honored name. So had Alfred, and her failure to conceive again had put a strain on their marriage.

She was aware of the distant barking of a dog, the clatter of the carriage wheels, the clopping of hooves as the phaeton went over a rise and descended a stretch of wooded slope toward the vastness of the moor.

Barren. She flinched at the thought of saying the word aloud.

But it had to be done. In a matter of minutes they would arrive at Snow Manor.

She forced herself to look at Burke. He was gazing at her with an unguarded tenderness that broke her heart. She had to tell him the truth. She had to reveal her most wrenching secret—that she was not a whole woman. Only then would he would understand and accept her refusal.

His hand still rested on hers. She turned hers palm up to his and took a deep breath. "I can't marry you, not now or ever. You see, I'm—"

A loud report split the air. Something struck her upper body with stinging force. She felt herself falling, falling toward the open side of the phaeton. A blow struck her head.

Burke's voice shouted her name as if down a long tunnel. Then the blackness swallowed her.

Chapter 17

"Catherine!"

Burke seized her in the instant before she would have toppled from the phaeton. At the same time, he held tight to the reins to keep the frightened horses under control. Trees and fields whirred past in a blur of green and brown.

She lay slumped against his chest. Her eyes were closed. He could see a hole in the side of her gown. Blood spread in an ever-widening stain, red against primrose pink.

Shot. She had been *shot.*

His heart thrummed in his ears. Not again. Not again. Not *Catherine.*

Staving off panic, he lowered her to his lap. With clumsy fingers, he yanked off his neckcloth and pressed it to her side. One-handedly, he snapped the reins and the carriage jolted faster along the rural lane.

Catherine lay unmoving. Deathly still.

Fear transported him back to the battlefield at Waterloo. He heard the whine of bullets. Smelled the stench of blood and smoke. Tasted the sickness in his throat. Saw men crying out in the agony of death.

No!

Think. Where had the shot come from? He had seen no hunter lurking among the trees. Had the attack been deliberate?

Rage burned through his veins. But he couldn't turn back and pursue the gunman. He must get Catherine to safety, to help.

He wanted to shake her, but didn't dare. "Catherine. Wake up. Talk to me."

She made no response. With stark clarity, her beloved face imprinted itself on his mind. The inky curve of lashes against pale skin. The dainty chin and exquisite bone structure. The cameo profile framed by that absurd little bonnet.

An hour ago they had shared the sweetest ecstasy he had ever known. Now he would trade away the precious memory if only she would open her eyes. He would barter his own life in exchange for hers.

Her blood heated his hand. Was she dying? Would her experience with death be like his? Against his will, he imagined her spirit separating from her body, rising toward the tunnel of light, reaching the radiance of perfect peace.

Lost to him.

For the first time since he had huddled in the wine cellar while his brother lay dying, Burke prayed. *Let her live. Please, God, let her live.*

An eternity passed before he spied Snow Manor, a stately stone box at the end of the long curving drive. The instant the phaeton came to a halt, he caught Catherine against him and leaped to the ground. He strode up the front steps and banged open the door.

"Humphrey!" he roared.

The echo of his voice died away against the walls of the foyer. From the end of the long passageway, the cadaverous butler advanced at a stately pace. "M'lord?"

His servile expression betrayed shock when he saw Catherine. "Mrs. Snow? Whatever is the matter—"

"Send for a doctor. Now."

"Straightaway, m'lord." At an undignified lope, Humphrey hastened toward the back of the house.

Burke carried her into the drawing room. His hands shaking, he settled her on the nearest chaise. Her pallor alarmed him. Pressing his ear to her breast, he was rewarded by the sound of a thready pulse. Thank God she was alive.

"My dear lord! Why were you shouting? Is that Catherine? What do you think you're doing?"

Lorena swept through the doorway and advanced on them. Heedless, Burke carefully lifted Catherine and opened the back of her gown. He eased the sleeves downward and lowered the bodice.

"Stop this violation at once!" Lorena snapped. "Have you lost all sense of decency? Oh!" Her tirade ended on a shriek as she came close enough to see past him. Her gold shawl slipped off her shoulders and fell into a glittering puddle on the rug. "What's happened? Why is she bleeding?"

"She's been shot." He paused to master his emotions, willing away the stinging in his eyes. "Fetch me some towels. Quickly."

Lorena stood staring at Catherine's supine form. "Shot, you say? Are you quite sure?"

"Yes, dammit! I was there. It happened on the road from West Scrafton."

"Did you see . . . did you see who fired the gun?"

"No. Now get on with you."

The older woman shook her head as if emerging from a trance. "Of course."

She yanked on the bell rope by the fireplace. Without waiting for a servant, she rushed from the room.

Painstakingly, Burke peeled away Catherine's red-smeared chemise and found an ugly gouge scoring the tender flesh of her side. Blood oozed from the long, shallow furrow.

The breath shuddered out of him. A graze. Not a life-threatening injury. A healthy young body could survive this. Yet she was so much more delicate than a battle-hardened soldier.

He folded Lorena's shawl and used it as a compress. Catherine moaned, turning her head from side to side. He untied the bow beneath her chin and removed her bonnet. Above her ear stood a lump the size of a plover's egg.

He smoothed the tumbled silken strands. "Catherine," he murmured, kissing her pale brow. The words welled from the empty place deep inside him. "Catherine, my love."

She heard him as if from a distance. His voice drew her from the soft folds of darkness and into the brilliance of pain.

She hurt. Pinpricks of color danced against her weighted lids. The left side of her body burned while the rest of her felt cold. So cold. A shiver coursed through her, then another until she trembled violently, her teeth chattering.

Something warm settled down on her. A blanket. She recognized the masculine scent of it even as her shaking subsided. "Burke?"

Her voice came out thin and reedy. She sensed his presence, felt him stroking her cheek and heard him whispering her name.

Had he truly called her his love?

No, he didn't believe in love.

Catherine opened her eyes. She was covered not by a blanket but by his coat. Two images of his face swam before her.

She blinked, and the forms merged into one. He had an odd watchfulness about him, his mouth set in a grim line. When she tried to push herself upright, pain stabbed her skull. The breath came out of her in a groan. "My head."

He held her close a moment. "Thank God you're all right." Then he pressed a cup to her lips. "Drink this."

She swallowed on reflex. The liquid seared a path down her throat, making her cough. "Brandy. I loathe the stuff."

He chuckled. "It does have a medicinal purpose." The gentle pressure of his hands guided her back down. The pulsing in her head began to subside and a mellow warmth trickled through her chest, numbing the pain in her side.

"What happened?" she asked.

He hesitated. "When you fell, you struck your head on the carriage hood."

Carriage? She had a hazy recollection of riding through the countryside with Burke. And hearing a sudden loud noise.

She focused on him again. Rusty spots smeared his white shirt. Blood. *Her* blood.

Memory returned in a bewildering jolt. She had felt something sting her; then she had fallen backward into blackness. "I've been shot."

A muscle worked in his jaw. "Yes."

"But . . . who would . . . ?"

"I don't know. But I intend to find out."

Then she could ask him no more questions, for several people hurried into the drawing room. Leading the contingent were Martha and Mrs. Earnshaw. Between them, they carried enough linen towels to bandage Napoleon's army.

"Poor child!" the cook exclaimed, her doughy face wreathed in concern. "What has become of thee?"

Lorena clapped her hands. "Don't just stand there, put a cloth beneath her. She's bleeding all over a very expensive chaise. And my shawl—it's ruined!"

Burke surged to his feet. "Yes, do let's have a care for

the clothing and furniture," he said in a hard tone. "After all, a mere servant can be replaced."

Pinned by his sharp gaze, Lorena lowered her eyes. "Forgive me," she said. "I meant no insult to Catherine. Of course, her safety and comfort are of the utmost importance to me."

"I should hope that's the case—"

"M'lord," Humphrey said from the doorway. "There's someone to see you."

Burke shot him a distracted glance. "The doctor? Already?"

"No, m'lord. A visitor."

"Not *now,* man."

The butler remained in the doorway. "Beg pardon, but he was most insistent upon seeing you immediately."

"Curse it, I don't care if it's the Regent himself. Tell him I'm busy. He can return later."

A man marched past the butler and into the drawing room. "You'll see me now."

At that imperious tone, the throng of servants parted like the Red Sea. Even Lorena stepped back, her eyes avid on the newcomer.

His bearing straight and tall, the stranger wore a coat of military blue over dark trousers and polished boots. White strands salted his black hair. Harsh lines of experience lent dynamic character to a face more striking than handsome. His eyes were an icy, penetrating gray.

He looked from Burke in his bloodied shirt to Catherine, lying on the chaise. His disdainful gaze reminded her she was half-clothed. Mortified, she drew the coat up to her neck.

Then he was watching Burke again, looking him up and down almost greedily. "Well." The single word held both judgment and punishment. "I see you've landed yourself in trouble, as usual. What's happened here?"

Burke's face had paled. "It's no concern of yours. *Father.*"

Catherine's heart pounded in painful strokes. Now she could see the resemblance in the eyes, the set of the cheekbones. This granite-faced stranger was Roderick Grisham, marquis of Westhaven. The man who blamed Burke for the death of his elder brother. The man who had denied his younger son the affection and support every child deserved. The man who had turned Burke into a rake who despised himself and scorned love.

Why was he here?

Lorena sank into a deep curtsy. "What a welcome surprise, my lord. Do permit me to introduce myself. I am your hostess, Mrs. Lorena Snow." Beaming, she shooed the servants out of the drawing room. "You must have had a long ride. May I offer you refreshment? Tea and cakes, perhaps? In the morning room, away from this unfortunate mess."

Ignoring her, Westhaven walked closer to Burke. Of the same height, they stood face to face as if they were the only two people in the room. "Answer me. Why do you have blood on your shirt? What have you done to this woman?"

"What have *I* done?" Burke laughed, a dark ripple of irony. "No, I'll ask the questions for once. It's been ten years. To what do I owe this honor?"

His father hesitated. "I wanted to quash a rumor that my son was about to make a most unsuitable marriage."

"You, listen to gossip? I don't believe it. You must have had a more reliable source of information." Burke turned to Lorena. "Let me guess. You wrote to him."

"I . . ." She lowered her gaze and wrung her hands. "I humbly beg your pardon, my lord. I merely thought your father might wish to counsel you. Before you were led astray."

"Led astray, is it? You're too late, then. Both of you."

Struck by dismay, Catherine clutched the coat to her

bosom and struggled to sit up. To protest their high-handed interference in her life. To stop Burke from making an announcement he would have to retract later.

"Wait," she said.

But no one heard her feeble whisper. A hot trickling pain seared her side.

Westhaven stared stonily at his son. "Is this the woman?"

His gaze cut to Catherine in a freezing glare that sparked a shudder in her. His image split into two, then four identical likenesses.

As if from a distance, she heard Burke reply, "The lady's name is Catherine. Soon to be the countess of Thornwald."

She opened her mouth to correct him. But the room seemed to tilt. Blackness nibbled at the edge of her vision.

For the second time in her life, Catherine swooned.

"Is she all right?" Roderick Grisham asked.

As Burke entered the library two hours later, his father walked toward him with the same square-shouldered carriage that Burke had tried to imitate as a child. There were so many things the same about his father: the ice-chip eyes, the forceful manner, the stern countenance. Yet in the past decade he had changed, too. Deep grooves cut into either side of his mouth, and his hair and brows were graying. Burke steeled himself against the shock of it. His once invincible father was growing old.

Not, of course, that Burke cared.

He went to the sideboard, poured himself a drink, and took a long swallow. He had replaced his shirt and freshened up, yet he still felt shaken by the memory of Catherine's blood. "The doctor's tending to her now. It's only a flesh wound, more's the pity to you."

"Don't be stupid. I wouldn't wish the woman dead."

Burke pivoted, the brandy sloshing in the glass. "Now that you mention it, how odd it is that you rode up to the house so shortly after Catherine had been shot. Tell me, Father, to what lengths would you go to stop me from marrying her?"

Roderick's face went ashen. "Dare you suggest I skulked in the bushes and attempted to murder a *woman?*"

Even now, his father had the power to inflict shame in Burke. He fought to keep his gaze level. "You have ample motive."

"That is a foul accusation, even coming from you. And here I'd begun to hope you'd changed."

"Changed?" Burke released an uneasy laugh. "Whatever gave you that idea?"

"You've spent the past year in Cornwall tending to estate matters. Ever since your surprising performance at Waterloo, you seem to have given up gambling, wenching, carousing."

So, Roderick had kept a close watch on him. Burke felt a strange warmth in his chest, then damned himself for clinging to childish dreams. His father's interest had nothing to do with love or caring. He hadn't even bothered to visit his recuperating son. "Who did you pay to spy on me? Trotter? Or better yet, Dibell?"

At the mention of the old steward, Roderick pursed his lips slightly. "I never paid him. He sent me reports because he was concerned about you, too."

"You're concerned only for the family name." Burke tilted his drink, downed the contents in one fiery gulp, and set the glass on the sideboard.

"Yes," Roderick stated, "I am troubled. Especially when I walk in here and find your intended wife lying with a bullet wound. What the devil happened today? Who shot her?"

Burke walked to the window and braced his hands on

the sill. Suspicion cudgeled his brain, but he couldn't speak until he knew more. "It was an accident, that's all you need to know."

"I hope to God you haven't embroiled yourself in some sordid scandal. Who is this Catherine Snow? How much do you know of her background? Who are her people?"

"I don't give a bloody damn about her pedigree." Arms folded across his chest, Burke turned to face his father. "Rest assured, I'm as irredeemable as ever. Nothing you can say or do will stop me from marrying this woman."

"So you're marrying her to spite me."

"Don't flatter yourself. I'll marry to please myself, not anyone else. Least of all you." *If* Catherine accepted his offer. Burke could still see the denial in her eyes, the shock that he would lie about their betrothal. Yet he burned with love and hatred for this man who had given life to him, then withheld all kindness and affection.

His father paced the room, his hands clasped behind his back. It brought back memories of standing in his study, of listening to the creak of shoe-leather as Roderick Grisham strode back and forth, firing punishing words like bullets.

Now, he gave his son a hard stare. "I thought you were finally ready to meet me as an adult. It seems I was wrong."

Burke shaped his mouth into a devil-may-care grin. "God forbid I should become like you. So go on back to your government office and your House of Lords and your circle of highborn snobs."

"I'm staying. It's my duty to make sure you're not throwing your life away on a fortune hunter. If I can stop this mésalliance, I will."

"Your meddling will accomplish nothing. If you dare upset Catherine in any way, you'll answer to me." Yet a turmoil of emotion churned in Burke, darkest of all, the fear that his father might succeed.

"It was that robber who shot Catherine yesterday," Prudence said, her blue eyes wide. "It has to be him. He stole Lady Beaufort's jewels."

Priscilla batted her lashes at Lord Westhaven across the tea table. "It was the oddest thing. The thief emptied her strongbox and left a single copper farthing as a joke."

Roderick Grisham paused, his tea cup half-raised. "A copper farthing, you say?"

"Yes, we know because Lady Beaufort is Mummy's dearest friend. She sent Mummy a letter about it."

Lorena poured cream from a silver pitcher into her cup. "The incident happened weeks ago. I'm sure his lordship isn't interested in our neighborhood gossip."

"On the contrary," the marquis mused. "I seem to recall a jewel thief in London some thirty years ago who left a coin in precisely the same manner."

Lorena's cup clattered against the saucer and turned over. The dark liquid stained the white lace on the tea table. "Oh, how clumsy of me. Owen," she snapped at the footman, "come clean this up."

Burke lifted his cup in a mocking salute. "That's my father. Always did have a mind as tight as a rabbit trap. Never forgets even the most obscure detail."

The marquis leveled a glare. "And you're still as insolent as ever."

Observing them from the doorway of the drawing room, Catherine felt a sinking in the pit of her stomach. No one had noticed her pause here a few moments ago. No one expected her to leave her sickbed. But, despite the stinging of her wound, she couldn't bear to lie there any longer. She had to see for herself how Burke and his father were getting on.

Thus far, it wasn't encouraging.

The previous night was still a haze in her memory. She recalled the doctor bending over her, the sense of floating from the dose of laudanum, and once, awakening to a dark room and seeing Burke dozing in the wing chair beside her bed. She had slept deep and late, until sunlight poured in her window and it was Mrs. Earnshaw sitting in the chair, her knitting needles clacking away. The fog over Catherine's senses lifted, enabling her to think clearly. For hours she had pondered the chain of events, and most of all, Lord Westhaven's unexpected arrival.

Against the cook's protests, Catherine donned a loose gown of sea-green muslin and an amber shawl that deepened the color of her eyes. Unable to contain her anxiety, she had pinched her wan cheeks and gone in search of Burke.

Now, she took a shallow breath, gathered her strength, and walked toward the group seated around the fireplace. "Good day," she said in her brightest voice.

Everyone turned to stare. Their mouths agape, the twins sat side by side, clad in complementary dresses of claret-red and toast-brown. Lorena pressed a hand to her pillowy bosom. Roderick Grisham coolly sat back on the gilt settee, looking for all the world like a despot on his throne.

Burke half-threw his cup onto the table and sprang to her side, leaving Owen to mop up another mess. "What the devil are you doing out of bed? Did you need more laudanum? I told Mrs. Earnshaw not to leave you on any account."

"It isn't her fault. I feel decidedly better."

"You look pale as a ghost. I'll carry you back upstairs."

Burke made a move to pick her up, but she stepped away, though smiling at his protectiveness. She felt the giddy urge to kiss him right there, in front of their gawking audience. "Do stop fussing. I shall be fine so long as I'm seated."

Radiating dour disapproval, Roderick Grisham rose to his feet. "Allow me." He helped her to the settee, then brought over a Sheridan chair for himself. His gentlemanly act surprised her.

Prudence sat, pouting. "We've been wondering who shot you."

That question had troubled Catherine as well. She could draw only one conclusion. "It was surely an accident. A stray bullet from a hunter's gun. Likely he wasn't even aware I'd been injured."

"My thoughts precisely." A sympathetic smile on her face, Lorena poured a cup of tea and brought it to Catherine. "There, my dear. It was a terrible mishap, nothing more. Even the parish constable thought so."

"Then again, perhaps not," Burke said with deadly calm.

The darkness in his eyes alarmed Catherine. "What do you mean? What other explanation could there be?"

"This morning I returned to the place where the shooting occurred. It was at a vantage point where the gunman had a clear view of the road. Behind a large tree trunk, I found the crumbs from someone's luncheon. And a linen patch used in loading a bullet in a gun."

Roderick Grisham stared unblinking at his son. "You're saying someone really was lying in wait to shoot Mrs. Snow?"

"Yes. I am."

His words sank like stones into the silence of the room. Catherine swallowed a sip of tea without tasting it. The notion was outrageous. Unthinkable. She had no enemies, no one who would wish her dead.

"See, I was right," Prudence said. "It was the robber. He was waiting for an unsuspecting traveler to come along."

"It might have been us on that road," Priscilla added with a delicate shiver. "My sister and I were out making calls all afternoon."

"What about Fabian?" Burke asked. "Does anyone know where he was yesterday?"

Catherine leaned forward, heedless of the throbbing in her side. "Surely you can't accuse him of wrongdoing." Burke gazed steadily at her. She knew with a sickening lurch in her stomach that he was thinking of how distraught Fabian had been when she had turned down his proposal of marriage. "He would never hurt me. Never."

At his post near the wall, Owen shuffled his feet. "Pardon, ma'am. Mr. Snow was out hunting yesterday. Brought in a brace of pheasants for tonight's table. Seemed in a hurry, he did. Said he had other duties to attend."

"There, you see," Lorena said as she helped herself to a generous slice of plum cake. "The mystery is solved. Poor Fabian accidentally shot Catherine and won't own up to it."

"This is nonsense," Catherine said heatedly. "Fabian paid me a visit this afternoon, and he couldn't have been more solicitous of my welfare."

"Perhaps so." Burke tapped his fingers on his empty china cup and looked straight at Lorena. "The other possibility is Ezekiel Newberry."

The name struck Catherine like a slap. She remembered too well his groping attack on her only a few days ago. Could the shooting be connected somehow to Alfred's secret? Her head ached from trying to find a logical answer. Even if Alfred had been Newberry's son, that had nothing to do with *her.*

Lorena stabbed a morsel of cake with her silver fork. "Are you referring to that poltroon who intruded upon my ball?"

Burke's smile failed to reach his eyes. "Yes. Two days

ago, Newberry settled his account at the Fox and Hound. No one has seen him since. I thought you might know his whereabouts."

"I?" Lorena pinched her lips tight. Abruptly she turned to her daughters and clapped her hands. "Run along to the music room, girls. It's time for your pianoforte practice."

"I want to hear about Mr. Newberry," Prudence objected. "He was a fine dancer and a handsome gentleman."

"Why does Catherine get to stay?" Priscilla asked, glowering. "She shouldn't have special privileges just because his lordship has taken a fancy to her."

So they knew, Catherine thought in dismay. She wanted to deny the betrothal, but she couldn't. Not until she had spoken to Burke in private.

"Do as I say," Lorena told her daughters, "and I shall take you to the milliner's on Thursday."

"Oh, thank you!" the girls cried in unison. They each kissed their mother on the cheek and then sauntered out, whispering behind their hands.

"Now," Burke said, "answer my question. Where is Newberry?"

"La, his whereabouts are a mystery to me. And I must take you to task for mentioning the cad in front of my daughters. They are so innocent in the ways of the world."

"Who is this Newberry?" Roderick asked, setting down his cup. "Why would he shoot Mrs. Snow?"

"It's none of your concern," Burke growled. "In fact, you should leave the room, too."

His father's eyes narrowed. "Are you so sure the bullet wasn't meant for you?"

Burke laughed, a harsh sound of denial. "Don't be absurd."

"Is it absurd?" Roderick rose from his chair and paced back and forth, his hands behind his back. "Is a threat against you any more peculiar than someone wanting to harm a lady from the country? The gunman could have been the husband of one of your former lovers, or someone who lost a fortune in cards to you."

Lorena gasped. "Now there's a notion! Could it be true?"

Ignoring her, Burke stared at Roderick. "Or hired by a father wanting to get rid of his embarrassment of a son?"

"It's a pity you didn't stop the carriage," Roderick snapped, giving Burke a piercing glare. "You might have caught the villain right then and there."

Burke crossed his booted legs at the ankles. "Who, me? Never."

Catherine knew his careless manner hid the hurting little boy who had fled after his older brother had been shot. The boy who had endured his father's scathing denunciation.

She sat thunderstruck by the tension between the two men. Their hostility vibrated the air like a gust of frigid wind. After all these years, Colin's ghost still separated them.

Catherine pressed her palm to her aching side. "Burke would never have left me to bleed while he went chasing through the woods. He had the good sense to consider my safety first."

"Be that as it may," Roderick said, "the fact remains that we don't know if the gunman held a grudge against my son or against you." His frosty gaze chilled her from head to toe. "So tell me more about this Newberry fellow. Were you and he lovers?"

Like a streak of dark lightning, Burke surged from his chair. He twisted his fist into the front of Roderick's shirt. "One more insult to her character, and I'll send you to hell."

"Stop it. Both of you." Bracing one hand on the settee, Catherine pushed to her feet. Their strife made her head pound abominably. "I can't mend what's gone wrong between you two, but I can forbid you to use me as your gauntlet."

Roderick Grisham regarded her in tight-lipped fury. "God preserve me from interfering females. I can handle my own son."

"Nevertheless, I will have no more of your boorish behavior." She turned to Burke, who appeared equally irate. In truth, father and son looked remarkably similar, from icy gray eyes to obstinate jaws to belligerent stance. "As to you, my lord, you should know by now that I don't need you to threaten anyone on my behalf. Least of all, your own father."

"Catherine, that gunshot must have addled your wits," Lorena said, clutching her napkin to her bosom. "Apologize at once to our guests."

"Feel free to do so on my behalf. You simper so much better than I."

Lorena's breast puffed up like a pigeon's. "Well!"

Catherine took one last glance at Burke, who somehow managed to look both sheepish and irate at the same time. Curbing an untimely swell of yearning, she said, "You disappoint me, all of you. Don't expect me to be a party to your quarreling any longer."

Turning on her heel, she walked out of the drawing room.

Chapter 18

Mentally flaying himself, Burke strode into the foyer. He hadn't meant to cause Catherine more pain. He caught up to her at the grand staircase and slid his arm around her slender form. Though she held her spine erect, he could feel the quivering of her muscles, as if the mere act of standing were a strain. The dark smudges beneath her eyes enhanced her aura of fragility.

"I told you," she said, "I can manage on my own."

She reminded him of a rose, fragrant and exquisite—and thorny as the devil. "You might swoon on your own, too. So humor me this once."

He drew her up the marble steps. Her movements had a stiffness he recognized from his own convalescence. As they reached the top of the staircase, she stopped.

Her eyes glowed like gemstones in the dusky light. "You've done your duty. Go back downstairs now and make peace with your father."

Burke felt a burning pressure inside his chest. "Spare me that punishment. With any luck he'll leave."

It was proof of her exhaustion that Catherine didn't

protest his assistance again. He guided her down the dim passage, their footsteps echoing.

She frowned at him as if pondering a puzzle. "Perhaps if you two talked as adults instead of snarling at each other, you might find a common ground. Can't you see you're hurting each other?"

"I've nothing to say to that pompous paragon."

"You had plenty of insults."

"I learned verbal sparring at his knee."

"I'm appalled at you, threatening to send your own father to hell." Catherine shook her head. "No wonder you two don't get along. Neither of you even tries."

Though shame stirred inside him, Burke denied her indictment. "Shall I welcome him with open arms? Let him order me around like a stripling? By the time I was seven, I'd learned to fight back or die."

She shushed him with a finger to his lips. "I'm not excusing him for hurting you in the past. But you might try reaching out to him now. Did you ever stop to consider how lucky you are to have a father?"

The earnestness of her voice gave Burke pause. What had it been like for Catherine, to lose her parents at a tender age, to be thrust into a strange household and forced to labor for a living? He had grown up with all the privileges of his rank: a superior education, an inherited fortune, a grand estate.

And a father who damned his son as a stinking coward.

The old embers of rebellion smoldered inside Burke. "I might as well be dead. He hasn't bothered to visit me in over ten years."

Outside her door, Catherine drew him around to face her. "You never went to see him either, did you? Perhaps he thought you didn't want him in your life."

"There's no *perhaps* about it. He and I get along like two rams locking horns. The less I see of him, the better."

"Yet he's here now. That must mean he cares about you."

Hating the empty ache inside him, Burke thrust open the door and conducted her inside. "Trust me, he wouldn't have come except to put a damper on my marriage plans."

She drew a breath and expelled it slowly. Leaving his side, Catherine walked to the bed and slumped against the post. "Oh, Burke. You knew I hadn't agreed to marry you. Why didn't you tell him the truth?"

Her words hit him like a blow to the stomach. The pain traveled upward, causing his temples to throb.

The truth. Tell him the truth.

A chill tingled over his arms and chest and neck. He tensed his muscles against the memory. He needed to answer Catherine, to romance her into accepting his proposal. Yet the shadowed walls of the bedroom dissolved into blinding light.

Burke slowed the carriage on the road to the battleground. The stench of smoke and the snap of gunfire made a vulgar contrast to the sunny afternoon. He looked carelessly elegant in a dark suit and snowy cravat as if he were off to a day at the races. He said, "I'm joining our illustrious fighting men. Now get down with you."

Alfred blinked his gritty eyes at the distant fighting. Like tin soldiers, a company of red-coated cavalrymen was charging a line of blue-clad French infantrymen. Screams and shouts carried across the trampled field, where bodies scattered the ground in horrifying numbers. So many Englishmen lay dying.

He had been too caught up in his own troubles to consider them, but now he imagined himself out there. Feeling the agony of a bullet cutting through flesh and bone. Experiencing the slide into blackness. Then . . . nothing. The end of earthbound torment.

The dark appeal of it gripped Alfred in a cold shudder.

Christ. Why couldn't he be more like Burke, sitting tall and confident, unafraid even in the face of death?

Because Burke wasn't an imposter. He had a code of honor, an unwavering valor. A sense of fairness and loyalty.

Tell him the truth. Tell him what Newberry knows. This may be your last chance.

But more than death itself, Alfred feared Burke's pity. He uptilted the silver flask and let the brandy sear him with false courage. "I'm going with you."

"No!" Burke bit out. "You're drunk. Besides, you've a wife waiting for you at home."

A wife he'd failed. A wife he'd reduced to weeping and begging for a husband who was nothing but a fraud.

Alfred twisted the gold ring on his finger. "Perhaps Catherine is better off without me."

Burke cast him a moody, inquiring look. "No woman is worth dying for."

If only he knew. Alfred had the sudden, futile wish that Burke had been the one to see Catherine for the first time as an amber-eyed girl smiling shyly in a church vestry. Burke should have married her. If ever he found the devotion of a good woman, he wouldn't squander it, the way Alfred had done.

"On the contrary," Alfred said slowly, "I pray you'll someday know such love yourself."

The scene wavered and vanished, leaving Burke with a dream-like memory of hot sunshine, ringing gunfire, and faroff cries. And a heavy sorrow for Alfred, who had given up on life even before a French bullet had struck him down.

Why? What secret did Newberry know?

The questions faded as Burke struggled with another puzzle. Alfred was wrong about him. Burke hadn't been courageous. He had been driven by the need to outrace his own demons, the demons of cowardice.

He sank onto the edge of the bed and bowed his

head, his fingers ploughing into his hair. Alfred had viewed him as a soul worth redeeming, as a man of honor and conviction. The shock of it was as mind-opening as a plunge into icy water. Burke had always regarded himself as undeserving of admiration. Undeserving of love. He thought the whole world had looked at him and jeered.

Had he been wrong all these years?

"Burke? Answer me."

He looked up to see Catherine standing against the bedpost, her expression stern. The sea-green gown with its high waist enhanced her alabaster complexion, and the dusk light lent a luminous, almost unearthly quality to her skin. He couldn't for the life of him remember the question he was supposed to answer.

"We can't ignore what you've done," she added. "We have to talk about this."

This? His mind went blank to all but the rise and fall of her breasts, the way she stood straight and proud despite the injury that would have turned any other woman into a whining invalid. How beautiful she was, inside and out.

A fathomless love escaped the iron bonds around his emotions. A love so brilliant he had felt it only once before—in the tunnel of heavenly light.

The radiance spread through him with frightening intensity. Burke sprang up from the bed and gathered her close, treasuring the warmth of her. She melted into him, her silken hair brushing his cheek, her breasts soft against his chest. A river of excitement flowed through him. Surely that was all he felt—a physical need. He was terrified to feel more. And yet he did. How sweet and artless she was, how he wanted to make love to her again, to give tangible form to his feelings, to lose himself in the instinctual bond between man and woman.

Still caught up in the memory, he murmured, "It's

odd how things have turned out. He wanted me to have the devotion of a good woman. To find . . . love."

She arched back and frowned. "Your *father* said that?"

"Not him. Alfred."

Catherine stiffened in his arms. "You remembered something else," she whispered. "That's why you had a glazed expression. When are his memories going to stop haunting you?"

"Perhaps when my own replace them."

She lowered her gaze, and he noticed again the paleness of her cheeks. Then she cautiously looked up again, her eyes huge and wary, framed by thick dark lashes. "What exactly did you recall?"

He kissed the tip of her nose. "Don't look so worried. For once, the memory had little to do with you."

"I still want to know what you saw."

"And you shall. But you'll get yourself to bed first. Turn around now."

"It's highly improper for you to be here in my bedroom."

"If it's Lorena you're worried about, I'll explain matters to her. She can hardly think I would take advantage of you in your condition."

But he wanted to. As he unbuttoned the back of her gown, Burke found himself fascinated by her swan-like neck. Resisting the urge to kiss her there, he helped Catherine step out of her dress.

As he guided her against the pillows, she seemed perfectly at ease in her undergarments, the clinging chemise, the lacy drawers, the silk stockings. His physical response was swift and hot. And discomfiting, for he could also see the faint bulge of the bandage on her side.

"Now," she said, folding her hands in her lap, "tell me everything."

Restlessly pacing the small bedroom, Burke forced

his mind from the temptation of her. "It was a memory of Waterloo. I tried to convince Alfred to keep away from the battlefield. But he insisted on helping our wounded soldiers, and I couldn't stop him. That's all."

"That can't be all. You looked so intense. What exactly did he say? What was he thinking? And feeling?"

Burke hesitated, uneasy at betraying Alfred's private torments. Better that Alfred should remain a hero in the eyes of his widow. "If I appeared engrossed in the memory, it was out of amazement to see myself through the eyes of another person."

"And what did you see?"

Unable to bear her scrutiny, he roamed to the window to peer at the sunset spreading rosy fingers of light over the garden. "Something quite the opposite of my reputation."

"Namely?"

Burke shrugged. "He believed me confident . . . commendable . . . a man of honor. Little did he know."

"On the contrary, it was amazingly perceptive of Alfred." Catherine's smile illuminated her face. "You've changed since the first time I saw you. Certainly you've committed your share of sins, but you've also shown yourself to be considerate. Generous. Brave. And you've a bad habit of downplaying your virtues and letting the world think you a rogue."

He *was* a rogue. Only a rogue would be eyeing her shadowy cleavage and contemplating ways to get her undressed, to slake his own need when she was sorely in need of rest. With any other woman he would already have put his plan into action. But this was Catherine, and he was committed to protecting her. It was a strange new feeling for him.

The deep beauty of her eyes slowed his prowling. How compelling they were, a hue somewhere between brown and gold, glowing as rich and mysterious as amber. He could gaze into them for a lifetime. Somehow he felt complete when they were together like this, talking companionably, sharing their thoughts much as a husband and wife must do.

"Burke? You have that faraway look again."

He blinked, realizing he was staring, caught up in the fantasy that he was the paragon she considered him. But a true hero wouldn't use her mistaken belief to his own advantage, as he was about to do.

He sat beside her, the bedropes creaking under his weight. Gathering the delicate weight of her hands in his, he said, "Since you think so highly of me, you admit I'll make you the perfect husband. You'll marry me."

Catherine felt her throat close on a knot of yearning. Gazing into the smoky depths of his eyes, she knew Burke embodied the man of her dreams—exciting, strong, humorous, tender. Yet she couldn't have him; she mustn't have him. She couldn't give him what he truly needed. A family.

"Burke, I—"

He put his finger to her lips. "Before you say no again, let me say that as lovely as Gilly Grange is, Thorncroft Castle is a hundred times more beautiful."

"You live in a castle?"

"In a manner of speaking. The house was built by my great-grandfather on the site of a ruined castle, and the present great hall incorporates the old stone keep." The fervor of pride burned on his face. "There's a sense of history about the place, a majesty that defies description. You'll have to see the house and judge for yourself."

If only she could. "It sounds utterly fascinating."

"You haven't heard the half of it. Thorncroft Castle stands on a cliff overlooking the sea. At night you can hear the waves crashing onto the shore." He went on to describe the sandy beaches, the hills laced with lush river valleys, and the moor with its glistening bogs and windswept freedom.

Catherine hung on his every word. She would live happily in a hovel—if only she could be his wife. But that was the one role she must never fulfill.

Her heart breaking, she raised his hands to her mouth and tenderly kissed them. "You do me a great honor. Yet there's something you don't know, or you wouldn't have offered for me. I was trying to tell you in the carriage yesterday, right before I was shot."

"It's Alfred, isn't it?" Burke asked on a sharp note. "You said once that your one true love is dead."

Catherine shook her head. "I did love him, but . . ." She paused, aching to express her feelings for Burke, yet reluctant to give him false hope. "But this is a different matter entirely."

"There's nothing you can say that could change my mind," Burke insisted. "But go ahead. I'm listening."

She gazed down at their clasped hands, his fingers brown against her fair skin. It was easier than looking at his face. "I can't ever have your children. I'm barren."

So small a word it was—*barren.* Yet it echoed like a curse in the silence of the bedroom.

She waited for Burke to recoil in shock, to withdraw from her. Instead, he tipped her chin up to meet his steady gaze. "You became pregnant at least once, didn't you? I remember Alfred telling me you'd miscarried."

"Yes." She drew a deep breath to ease the aching in her chest. "Do you remember the time I said I'd gone to London four years ago and witnessed the party you gave for him?"

"How could I forget? It's a wonder you'll even speak to me."

"I'd gone to tell Alfred that I was pregnant. But after seeing him with Stella Sexton, I was so distraught, I ran out of the house and into the street. Straight into the path of a carriage." In her mind she heard the shout of the coachman, saw the rearing horse, felt the terrible pain strike her belly. Even now tears burned her eyes at the memory. "I lost the baby. The doctor said my womb had been damaged forever."

Quiet settled over the room. She lifted her eyes to see Burke staring at her. "The scar," he muttered. "On your abdomen."

"It's from the horse's hoof."

He sat still on the bed. Then he bowed his head and raked his fingers into his hair. "My God. How you must hate me."

"No." Trembling from the force of her feelings, she caressed his cheek. "It was an accident. No one planned it. *I* was as much to blame as anyone for not warning Alfred about my visit."

Burke looked unconvinced. He got up from the bed and paced the room. "This doctor, he was a reputable man?"

"The very best in London. And his diagnosis was right. I never conceived again in three years."

"How could you have?" In sudden savagery, Burke struck his fist on the bedpost. "Alfred spent so much of his time in London. He left you here for weeks on end. It won't be that way with us, Catherine."

He still wished to marry her? She braced her shaking fingers in her lap. "You'll go off to London, too."

"If I do, you'll accompany me. We shan't spend a night apart for the rest of our lives. If there's the slightest chance of your bearing a child, I want it to be mine."

Catherine understood his disbelief; she herself had wrestled with the same poignant determination to prove the doctor wrong. She remembered the hope that had flared each time Alfred had come to her bed, and then the crushing disappointment each month.

And now that same hope sparked anew. Against her will, she felt the awakening of dreams that had slept so deeply she thought them gone forever. The dream of having a husband and a family, a baby to cuddle to her breast. A baby with black hair and laughing gray eyes.

Burke deserved a son, a mischievous boy to guide as he had done Peter Guppy. And a beautiful daughter to put a prideful shine in his eyes. A whole clan of children to give him the love he had never known in his own youth. If she failed . . .

She swallowed hard. "You must have an heir. It's expected of you."

"I'll leave the dynasty-building to men like my father. If we don't have children, then it wasn't meant to be." He sat down on the bed and looked at her with a steady flame burning in his eyes. "I know little about love, Catherine. I've considered it a useless emotion for so long that I don't know if I can change. But I do know that I want you—only you as my wife."

Wonderment trembled inside her. In a daze, she reached out and traced his jaw, his skin faintly rough to her fingertips. She wanted so badly to take a chance on him. Yet a shadow haunted her joy. Burke didn't realize, as she did, that the luster of romance could tarnish under the day-to-day strain of marriage. Regrets would take root in him, withering love before it had a chance to grow. She had seen that happen once, and this time would be a thousandfold worse.

"I love you," she whispered. "With all my heart. Don't let's think beyond that for now."

She placed her hands on either side of his face and drew him closer for a kiss. He held her as if she were made of spun glass. But Catherine wanted him to treat her like a woman, not a breakable treasure. She licked the seam of his lips in tiny, stinging strokes until a groan broke from him and his hard body settled over her uninjured side.

The kiss deepened into a creation of his own making, his tongue tasting and teasing, wooing and warming. He slipped his fingers along her neck, caressing the hollow of her throat, stroking the underside of her jaw, rubbing the tender base of her ear. The sensations he aroused rippled downward to her very core, pulsing and shimmering like a pool of liquid heat. Restless and aching, Catherine reached between them and showed him exactly what she needed.

For one heady moment he thrust against her fingers. Then with a sharp breath, he pushed himself back and braced his hands on either side of her, tension quivering from his every muscle. "What the devil am I doing?"

"You?" Smiling, she reached for the buttons of his shirt. "I could have sworn we were partners in this seduction."

"Stop that." Speaking in his most imperious tone, he caught her wrist in a gentle vise. "There will be no seduction while you're lying on your sickbed."

She did indeed feel an uncomfortable burning in her side. But the fire inside her glowed brighter. "Ah, but the rest of my body aches for you, Burke."

"I won't permit you to exert yourself."

"Who said anything about exertion? I promise to lie here quietly while you do all sorts of wicked and wonderful things to me."

One corner of his glowering mouth twitched. "Quietly?"

She blushed. "Well, perhaps I'll utter a sound or two. But I'll endeavor not to strain myself. Now, don't gainsay a wounded woman." She deftly untied his cravat, then slid her hands inside his opened collar, savoring the smooth warmth of his skin.

It was all the persuasion he required. He got off the bed and locked the door. In the lavender light of dusk, he shed shirt and boots and breeches. Lying against the pillows, Catherine admired the play of his muscles, the brownness of his skin, the expanse of his chest. The scar on his shoulder added to his rakish appeal, and the sight of him naked took her breath away.

She held out her hand, whispering, "Come."

"With pleasure."

Stretching out full-length beside her, he hooked his leg over her thighs so that his knee touched her center with insistent pressure. They kissed long and slow and deep, and she gloried in the feel of their warm skin pressed together and the heat building steadily into a consuming blaze. He withdrew to peel away her undergarments, tarrying over the stockings, his mouth flowing like warm silk over all the places his fingers touched. His lips lingered a moment over the scar on her belly.

Catherine tried to sit up, to draw him down on her again, but he forestalled her. "Lie still," he commanded. "Mind your promise."

She sank back onto the pillows, not so much from obedience as from surprise when he lifted her foot and kissed each toe in turn. Never would she have thought such an action could excite her, yet anticipation curled inside her, coiling tighter as he moved up the slim length of her leg, anointing her with kisses. And then he parted her softness and put his mouth to the mystery of her.

Always before, this aspect of intimacy had seemed bestial, embarrassing. But this time it was an act of love. The laving of his tongue wrested a gasp from her, and in wordless encouragement, she slid her fingers into the thickness of his hair, needing to touch him while the tide of feelings swelled and crested, and she gave herself up to radiant release.

As her pleasure subsided to slow sensual ripples, he knelt in the nave of her legs and smiled, his gaze alight with tenderness. "This is how I want to spend the rest of my life. Be forewarned, I intend to make that your dream, too."

On that, he joined their bodies, and a rich surge of feeling flooded Catherine. It would be so simple to fall into the fantasy of becoming his wife. Yet it would also be the ultimate act of selfishness. As powerful as he was, the earl of Thornwald could not command her to conceive.

He feathered his fingertips over her belly and breasts, and when he touched the place where they were linked, she felt a leap of longing that drove all thought from her mind. The mystical bond between their souls enhanced the sweet sensations in her body until she cried out her joy to the heavens and he spilled his seed inside her.

He lay beside her, caressing her, though with more tenderness than fire now. Dusk had darkened to the deep purple of evening and veiled the room in shadow. With gentle fingers, he probed her bandage, a padding of bleached linen tied with strips around her midsection. "Are you in pain?"

Sighing, she snuggled into the warmth of his chest. "If this is pain, I certainly like it."

He smoothed back the cloud of her hair. "How's the bump on your head?"

"I'm fine, truly." She turned her head and kissed his throat, savoring the scent of his skin. "You can minister to my wounds any time."

He braced himself on his elbow, his features solemn through the gloaming. His brow was furrowed as if his mind roamed far from this bedroom.

A sudden notion darkened Catherine's bliss. "You're thinking about who shot me."

Though he continued to stroke her hair, his eyes glittered with cold purpose. "It needn't trouble you. Just rest and heal."

"The shooting was surely an accident," she said, trying to convince herself, too. "It won't happen again."

His cocked eyebrow conveyed disbelief. "We can't know that for certain. That's why you're leaving here in a day or two, as soon as you're able to travel."

His dark tone evoked a shiver in her. Heedless of the

throbbing in her side, she pushed up against the pillows. "Where will I go?" she asked in bewilderment.

"Where you belong," he said firmly. "You'll live at my estate in Cornwall."

Lorena sat preening at the satinwood dressing table. Her boudoir lay in shadow except for the lamp flickering amid the clutter of perfume flagons and rouge pots. A purple turban hiding her hair, she performed the nightly regimen that preserved her beauty. Over her face, she smoothed a pomade of onion juice, honey, and wax. The miracle ointment was one of Catherine's creations, a fact that did not mollify Lorena in the least.

Ordinarily, she would have been triumphant to host both a marquis and an earl under her roof. But tonight she felt an ugly fury directed at Catherine. At this very moment, the chit was entertaining the earl in her bedroom.

Lorena considered marching there, sweeping the door open on their tryst, acting the outraged mother-in-law and ruining Catherine's reputation in the process. Only the likelihood of angering his lordship stopped her. If there was one thing men found unforgivable, it was having their pleasure interrupted.

Lifting her chin, she stroked a thin layer of paste over her fleshy neck. It went on with a soothing, sensual coolness that calmed her. In the morning, when she removed the cream, her skin would be dewy fresh and nearly unwrinkled.

Wiping her fingers on a linen towel, Lorena turned her head to and fro, and smiled at her ghostly white face in the glass. For a woman approaching the half-century mark, she looked remarkably fine. Certainly she had put on a few pounds over the years, but the weight only added to her majesty. She wondered if the marquis of Westhaven liked his women pleasingly plump.

The thought was only fleeting. Judging by his animosity toward his son, Roderick Grisham might wish to father a whole new family. And Priscilla would make a lovely marchioness.

A small scraping noise came from behind her. Lorena's eyes widened. In the mirror loomed the dark face of a man.

"Arrghh!" Snatching up a perfume bottle as a weapon, Lorena rotated on the stool. The delicate wood creaked beneath her bulk.

The interloper struck a pose in his black superfine coat and nankeen pantaloons, the ivory-topped cane adding to his dapper appearance. Her heart thundered and the breath squeaked out of her. "Zeke."

"Evening, darling. What is that smelly stuff? If you want to attract a man, I'd suggest you stop eating cake instead."

She barely noticed his insult. Through dry lips, she asked, "How did you get in here?"

"As you well know, m'dear, there ain't a lock in this world that I can't pick." Zeke Newberry sauntered around the gloomy bedroom, opening drawers and wardrobes, even peering into the bidet cabinet. "You do keep this house buttoned up as tight as Newgate Prison. A bloke might think you're afraid of robbers here."

Those keen blue eyes were laughing at her. She wanted to scream, *Get out!* But he would never leave until he'd gotten what he wanted.

Striving for calm, she placed the bottle back on the dressing table. "Lord Thornwald has been looking for you. Into what hole have you scuttled?"

Zeke prowled closer, found her brocaded jewelry box, and opened it. "Ah, Peg, m'love, if I told you, would you surprise me one night? Would you set me afire like you used to do?"

She sat rigid, the unwelcome images tumbling from the secret reaches of memory. He exuded the same spicy aroma, yet now the scent roused disgust in her. "If his lordship finds you in this house he'll kill you."

"And you'd hand him the pistol, no doubt." Zeke took out her diamond necklace and examined it in the lamplight. "What a fine lady you've become, my own. These stones must be worth a bloody fortune."

"That's a family heirloom. Give it to me." Lorena snatched the necklace from him and clutched it to her bosom. "You're a fool for taking that shot at Catherine. What if his lordship had stopped the carriage and come after you?"

"Ah, such concern for my well-being." He rocked back and forth on his heels, using the cane as a lever. "A shame I missed, eh? That's two thousand pounds we could be spending right now. And we could've split the estate revenues from now on." He had the audacity to wink at her. "It'd be just like old times."

"There is no *we,*" she snapped. "Not anymore."

"Ah, darling. And here, I thought you'd be even more generous than dear Freddie."

At the mention of her son, Lorena lost all restraint. "You blundering idiot. I've no money to spare so long as Catherine lives. So get your filthy carcass out of here."

"My, old age has made you forgetful." Lightning quick, Zeke twisted the cane apart and held a rapier to her throat. "Like it or not, you owe me a debt until death do us part. You'll not be cheating me, my plump little pigeon."

The tip of the sword nicked her skin. Lorena imagined it slicing across her throat, and terror descended to her bowels. "I-I'm sorry," she forced out.

"Now that's more like it. You can hand over your first payment straightaway." He moved the sword lower and poked the necklace. She clung to the gems for a moment, then with a whimper, loosened her sweaty grip. The diamonds flashed as he tossed the necklace in the air. He neatly caught it in one hand and let it slither into his coat pocket. "Thank you, m'dear."

Feeling suddenly old, Lorena groped for a cloth and held it to her bleeding throat.

A metallic rattle sounded as he slid the rapier back into the cane. "If you must know, I missed Catherine on purpose. Just as I was aiming the pistol"—he held up the cane and pointed it at Lorena—"I had a brilliant idea."

Lorena glowered at him. "What might that be?"

"Catherine's quite the handsome female. And here I am, a poor bloke having to do without. So I thought, Zeke, old boy, maybe you should marry the chit yourself." He grinned like a wizened monkey. "Imagine, I could be living in this fancy house with you."

Only fear kept Lorena from leaping up and clawing his eyes out. She reminded herself that he could never succeed; the earl had already laid claim to Catherine.

A half-formed plan sprang to her mind. A plan to get rid of Ezekiel Newberry for good. His lust might just be the key.

She pasted on an affable smile. "If it's Catherine you want, you should have said so. La, I'll even help you kidnap her."

Chapter 19

Summer was ending, but Catherine felt poised on the brink of a new beginning. She sat on the stone bench beneath the rose arbor and breathed deeply of the crisp September air. A few years ago, this place had been her retreat after quarreling with Alfred. Now it held a happier memory.

Here on the soft grass near the sycamore tree, she and Burke had shared an impassioned kiss. It had happened the night of the ball, the same night he had come to her bed for the first time and roused her slumbering heart.

Smiling, she reflected on the love they shared now. For a man who showed the world the demeanor of a jaded gentleman, Burke had proven himself a tender and considerate lover. Soon he would be more than her lover. He would be her husband.

Catherine drew a shuddering breath, inhaling the scent of late season roses blooming on the arched trellis. The wind swirled a petal downward onto her outstretched palm. She added the velvet petal to the pile in her lap, pink and scarlet and cream against the honey hue of her gown.

Sometime during the darkest hour of night, she had awakened in his arms while Burke lay asleep. Gazing at his beloved face through the shadows, she had felt the uplifting of hope and the quieting of doubt. Why had she resisted the one man who could give her such perfect happiness? Even though she might never bear him a baby, she could work harder to fill his days so that he never noticed a lack. She would open a school so that the children of his estate could satisfy his need for being a father. She would devote every moment of her life to making him happy.

Impatient to tell Burke of her decision, she stirred restlessly on the bench. From this vantage point, she could see over the garden wall to the moor beyond, and for an hour now, she had watched for his big black horse. He'd been gone when she'd awakened to the sun streaming through the window. Gone on his errand to find the gunman.

Catherine refused to let dark suspicion shadow her joy. All morning, she had basked in a mood of splendid bliss. The buoyant feeling had carried her through breakfast, when she had informed the family that she and Burke would be leaving for Cornwall on the morrow. It had lasted despite the veiled insults from Lorena about Catherine spending the night with the earl. It had borne her through the packing of her few belongings and the frequent rests she'd had to take in deference to her injury. And now she waited in dreamy contentment, spinning fantasies of them sitting by the fire on a winter's eve, dancing together at a country ball, sharing a kiss in the middle of the sheepshearing.

Not that she knew anything about sheep. But she could learn. She intended to participate in every part of her husband's life.

The sound of approaching footsteps startled Catherine from her reverie. She turned to see Roderick Grisham marching into the clearing.

"If I may have a word with you, Mrs. Snow."

He radiated disapproval from his frosty gray eyes to the tips of his polished shoes. This stern nobleman would be her father-in-law. Somehow, the thought didn't bother Catherine in the least.

Riding on a crest of happiness, she curved her lips in a serene smile. "Good afternoon, m'lord. It's a beautiful day, is it not?"

She started to rise, to dip a dutiful curtsy, but he waved her back to her seat. "You may dispense with the formalities," he said. "Though I will ask after your health."

"I'm feeling much better today. The brisk air does me well."

His hands clasped behind his back, the marquis regarded her with an intent look. "I am sure you know why I asked to speak with you."

Determined not to be intimidated, she returned his direct gaze. "I am sure that I do not."

His lips tightened. "I'm here to ask you to reconsider your betrothal to my son. Your impertinence only confirms my belief that you're the wrong woman for him."

Her smile slipped a little. "Burke thinks otherwise."

"He only wishes to annoy me."

"Please credit him with more sense than that."

Eyeing her, Roderick paced back and forth. "You are a very handsome woman, Mrs. Snow."

"Thank you."

"However, to be perfectly frank, your background has ill-prepared you for the role of countess of Thornwald. Therefore, I have advised my son not to marry you."

The old doubts crept back. Ignoring them, she asked, "Why did you not visit Burke when he was convalescing after Waterloo?"

The marquis slowed his steps and aimed a wary look at her. "More than a month had passed before I learned he'd been shot. It seems Burke forbade anyone to write to me. By the time he returned to his estate and I received word of his injury, he was quite recovered. There was no point in calling on him then."

"Why not? He is your son."

Roderick scowled. "I'm not here to explain myself to you. The incident has nothing to do with the unsuitability of his marriage plans."

Catherine crushed a handful of rose petals, releasing their fragrant perfume. "I beg to differ," she said softly. "It's proof that you've neglected Burke all these years. And that you have no right to expect him to take your advice now."

"Rights! If Burke had behaved like a man of business instead of a worthless wastrel, I would have been proud to associate with him."

"You still blame him for Colin's death, don't you?"

Roderick spun toward her. Redness tinged his cheeks. "Colin? How dare you presume to speak of him. You know nothing of the situation."

Pressing her trembling hands to the cold bench, she didn't flinch from his fury. "I know that you branded a seven-year-old boy a coward. If Burke grew up to drink and gamble, it was only to forget the pain of his father's cruelty."

Roderick stood like a statue, his expression carved in stone. Though buffeted by a gust of wind, every strand of his graying hair remained perfectly in place. The silence grew as thick as the sycamore leaves lying beneath the tree. Then abruptly he passed his hand over his face. "You can't imagine what it's like to lose a son."

Her throat closed. "Since you can, why have you driven away your only remaining son?"

Roderick resumed pacing, cutting a swath in front of her. "Driven him away? I want to advise him, but he pushes *me* away at every turn. He must realize it is his duty to make a good match with a lady of his own class."

Catherine was through being insulted. She stood up,

the rose petals showering the grass. "Then kindly address your concerns to Burke when he returns. I have nothing more to say to you."

Before she could walk off, the marquis stopped in front of her. He said, "In exchange for your crying off this engagement, I am prepared to offer you the sum of five thousand pounds."

His proposal pierced her breast as cleanly as a bullet. Roderick Grisham thought her nothing but a fortune hunter.

His opinion shouldn't matter. Yet it did.

He watched her keenly. "You're staring, Mrs. Snow. That's hardly the mark of the lady you profess to be."

"Offering a bribe is hardly the mark of the honorable gentleman *you* claim to be. I refuse your money."

Head held high, Catherine marched past him, down the trail of flagstones that led back to the manor. His quick footsteps dogged her heels. Rounding in front of her, he blocked her path.

"If five thousand doesn't suit you," he said, "I can increase the amount—"

"You don't seem to comprehend," she broke in. "I love your son with all my heart. You could not dissuade me from marrying him if you were to offer me the crown jewels."

The marquis lowered his graying eyebrows. For a long moment he looked her up and down. "You force me to broach an indelicate topic, then. Your inability to bear a child."

Nausea burned at the back of Catherine's throat. She swallowed hard, but the bitter taste lingered. "Burke said it didn't matter to him."

"Having an heir matters to all men of property and distinction. Burke will come to realize that very soon, as soon as the fire of youthful lust dies to the reality of marital duty. Especially considering the change he's made in his life."

"Change?"

The harsh lines of Roderick's face softened. "This past year, for the first time, Burke has spent a considerable amount of time at his country estate. He's taken a keen interest in running his own business affairs. Already he's increased the revenues from the estate's wool production. So you see, now more than ever, he'll want a son, an heir to his holdings."

Burke really had changed. All of his jesting about sheep-breeding was in fact the truth.

Catherine crossed her arms in a vain effort to ward off the agony of truth. He would wish to improve his lands for a purpose. To create a legacy for his children.

Dear God. She had let herself be seduced by romantic dreams. But the marquis was right. Someday, the lack of a son would cause an aching hole in Burke's life. No matter how he avowed to the contrary, no matter how hard she worked to fill the gap, in time he would come to regret his choice of a wife.

"You really do love him." His gaze unexpectedly kind, Roderick placed his hands on her shoulders. "I came here convinced you wanted my son solely for his fortune and position. I apologize for judging you so harshly—and for causing you distress. Yet if your feelings for Burke are true, then you won't condemn him to a childless marriage."

"Ouch!"

Lorena flinched at the tugging pain in her scalp. Swiveling on the stool, she snatched the hairbrush from Martha. "Clodpate! You'll find yourself scrubbing pots in the scullery if you can't dress hair better than that."

The maid pursed her cherry lips. "Sorry, ma'am. I'm doing as best I can."

Those bold brown eyes held no respect. Lorena had seen that same brazen look in Catherine.

Catherine, who was leaving in the morning. She had

risen from her sickbed and made the announcement to the family over breakfast. The shock of it still stormed inside Lorena, giving rise to a whirlwind of frustration.

She surged up from the stool and swung the hairbrush at Martha. "Insolent chit."

With a loud smack, the silver brush met flesh. Gasping, the maid staggered backward, cradling her cheek. Her lower lip quivered, yet she held her chin high. "Thee shouldn't have done so. I'll have a mark. And I'll have to tell where I got it."

"Don't threaten me, you plebeian. Who could you possibly tell?"

"Me," came a voice from the doorway. "She can t-tell me."

Lorena turned to see Fabian entering the boudoir. As always, the floppy-eared dog trotted at his heels. The gangly man walked to Martha, gently moved her hand from her cheek, and examined the redness that marred her creamy skin.

He pivoted toward Lorena on the heels of his jackboots. "You oughtn't have hit her. I-I demand an apology."

His tone had a sharpness that Lorena had never heard before. He held his shoulders straight, and despite his drab country tweeds and ill-tied cravat, he looked like a man to be reckoned with. Even odder, he gripped Martha's hand as if they were sweethearts.

So that was the way of it, Lorena thought, reeling from her second shock of the day. No wonder he had never taken an interest in Prudence. This common chit had lifted her skirts for the master of Snow Manor. Even an idiot like Fabian would be mesmerized by a taste of warm female flesh.

Lorena fought down her ire. For now, she must pacify him. She had summoned him here because his unwitting assistance was crucial to her scheme.

"You're absolutely right, Nephew," she said, working

her lips into a contrite smile. "I made a terrible error of judgment. Do forgive me, Martha."

Wary-eyed, the maid dipped a curtsy. "Aye, ma'am."

"Now run along, dear. Mr. Snow and I must have a private chat."

A soft insistent rapping interrupted Catherine as she knelt before the trunk in her bedroom. Her gaze flew to the door. Burke. He must have returned at last.

Her heart took a joyful leap, then plummeted deep in her chest. The time had come for her to tell him.

Slowly she unclenched her fingers, dropped the petticoat back into the trunk, and rose stiffly. Pain prickled her side. Other than sitting down to write one letter, she had kept busy all afternoon, nervously arranging and rearranging her belongings.

Taking shallow breaths, she walked to the door and opened it. Just as she hoped and feared, Burke filled the doorway with his broad shoulders and commanding presence. A ray of late afternoon sunshine enveloped him in golden light. His hair was mussed from the wind and a strand dipped rakishly onto his brow.

His smile flashed white across his bronzed features. "You're looking fit, thank God."

"I am better." She couldn't resist adding, "Now."

He bent to kiss her, his lips tender and firm, infusing her with the unique scent and taste of him. Catherine's weariness slid away on a rush of love so poignant it sparked stinging tears in her eyes. She savored the precious moment, the sense of completeness she felt only in his embrace.

When she slid her arms around his muscled waist, she encountered a cold metal object. Rearing back, she gasped. "Jervis's dueling pistol. Why are you carrying it?"

Burke drew the long-barreled pistol from his waistband and placed the gun on her dressing table. "It's best to be prepared when dealing with rats like Ezekiel Newberry."

In her preoccupation with the future, she had nearly forgotten the man. "Did you find him?"

Grimacing, Burke shut the door. "No. Though a tavern keeper in West Scrafton thinks a man answering Newberry's description might have bought food at the pub yesterday."

"Might have?"

"It was dinner hour and the place was busy, so he couldn't say for certain." Burke stripped off his riding gloves and flung them down beside the gun. "The bastard is still at large."

Catherine touched his tight fist. "Don't torture yourself over it. Surely Newberry has left Yorkshire, just as you told him to do. He's likely far away in London by now."

Burke slowly unclenched his fingers. When he stroked her face, she nestled her cheek in his palm. He smelled of wind and saddle leather and the heady essence of man. In defiance of all wisdom, she felt the rise of wildness inside her, the need of her body for his, the cry of her soul to its mate.

He tipped her chin up, his gaze penetrating. "While I was out riding, I had quite a lot of time to think. I remembered something that might interest you."

"Another of Alfred's memories?" She shook her head, her old reservations a mere trifle beside the torment of saying what must be said now. "They don't matter to me anymore."

"I'm not speaking of Alfred. I wanted to tell you about the Cerne Giant."

"The . . . who?"

He guided her to the bed and sat her down beside him. "The Cerne Giant is an ancient Celtic figure cut into the turf on a chalk hill in Devon. It's a huge naked man outlined white against the green grass."

She smiled at the unexpected image. "Upon my word. What have antiquated drawings to do with me?"

His gaze roved hers with a strange sort of excitement. "The figure was carved many hundreds of years ago as a fertility god." Burke settled his palm over her stomach. "He's said to bring fruitfulness to infertile women."

Catherine sat paralyzed. His smoky eyes were alight with a tender hope that called to her dearest and most futile dreams. The warm weight of his hand covered her womb. As if he yearned to feel his baby kick and grow inside her.

If your feelings for Burke are true, then you won't condemn him to a childless marriage.

"Perhaps it's a lot of superstitious nonsense," Burke went on, "but I thought we might stop there on our way to Cornwall."

She cast away his hand and surged to her feet, backing away from him. "No."

His smile faded. "As you wish. I merely thought the visit might lift your spirits." Rising, he stalked after her. "Considering your injury, it might be best for us to go straight to Thornwald Castle, anyway."

The pain in her heart superceded the pain in her side. Regretting the necessity to hurt him, she hugged herself and forced out the words. "I'm not going to Cornwall."

His eyes darkened. "Of course you're going. I thought we agreed it isn't safe for you here."

"You decided that. I've never felt convinced that someone shot me on purpose." She shook her head. "Ezekiel Newberry has no reason to want me dead."

Burke gathered her against his hard form. "There is a reason. Lorena could have talked him into it. Because she wants to keep your portion of the dower right."

Icy denial spilled through Catherine. "That's unthinkable," she whispered. "Of course Lorena resents giving up the money. But she wouldn't . . . murder me."

"I don't mean to frighten you. Let me do the worrying." Bending, he brushed his lips over hers. "I want to protect you, Catherine, to give you the pampered life you deserve. I want you to be my wife."

Her chest ached with the need to commit herself to him. But indulging herself would mean depriving him of a family. An heir.

Wrenching herself from his embrace, she stepped back until her spine met the hard edge of a wardrobe. "I'm afraid you ask the impossible, Burke. I've thought about it all day. And I've come to the conclusion that we would never suit."

His arms were still lifted as if to hold her again. Slowly he lowered them to his sides. "The devil you say. You can't claim the past few weeks have meant nothing to you." In a husky murmur haunted by disbelief, he added, "Just last night you said you loved me with all your heart."

She regretted remembering the closeness they had shared. Even more, she regretted the stark hurt shadowing his face. But she had no other choice. "I tried marriage once, and that was enough for me. I want my freedom. I want to live on my own and open a school as I'd planned. I've already posted a letter to Mr. Harewood, making an offer for Gilly Grange."

Burke reared back as if she'd slapped him. His chest rose and fell beneath the snowy linen shirt and the dark plum coat that hugged the breadth of his shoulders. Then his eyes hardened with a peculiar intensity. "My father spoke to you, didn't he? He poisoned your mind against me."

She had no wish to broaden the gulf between father and son. Nor to let him blame anyone else. "It was my own decision. My final decision." Her voice caught. "I'll have to ask you to go now."

His lips tightening, he took a step closer. "I'm not leaving you alone tonight."

Catherine thought about being confined with him inside these four walls, with love burning in her heart and the bed so temptingly near. He could so easily lead her from the path of resolution. Unless she turned him away, once and for all.

Chilling her voice, she said, "You were right to call love a useless emotion. I enjoyed our little interlude while it lasted. But it's over now. Over for good."

The noise startled Catherine awake.

She sat up in bed so quickly that pain stabbed her side. The ray of silvery moonlight that trickled through the window barely penetrated the veil of darkness in the bedroom. The wind wuthered around the eaves like the call of a lonely voice. Somewhere outside, a loose shutter banged against the house. That must have been what she'd heard.

As she lowered her head to the pillow, the sound came again. A scratching on the door.

Her heart thumped erratically. Before Burke had departed, before she had wept herself to sleep, he had warned her to take care. He had left the dueling pistol on her dressing table, though she had been too heartsick to heed his instructions on how to use it. He had frightened her with his talk of a murder plot, and she had promised to lock herself in, to trust no one.

Yet she couldn't lie here, paralyzed by fear.

Rising, she felt for her dressing robe and put it on. Then she picked up the heavy pistol and crept through the gloom to the door. "Who is it?"

" 'Tis Martha," came the muffled reply.

Awash with relief, Catherine lay down the gun, turned the key, and opened the door. The maid stood shivering in a voluminous nightdress and mobcap. The candle she held cast quivering shadows over her wide-eyed face.

Martha peered past Catherine into the darkened bedroom. "Thee are alone?"

A pang struck Catherine. "Yes, but what matter is that?"

"The missus told me not to disturb his lordship. She's worked herself into a state and won't have nobody but thee to calm her."

"A state? What about?"

"Her diamond necklace is missing. She roused me out of bed and accused me of snitching it!" Martha clutched Catherine's arm. "But I didn't, Mrs. Catherine. I swear on me Mum's own grave I didn't."

Catherine considered Burke's advice to remain safely in her room. But how could she ignore the maid's tear-dampened face? Someone had to defend her against Lorena.

"Come along." Catherine stepped over the threshold and they started down the gloomy corridor.

"What will thee do?" Martha asked, her voice wobbling.

"I'll make her see your side. Doubtless she misplaced the piece. Or one of the twins borrowed it without her knowledge."

"She already asked Miss Priscilla and Miss Prudence. And they don't have it." Martha sucked in a woebegone breath. "Oh, what if Mr. Fabian believes her? What if he thinks me a thief?"

Her concern for Fabian's opinion surprised Catherine. "He's a fair-minded man. He'll listen to you."

"I pray so," Martha said fervently. "I wouldn't want him thinking me a bad sort."

As they turned a corner, the candlelight illuminated a large brownish mark on her cheek. Catherine angled the girl's face to the light and drew an appalled gasp. "This is a bruise. How did it happen?"

Martha cupped her fingers over the spot. " 'Tis naught."

"Did someone strike you?"

Catching her full lower lip between her teeth, the

maidservant lowered her eyes. And Catherine guessed the truth. "It was Lorena, wasn't it?"

The girl nodded reluctantly. " 'Tis no matter, truly."

Anger swelled in Catherine. She had witnessed Lorena's petty rages before, though usually her mother-in-law exercised more restraint. How dare she raise a hand to a defenseless girl.

Energized by the need to speak her mind, Catherine marched to Lorena's suite and knocked. Lorena flung open the door as if she'd been waiting just inside.

"Praise heavens you're here." She glided forward, her white nightgown spread like the broad side of a sail. The burgundy turban hiding her hair emphasized the pallor of her face. She clutched a frilly handkerchief and pointed a finger at Martha. "There she is, the little thieving baggage! Have you returned to steal more of my jewels?"

The servant hung back in the shadowed passageway. "I didn't take nothing! I told thee so already."

"Liar. I'll summon the magistrate come morning. He'll have you transported for your crime. Lord knows, you must have filched Lady Beaufort's jewels, too."

Martha fell sobbing to her knees. "Thee cannot send me away. I done no wrong. Please, I have nowhere to go."

"No one shall punish you. Run back up to bed now." Catherine gently helped Martha to her feet and shooed her toward the servants' staircase. Then she swung toward Lorena. "Bullying the servants won't help you find the necklace," she snapped. "Nor will making false accusations."

"Well! How do you know it is false? Such a necklace would be a great temptation to a girl in her position."

"Martha has been with us for two years now, and she's never shown the slightest dishonesty." Painfully aware that once she left there would be no one to defend the servants, Catherine stepped closer to her mother-in-law. "If you wish to keep a good staff, you'll refrain from striking them. No servant will stay in a household where the mistress might beat her."

Heaving a sigh, Lorena hung her head. "You are right, of course. La, if you're certain of the girl's character, then that is enough for me. Come, help me inside now."

Catherine automatically extended a supporting arm as Lorena sagged heavily against her uninjured side. Her mother-in-law's abrupt turnabout was startling. Yet it was heartening to think she had realized her error.

As they walked inside, Catherine stopped short. Lit by a pair of flickering lamps, the chamber lay in shambles. Drawers were pulled out of dressers. Wardrobes stood open. Clothing strewed the Savonnerie carpet and the grand four-poster with its hangings of gold silk.

"Upon my word," she breathed. "What happened?"

"I wanted to find the necklace," Lorena said testily. "My dear Henry gave it to me on our wedding day. It was a Snow family heirloom." She lowered her bulk to a chaise and began sniffling into her handkerchief.

Her mother-in-law looked genuinely distraught, and the sight roused a reluctant sympathy in Catherine. "Could it have fallen behind your dressing table?"

"I never thought to look there." Lorena loudly blew her nose. "You always were a helpful girl. I don't know how I shall manage without you."

Subduing a niggling guilt, Catherine made a systematic inspection of the bedroom and boudoir, checking cabinets and jewel box, even moving furniture aside as best she could manage. At last, she threw up her hands in frustration. "I'm afraid I can't find the piece, either."

Lorena fanned her face, devoid of its usual coating of night cream. "What am I to do? The necklace was to be Priscilla's upon her marriage. And now it's gone. Gone!"

"It'll turn up." Surreptitiously, Catherine pressed her

hand to her bandaged side. "We're both weary. We'll look again in the morning, when there's better light."

"You're leaving then. Leaving me to fend for myself."

Catherine swallowed hard. "There's been a slight change in my plans. I shan't be moving out just yet."

Lorena peered over the lace edge of the handkerchief. "Whyever not?"

"His lordship and I have called off the betrothal." There. It was out. Catherine told herself she ought to feel relieved. Yet bleakness swept through her like a winter storm over the moor.

Wriggling herself into an upright position on the chaise, Lorena said, "My dear girl. I'm terribly sorry. You've a place here for as long as you like."

"I appreciate that," Catherine said sincerely. "But I shall be moving to my own house shortly."

"Deserting me. After all I have done for you." Lorena propped her fingers against her temples. "Oh, I feel dizzy of a sudden. As if I might . . . might swoon."

Her head wobbled and her eyes rolled back. With a gasp, Catherine rushed to help Lorena recline against the cushions. "Have you any hartshorn here?"

Lorena waved her weakly away. "Never mind that horrid-smelling stuff. A nice hot tisane would revive me. Yes. But you're exhausted. I could never ask you . . ."

The bellrope connected to the kitchen, but all the servants would be sleeping in the attic at this time of night. Catherine sighed. No matter how her wound ached, she would have to go herself.

"Lie still," she told her mother-in-law. "I'll return as quickly as I can."

"Thank you, my dear. You're so kind."

Catherine took one of the lamps and made her way down the darkened passageway. As she passed Burke's bedroom, she noticed that no light shone beneath the door. He must be asleep. If only she could steal inside and lie down beside him. If only she could seek comfort in his encircling arms, a warm respite from the loneliness that dwelt inside her already.

Yet the love that fed her longings also kept temptation at bay. She must hold firm to her decision. For his sake.

Far in the distance, a clock bonged the hour of two. The eerie sound echoed through the sleeping house. As Catherine descended the servants' staircase, the lamp cast weird shadows over the walls. Gooseflesh prickled over her spine and down her arms. Perhaps she ought to have heeded Burke's warning.

Nonsense. She was safe within the house. Who could possibly hurt her here? Not Lorena, who lay weak from an attack of the nerves.

Catherine descended the last few steps and emerged into the kitchen. The huge room looked eerie in the darkness, the massive range crouched like a giant at the far wall. The flagstones chilled her bare feet. It was odd to see the place deserted—and quiet except for the rush and swoop of the wind against the house.

She took a deep breath; the room was redolent of roasted beef and onions from dinner, along with the ever-present tang of smoke. She would have to stir the banked coals into a fire, heat a kettle, and fetch the herbs from the pantry.

After setting down the lamp, she walked to the woodpile for kindling. From the shadows by the pile, a pair of glowing yellow eyes peered out at her.

A gasp strangled her throat. She froze, her heart thundering. Then she laughed aloud.

Bending, she scooped up the small warm body. "Tigress. Who let you in?"

The kitten dug its tiny claws into Catherine's nightrobe and tried to climb onto her shoulder. Its heart was beating madly.

Stroking the soft fur, Catherine walked to the back door. "There's naught to fear, darling. But you can't stay here. Lorena would have another fit of the vapors if she found you roaming the house. It's back to the stable now."

She put the cat outside, and Tigress bolted into the shadows of the garden. The trees swayed and dipped like ghostly dancers in the moonlight. Catherine shivered as a gust of wind plastered the nightgown against her legs. How terrified the animal had acted. Even odder, Catherine realized as she stepped back inside, the door had been unlocked.

Humphrey was responsible for securing the house each night. Lorena had given the butler explicit instructions after Lady Beaufort had been robbed. Usually, the old retainer was meticulous to a fault. Subduing a vague sense of alarm, Catherine turned the key in the lock and resolved to have a word with him in the morning.

Within moments, she had the fire blazing and a copper kettle hung over the flames. She opened the pantry door and stepped into the fragrant darkness. Peppermint would make a good tisane, she thought, along with a pinch of chamomile to soothe Lorena's nerves.

She was reaching for the spice cabinet when a muffled noise emanated from deep within the pantry.

Even as she turned in surprise, a black shadow moved toward her. A scream formed in her throat. But a hand clamped over her mouth. Another caught her by the waist and yanked her off balance, slamming her backward against a man's body.

Chapter 20

The bone-deep cold awakened him. Slumped in a chair, his long legs stretched out, Burke opened his eyes to the darkness of his bedchamber. The odor of spilled brandy tainted the air. Memory slapped him to full awareness. A few hours ago, he had returned from Catherine's room, gripped by the ferocious need for a drink. Then, struck by the bitter realization that alcohol could never alleviate the pain in his heart, he had smashed the decanter on the hearth.

Now he sat up stiffly, shivering in his shirtsleeves. The fire had died to embers, yet it couldn't account for the unseasonal chill in the room. A harbinger of winter must have blown in from the north. The moaning of the wind sounded almost human, and the eerie wail pulled at him, somehow made him turn.

And then he saw it.

Against the dense shadows hovered a shimmering patch of light. As he watched, it seemed to pulse and grow until the bluish white radiance took on the shape of a man. Alfred.

Burke rubbed his eyes and stared again. The apparition loitered against the darkness of the bedroom. A hand as pale as mist beckoned to him. Then the glowing figure drifted toward the door and vanished through the wood panel.

Catherine. Hurry.

The words penetrated Burke's mind as if the specter had spoken aloud. His heart slammed against his rib-cage. Without making a conscious decision, he found himself striding forward, following the phantom.

Catherine. Hurry.

Burke yanked open the door. The passageway lay in pitch darkness and the air was curiously warmer here. Alfred's ghost had melted away.

Ghost? No, madness. Burke shook his head quickly, impatient to rid himself of the dream-like image. His own mind had conjured up that unearthly form.

Yet a sense of urgent foreboding lingered. Clung to him like a sticky cobweb.

Catherine. Hurry.

She was in danger. The certainty of it enflamed Burke.

He ducked back into the bedroom and lit a candle from the embers on the hearth. Then he dashed through the rabbit warren of corridors.

You were right to call love a useless emotion. I enjoyed our little interlude while it lasted. But it's over now. Over for good.

The agony of her rejection pounded through his head with every step he took. The devil take her wishes. Whether she liked it or not, he should never have left her alone. He needed desperately to hold her in his arms and let her warmth chase away the cold inside him.

It was his own fault for failing to admit his love for her. He was a coward for holding back. Even if it stripped him of his pride, even if it were too late to restore her love, he would tell her the truth.

Doubtless he would find her sleeping peacefully. An angel with her dark hair fanned out on the pillow and a gossamer nightgown veiling her body. He would awaken her slowly, with gentle caresses, reenacting the first night they'd made love. Only this time, he would reveal his true feelings for her. This time he would lay bare his soul and hope that Catherine would have him back. He wanted to spend the rest of the night with her—and every night for the remainder of their lives.

Her door stood ajar. Shock sucked the fantasy out of him. He stormed inside and stopped short. The circle of candlelight quivered on the thrown-back coverlet and the indentation left by her head on the pillow.

She was gone.

Her trunk stood in the corner. The dueling pistol lay where he had left it on the dressing table.

Bracing one hand on the bedpost, he struggled to think. Where might she have vanished at this hour of the night? To help one of the twins? To aid a servant? To answer a summons from Lorena?

Yes. Catherine might have been lured to her mother-in-law's bedroom on a pretext. She steadfastedly refused to believe the woman could harm her.

But Burke feared otherwise.

Praying he was wrong, he snatched up the pistol and sped from the room.

In the darkness of the pantry, Catherine fought her captor. Panic roared in her ears. She couldn't see his face. But her senses registered the scent of his shaving soap, the wiry strength of his muscles.

She kicked backward and her bare heel struck his shin. He grunted, his elbow jabbing her wound. Pain seared her side like a brand of fire. The air whooshed out of her lungs. As she struggled to catch her breath, he loosened his hold long enough to thrust a cloth over her mouth.

She jerked her head aside. When he tried to fit the gag on her again, she bit down hard on a finger. Her teeth sliced through skin and she tasted a spurt of salty blood.

He cursed. The instant the hand left her mouth, she screamed. Loud and piercing. Blasting the confines of the pantry.

"Bitch!"

He cuffed her ear. Stars burst before her eyes. Before she could regain her senses, he secured the gag and pressed a cold steel blade against her throat.

Dear God. He meant to kill her.

"Easy, m'dear, or your blood will spill. This time, I won't miss."

Ezekiel Newberry.

With a chill of horror, she recognized his voice. Burke had been right. Newberry had shot her. He had caused the crippling pain in her side.

Did he want money? If only he would remove the gag, she would offer him every last penny of the two thousand pounds. Giving up Gilly Grange was worth having the chance to tell Burke that she had never meant to hurt him. The chance to retract her denial of their love.

Newberry dragged her out of the pantry and into the kitchen. The lamp shed yellow light over the long table, but the corners of the cavernous room lay in shadow. She could see that he held not a knife to her throat, but the edge of a deadly-sharp rapier. The kettle bubbled on the hearth, a merry note in the dirge of her fear.

"Wait till his fancy lordship knows I've got you," he said, chortling as he hauled her toward the back door. "Nobody tosses Zeke Newberry in the drink and gets away with it. There's a little cottage on the moor where no one will find us—"

The door to the outer passage swung open. "Release her at once."

The ringing command sparked a blaze of joy in Catherine's heart. Burke entered the kitchen, pulling Lorena with him. He wore no cravat or coat, and his white shirt was unfastened at the throat, revealing a wedge of bronzed chest.

He held the dueling pistol pointed at Newberry. And Catherine. "If you release her," he said, "I'll lay down the gun. And I'll pay you handsomely to leave England for good."

"Please, m'lord," Lorena squeaked. "He won't honor your bargain. Shoot the devil."

Newberry gave a hard laugh that reverberated in Catherine's ear. "You won't shoot, m'lord. You're too much the gentleman to risk striking the lady."

"And you're a knave to hide behind the skirts of a woman. A craven coward."

Newberry shook with tension. "Put down the gun. Now. Or I'll slice her throat." The edge of the rapier pressed harder on Catherine's tender skin, and she couldn't stop a little whimper of terror against the gag.

Burke stood very still. The lamplight cast his cold features into sharp relief, and a strand of tousled black hair tumbled onto his forehead. It was the only softness about his grim expression, the taut mouth, the firm jaw. His eyes bore an arrogance so frosty that Catherine thought for a moment he might take a rash chance.

Then his gaze touched hers and in that brief moment she glimpsed his tortured fear for her and the frustration of having no choice. Slowly he lowered the gun.

"Shoot him," Lorena urged again. "You can't let Newberry go. He'll murder her."

Burke shook off her clinging hand. He walked toward Newberry, the pistol balanced in his palm. "Where do you want it?"

"Stop right there. Put the gun on the table. Good and easy, that's it."

The weapon met the table with a tiny clink.

"Now step away," Newberry advised. "Back to the cupboard there in the corner. And let me see your hands while you do so."

Burke retreated, his palms up. "I've done as you asked. Now let Catherine go. Whatever your quarrel with Lorena, Catherine isn't a part of it."

"You know nothing of my quarrel with that bitch." His breath heated Catherine's neck, and she felt the rage tremble in his body, pressed so close to hers. "Tell 'em, my plump little pigeon, how you tried to double-cross me tonight."

"Liar," Lorena retorted. "You'll babble anything to avoid the hangman's noose." For a woman who had been near swooning a short while ago, she looked remarkably recovered. Her blue eyes flashed beneath the burgundy turban that crowned her head. "Loose the girl and get out of here. If you ride fast, you might escape the magistrate."

"And what will these fine folks think when they find Mr. Fabian Snow tied up in the pantry? You told him to lie in wait for me. You told him I'd threatened Catherine and meant to come for her tonight. You told him to shoot me on sight."

"What is this ruckus? What's going on here?" The male voice resounded from the doorway of the kitchen. Roderick Grisham stood there, clad in a dark dressing gown, his hair perfectly groomed. His gaze flicked from Burke to Catherine, clutched against Newberry. "What the devil! Unhand her at once."

"Who's this now?" Newberry tightened his grip, and she smelled the acrid sweat of desperation on him. "Well, no matter. 'Tis another witness to your unveiling, Peg New—"

"No!" Lorena screamed. "I'll shut your foul mouth for good."

She lunged for the table and snatched up the pistol.

Catherine saw the round circle of the barrel pointed straight at her. Instinct told her to duck. But the rapier blade held her immobile.

Even as Lorena's finger curled around the trigger,

Burke sprang from the corner in a streak of motion. He threw himself between the two women.

The shot exploded. Burke staggered backward and pivoted toward Catherine. He swayed on his feet. A red stain spread against the white of his shirt.

His eyes widened on her as if to assure himself of her safety. Then he slumped to the floor.

Roderick seized Newberry's arm and wrenched it behind his back. The rapier clattered to the flagstones. Catherine wasted no time tearing off her gag and falling to her knees beside Burke.

She lifted his head onto her lap and felt his wrist. A pulse thrummed erratically, to her great relief. "Burke. Burke, speak to me, my love. Open your eyes."

He lay silent, as still as death. With trembling fingers she parted his shirt. The wound appeared to be high on his shoulder, the free-flowing blood obscuring the scar that lay slightly lower on his chest. From the depths of her horror, she uttered a swift, fervent prayer for him.

Several staff members came rushing down the servants' staircase. "We heard a shot, ma'am," Martha said. Her brown eyes grew as big as buttons when she spied Burke stretched out on the floor.

"Fetch me a towel," Catherine said. "Quickly now."

The maid obliged, and Catherine pressed the linen square to Burke's wound. He stirred and muttered in pain.

Owen hovered nearby, looking sleep-mussed in his nightshirt. "Ride for the doctor," she told him. "Immediately."

"Yes, ma'am."

Even as the footman scurried out the door, Burke opened his eyes and looked straight at her. His face was pale, yet incredibly, a jaunty smile curved his whitened lips. "The voice of an angel. Snapping orders as always."

"I'm only a woman," she whispered, bending closer so that he alone could hear. "You're the angel. My hero."

He felt for her hand and squeezed tightly. The unguarded fervency of his expression made her light-headed. Dare she hope he might forgive her for rejecting him so cruelly?

Then he struggled to rise, his face contorted with pain.

Catherine said swiftly, "You mustn't tax yourself."

"I'm perfectly capable," he protested, though his voice was raspy with effort. "Just give me a moment."

"Allow me," Lord Westhaven said.

Only then did Catherine notice him standing over them, his face nearly as ashen as his son's. Somewhere, the marquis had found some twine and tied Newberry's hands behind his back. Now he held his prisoner in a firm grip. His eyes were no longer icy, but warm with concern. He thrust Newberry at another footman, saying, "Take this knave and follow us."

Roderick slipped his arm around Burke, helping him to his feet. A long look passed between them, and Catherine thought he might refuse his father's aid. Then he leaned against Roderick.

"Help him upstairs," Catherine said. "My room is closest. I'll show you the way."

"Wait!" Lorena burst out. "You can't mean to take that criminal upstairs, too. He should be locked up. Someone, send for the constable!" Wild-eyed, she waved the pistol.

"Madam," Roderick said in his chilliest tone, "you shot my son. I suggest that you put the gun down at once and come with us. You've some explaining to do."

Pinned by his glare, Lorena shrank back and carefully placed the pistol on the table. "I need to lie down," she said, her voice going faint. "Such a shock . . . you must forgive me . . . a terrible mistake . . ."

"Walk." Loosing his grip on Burke only an instant, Roderick snatched up the rapier. He pointed it toward the servants' stair. "Now."

She hesitated, her face pasty white. "Yes, m'lord."

Catherine turned to Martha. "Fabian is tied up in the pantry, I think. Tend to him, if you will."

"Aye, ma'am." Eyes agog, the maid took the lamp and hastened away.

Within moments, the group was assembled in Catherine's bedroom, with Burke propped against the pillows. His color was a little better, though Catherine felt a stab of renewed alarm when she changed the makeshift bandage. The wound oozed blood, dark as wine in the candlelight.

"You need rest," she said. "All of this can wait until after the doctor's tended to you."

"Never mind me." Burke caught her hand, his eyes intent on her. "What of you? How is your side? You ought to be lying down instead of me."

In all the chaos, Catherine had forgotten her own wound. The discomfort lingered from her struggle with Newberry, yet how could she complain when Burke had risked his life for her?

"I'm perfectly content so long as you are alive," she said softly.

When she started to move away, he held tight to her hand. "Sit beside me. Please."

He looked so weary, his mouth pinched by pain, that Catherine obeyed without a murmur.

Newberry lolled against the wall, his hands tied behind his back, while Lorena perched sullenly on the edge of the wing chair. "This is absurd," she protested. "That villain belongs behind bars."

"No one's arguing that," Burke said. "But I've some questions for the both of you first."

Holding the purloined rapier, Roderick paced the length of the small bedroom. "Allow me to do the talking, son. You've had a rough time of it tonight."

Burke nodded, and Catherine felt a surge of giddy hope that the two men might settle their differences.

Roderick stopped in front of Newberry. "Tell me why you entered this house in the middle of the night."

Newberry smiled, his teeth flashing white against his teak dark face. "I didn't come to steal the silver, m'lord."

"Answer the question, or I'll see to it you're swinging from the gallows within the passing of a day."

"I came to kidnap Catherine Snow. But before you toss me in the clink, let me say that her mother-in-law put me up to it."

Lorena gripped the arms of her chair. "That is a vile lie! Don't heed his vulgar mouth, your lordship. He would pose as Saint George himself if it meant saving his scrawny neck."

"It seems you two are well acquainted," Roderick observed, glancing from one to the other. "I should like to know the nature of your relationship."

"There is naught to know," Lorena said, spots of high color on her cheeks. "I only met the man when he invaded my ball last week. I am appalled that anyone would think there is more between us—"

"Cut the play-acting, Peg." Newberry's gaze held a note of triumph as he looked over his audience. "I'll tell you who she is. She's me wife."

Burke's fingers tensed around Catherine's. She stared in amazement, first at Newberry's smirking face, then at Lorena. The older woman breathed heavily, her bosom heaving and her features mottled red.

All of a sudden she flew at Newberry, her fingers arched like claws to scratch out his eyes. "You nodcock," she screamed. "You never did know when to keep your mouth shut."

Though his hands were tied, Newberry lashed out with a swift kick that knocked her on her backside. The floorboards shook from the thump of her weight. She landed in a sprawl, her pale legs thrust out like plump sausages.

Catherine blinked at the incongruous image of her so-proper mother-in-law who now resembled a fishwife. His lip curled in distaste, Roderick helped Lorena to her feet.

He stood over her, his fingers clenched on the rapier. "Try that again," he said coldly, "and I shall truss your hands just as I did your husband's."

But the fight seemed to have gone out of Lorena. The burgundy turban hung askew, and she made no move to right it. Her face looked saggy and old as she slouched in the chair.

"I don't understand," Catherine said in bewilderment. "When did you two marry? After Mr. Snow died twelve years ago?"

" 'Twas long before that," Newberry said. "Long before she invented her wellborn background, she was known as plain Peg Newberry."

Burke let out a low whistle. "Bigamy. Lorena's marriage to Alfred's father was invalid. That's the secret Alfred wanted to hide."

"Righto, mate. Peg and me, we got wed on Fleet Street when we were youngsters of eighteen."

"Then where have you been all these years?" Catherine asked Newberry.

His face darkened. " 'Tis a long story, and best to start at the beginning. Peg knows the whole of it." To Lorena, Newberry said, "Go on, pigeon. Talk. Tell 'em how hard we worked to make our living thirty years ago."

Lorena muttered, "It's a lie. I'm a lady. A *lady.*"

"You're no more a lady than the lowest scullery maid. Born in a Whitechapel gutter, you were." When she uttered a small moan and covered her face, Newberry lifted his insolent gaze to the others. "Peg and me, we were more than husband and wife. We were partners, robbing the rich nobs of London. Peg looked so innocent, no one would've believed she had a dishonest bone in her shapely body."

Catherine recalled the time Lorena had admitted to stealing money from the household accounts to pay the dressmaker's bill. But that was a far cry from committing a crime punishable by law. "I can hardly credit this tale."

"You haven't heard the best of it. We had a regular scheme going. She'd take a post as a governess or a lady's maid. Then she'd let me into the house at night so I could crack open the safe. Always left a farthing. Just to poke a little fun at the nobs."

"The Copper Farthing Robberies." Roderick stopped pacing and gave him a piercing stare. "So I did remember correctly."

Newberry grinned as if proud of his exploits. Then his smile died. "At our last caper, the biggest one of all, we cleaned out the earl of Nottingham. Just as I stuck my arm in the safe to leave the farthing, a young sod of a footman burst in and slammed the door on my hand. Peg here snatched the sack of jewels and ran. She left me to rot in Newgate. Loyal, ain't you, Peg?"

Lorena said nothing. She sat plucking at a thread in her dressing gown as if it were the most important task in the world.

"Because of her," Newberry went on, "I got sent off in one of the first shiploads of convicts transported to Botany Bay. In case you fine folks don't know, 'tis halfway 'round the world in Australia. I served near thirty years in that stinking hellhole before they finally let me loose."

His incredible story explained his leathery skin and his peculiar accent, Catherine thought. "If she changed her name, how did you trace her?"

"She always talked of turning herself into a real lady. But I knew she didn't dare show her face in London society for fear of somebody recognizing her. I figured she'd find herself a rich gull in an outlying province, and she wouldn't be able to resist announcing the union in the London papers. Still, it took me nigh on a year of tracking down names to find the wily bitch."

"You robbed Lady Beaufort, too," Catherine said. "No wonder Lorena swooned when she read her ladyship's note mentioning the copper farthing."

"Now, you'll never prove I'm guilty of that," Newberry said with a sly grin.

"You did it," Lorena said in a creaky voice. "You wanted me to know you were still lurking around. Wasn't it enough that you tormented poor Freddie?"

Everyone turned to look at her. Her eyes anguished, she clutched a fistful of her dressing gown. "After you milked my Freddie dry, you promised to go away and never come back."

Newberry took a step toward her. "Ah, Peg. How could you have thought such a pittance would repay the debt you owe me? All the years I was working in chains, you were living in this fancy house with your fancy family and putting on fancy airs."

"You should have died," she whispered. "Died on that forsaken island with the other convicts."

"Sorry to disoblige. But the fact remains, I'm still your lawful husband. I kept the paper to prove it."

"And used it to blackmail Alfred," Burke said in a hard voice. "If the truth came out, it would nullify Lorena's second marriage. Alfred and his sisters would have been illegitimate—left without a penny to their ruined name."

Catherine felt a flood of understanding mixed with pity. "It wasn't my fault, then," she whispered. "No wonder Alfred was so melancholy. He knew he would have lost everything—honor, social standing, even the roof over our heads."

"And now," Burke said, flashing a steely look, "Lorena was willing to hand you over to Newberry. He would have used you, then murdered you. And the both of them would have profited from your portion of an ill-gained inheritance."

"I deny it all," Lorena said weakly. "You have only the word of a convicted thief."

"But I'll tell my tale in court," Newberry taunted. "Wait till the whole of England hears you're really Peg Newberry. You'll be back living in the gutter. Your daughters will be forced to work as whores. Perhaps you, too, if any man will still have you."

She sat on the chair, her shoulders slumped in defeat and her eyes dull with shock. Catherine felt sorry for her, in spite of the evil plotting that had almost cost Catherine her life. The whole story seemed inconceivable, a terrible nightmare that made her glad for the warmth of Burke's hand around hers.

At that moment, a knock on the door jarred the tense silence. Roderick propped the rapier against the bedpost. "That'll be the doctor."

As he went to answer the summons, Lorena sprang to life. With a feral cry, she snatched up the sword and hurled herself at her husband.

It happened so fast that Catherine could only stare in horror. Burke scrambled out of bed and Roderick hastened from the door. But they were too late. The razor-thin blade pierced Newberry's chest to the hilt. His eyes were wide, already glazing as he crumpled to the floor.

Burke stood swaying while the shocked doctor knelt beside Newberry, felt for a pulse, and then shook his head. Catherine guided Burke back to the bed, where they sat close, his body shielding her from the sight.

Roderick had caught Lorena in a firm grip. As he led her out of the room, she spat a string of vile curses at her dead husband, gutter terms that added to the sickened sadness in Catherine's heart.

In due course, the two footmen carried off Newberry's body, and the doctor tended to Burke's wound.

The bullet had passed cleanly through and he needed only a padding of linen to bandage the injury.

As the doctor departed, Roderick returned to the bedroom, his face gray with fatigue. "I thought you would like to know. Mrs. Snow—or rather, Peg Newberry—is in the hands of the constable now."

Catherine imagined the once-proud woman confined to a cold cell. "What will happen to her?"

"She'll spend the rest of her days behind bars," Burke said. "And good riddance to her. She'll never hurt you again."

Roderick walked to the bed and looked down at Burke, who sat up against the pillows. "You made me proud tonight. Proud to call you my son."

Burke gazed steadily at him, the glitter of his eyes revealing the depth of his feelings. In a low voice, he said, "I'm pleased to have my father back."

The two men embraced, a brief awkward clasp that sealed their reconciliation. The sight of their heads together, one jet-black, the other graying, brought a lump to Catherine's throat. And reminded her of how vital it was for a man to have a son.

Or perhaps it was simply having someone to love.

Roderick straightened, a tinge of color on his cheeks as he looked at Catherine and Burke. "If you'll excuse me, I'll leave the two of you alone."

When he had gone, closing the door behind him, Burke said, "He approves of you now. Maybe it doesn't matter, but I feel better having his blessing."

Yearning to believe Burke could forgive her, Catherine walked to the darkened window. A pink glow on the horizon portended the dawn of a new day. "Even though scandal has tainted my family?"

"They're not your family," Burke said roughly. "You never fit in here."

It was true. Yet in spite of all that had happened, she felt a wistful affection for the Snows. "I'll have to break the news to Prudence and Priscilla. How shocking this will be to them, to have their mother exposed as a criminal and thrown in gaol. They won't even have a home anymore. The house, the money, even their wardrobes —all of it belongs to Fabian. He's the true heir."

"He's a kind man. No doubt he'll permit them to keep their clothing. However, if it makes you happy, I'll buy them a modest cottage and give them a small stipend. They won't starve."

His generosity overwhelmed her. "You would do that?"

He nodded. "Since you consider them as your sisters. But I draw the line at finding them husbands. No man would ever please either of them. They'll probably spend the rest of their lives sniping at each other." Burke's voice grew softer. "But you're fretting over them when you ought to be worrying about yourself. You've lost your inheritance, too."

He was right. Now she lacked the means to purchase Gilly Grange. Yet she felt no sense of loss for the lovely dwelling, only a soul-deep hunger for the man who occupied her bed—and her heart. Would he think she had changed her mind only because she had no money, nowhere else to turn?

Burke sat watching her, his chest bare except for the bandage anchored to his shoulder by strips of linen wound beneath his arm. "There's something else you should know," he said in a low voice. "Something I didn't have the courage to admit before now. I love you, Catherine."

His eyes held a raw sincerity, as if his soul were laid bare. Laid at her feet.

Her throat tightened. He meant it. He truly meant it.

In a rush, she confessed, "I'm sorry for those awful things I said to you. I let you think I didn't love you, and I won't blame you if you never forgive me."

His eyes glowed with a fire that gave her hope. He held out his hand to her. "Come here."

She went. The moment she sat beside him on the bed, he took her hands in his. "If you truly love me, Catherine, I'll forgive you anything."

She raised his hands to her lips. "Oh, Burke, I'll love you forever."

"Then you'll come live with me. As my wife."

"Yes." She released a fervent breath. "So long as you don't mind if we never have children."

"We'll have each other. That's a far richer life than I ever expected to live."

Mindful of his shoulder, Catherine pressed herself to him, and their kiss lasted a long, tender moment. When she drew back, she said, "Tonight might have turned out so differently. Thank heaven you came down to the kitchen when you did."

"Heaven," he mused. An odd intensity on his handsome features, he gazed out the window at the lightening sky. "Now there's a thought. Heaven did have something to do with it."

Cupping his cheek in her hand, she turned his face toward her. "What do you mean?"

"It's the oddest thing. I'm not sure I understand completely. But Alfred's ghost warned me that you were in danger." Quickly he explained about the apparition he had seen in his bedroom.

"Then there's still a link between you two," she said in wonderment. "Do you suppose he's our guardian angel?"

Burke chuckled. "If he is, I hope to hell he isn't watching us right now."

With that, Burke brought his mouth down on hers. And as sunrise banished the shadows of night, they found their own heaven on earth.

Epilogue

Cornwall, April 1822

"She's sucking on my thumb, Mother. Look!"

Laughing, Colin stood beside a curly-wooled lamb that suckled greedily on his hand. Catherine smiled from her perch on the beech stump, and her heart contracted with the fierceness of love. Her son looked untidy as ever, from his rumpled black hair to his muddy boots. The pockets of his suit bulged with a treasure trove of sticks and stones and feathers he had found in the sunny meadow.

"She's hungry," Catherine said. "It's been two hours since her last meal."

"This is what she wants, son."

Burke walked out of the shepherd's hut with a bottle in his hand. He hunkered down beside the boy, and the lamb nuzzled the makeshift teat made of cork pierced by a slender, hollow pipe. Within moments, the animal's contented smacking blended with the twittering of linnets in the furze bushes.

"Why doesn't her mother feed her?" Colin asked.

Burke ruffled the boy's hair. "Unlike you, she hasn't a mother or father to love her. She's an orphan. All alone in the world."

Colin's gray eyes grew big. "Can she be mine?"

"Well, now. Caring for a lamb is a big job."

"I can do it. I'm almost this many." He held up four grubby fingers.

Burke set the empty bottle in the grass, then placed his hands on the boy's shoulders. "You must give me your word you'll visit her every day and help the shepherds feed her."

"I will. Cross my heart." Colin did so solemnly.

"Very well, then. Wait here." Burke ducked into the hut a moment and emerged with a canister bell, which he handed to his son. "Sound this whenever you want her to come to you."

"Thank you, Father." Colin threw his arms around Burke in an exuberant hug, then dashed off into the meadow, the lamb frolicking after the clanking bell.

Smiling, Burke walked toward Catherine. In the blousy white shirt and buckskin breeches, his tall black boots shining, he looked every inch the beloved rake she had married. Yet he had proven himself a steady, devoted husband, the man of her dreams.

She moved over to make room for him on the stump. He sat down behind her and drew her against him, and she leaned into the hard cradle of his chest and thighs. Even after six years of his loving, she felt a thrill at the feel of his strong body. They made love often, and she marveled that their pleasure in each other had mellowed and deepened with the passage of time.

He kissed the back of her neck, then caressed the gentle mound of her belly. "How's our daughter today?"

"Asleep at the moment." Catherine tilted her head back. "But she might be a he. In fact, your father insists it's to be so."

Burke smiled. "Still as imperious as ever. Well, I suspect he'll act the doting grandfather, no matter if the baby is a boy or a girl."

Relaxing against him, Catherine sighed in contentment. The spring breeze carried the scent of violets and the richness of the awakening land. The occasional bleating of sheep drifted from the green hills.

On the cliff in the distance stood the rambling stone structure of Thornwald Castle, the home she had grown to cherish, the place she truly belonged. A suite of rooms in the west wing served as a school for the children of the estate, and she had promoted one of the studious older girls to the role of assistant teacher.

In the meadow, Colin gamboled with his lamb amid colorful clumps of wild arum and dog's mercury. She could still scarcely believe he was hers. For a long time, even though Burke made good on his promise to love her well and often, her infertility had seemed irreversible. They had been married for more than a year before she had become pregnant with her son. This second baby seemed no less miraculous.

She shifted position and studied Burke's clean-shaven features. "I received a letter from Peter Guppy this morning."

"Ah, the incorrigible lad has stirred up trouble at school again. He'll never earn his commission in the cavalry that way."

"He vows he's working hard. But he also mentioned that Martha Snow gave birth on Easter Sunday to her fifth son."

Burke chuckled. "That sly fox, Fabian. It seems he's lost his bashfulness—especially in the bedroom."

She sighed. "Five sons. What a brood that must be."

He tilted her chin up and brushed his lips over hers. "Ah, Countess, our two children are surely a gift from heaven. You've given me more love than I ever imagined possible. I doubt there's a man in England more content than I."

At the devilish warmth in his eyes, she felt her heart brim with happiness. No more these days did she see the glazed look that had once indicated he was viewing a scene from Alfred's past. Oddly, those mysterious memories had stopped after Burke had been shot while saving her life. Not that she had anything to hide anymore. The hardships of long ago had brought Burke into her life, and for that she would always be grateful.

She kissed him back with a fervency that arose from her soul. "We've been truly blessed," she said softly. "We've created so many wonderful memories together."

Reaching down, he plucked a cluster of violets and tucked them behind her ear. "With many more to come, my love."

Burke helped Catherine to her feet. Arm in arm, they walked through the sunlit meadow toward their son.